THINGS GET UGLY

SELECTED WORKS BY JOE R. LANSDALE

HAP AND LEONARD

Savage Season (1990)

Mucho Mojo (1994)

The Two-Bear Mambo (1995)

Bad Chili (1997)

Rumble Tumble (1998)

Veil's Visit: A Taste of Hap and Leonard
    (with Andrew Vachss, 1999)

Captains Outrageous (2001)

Vanilla Ride (2009)

Hyenas (2011)

Devil Red (2011)

Dead Aim (2013)

Honky Tonk Samurai (2016)

Hap and Leonard (2016)

Rusty Puppy (2017)

Blood and Lemonade (2017)

The Big Book of Hap and Leonard
    (2018)

Jack Rabbit Smile (2018)

The Elephant of Surprise (2019)

Of Mice and Minestrone (2020)

Born for Trouble (2022)

OTHER NOVELS

Act of Love (1981)

Dead in the West (1986)

The Magic Wagon (1986)

The Nightrunners (1987)

The Drive-In (1988)

Cold in July (1989)

Batman: Captured by the Engines (1991)

Tarzan: The Lost Adventure
    (with Edgar Rice Burroughs, 1995)

The Boar (1998)

Freezer Burn (1999)

Waltz of Shadows (1999)

The Big Blow (2000)

The Bottoms (2000)

A Fine Dark Line (2002)

Sunset and Sawdust (2004)

Lost Echoes (2007)

Leather Maiden (2008)

Flaming Zeppelins (2010)

All the Earth, Thrown to Sky (2011)

Edge of Dark Water (2012)

The Thicket (2013)

Paradise Sky (2015)

Fender Lizards (2015)

Bubba and the Cosmic Bloodsuckers
    (2017)

Jane Goes North (2020)

More Better Deals (2020)

Moon Lake (2021)

Donut Legion (2022)

THINGS GET UGLY

THE BEST CRIME STORIES OF

JOE R. LANSDALE

T A C H Y O N

To my readers, who've kept me in beans and biscuits.

C O N T

8 N T S

Introduction by S. A. Cosby

Back in 2019, I was in Dallas for a huge crime-writing convention and I found myself sipping on a whiskey sour as I waited to read at a Noir at the Bar event. The crowd that night was boisterous and a bit rowdy, and I was a little concerned we wouldn't be able to grab the attention of the patrons.

Then, a hush fell over the room.

There were all kinds of writers in attendance that night—debut authors, bestsellers, millionaires with names that were industries unto themselves. But we all sat in awe of the man who had come up to the lectern . . . a square-jawed Texan with a sparkle in his eye. The man who could grab your attention without saying a word

That's the effect Joe Lansdale has on people.

The thing I've always admired about Joe is his steadfast defiance of genre constriction. If he wants to write a rural noir, he writes it. If he wants to write a supernatural Western, he writes it. If he wants to write a creature feature set at a cursed drive-in, by God, he writes it and throws in a T-Rex, because why the hell not?

In this amazing collection, you'll see the width and breadth of Joe's staggering talent. The kind of talent that only inspires adulation not envy. Reading a Joe Lansdale story is what it must have been like when listening to Mozart compose, or watching Picasso paint, or seeing Lawrence Oliver live onstage.

You realize you're in the presence of a true master. A master who has honed their natural ability to a wicker edge. But don't be afraid . . . he isn't going to cut you, just slice away your inhibitions. Expand your mind, break your heart, make you laugh, move your soul.

Now, let me get out of the way. You didn't pick up this book to hear me prattle on. You came for the stories, and Joe Lansdale is definitely in the story business.

And folks, business is booming.

Introduction by Joe R. Lansdale

THESE STORIES WERE written over the course of my career. There are other crime stories I'm quite fond of that didn't end up here, but a book can only be so long. I'd love for there to be a second volume of my crime stories. Some of the stories we left out are better known than these, but for this volume, these were mine and the editor's choices. As a way of throwing that editor a well-deserved bone—hell, let's make it an entire fresh carcass—his name is Rick Klaw.

I should also note that some of my favorite short crime stories include my series characters, Hap and Leonard. I'm especially fond of those in *Blood and Lemonade* and *Of Mice and Minestrone*. These stories show them in their youth. Mostly Hap. None of those ended up here, because both of those volumes, as well as two others, *Hap and Leonard* and *Born for Trouble*, are still in print from Tachyon. I invite you to check them out.

I don't love labels, but I do love packaging my stories for new readers. Some of these hit the crime classification securely enough, and others, not so much. But they can all be easily justified as crime stories. I like to think there's no question they are good stories.

I'll let the reader decide.

I will also say that if you have a lot of my collections, you may have most of these already. But new readers may want to find an available volume that collects the best of them. Older readers may like the idea of a fresh volume with a few they don't have.

Another thing: I don't do trigger warnings. No way a writer knows what triggers someone. Look at it this way. I wrote it, that's advisable enough. If you're of a sensitive nature, my work is not for you in any arena.

I'm proud of these.

I hope you enjoy them.

"The Steel Valentine" was my attempt to write a more graphic, Alfred Hitchcock–style story. I thought it was a solid, workmanlike story. Sometimes you build a cathedral, sometimes a chair. I thought it was a solidly good chair. I thought it was a chair. I discovered it was more than a chair, and not a cathedral, but in fact a story that had resonance with a lot of readers. It got a lot of attention when it came out, was reprinted more than I expected, and even had its own chapbook. It still lives on, and I've come to think of it as one of my better crime and suspense stories, having reread it for the first time in years. As to exactly what inspired it, I'm uncertain. Too much time has passed, and I may not have known the true source even when I wrote it. Stories sometimes have a way of hiding in the shadows, forming their shape, and then leaping out of the shadows to surprise you. I do remember that I originally wrote it for a crime Valentine anthology, and it was rejected because it offended the editor. It was good to know I hadn't lost my touch.

THE STEEL VALENTINE

For Jeff Banks

EVEN BEFORE MORLEY told him, Dennis knew things were about to get ugly.

A man did not club you unconscious, bring you to his estate and tie you to a chair in an empty storage shed out back of the place if he merely intended to give you a valentine.

Morley had found out about him and Julie.

Dennis blinked his eyes several times as he came to, and each time he did, more of the dimly lit room came into view. It was the room where he and Julie had first made love. It was the only building on the estate that looked out of place; it was old, worn, and not even used for storage; it was a collector of dust, cobwebs, spiders and desiccated flies.

There was a table in front of Dennis, a kerosene lantern on it, and beyond, partially hidden in shadow, a man sitting in a chair smoking a cigarette. Dennis could see the red tip glowing in the dark and the smoke from it drifted against the lantern light and hung in the air like thin, suspended wads of cotton.

The man leaned out of shadow, and as Dennis expected, it was Morley. His shaved, bullet-shaped head was sweaty and reflected the light. He was smiling with his fine, white teeth, and the high cheekbones were round, flushed circles that looked like clown rouge. The tightness of his skin, the few wrinkles, made him look younger than his fifty-one years.

And in most ways he was younger than his age. He was a man who took care of himself. Jogged eight miles every morning before breakfast, lifted weights three times a week and had only one bad habit—cigarettes. He smoked three packs a day. Dennis knew all that and he had only met the man twice. He had learned it from Julie, Morley's wife. She told him about Morley while they lay in bed. She liked to talk and she often talked about Morley; about how much she hated him.

"Good to see you," Morley said, and blew smoke across the table into Dennis's face. "Happy Valentine's Day, my good man. I was beginning to think I hit you too hard, put you in a coma."

"What is this, Morley?" Dennis found that the mere act of speaking sent nails of pain through his skull. Morley really had lowered the boom on him.

"Spare me the innocent act, lover boy. You've been laying the pipe to Julie, and I don't like it."

"This is silly, Morley. Let me loose."

"God, they do say stupid things like that in real life. It isn't just the movies . . . You think I brought you here just to let you go, lover boy?"

Dennis didn't answer. He tried to silently work the ropes loose that held his hands to the back of the chair. If he could get free, maybe he could grab the lantern, toss it in Morley's face. There would still be the strand holding his ankles to the chair, but maybe it wouldn't take too long to undo that. And even if it did, it was at least some kind of plan.

If he got the chance to go one-on-one with Morley, he might take him. He was twenty-five years younger and in good shape himself. Not as good as when he was playing pro basketball, but good shape nonetheless. He had height, reach, and he still had wind. He kept the latter with plenty of jogging and tossing the special-made, sixty-five-pound medicine ball around with Raul at the gym.

Still, Morley was strong. Plenty strong. Dennis could testify to that. The pulsating knot on the side of his head was there to remind him.

He remembered the voice in the parking lot, turning toward it and seeing a fist. Nothing more, just a fist hurling toward him like a comet. Next thing he knew, he was here, the outbuilding.

Last time he was here, circumstances were different, and better. He was with Julie. He met her for the first time at the club where he worked out, and they had spoken, and ended up playing racquetball together. Eventually she brought him here and they made love on an old mattress in the corner; lay there afterward in the June heat of a Mexican summer, holding each other in a warm, sweaty embrace.

After that, there had been many other times. In the great house; in cars; hotels. Always careful to arrange a tryst when Morley was out of town. Or so they thought. But somehow he had found out.

"This is where you first had her," Morley said suddenly. "And don't look so wide-eyed. I'm not a mind reader. She told me all the other times and places too. She spat at me when I told her I knew, but I made her tell me every little detail, even when I knew them. I wanted it to come from her lips. She got so she couldn't wait to tell me. She was begging to tell me. She asked me to forgive her and take her back. She no longer wanted to leave Mexico and go back to the States with you. She just wanted to live."

"You bastard. If you've hurt her—"

"You'll what? Shit your pants? That's the best you can do, Dennis. You see, it's me that has you tied to the chair. Not the other way around."

Morley leaned back into the shadows again, and his hands came to rest on the table, the perfectly manicured fingertips steepling together, twitching ever so gently.

"I think it would have been inconsiderate of her to have gone back to the States with you, Dennis. Very inconsiderate. She knows I'm a wanted man there, that I can't go back. She thought she'd be rid of me. Start a new life with her ex–basketball player. That hurt my feelings, Dennis. Right to the bone." Morley smiled. "But she wouldn't have been rid of me, lover boy. Not by a long shot. I've got connections in my business. I could have followed her anywhere. . . . In fact, the idea that she thought I couldn't offended my sense of pride."

"Where is she? What have you done with her, you bald-headed bastard?"

After a moment of silence, during which Morley examined Dennis's face, he said, "Let me put it this way. Do you remember her dogs?"

Of course, he remembered the dogs. Seven Dobermans. Attack dogs. They always frightened him. They were big mothers, too. Except for her favorite, a reddish, undersized Doberman named Chum. He was about sixty pounds, and vicious. "Light, but quick," Julie used to say. "Light, but quick."

Oh yeah, he remembered those goddamn dogs. Sometimes when they made love in an estate bedroom, the dogs would wander in, sit down around the bed and watch. Dennis felt they were considering the soft, rolling meat of his testicles, savoring the possibility. It made him feel like a mean kid teasing them with a treat he never intended to give. The idea of them taking that treat by force made his erection soften, and he finally convinced Julie, who found his nervousness hysterically funny, that the dogs should be banned from the bedroom, the door closed.

Except for Julie, those dogs hated everyone. Morley included. They obeyed him, but they did not like him. Julie felt that under the right circumstances, they might go nuts and tear him apart. Something she hoped for, but never happened.

"Sure," Morley continued. "You remember her little pets. Especially Chum, her favorite. He'd growl at me when I tried to touch her. Can you imagine that? All I had to do was touch her, and that damn beast would growl. He was crazy about his mistress, just crazy about her."

Dennis couldn't figure what Morley was leading up to, but he knew in some way he was being baited. And it was working. He was starting to sweat.

"Been what," Morley asked, "a week since you've seen your precious sweetheart? Am I right?"

Dennis did not answer, but Morley was right. A week. He had gone back to the States for a while to settle some matters, get part of his inheritance out of legal bondage so he could come back, get Julie, and take her to the States for good. He was tired of the Mexican heat and tired of Morley owning the woman he loved.

It was Julie who had arranged for him to meet Morley in the first place, and probably even then the old bastard had suspected. She told Morley a partial truth. That she had met Dennis at the club, that they had played racquetball together, and that since he was an American, and supposedly a mean hand at chess, she thought Morley might enjoy the company. This way Julie had a chance to be with her lover, and let Dennis see exactly what kind of man Morley was.

And from the first moment Dennis met him, he knew he had to get Julie away from him. Even if he hadn't loved her and wanted her, he would have helped her leave Morley.

It wasn't that Morley was openly abusive—in fact, he was the perfect host all the while Dennis was there—but there was an obvious undercurrent of connubial dominance and menace that revealed itself like a shark fin every time he looked at Julie.

Still, in a strange way, Dennis found Morley interesting, if not likeable. He was a bright and intriguing talker, and a wizard at chess. But when they played and Morley took a piece, he smirked over it in such a way as to make you feel he had actually vanquished an opponent.

The second and last time Dennis visited the house was the night before he left for the States. Morley had wiped him out in chess, and when finally Julie walked him to the door and called the dogs in from the yard so he could leave without being eaten, she whispered, "I can't take him much longer."

"I know," he whispered back. "See you in about a week. And it'll be all over."

Dennis looked over his shoulder, back into the house, and there was Morley leaning against the fireplace mantle drinking a martini. He lifted the glass to Dennis as if in salute and smiled. Dennis smiled back, called goodbye to Morley and went out to his car feeling uneasy. The smile Morley had given him was exactly the same one he used when he took a chess piece from the board.

"Tonight. Valentine's Day," Morley said, "that's when you two planned to meet again, wasn't it? In the parking lot of your hotel. That's sweet. Really. Lovers planning to elope on Valentine's Day. It has a sort of poetry, don't you think?"

Morley held up a huge fist. "But what you met instead of your sweetheart was this. . . . I beat a man to death with this once, lover boy. Enjoyed every second of it."

Morley moved swiftly around the table, came to stand behind Dennis.

He put his hands on the sides of Dennis's face. "I could twist your head until your neck broke, lover boy. You believe that, don't you? Don't you? . . . Goddamnit, answer me."

"Yes," Dennis said, and the word was soft because his mouth was so dry.

"Good. That's good. Let me show you something, Dennis."

Morley picked up the chair from behind, carried Dennis effortlessly to the center of the room, then went back for the lantern and the other chair. He sat down across from Dennis and turned the wick of the lantern up. And even before Dennis saw the dog, he heard the growl.

The dog was straining at a large leather strap attached to the wall. He was muzzled and ragged looking. At his feet lay something red and white. "Chum," Morley said. "The light bothers him. You remember ole Chum, don't you? Julie's favorite pet. . . . Ah, but I see you're wondering what that is at his feet. That sort of surprises me, Dennis. Really. As intimate as you and Julie were, I'd think you'd know her. Even without her makeup."

Now that Dennis knew what he was looking at, he could make out the white bone of her skull, a dark patch of matted hair still clinging to it. He also recognized what was left of the dress she had been wearing. It was a red and white tennis dress, the one she wore when they played racquetball.

It was mostly red now. Her entire body had been gnawed savagely.

"Murderer!" Dennis rocked savagely in the chair, tried to pull free of his bonds. After a moment of useless struggle and useless epithets, he leaned forward and let the lava hot gorge in his stomach pour out.

"Oh, Dennis," Morley said. "That's going to be stinky. Just awful. Will you look at your shoes? And calling me a murderer. Now, I ask you, Dennis, is that nice? I didn't murder anyone. Chum did the dirty work. After four days without food and water he was ravenous and thirsty. Wouldn't you be?

"And he was a little crazy too. I burned his feet some. Not as bad as I burned Julie's, but enough to really piss him off. And I sprayed him with this."

Morley reached into his coat pocket, produced an aerosol canister and waved it at Dennis.

"This was invented by some business associate of mine. It came out of some chemical warfare research I'm conducting. I'm in, shall we say . . . espionage? I work for the highest bidder. I have plants here for arms and chemical warfare. . . . If it's profitable and ugly, I'm involved. I'm a real stinker sometimes. I certainly am."

Morley was still waving the canister, as if trying to hypnotize Dennis with it. "We came up with this to train attack dogs. We found we could spray a padded-up man with this and the dogs would go bonkers. Rip the pads right off of him. Sometimes the only way to stop the beggars was to shoot them. It was a failure actually. It activated the dogs, but it drove them out of their minds and they couldn't be controlled at all. And after a short time the odor faded, and the spray became quite the reverse. It made it so the dogs couldn't smell the spray at all. It made whoever was wearing it odorless. Still, I found a use for it. A very personal use.

"I let Chum go a few days without food and water while I worked on Julie. . . . And she wasn't tough at all, Dennis. Not even a little bit. Spilled her guts. Now that isn't entirely correct. She didn't spill her guts until later, when Chum got hold of her. . . . Anyway, she told me what I wanted to know about you two, then I sprayed that delicate thirty-six, twenty-four, thirty-six figure of hers with this. And with Chum so hungry, and me having burned his feet and done some mean things to him, he was not in the best of humor when I gave him Julie.

"It was disgusting, Dennis. Really. I had to come back when it was over and shoot Chum with a tranquilizer dart, get him tied and muzzled for your arrival."

Morley leaned forward, sprayed Dennis from head to foot with the canister. Dennis turned his head and closed his eyes, tried not to breathe the foul-smelling mist.

"He's probably not all that hungry now," Morley said, "but this will still drive him wild."

Already Chum had gotten a whiff and was leaping at his leash. Foam burst from between his lips and frothed on the leather bands of the muzzle.

"I suppose it isn't polite to lecture a captive audience, Dennis, but I thought you might like to know a few things about dogs. No need to take notes. You won't be around for a quiz later.

"But here's some things to tuck in the back of your mind while you and Chum are alone. Dogs are very strong, Dennis. Very. They look small compared to a man, even a big dog like a Doberman, but they can exert a lot of pressure with their bite. I've seen dogs like Chum here, especially when they're exposed to my little spray, bite through the thicker end of a baseball bat. And they're quick. You'd have a better chance against a black belt in karate than an attack dog."

"Morley," Dennis said softly, "you can't do this."

"I can't?" Morley seemed to consider. "No, Dennis, I believe I can. I give myself permission. But hey, Dennis, I'm going to give you a chance. This is the good part now, so listen up. You're a sporting man. Basketball. Racquetball. Chess. Another man's woman. So, you'll like this. This will appeal to your sense of competition.

"Julie didn't give Chum a fight at all. She just couldn't believe her Chummy-whummy wanted to eat her. Just wouldn't. She held out her hand, trying to soothe the old boy, and he just bit it right off. Right off. Got half the palm and the fingers in one bite. That's when I left them alone. I had a feeling her Chummy-whummy might start on me next, and I wouldn't have wanted that. Oooohhh, those sharp teeth. Like nails being driven into you."

"Morley listen—"

"Shut up! You, Mr. Cock Dog and Basketball Star, just might have a chance. Not much of one, but I know you'll fight. You're not a quitter. I can tell by the way you play chess. You still lose, but you're not a quitter. You hang in there to the bitter end."

Morley took a deep breath, stood in the chair and hung the lantern on a low rafter. There was something else up there too. A coiled chain. Morley pulled it down and it clattered to the floor. At the sound of it Chum leaped against his leash and flecks of saliva flew from his mouth and Dennis felt them fall lightly on his hands and face.

Morley lifted one end of the chain toward Dennis. There was a thin, open collar attached to it.

"Once this closes, it locks and can only be opened with this." Morley reached into his coat pocket and produced a key, held it up briefly and returned it. "There's a collar for Chum on the other end. Both are made out of good leather over strong, steel chain. See what I'm getting at here, Dennis?"

Morley leaned forward and snapped the collar around Dennis's neck.

"Oh, Dennis," Morley said, standing back to observe his handiwork. "It's you. Really. Great fit. And considering the day, just call this my Valentine to you."

"You bastard."

"The biggest."

Morley walked over to Chum. Chum lunged at him, but with the muzzle on he was relatively harmless. Still, his weight hit Morley's legs, almost knocked him down.

Turning to smile at Dennis, Morley said, "See how strong he is? Add teeth to this little engine, some maneuverability . . . it's going to be awesome, lover boy. Awesome."

Morley slipped the collar under Chum's leash and snapped it into place even as the dog rushed against him, nearly knocking him down. But it wasn't Morley he wanted. He was trying to get at the smell. At Dennis.

Dennis felt as if the fluids in his body were running out of drains at the bottoms of his feet.

"Was a little poontang worth this, Dennis? I certainly hope you think so. I hope it was the best goddamn piece you ever got. Sincerely, I do. Because death by dog is slow and ugly, lover boy. They like the throat and balls. So, you watch those spots, hear?"

"Morley, for God's sake, don't do this!"

Morley pulled a revolver from his coat pocket and walked over to Dennis. "I'm going to untie you now, stud. I want you to be real good, or I'll shoot you. If I shoot you, I'll gut shoot you, then let the dog loose. You got no chance that way. At least my way you've got a sporting chance—slim to none."

He untied Dennis. "Now stand."

Dennis stood in front of the chair, his knees quivering. He was looking at Chum and Chum was looking at him, tugging wildly at the leash, which looked ready to snap. Saliva was thick as shaving cream over the front of Chum's muzzle.

Morley held the revolver on Dennis with one hand, and with the other he reproduced the aerosol can, sprayed Dennis once more. The stench made Dennis's head float.

"Last word of advice," Morley said. "He'll go straight for you."

"Morley . . . ," Dennis started, but one look at the man and he knew he was better off saving the breath. He was going to need it.

Still holding the gun on Dennis, Morley eased behind the frantic dog, took hold of the muzzle with his free hand, and with a quick ripping motion, pulled it and the leash loose.

Chum sprang.

Dennis stepped back, caught the chair between his legs, lost his balance. Chum's leap carried him into Dennis's chest, and they both went flipping over the chair.

Chum kept rolling and the chain pulled across Dennis's face as the dog tumbled to its full length; the jerk of the sixty-pound weight against Dennis's neck was like a blow.

The chain went slack, and Dennis knew Chum was coming. In that same instant he heard the door open, glimpsed a wedge of moonlight that came and went, heard the door lock and Morley laugh. Then he was rolling, coming to his knees, grabbing the chair, pointing it with the legs out.

And Chum hit him.

The chair took most of the impact, but it was like trying to block a cannonball. The chair's bottom cracked and a leg broke off, went skidding across the floor.

The truncated triangle of the Doberman's head appeared over the top of the chair, straining for Dennis's face. Dennis rammed the chair forward.

Chum dipped under it, grabbed Dennis's side. It was like stepping into a bear trap. The agony wasn't just in the ankle, it was a sizzling web of electricity that surged through his entire body.

The dog's teeth grated bone and Dennis let forth with a noise that was too wicked to be called a scream.

Blackness waved in and out, but the thought of Julie lying there in ragged display gave him new determination.

He brought the chair down on the dog's head with all his might.

Chum let out a yelp, and the dark head darted away.

Dennis stayed low, pulled his wounded leg back, attempted to keep the chair in front of him. But Chum was a black bullet. He shot under again, hit Dennis in the same leg, higher up this time. The impact slid Dennis back a foot. Still, he felt a certain relief. The dog's teeth had missed his balls by an inch.

Oddly there was little pain this time. It was as if he were being encased in dark amber; floating in limbo. Must be like this when a shark hits, he thought. So hard and fast and clean you don't really feel it at first. Just go numb. Look down for your leg and it's gone.

The dark amber was penetrated by a bright stab of pain. But Dennis was grateful for it. It meant that his brain was working again. He swiped at Chum with the chair, broke him loose.

Swiveling on one knee, Dennis again used the chair as a shield. Chum launched forward, trying to go under it, but Dennis was ready this time and brought it down hard against the floor.

Chum hit the bottom of the chair with such an impact, his head broke through the thin slats. Teeth snapped in Dennis's face, but the dog couldn't squirm its shoulders completely through the hole and reach him.

Dennis let go of the chair with one hand, slugged the dog in the side of the head with the other. Chum twisted and the chair came loose from Dennis. The dog bounded away, leaping and whipping its body left and right, finally tossing off the wooden collar.

Grabbing the slack of the chain, Dennis used both hands to whip it into the dog's head, then swung it back and caught Chum's feet, knocking him on his side with a loud splat.

Even as Chum was scrambling to his feet, out of the corner of his eye Dennis spotted the leg that had broken off the chair. It was lying less than three feet away.

Chum rushed and Dennis dove for the leg, grabbed it, twisted and swatted at the Doberman. On the floor as he was, he couldn't get full power into the blow, but still it was a good one.

The dog skidded sideways on its belly and forelegs. When it came to a halt, it tried to raise its head, but didn't completely make it.

Dennis scrambled forward on his hands and knees, chopped the chair leg down on the Doberman's head with every ounce of muscle he could muster. The strike was solid, caught the dog right between the pointed ears and drove his head to the floor.

The dog whimpered. Dennis hit him again. And again.

Chum lay still.

Dennis took a deep breath, watched the dog and held his club cocked.

Chum did not move. He lay on the floor with his legs spread wide, his tongue sticking out of his foam-wet mouth.

Dennis was breathing heavily, and his wounded leg felt as if it were melting. He tried to stretch it out, alleviate some of the pain, but nothing helped.

He checked the dog again.

Still not moving.

He took hold of the chain and jerked it. Chum's head came up and smacked back down against the floor.

The dog was dead. He could see that.

He relaxed, closed his eyes and tried to make the spinning stop. He knew he had to bandage his leg somehow, stop the flow of blood. But at the moment he could hardly think.

And Chum, who was not dead, but stunned, lifted his head, and at the same moment, Dennis opened his eyes.

The Doberman's recovery was remarkable. It came off the floor with only the slightest wobble and jumped.

Dennis couldn't get the chair leg around in time and it deflected off of the animal's smooth back and slipped from his grasp.

He got Chum around the throat and tried to strangle him, but the collar was in the way and the dog's neck was too damn big.

Trying to get better traction, Dennis got his bad leg under him and made an effort to stand, lifting the dog with him. He used his good leg to knee Chum sharply in the chest, but the injured leg wasn't good for holding him up for another move like that. He kept trying to ease his thumbs beneath the collar and lock them behind the dog's windpipe.

Chum's hind legs were off the floor and scrambling, the toenails tearing at Dennis's lower abdomen and crotch.

Dennis couldn't believe how strong the dog was. Sixty pounds of pure muscle and energy, made deadlier by Morley's spray and tortures.

Sixty pounds of muscle.

The thought went through Dennis's head again.

Sixty pounds.

The medicine ball he tossed at the gym weighed more. It didn't have teeth, muscle and determination, but it did weigh more.

And as the realization soaked in, as his grip weakened and Chum's rancid breath coated his face, Dennis lifted his eyes to a rafter just two feet above his head; considered there was another two feet of space between the rafter and the ceiling.

He quit trying to choke Chum, eased his left hand into the dog's collar, and grabbed a hind leg with his other. Slowly, he lifted Chum over his head. Teeth snapped at Dennis's hair, pulled loose a few tufts.

Dennis spread his legs slightly. The wounded leg wobbled like an old pipe cleaner, but held. The dog seemed to weigh a hundred pounds. Even the sweat on his face and the dense, hot air in the room seemed heavy.

Sixty pounds.

A basketball weighed little to nothing, and the dog weighed less than the huge medicine ball in the gym. Somewhere between the two was a happy medium; he had the strength to lift the dog, the skill to make the shot—the most important of his life.

Grunting, cocking the wiggling dog into position, he prepared to shoot. Chum nearly twisted free, but Dennis gritted his teeth, and with a wild scream, launched the dog into space.

Chum didn't go up straight, but he did go up. He hit the top of the rafter with his back, tried to twist in the direction he had come, couldn't, and went over the other side.

Dennis grabbed the chain as high up as possible, bracing as Chum's weight came down on the other side so violently it pulled him onto his toes.

The dog made a gurgling sound, spun on the end of the chain, legs thrashing.

It took a long fifteen minutes for Chum to strangle.

When Chum was dead, Dennis tried to pull him over the rafter. The dog's weight, Dennis's bad leg, and his now aching arms and back, made it a greater chore than he had anticipated. Chum's head kept slamming against the rafter. Dennis got hold of the unbroken chair, and used it as a stepladder. He managed the Doberman over, and Chum fell to the floor, his neck flopping loosely.

Dennis sat down on the floor beside the dog and patted it on the head. "Sorry," he said.

He took off his shirt, tore it into rags and bound his bad leg with it. It was still bleeding steadily, but not gushing; no major artery had been torn. His ankle wasn't bleeding as much, but in the dim lantern light he could see that Chum had bitten him to the bone. He used most of the shirt to wrap and strengthen the ankle.

When he finished, he managed to stand. The shirt binding had stopped the bleeding and the short rest had slightly rejuvenated him.

He found his eyes drawn to the mess in the corner that was Julie, and his first thought was to cover her, but there wasn't anything in the room sufficient for the job.

He closed his eyes and tried to remember how it had been before.

When she was whole and the room had a mattress and they had made love all the long, sweet, Mexican afternoon. But the right images would not come. Even with his eyes closed, he could see her mauled body on the floor.

Ducking his head made some of the dizziness go away, and he was able to get Julie out of his mind by thinking of Morley. He wondered when he could come back. If he was waiting outside.

But no, that wouldn't be Morley's way. He wouldn't be anxious. He was cocksure of himself, he would go back to the estate for a drink and maybe play a game of chess against himself, gloat a long, sweet while before coming back to check on his handiwork. It would never occur to Morley to think he had survived. That would not cross his mind. Morley saw himself as Life's best chess master, and he did not make wrong moves; things went according to plan. Most likely, he wouldn't even check until morning.

The more Dennis thought about it, the madder he got and the stronger he felt. He moved the chair beneath the rafter where the lantern was hung, climbed up and got it down. He inspected the windows and doors. The door had a sound lock, but the windows were merely boarded. Barrier enough when he was busy with the dog, but not now.

He put the lantern on the floor, turned it up, found the chair leg he had used against Chum, and substituted it for a pry bar. It was hard work and by the time he had worked the boards off the window his hands were bleeding and full of splinters. His face looked demonic.

Pulling Chum to him, he tossed him out the window, climbed after him clutching the chair leg. He took up the chain's slack and hitched it around his forearm. He wondered about the other Dobermans. Wondered if Morley had killed them too, or if he was keeping them around. As he recalled, the Dobermans were usually loose in the yard at night. The rest of the time they had free run of the house, except Morley's study, his sanctuary. And hadn't Morley said that later on the spray killed a man's scent?

That was worth something; it could be the edge he needed.

But it didn't really matter. Nothing mattered anymore. Six dogs. Six war elephants. He was going after Morley.

He began dragging the floppy-necked Chum toward the estate.

Morley was sitting at his desk playing a game of chess with himself, and both sides were doing quite well, he thought. He had a glass of brandy at his elbow, and from time to time he would drink from it, cock his head and consider his next move.

Outside the study door, in the hall, he could hear Julie's dogs padding nervously. They wanted out, and in the past they would have been in the yard long before now. But tonight he hadn't bothered. He hated those bastards, and just maybe he'd get rid of them. Shoot them and install a burglar alarm. Alarms didn't have to eat or be let out to shit, and they wouldn't turn on you. And he wouldn't have to listen to the sound of dog toenails clicking on the tile outside of his study door.

He considered letting the Dobermans out, but hesitated. Instead, he opened a box of special Cuban cigars, took one, rolled it between his fingers near his ear so he could hear the fresh crackle of good tobacco. He clipped the end off the cigar with a silver clipper, put it in his mouth and lit it with a desk lighter without actually putting the flame to it. He drew in a deep lungful of smoke and relished it, let it out with a soft, contented sigh.

At the same moment he heard a sound, like something being dragged across the gravel drive. He sat motionless a moment, not batting an eye. It couldn't be lover boy, he thought. No way.

He walked across the room, pulled the curtain back from the huge glass door, unlocked it and slid it open.

A cool wind had come along and it was shaking the trees in the yard, but nothing else was moving. Morley searched the tree shadows for some telltale sign, but saw nothing.

Still, he was not one for imagination. He had heard something. He went back to the desk chair where his coat hung, reached the revolver from his pocket, turned.

And there was Dennis. Shirtless, one pants leg mostly ripped away. There were blood-stained bandages on his thigh and ankle. He had the chain partially coiled around one arm, and Chum, quite dead, was lying on the floor beside him. In his right hand Dennis held a chair leg, and at the same moment Morley noted this and raised the revolver, Dennis threw it.

The leg hit Morley squarely between the eyes, knocked him against his desk, and as he tried to right himself, Dennis took hold of the chain and used it to swing the dead dog. Chum struck Morley on the ankles and took him down like a scythe cutting fresh wheat. Morley's head slammed into the edge of the desk and blood dribbled into his eyes; everything seemed to be in a Mixmaster, whirling so fast nothing was identifiable.

When the world came to rest, he saw Dennis standing over him with the revolver. Morley could not believe the man's appearance. His lips were split in a thin grin that barely showed his teeth. His face was drawn and his eyes were strange and savage. It was apparent he had found the key in the coat, because the collar was gone.

Out in the hall, bouncing against the door, Morley could hear Julie's dogs. They sensed the intruder and wanted at him. He wished now he had left the study door open, or put them out in the yard.

"I've got money," Morley said.

"Fuck your money," Dennis screamed. "I'm not selling anything here. Get up and get over here."

Morley followed the wave of the revolver to the front of his desk. Dennis swept the chess set and stuff aside with a swipe of his arm and bent Morley backwards over the desk. He put one of the collars around Morley's neck, pulled the chain around the desk a few times, pushed it under and fastened the other collar over Morley's ankles.

Tucking the revolver into the waistband of his pants, Dennis picked up Chum and tenderly placed him on the desk chair, half-curled. He tried to poke the dog's tongue back into his mouth, but that didn't work. He patted Chum on the head, said, "There, now."

Dennis went around and stood in front of Morley and looked at him, as if memorizing the moment.

At his back the Dobermans rattled the door.

"We can make a deal," Morley said. "I can give you a lot of money, and you can go away. We'll call it even."

Dennis unfastened Morley's pants, pulled them down to his knees. He pulled the underwear down. He went around and got the spray can out of Morley's coat and came back.

"This isn't sporting, Dennis At least I gave you a fighting chance."

"I'm not a sport," Dennis said.

He sprayed Morley's testicles with the chemical. When he finished, he tossed the canister aside, walked over to the door and listened to the Dobermans scuttling on the other side.

"Dennis!"

Dennis took hold of the doorknob.

"Screw you, then," Morley said. "I'm not afraid. I won't scream. I won't give you the pleasure."

"You didn't even love her," Dennis said, and opened the door.

The Dobermans went straight for the stench of the spray, straight for Morley's testicles.

Dennis walked calmly out the back way, closed the glass door. And as he limped down the drive, making for the gate, he began to laugh.

Morley had lied. He did too scream. In fact, he was still screaming.

I love stories with young people as protagonists. I love coming-of-age stories. People have asked, How do you write about young people? Well, we've all been one, haven't we? I am also interested in the Great Depression, as my parents lived through it. They were older when I was born, so the Great Depression had colored the totality of their existence. My wife and I save everything. Too much. We have a lot of crap that we are just now divesting ourselves of, and should have long ago. This is the Depression-era mindset: "Save that. You might need it." There was a time, growing up, when it always seemed we did. Now, we save things and put them up, forget where they are, buy replacements when needed, put up extra materials—rubber bands, paper clips, as well as items much larger—and then forget where they are. The process starts over. I have always been interested in Geronimo as well. He was an amazing warrior and held off the United States Army with slightly more than twenty warriors for years. So, my interest in the Western era and the Great Depression, coming-of-age stories, and being asked by my friend Patrick Miliken to write a story having to do with an automobile for an anthology he was editing produced this. It's also a road story. Lot of bases are covered with this one, and it is one of my personal favorites. I have quite a few. More than fifty years of writing, or close to it, have allowed me to produce a lot, so I don't have to pick one or two stories out of a dozen. I'm into hundreds of stories, and I've made no secret that of all my writing, the short story is my favorite form of expression.

DRIVING TO GEROMINO'S GRAVE

We ought to never do wrong when people are looking.
—Mark Twain

I HADN'T EVEN been good and awake for five minutes when Mama came in and said, "Chauncey, you got to drive on up to Fort Sill, Oklahoma, and pick up your Uncle Smat."

I was still sitting on the bed, waking up, wearing my nightdress, trying to figure which foot went into what shoe, when she come in and said that. She had her dark hair pushed up on her head and held in place with a checkered scarf.

"Why would I drive to Oklahoma and pick up Uncle Smat?"

"Well, I got a letter from some folks got his body, and you need to bring it back so we can bury it. The Wentworths said they were gonna leave it in the chicken house if nobody comes for it. I wrote her back and posted the letter already telling her you're coming."

"Uncle Smat's dead?" I said.

"We wouldn't want to bury him otherwise," Mama said, "though it took a lot longer for him to get dead than I would have figured, way he honky-tonked and fooled around with disreputable folks. Someone knifed him. Stuck him like a pig at one of them drinking places, I figure."

"I ain't never driven nowhere except around town," I said. "I don't even know which way is Oklahoma."

"North," Mama said.

"Well, I knew that much," I said.

"Start in that direction and watch for signs," she said. "I'm sure there are some. I got your breakfast ready, and I'll pack you some lunch and give you their address, and you can be off."

Now this was all a fine good morning, and me hardly knowing who Uncle Smat was, Mama not really caring that much about him, Smat being my dead daddy's brother. She had cared about Daddy plenty, though, and she had what you could call family obligation toward Uncle Smat. As I got dressed she talked.

"It isn't right to leave a man, even a man you don't know so well, laying out in a chicken house with chickens to peck on him. And there's all that chicken mess too. I dreamed last night a chicken snake crawled over him."

I put on a clean work shirt and overalls and some socks that was sewed up in the heels and toes, put on and tied my shoes, slapped some hair oil on my head and combed my hair in a little piece of mirror I had on the dresser. I packed a tow sack with some clothes and a few odds and ends I might need. I had a toothbrush and a small jar of baking soda and salt for tooth wash. Mama was one of the few in our family who had all her teeth, and she claimed that was because she used a brush made from hair bristles and she used that soda and salt. I believed her, and both me and my sister followed her practice.

Mama had some sourdough bread, and she gave that to me, and she filled a couple of my dad's old canteens with water, put a blanket and some other goods together for me. I loaded them in a good-sized tow sack and carried it out to the Ford and put the bag inside the turtle hull.

In the kitchen, I washed up in the dish pan, toweled off, and sat down to breakfast, a half a dozen fried eggs, biscuits, and a pitcher of buttermilk. I poured a glass of milk and drank it, and then I poured another, and ate along with drinking the milk.

Mama, who had already eaten, sat at the far end of the table and looked at me.

"You drive careful now, and you might want to stop somewhere and pick some flowers."

"I'm picking him up, not attending his funeral," I said.

"He might be a bit stinky, him lying in a chicken coop and being dead," Mama said. "So I'm thinking the flowers might contribute to a more pleasant trip. Oh, I tell you what. I got some cheap perfume I don't never use, so you can take that with you and pour it on him, you need to."

I was chewing on a biscuit when she said this.

I finished chewing fast as I could, said, "Now wait a minute. I just got to thinking on this good. I'm picking him up in the car, and that means he's going to go in the backseat, and I see how he could have grown a mite ripe, but Mama, are you telling me he ain't going to be in a coffin or nothing?"

"The letter said he was lying out in the chicken coop, where he was living with the chickens, having to only pay a quarter a week and feed the chickens to be there, and one morning they came out to see why he hadn't gathered the eggs and brought them up—that also being part of his job for staying in the coop—and they found him out there, colder than a wedge in winter. He'd been stabbed, and he had managed to get back to the coop where he bled out. Just died quietly out there with their chickens. They didn't know what to do with him at first, but they found a letter he had from his brother, that would be your father—" She added that like I couldn't figure it on my own.

"—and there was an address on it, so they wrote us."

"They didn't move the body?"

"Didn't know what to do with it. They said in the letter they had sewed a burial shroud you can put him in; it's a kind of bag."

"I have to pour perfume on him, put him in a bag, and drive him home in the backseat of the car?"

"Reckon that's about the size of it. I don't know no one else would bother to go get him."

"Do I have to? Thinking on it more, I'm not sure it's such a good idea."

"Course you got to go. They're expecting you."

"Write them a letter and tell them I ain't coming. They can maybe bury him out by the chicken coop or something."

"That's a mean thing to say."

"I didn't hardly know him," I said, "certainly not enough to perfume him, bag him up, and drive him home."

"You don't have to have known him all that well, he's family."

My little sister, Terri, came in then. She's twelve and has her hair cut straight across in front and short in back. She had on overalls with a work shirt and work boots. She almost looked like a boy. She said, "I was thinking I ought to go with you."

"You was thinking that, huh," I said.

"It might not be such a bad idea," Mama said. "She can read the map."

"I can read a map," I said.

"Not while you're driving," Mama said.

"I can pull over."

"This way, though," Mama said, "you can save some serious time, just having her read it and point out things."

"He's been dead for near two weeks or so. I don't know how much pressure there is on me to get there."

"Longer you wait, the more he stinks," Terri said.

"She has a point," Mama said.

"Ain't they supposed to report a dead body? Them people found him, I mean? Ain't it against the law to just leave a dead fella lying around?"

"They done us a favor, Uncle Smat being family and all," Mama said. "They could have just left him, or buried him out there with the chickens."

"I wish they had," I said. "I made that suggestion, remember?"

"This way we can bury him in the cemetery where your daddy is buried," Mama said. "That's what your daddy would have wanted."

She knew I wasn't going to say anything bad that had to do with Daddy in any manner shape or form. I thought that was a low blow, but Mama, as they say, knew her chickens. She knew where I was the weakest.

"All right then," I said, "I'm going to get him. But that car of ours has been driven hard and might not be much for a long trip. The clutch hangs sometimes when you press on it."

"That's a chance you have to take for family," Mama said.

I grumbled something, but I knew by then I was going.

"I'm going, too," Terri said.

"Oh, hell, come on then," I said.

"Watch your cussing," Mama said. "Daddy wouldn't like that either."

"All he did was cuss," I said.

"Yeah, but he didn't want you to," she said.

"I think I'm gonna cuss," I said. "My figuring is Daddy would have wanted me to be good at it, and that takes practice."

"I ain't forgot how to whip your ass with a switch," Mama said.

Now it was figured by Mama that it would take us two days to get to the Wentworths' house and chicken coop if we drove fast and didn't stop to see the sights and such, and then two days back. As we got started out early morning, we had a pretty good jump on the first day.

The clutch hung a few times but seemed mostly to be cooperating, and I only ground the gears now and again, but that was my fault, not the car's, though in the five years we had owned it, it had been worked like a stolen mule. Daddy drove that car all over the place looking for spots of work. His last job had been for the WPA, and we seen men working those jobs as we drove along, digging out bar ditches and building walls for what I reckoned would be schools or some such. Daddy used to say it was mostly busywork, but it paid real money, and real money spent just fine.

Terri had the map in her lap, and from time to time she'd look at it, say, "You're doing all right."

"Of course I am," I said. "This is the only highway to Marvel Creek. When we need the map is when we get off the main road and onto them little routes back in there."

"It's good to make sure you don't get veered," Terri said.

"I ain't getting veered," I said.

"Way I figure it, it's gonna take three days to get there, or most near a full three days, not two like Mama said."

"You figured that, did you?"

"I reckoned in the miles and how fast the car is going, if that speedometer is right, and then I put some math to it, and I come up with three days. I got an A in math."

"Since it's the summer, I reckon you've done forgot what math you learned," I said.

"I remember. Three days at this pace is right, and this is about as fast as you ought to go. Slowing wouldn't hurt a little. As it is, we blowed a tire, they wouldn't find nothing but our clothes in some bushes alongside the road, and they'd be full of shit."

End of that day we come near the Oklahoma border. It was starting to be night, so I pulled us over and down a little path, and we parked under a tree for the night. We had some egg sandwiches Mama had made, and we ate them. They had gotten kind of soggy, but it was that or wishful thinking, so we ate them and drank some water from the canteens.

We threw a blanket on the ground and laid down on that and looked up through the tree limbs at the stars.

"Ever wonder what's out there?" Terri said.

"I read this book once, about this fella went to Mars. And there was some green creatures there with four arms."

"No joke?"

"No joke."

"Must have been a good book."

"It was," I said. "And there was four-armed white apes, and regular-looking people too, only they were red-skinned."

"Did they have four arms too?"

"No. They were like us, except for the red skin."

"That's not as good," Terri said. "I'd like to have had me four arms, if I was one of them, and otherwise looked regular."

"You wouldn't look regular with four arms," I said.

"I could stand it," Terri said. "I could pick up a lot of things at once."

When we woke up the next morning, my back hurt considerable. I had stretched the blanket out on an acorn, and it had stuck me all night. I come awake a few times during the night and was going to pull back the blanket and move it, but I was too darn tired to move. In the morning, though, I wished I had. I felt like I had been shot with an arrow right above my belt line.

Terri, however, was as chipper as if she had good sense. She had some boiled eggs in the package Mama had ended up giving her after it was decided she was going, and we had one apiece for breakfast and some more canteen water.

After wrapping up the blanket, we climbed back in the car and started out again, drove on across the line and into Oklahoma, crossing the Red River, which wasn't really all that much of a river. At that time of the year, at least where we crossed, it wasn't hardly no more than a muddy trickle, though as we crossed the bridge, I could see down a distance to where it was wider and deeper-looking.

We come to a little town called Hootie Hoot, which seemed to me to be a bad name for most anything, and there was one gas pump outside a little store there, and by the door going into the store was a sign that said they was looking for a tire-and-rim man. We could see the gas in the big jug on top of the pump, so we knew there was plenty, and we pulled up to it. Couple other stations we had passed were out of gas.

After we had sat there awhile, an old man with bushy white hair wearing overalls so faded they was near white as his hair came out of the station. He had a big red nose and looked like he had just got out of bed. We stood outside the car while he filled the tank.

"They say the Depression has done turned around," he said. "But if it did, it darn sure didn't turn in this direction."

"No, sir," I said.

"Ain't you a little young to be driving around?" he said.

"Not that young," I said.

He eyed me some. "I guess not. You children on an errand?"

"We are," I said. "We're going to pick up my Uncle Smat."

"Family outing?"

"You could say that."

"So we will," he said.

"We might want something from the store too," I said.

"All right, then," he said.

Me and Terri went inside, and he hung up the gas nozzle and trailed after us.

I didn't have a lot of money, a few dollars Mama had given me for gas and such, but I didn't want another soggy egg sandwich or a boiled egg. I bought some Vienna sausages, some sardines and a box of crackers, and splurged on Coca-Colas for the two of us. I got some shelled and salted peanuts to pour into the Coca-Colas, bought four slices of bread, two cuts of bologna, and two fat cuts of rat cheese. The smell of that cheese made me seriously hungry; it was right smart in aroma and my nose hairs tingled.

We paid up, and I pulled the car away from the pump, on around beside the store. We sat on the bumper and made us a sandwich from the bread, bologna and cheese. It was a lot better than those soggy egg sandwiches Mama had made us, and though we had two more of them, they had reached a point where I considered them turned, and I planned on throwing them out on the road before we left.

That's when a ragged-looking fellow come up the road to the store and stopped when he seen us. He beat the dust off the shoulders and sides of his blue suit coat. His gray hat looked as if a goat had bitten a hunk out of the front of it. The suit he was wearing had been nice at one time, but it was worn shiny in spots and hung on him like a circus tent. His shoe toes flapped when he walked like they were trying to talk. He said, "I hate to bother you children, but I ain't ate in a couple days, nothing solid anyway, and was wondering you got something to spare?"

"We got some egg sandwiches," Terri said. "You can have both of them."

"That would be right nice," said the ragged man.

He came over smiling. Up close, he looked as if he had been boiled in dirt, his skin was so dusty from walking along the road. One of his nose holes was smaller than the other. I hadn't never seen nobody like that before. It wouldn't have been all that noticeable, but he had a way of tilting his head back when he talked.

Terri gave him the sandwiches. He opened up the paper they was in, laid them on the hood of our car, took hold of one, and started to wolf it down. When he had it about ate, he said, "That egg tastes a might rubbery. You ain't got nothing to wash it down?"

"We could run you a bath if you want, and maybe we could polish your shoes for you," Terri said. "But we ain't got nothing to wash down that free sandwich."

The dusty man narrowed his eyes at Terri, then gathered himself.

"I didn't mean to sound ungrateful," he said.

"I don't think you give a damn one way or the other," Terri said.

"Look here," I said. "I got the last of this Coca-Cola; you don't mind drinking after me, you can have that. It's got a few peanuts in it."

He took the Coca-Cola and swigged some. "Listen here, could you spare a few other things, some clothes, some more food? I could give you a check."

"A check?" Terri said. "What would it be good for?"

The man gave her a look that was considerably less pleasant than a moment ago.

"We don't want no check," Terri said. "We had something to sell, and we don't, we'd want cash money."

The man's eyes narrowed. "Well, I ain't got no cash money."

"There you are, then," Terri said. "A check ain't nothing but a piece of paper with your name on it."

"It represents money in the bank," said the man.

"It don't represent money we can see, though," Terri said.

"That's all right," I said. "Here, you take this dollar and go in there and buy you something with it. That's my last dollar."

It wasn't my last dollar, but when I pulled it out of my pocket, way he stared at it made me nervous.

"I'll take it," he said. He started walking toward the store. After a few steps, he paused and looked back at us. "You was right not to take no check from me, baby girl. It wouldn't have been worth the paper it was written on. And let me tell you something. You ought to save up and buy yourself a dress and some hair bows, a dab of makeup, maybe take a year or two of charm lessons."

He went on in the store, and I hustled us up, taking what was left of our sandwiches with us and getting into the car.

"Why you in such a hurry?" Terri said, as I drove away.

"Something about that fella bothers me," I said. "I think he's trouble."

"I don't know how much trouble he is," Terri said, "but I darn sure had him figured on that check. As for a dress and hair bows, he can kiss my ass. I wish him and all fools like him would die."

"You can't wish for all fools to die, Terri. That ain't right."

Terri pursed her lips. "I guess you're right. All them fools died, I'd be pretty lonely."

I guess we went about twenty miles before the motor steamed up and I had to pull the Ford over. I picked a spot where there was a wide place in the road, and stopped there and got out and put the hood up and looked under it like I knew what was going on. And I did, a little. I had developed an interest in cars, same as Daddy. He liked to work on them and said if he wasn't a farmer he'd like to fix engines. I used to go with him when he went outside to put water in the radiator and mess with the motor. Still, I wasn't what you'd call a mechanic.

"You done run it too long without checking the water," Terri said.

I gave her a hard look. "If you weren't here, I don't know what I'd think was wrong with it."

I got a rag out of the turtle hull, got some of our canteen water, and using the rag, unscrewed the radiator lid. I had Terri stand back, on account of when I poured the water in some hot, wet spray boiled up. Radiator was bone dry.

We got enough water in the car to keep going, but now we were out of water to drink. We poked along until I saw a creek running alongside the road and off into the woods. We pulled down a tight trail with trees on both sides, got out and refilled the canteens from a clear and fast-running part of the creek. The water tasted cold and clean. I used the canteens to finish filling the radiator, and then we filled them for us to drink. I decided to take notice of this spot, in case we needed it on the way back. While I was contemplating, Terri picked up a rock and zinged it side-arm into a tree, and a red bird fell out of it and hit the ground.

"You see that," she said. "Killed it with one shot."

"Damn it, Terri. Wasn't no cause for that."

"I just wanted to."

"You don't kill things you don't eat. Daddy taught you that."

"I guess we could eat it."

"No. We're not eating any red birds. And don't you never kill another."

"All right," she said. "I didn't really know I'd hit it. But I'm pretty good with rocks. You know Gyp Martin? Well, he called me a little bitch the other day, and I hit him with a rock so hard it knocked him cold out."

"No it didn't."

"Yes it did. Sharon Miller was with me and seen it."

"Terri. You got to quit with the rocks. I mean, well, I give you this. That was a good shot. I don't know if I can even throw that far."

"I'd be surprised if you could," she said. "It's a natural talent for a rare few, but then you got to develop it."

We got to where we were going about dark that day.

"I thought you said three days," I said. "We made it in two, way Mama said."

"Guess I figured in too many stops and maybe a cow crossing the road or something."

"You did that, did you?"

"I was thinking you'd want to stop and see the sights, even though you said you didn't."

"What sights?"

"That turned out to be the problem. No sights."

"Terri, you are full of it, and I don't just mean hot wind."

The property was off the road, up in the woods, and not quite on top of a hill. We could see the house as we drove up the dirt drive. It was big, but looked as if it might slip off the hill at any moment and tumble down on us. It was even more weathered than our home place.

The outhouse out back was in better shape than where they lived.

As we came rest of the way up the hill, we saw there were hog pens out to the side with fat black-and-white hogs in them. Behind that we could see a sizable run of henhouses. I had expected just one little henhouse, but these houses were plentiful and had enough chicken wire around them you could have used it to fence in Rhode Island.

I parked the Ford and we went up and knocked on the door. A man came to the door and looked at us through the screen. Then he came out on the porch. He had the appearance of someone that had been thrown off a train. His clothes were dirty and his hat was mashed in front. His body seemed about forty, but his face looked about eighty. He was missing all his teeth, and had his jaw packed with tobacco. I figured he took that tobacco out, his face would collapse.

"Who are you?" he said, and spat tobacco juice into a dry flower bed.

"The usual greeting is hello," Terri said.

I said, "Watch this, sir." And I gave Terri a kick in the leg.

"She had that coming," he said.

Terri hopped off the porch and leapt around yipping while I said, "We got a letter from your missus, and if we got the right place, our Uncle Smat is in your chicken house."

"You're in the right place. When she quits hopping, step around to the side, start up toward the chicken houses, and you'll smell him. He ain't actually up in a henhouse no more. A goddang old dog got in there and got to him, dragged him through a hole in the fence, on up over the hill there, into them trees. But you can smell him strong enough you'd think he was riding on your back. You'll find him."

"You didn't have to kick me," Terri said.

"I got a bit of thrill out of it," said Mr. Wentworth. "I thought maybe you was a kangaroo."

Terri glared at him.

A woman wiping her hands with a dish towel, and looking a lot neater, came to the door and stepped out on the porch.

"You take these kids to their uncle," she said to the man.

"They can smell him," he said.

"You take them out there. I'll go with you."

She threw the dish towel inside the door, said, "But I got something you'll need."

Mrs. Wentworth went in the house and came out with a jar of VapoRub and had us dab a good wad under our noses so as to limit the smell of Uncle Smat. I was beginning to get a bit weak on the whole idea of a Christian burial for a man I'd never seen, and by all accounts wasn't worth the water it'd take to put him out if he was on fire.

Dabbed up, we all started around the house and up the higher part of the hill. We passed the chicken coops, and as we did, this gave Mrs. Wentworth a moment for a bit of historical background concerning their time with Uncle Smat.

"He walked up one day and said he needed a job, most anything so he could eat. So we put him out there chopping firewood, which he did a fair job of. We let him sleep in one of the coops that didn't have a lot of chickens in. We couldn't have some unknown fella sleeping in the house. Next day he wanted more work, and so he ended up staying and taking care of the chickens, a job at which he was passable. Then one night he come up on the porch, a-banging on the door, drunk as Cooter Brown. We wouldn't let him in and told him to go on out to the coop and sleep it off."

Mr. Wentworth picked up the story there. "Next morning he didn't come down to the back porch for his biscuits, so I went up there and found him dead. He'd been knifed. I guess maybe he wasn't drunk after all."

"He was drunk all right," Mrs. Wentworth said. "That might have killed some of the pain for him. Fact was, I don't know I'd ever heard anyone drunk as he was that was able to stand. I went through his clothes, and he had some serious money on him, and I won't lie to you, we took that as his room and board money."

"You robbed a dead man for sleeping in your chicken coop?" Terri said. "Why didn't you just take his shoes too?"

Mr. Wentworth cleared his throat. "Well, they *was* the same size as mine, and he didn't need them."

Wentworth lifted a foot and showed us a brown brogan.

"Them toes was real scuffed up," Mrs. Wentworth said, "so I put some VapoRub on them, rubbed it in good, and put a solid shine on them, took out some of that roughness."

"Damn," Terri said, looking down at the shoes on Mr. Wentworth's feet. "You did take his shoes."

"You're talking like a gun moll," Mrs. Wentworth said to Terri.

"I'm talking like someone whose uncle was robbed of money and shoes, that's how I'm talking," Terri said.

"It's all right," I said. "Let's see him."

As we walked along, Mr. Wentworth said, "When I come to look in on his body yesterday, he wasn't in the coop, but the coop was broke open, and something had dragged him off. It was either a pack of dogs or coyotes. They dragged him up there a ways and chewed off one of his feet. They got a toe off the other foot."

Terri looked at me. I gently shook my head.

Top of the hill near a line of woods, we seen his body. The smell was so strong that VapoRub might as well have been water. I ain't never smelled nothing that bad in all my life. If at the bottom of the hill it had been strong as a bull, at the top it was a bull elephant.

Uncle Smat wasn't a sight for sore eyes, but he damn sure made the eyes sore. He was up next to a line of woods, half in a feed bag. It was over his head and tied around his waist with twine.

His legs stuck out, and his pants legs was all ripped from animals dragging him out of the coop, on up where he lay. One foot, as Mr. Wentworth had said, was gnawed off, and Mr. Wentworth was right about that missing toe on the other foot; the big toe, if you're curious.

"So the man dies, you put a bag over his head and leave him with the chickens and write us a letter?" Terri said.

Mr. Wentworth nodded.

"Yeah," Terri said. "I guess there ain't no use denying any of that."

"It's been too hot for digging, and thing is we don't know him. We found he had his name and your address on a letter in his billfold, and we wrote your family. We figured we'd leave the rest to his kin."

I went over and untied the twine around his waist and pulled the bag off his head. Uncle Smat was not a pretty man, but I recognized the family nose. His eyes was full of ants and worms and such. His stomach was bloated up with gas.

"He's all yours," Mr. Wentworth said.

"Oh," said Mrs. Wentworth. "I guess you ought to have his hat. I put it on the back porch and put corn in it for the squirrels. I like squirrels. Oh, one more thing. He had a car, but the night he died, he didn't bring it back with him. He come on foot or someone dropped him off. Didn't want you to think we took his car."

"Just his billfold and what was in it," Terri said.

"Yeah," Mrs. Wentworth said, "just that."

In the car, Uncle Smat laying in the backseat, tucked completely inside a big burlap bag, we started out. I had paid a quarter for the used jar of VapoRub, which was far too much, but at the time seemed a necessity. I poured Mama's perfume over him, but if it knocked back the smell any, I couldn't tell it. We drove through the night with the windows down and the car overflowing with the aroma of Uncle Smat. Terri hung out of her window like a dog.

"Oh baby Jesus," she said. "This here is awful."

I was driving and leaning out my window as much as was reasonable and still be able to drive. The air was helping a little, but there wasn't nothing that could defeat that smell short of six feet of dirt or the bottom of the deep blue sea.

The Ford's headlights was cutting a path through the night, and I felt we were making pretty good time, and then I seen the smoke from under the hood. It was the radiator again.

I pulled over where the road widened against the trees, and parked. I got the hood up and looked at the radiator. It was really steaming. I knew then it had a hole in it. I decided it was a small hole, and if I could keep water in the radiator and not drive like John Dillinger in a getaway car, I might make it home.

With the car not moving, Uncle Smat's stink had taken on a power that was beyond that of Hercules.

"Oh, hell." Terri was in the woods throwing up and calling out. "I holler calf rope. You win, Uncle Smat. Lord have mercy on all His children, especially me."

I used most of our water to fill the radiator, and was going to call Terri up from the woods, when the wind changed and the smell hit me tenfold. It was like I was in that bag with Uncle Smat.

Terri was coming up the hill. I said, "You're right. We can't keep going on like this. Uncle Smat deserves a burial."

"We ain't got no shovel," Terri said.

This was an accurate observation.

"Then he deserves a ditch and some Christian words said over him."

"I'm all for that ditch, but we ain't got no preacher neither."

"Damn it," I said.

"I say we just put him in a ditch and go on to the house," Terri said.

"That ain't right," I said.

"No, but it sure would be a mite less smelly."

We packed our noses with VapoRub, dragged Uncle Smat out of the car by the bag he was in, and pulled him down a hill that dropped off into the woods. The bag ripped on a stob. Uncle Smat came out of the bag and

rolled down the hill, caught up on a fallen tree branch, and stopped rolling. I could see that Uncle Smat's coat had ripped open. The pale lining
was fish-belly white in the pale moonlight.

"Ah, hell," Terri said. "Can't believe that bag was holding back the
smell that much. Oh heavens, that is nastier than a family of skunks rolled
up in cow shit."

I was yanking the branch away from under Uncle Smat so he could roll
the rest of the way down, when Terri said, "Hey, Chauncey. Something fell
out of his coat."

I looked at what she had picked up. It was a folded piece of paper.

Dark as it was, we went up to the car and I turned on the headlights,
stood in front of them, and looked at the paper. It had some lines on it, a
drawing of some tombstones, and the words *Fort Sill* and *Geronimo's grave*
written on it. There was a dollar sign drawn on one of the tombstones.

"It was in his coat," Terri said.

"Probably stitched up in the lining."

"He must have had a reason for hiding it," Terri said.

"If he hadn't, Wentworths would have found it."

"What you think it is?"

"A map."

"To what?"

"You see what I see," I said. "Where do you think?"

"Geronimo's grave?"

"Domino," I said.

"I ain't going there," she said.

"Me neither. We're going home. Remember, Terri. The hogs ate him.
Nobody is going to believe the chickens did it. It would take them too
long."

Back with Uncle Smat, I finally managed to pull the branch aside that was
holding him, and as there was a deep, damp sump hole at the bottom of
the hill between two trees, I gave him a bit of a boost with my foot and he
rolled down into it. One of his legs stuck out, and it was the one with the
chewed-off foot. I scrambled down and bent his leg a little and got it into
the sump, and then I tossed the ripped bag over him, kicked some dirt in

on top of that, but it was like trying to fill in the ocean with a pile of dirt, a spoon, and good intentions.

"Hell with it," Terri said.

"Maybe we can come back for him later," I said.

"Ha," Terri said. "I say we stick to that story about how the Wentworths' hogs got to him and ate him."

"I can live with that," I said.

"Mostly I can live with him being out of the car," Terri said.

"It ain't much of a Christian burial," I said.

Terri inched closer to the sump hole, put her hand over her heart, said, "Jesus loves you. . . . Let's go."

We drove with all the windows down, trying to drive out memories of Uncle Smat. When we got to the Red River, and was about to cross, the car got hot again and I had to pull over. We didn't have any more water, other than a bit for drinking, so I decided wasn't no choice but for me to take the canteens and go down the hill and under the bridge and dip some out of the river.

Terri stayed with the car. I took the canteens with me and dipped water out of the river, and when I came back up the hill, there, sitting on the hood with Terri, was the man we had seen the other day. He was sitting there casual-like with his hand clutched in the collar of Terri's shirt, and the moonlight gleamed on a knife blade he had in his hand, resting it on his thigh.

"There he is," the man said. "Good to see you and Miss Smart Ass again."

I placed the canteens gently on the ground and picked up a stick lying by the side of the road and started walking toward him. "Let go of her," I said, "or I'll smack you a good one."

He held up the hand with the knife in it.

"I wouldn't do that, boy. You do, I might have to cut her before you get to me. Cut her good and deep. You want that boy?"

I shook my head.

"Put down that limb then."

I dropped it.

"Come over here," the man said.

"Don't do it," Terri said.

"You shut up," the man said.

I came over. He got down off the car and dragged Terri off of it and flung her on the road.

"I'm gonna need this car," he said.

"All right," I said.

"First, you're gonna put water in it, and then you're going to drive me."

"You don't need me," I said. "I'll give you the keys."

"Now, this here is embarrassing, but I can't drive. Never learned."

"Just put your foot on the gas and turn the wheel a little and stomp on the brake when you want to stop."

"I tried to drive once and ran off in a creek. I ain't driving. You are. The girl can stay here."

"All right," I said.

"I ain't staying," she said. "He needs me to read the map and such."

"I ain't going the same place you was going," the man said.

"Where are you going?" I said.

"Back the way you come," he said.

He reached in his coat pocket and pulled out the folded sheet of paper I had left lying on the front seat. He pointed at the map.

"I'm going here, to see where my partner hid the bank money."

Damn you, Uncle Smat. I said, "You mean that dollar sign means real money?"

"Real paper money," he said.

After I put water in the radiator, the man sent me back down to get more water, while he stayed with Terri. I didn't have no choice but to do what he wanted. Next thing I knew I was turning the car around and heading back the way we had come.

"It stinks in here," said the man.

I was at the wheel; he was beside me, his knife hand lying against his thigh. Terri was in the backseat.

"You ought to be back here," Terri said. "I think I'm going to be sick."

"Be sick out the window," said the man.

"So you and Uncle Smat were partners?" I said.

"Guess you could say that. Ain't this just the peachiest coincidence that ever happened? You coming along, him being your uncle, and me being his partner."

"I think you stabbed your partner," Terri said.

"There is that," said the man. "We had what you might call a falling-out on account we split up after we hit the bank and he didn't do like he said he would. Let me tell you, that was one sweet job.

"I had a gun then. I wish I had it now. We come out of the bank in Lawton with the cash, and the gun went off and I shot a lady. Not on purpose. Bullet ricocheted off a wall or something. Did a bounce and hit her right between the eyes. Went through a sack of groceries she was carrying and bounced off a can in the bag or something, hit right and betwixt."

I didn't believe his story, but I didn't bring this to his attention.

"So Smat, he decides we ought to split up, to divide the heat on us, so to speak, and he was going to give me a map to where he hid the money. He said he'd hid it in haste but had made a map, and when things cooled, we could go get our money."

Terri leaned over the seat.

"So he come and told you he had a map for you, and he was right with you, and he didn't give it to you?"

"Get your nose back, before I cut it off," the man said, and he showed her the knife. Terri sat back in the seat.

"All right, here it is," he said. "It wasn't no bank job at all. We robbed a big dice game in Lawton. One that was against the law, but the law was there playing dice. This was a big game and there were all these mighty players there from Texas and Oklahoma, Arkansas, Louisiana, I think Kansas. Hot arms, they were. Illegal money earned in ways that didn't get the taxes paid. This was a big gathering, and the money was going into a big dice game and there was going to be some big winners. We were just there as small potatoes, me and Smat. Kind of bodyguards for a couple of fellas. And then it come to me and Smat we ought to rob the dice game. It wasn't that smart an idea, them knowing us and all, but it was a lot of money. Right close to a million dollars. Can you imagine? You added up every dollar I've ever made sticking up banks and robbing from folks here and there, and what I might make robbing in the future, it ain't anywhere near that. Me and Smat decided right then and there we was going to take the piles of money heaped there on the floor, and head out. We pulled our guns and took it. That woman I shot, it wasn't no damn accident. She started yelling at us, and I can't stand screeching, so I shot her. It was a good shot."

"Yeah," Terri said. "How far away were you from her?"

"I don't know."

"I bet you was right up near her. I bet it wasn't no great shot at all."

"Terri," I said. "Quiet."

"Yeah, Terri," the man said. "Quiet."

"Well, we robbed them, made a run for it in Smat's car, and then we hid out. Smat, after a few days, he starts thinking he's done shit in the frying pan. Starts saying we got to give it back, like they were gonna forgive and forget, like we brung a lost cat home. We hid the money near Geronimo's grave one night, took some shovels up there in the dark and buried it by an oak tree. There ain't nobody guards that place. There ain't even a gate. It was a lot of money and in a big tin canister—and I mean big. A million dollars in bills is heavier than you'd think. We took about ten thousand and split that for living money, but the rest we left there, so if we got caught by cops for other things we'd done, we wouldn't have all that big loot on us. If we went to jail, when we got out, there'd be a lot of money waiting. Right then, though, we didn't plan on being caught. That was just a backup idea. We were going to wait until the heat died down, go back and get it. But Smat, he got to thinking, considering who we robbed, the heat wasn't going to die down. He reckoned they'd start coming after us, and keep coming, and that worried him sick. It didn't do me no good to think about it either, but I didn't like what he wanted to do. He was planning on making a map and mailing it to them so they could come get the money. He showed me the map. We had driven to Nebraska by then, where we was hiding out. He was gonna send them the map with an apology, just keep moving, hoping they'd say, 'Well, we got our money, so let's forget it.' He thought he could go on then and live his life, go back to small stickups or some such, and steal from people who would forget it. But them boys at that dice game, I tell you, they aren't forgetters. With a million dollars, I tell him, we can go off to Mexico and live clear and good the rest of our lives. You can buy a señorita down there cheaper than a chicken. Or so I'm told. Shit, them boys were gonna forget it like they would forget their mamas. Wasn't going to happen."

"Yeah," Terri said. "I'd be mad, I was them. I can hold a grudge."

"Damn right," the man said. "What I told Smat. Mama Johnson didn't raise no idiots."

"I guess that's a matter of opinion, Mr. Johnson," Terri said.

"I swear, girl, I'm gonna cut you from gut to gill if you don't hush up."

Terri went silent. I glanced at her in the mirror. She was smiling. Sometimes Terri worries me.

"Thing was, I couldn't let him mail that map, now could I? So we had this little scuffle and he got the better of me by means of some underhanded tricks and took off with the car, left me stranded but not outsmarted. You see, I knew he had a gal he had been seeing up around Lawton, and the money was around there, so I figured he'd go back. He might mail that map, and he might not. Finding the map in your car when I come up on missy here, that was real sweet. I knew then you knew Smat, and that he was the uncle you were going to see."

"Did Uncle Smat ever mention us?" I said.

"No," Johnson said. "I hitched my way back to Oklahoma, went up to where we buried the money one night, had me a shovel and all, but I didn't use it. Wasn't nothing but a big hole under that tree. Smat had the money. I thought, damn him. He pulled it out of that hole on account of me. I didn't know if he reckoned to give the bad boys a new map with the new location of the money, or if he took it with him, deciding he wasn't going to give it back at all. Now he could keep it and not have to split it, which might have been his plan all along. I was down in the dumps, I tell you."

Terri was leaning over the seat now, having forgotten all about Johnson's harsh warning and the knife.

"Sure you were," she said. "That's a bitter pill to swallow."

"Ain't it?" Johnson said.

"I'd have been really put out," Terri said.

"I was put out, all right. I was thinking I caught up with him, I'd yank all his teeth out with pliers. One by one, and slow."

"He wouldn't have liked that," she said.

"No he wouldn't," Johnson said. "But like I said, I knew he liked a gal in Oklahoma, and I'd met her, and he was as moony over her as a calf is over its mother, though it wasn't motherly designs he had."

"It wouldn't be that, no, not that," Terri said.

I thought, How does Terri know this stuff? Or does she just sound like she knows?

"I got me a tow sack of goods I bought with some of that money I had, and I made my way to her house, and hid out in the woods across the road from her place. I lived off canned beans and beer for two or three days, sleeping on the dirt like a damn dog, getting eat up by chiggers and ticks, but he didn't come by. I didn't know where he was staying, but it wasn't with her. I was out of beer and on my last can of beans, and was about to call in the dogs on my plans, when I seen him pull up in front of her house. He got out of his car, and let me tell you, he looked rough, like he'd been living under someone's porch. He went inside the house, and I hid in the back floorboard of his car. When he come out and drove off, I leaped up behind him, and put my knife to his throat, which was all I had, having lost my gun in a craps game on the way back to Oklahoma. I had some good adventures along the way. If you two are alive later, I'll tell you about them."

Considering Johnson was telling us everything but what kind of hair oil he used, I figured he wouldn't want us around later. We knew too much.

"So there I was with my knife to his throat, and you know what he did?"

"How would we?" Terri said.

"He drove that car into a tree. I mean hard. It knocked me winded, and the next thing I know I'm crawling out through the back where the rear windshield busted out, and then I'm falling out on the ground. I realize I'm still holding the knife. When I got up, there was Smat, just wandering around like a chicken with its head cut off. I yelled at him about the money, and he just looked at me, and seemed drunk as a skunk, which I know he ain't. I say, 'Smat. You tell me where that money is, or I'm going to cut you a place to leak out of.' He says to me, 'I ain't got no mice.'"

"Mice?" Terri said.

"I'm sure that's what he said. Anyway, I got mad and stabbed him. I'm what my mama used to call real goddamn impulsive. Next thing we're struggling around, and he falls, and I fall, and I bang my head on the side of the car, and when I wake up I'm on my back looking at stars. I got up and seen Smat had done took off. So I went looking for him, high and low, thinking I'd got a good knife thrust or two on him, and he'd be dead thereabouts. But he wasn't. So, I went wandering about for a few days, thumbed a ride back to Texas, knowing Smat knew a fellow just over the river. But Smat wasn't there. I cut that guy good to find out if he knew anything about where he was, but I killed him for nothing. He didn't know shit. I went wandering for a couple days, and then I seen you two at that station. Ain't that something? Ain't life funny?"

"Makes me laugh," Terri said.

"I wandered a couple more days, finally caught a ride from a farmer and was dropped off at the Red River bridge, and when I got to the other side, what do I see but your car and this little fart outside of it, and I think, where's that boy? He's gonna drive me. Then I seen the map on the seat and knew you knew Smat and knew he hadn't mailed any map at all, 'cause there was the same one he'd drawn. I figured you knew where he was, that he'd been in your car, and then the rest of it you can put together."

Before Terri could say anything, I said, "He ain't alive no more, but before he died he said he done that map to trick you, so you'd think he was letting go of the loot, but he came back for it. He moved it all right, but it's still in the same graveyard, buried right behind Geronimo's grave. You missed it."

He studied me a moment, to see if there was truth in what I said, and he saw truth where there wasn't any, which goes to prove if I want to lie, I can do it. So we got our bearings and headed out in the direction of Geronimo's grave, after stopping at a station for gas, and at a General Store across the street from it to buy a shovel and some rope. Johnson gave me some money and I went in and bought the goods. Johnson sat in the backseat with Terri to make sure I didn't talk to anyone at the station or the store. He kept the knife close to her.

At the store I was supposed to ask how far it was to Fort Sill, where Geronimo was buried, and I did. When I told Johnson how far it was, he figured we could drive through the night and be there early morning before, or just about the time the sun came up.

It started raining that afternoon, and it was a steady rain, but we drove on, the wipers beating at the water on the windshield.

Johnson said, "Every time it rains, someone says, 'The farmers need it.' I don't give a hang about the farmers. Papa raised hogs and chickens and grew corn and such, and he spent a lot of time beating my ass with a plow line. To hell with the farmers and their rain. I hope their lands blow away. I can eat pork or beef or chicken, or a squirrel. I don't care about the farmers. The farmers can go to hell."

"If I'm reading you right, you don't seem to like farmers," Terri said.

"That's funny," Johnson said. "You're gonna funny yourself to death."

Johnson sat quiet after that and didn't say another word until we came close to Fort Sill. Now, it's supposed to be a fort and all that, but the grave-yard wasn't really protected at all. We parked up near it, Johnson grabbed the shovel and coiled the rope over his shoulder, and we all trudged into the graveyard, the rain beating down on us so hard we could barely see. We fumbled around in the dark a while, but Johnson, having been there before, found Geronimo's grave easy enough. A blind man could have found it. There was a monument there. It was made of cemented stones, and it was tall and thin at the top, wide at the bottom. There was a marker that said GERONIMO. On the grave itself were pieces of glass and bones and stones that folks had put there as some kind of tribute. The sun was rising and the rain had slackened, but we could see it had beat down the dirt at the back of the grave, behind the pile of rocks that served as Geronimo's marker, and damn if we couldn't see a tin box down in a hole there.

The rain had opened the soft dirt up so you could see it clearly as the sun broke over the trees in the graveyard.

I thought, Uncle Smat, you ole dog you. He had done exactly what I was pretending he did. The box really was there. Uncle Smat figured hiding it right near where it had been before would fool Johnson, and it would have, had I not told a lie that turned out to be the truth. Uncle Smat might actually have meant to mail that map, but then he got stabbed, went off his bean, and somehow ended back at the chicken coop where he'd been staying, and died of the stabbing.

Johnson handed me the shovel, said, "Dig it the rest of the way out."

"What happens to us then?"

"You drive me out of here. I can't carry that on my back, and I can't drive. Later, I tie you up with the rope somewhere where you can be found alongside the road."

"What if no one comes along?" Terri said.

"That's not my problem," Johnson said.

I scraped some dirt off the box with the shovel, and then I got down in the hole to dig. Water ran over the tops of my shoes and soaked my socks and feet. I widened the hole and worked with the shovel until I pried the box loose from the mud. I slipped the rope under the box, and fastened it around the top with a loop knot. I climbed out of the hole to help pull the box up. Me and Terri had to do the pulling. Johnson stood there with his big knife watching us.

When we got it up and out of the hole, he took the shovel from me, told us to stand back, and then he used the tip of the shovel to try and force open the lid. This took some considerable work, and while he was at it Terri stepped around beside Geronimo's grave.

Johnson stopped and said to Terri, "Don't think I ain't watching you, girly."

Terri stopped inching along.

Johnson got the box open and looked inside. I could see what the sunlight was shining on, same as him. A lot of greenbacks.

"Ain't that fine-looking," Johnson said.

"Hey, Johnson, you stack of shit," Terri said.

Johnson jerked his head in her direction, and it was then I realized Terri had stooped down and got a rock, and she threw it. It was like the day she killed that bird. Her aim was true. It smote Johnson on the forehead, knocking off his hat, and he sort of went up on his toes and fell back, flat as a board, right by that hole we had just dug.

I looked down at Johnson. He had a big red welt on his forehead, and it was already starting to swell into a good-sized knot.

"Girly, my ass," Terri said as she came up.

I bent down and took hold of his wrist, but didn't feel a pulse.

"Terri, I think you done killed him."

"I was trying to. Did you hear the way it sounded when it hit him?"

"Like a gunshot," I said.

"That's for sure," she said. "Let's get this money."

"What?"

"The money. Let's get it and put it in the car and drive it home with us."

"A million dollars? Show up at the house without Uncle Smat, and with a large tin box full of money?"

"Here's the way I see it," Terri said. "Uncle Smat has left enough of himself in the car it ought to satisfy Mama that it was best we didn't bring the rest of him home, his stink being more than enough. And this money might further soothe Mama's disappointment about us not hauling him back."

"We just pushed him in a sump hole and left him," I said.

"Really want to go pick him up on the way home?"

I shook my head, looked down at the box. It had handles on either side. I bent down and took one of them, and Terri took the other. We carried the money down to the car and put it in the backseat floorboard.

It was good and light by then, and I figured it might be best to leave without drawing a lot of attention to ourselves, or the dead body up by Geronimo's grave. I let the car roll downhill before starting it, and when we were going pretty fast, Terri said, "Oh goddamn it."

She was looking over the seat, and I glanced in the mirror, and there was Johnson. He wasn't dead at all. He was running after us, nearly on us, his arms flapping like a scarecrow's coat in the wind.

He grabbed onto the back door handle and got a foot on the running board. I could see his teeth were bared and he had the knife in his free hand and he was waving it about.

I jerked the car hard to the right and when I did, the car slid on the gravel road, and Johnson went way out, his feet flying in the air, him having one hand on the door handle, and then I heard a screeching sound as that handle came loose of the car and Johnson was whipped out across the road and into some trees.

"Damn it to hell," Terri said. "He done bent up in a way you don't bend."

I glanced back. I could see he was hung up in a low growing tree with his back broken over a limb so far he looked like a wet blanket hanging over it. That rock might not have killed him, but I was certain being slung across the road and into a tree and having his back snapped had certainly done it.

The motor hummed, and away we went.

It took us another two days to get home on account of having to stop more and more for the radiator, and by the time we pulled up in the yard, the car was steaming like a tea kettle.

We sat in the car for awhile, watching all that steam tumbling out from under the hood. I said, "I think the car is ruined."

"We can buy a bunch of cars with what's in that box."

"Terri, is taking that money the right thing to do?"

"You mean Sunday School right? Probably not. But that money is ill-gotten gains, as they say in the pulp magazines. It was Uncle Smat and Johnson stole it, not us. Took it from bigger crooks than they were. We didn't take any good people's money. We didn't rob no banks. We just carried home money bad people had and were using for bad reasons. We'll do better with it. Mama's always saying how she'd like to have a new car and a house, live somewhere out west, and have some clothes that wasn't patched. I think a rich widow and her two fine-looking children can make out quite well out west with that kind of money, don't you?"

"How do we explain the money?"

"Say Uncle Smat left us an inheritance that he earned by mining, or some such kind of thing. Oil is good. We can say it was oil."

"And if she doesn't believe that?"

"We just stay stuck to that lie until it sounds good."

I let that thought drift about. "You know what, Terri?"

"What's that?"

"I think a widow and her two fine-looking children could live well on that much money. I really think they could."

"Mr. Bear" is a story I truly love. I have always been a Smokey Bear fan. My wife and I both grew up reading Smokey Bear comics and being a member of the Smokey Bear Rangers, or some such. We have one of the comics framed and on our wall. It holds a place of honor with my wife's plaque proclaiming her as the prime architect of the Horror Writers Association, known as the Horror Writers of America back then. When I wrote this story, I was playing with a lot of things about Smokey Bear, but Mr. Bear is definitely not Smokey Bear. He is Mr. Bear. I have always loved cartoons and animals treated as being humanlike without so much as a blink from human companions. Some readers were appalled and proclaimed it was a tale of bestiality, which means some people really don't have enough to do, and, dare I say, are dumb as a brick. In a world where a bear can live a life like everyone else, then. . . . Oh, well, what's the use? I also had one person say in a comment online that bears couldn't fly on airplanes. I think these folks exist in some weird narrow universe where all things are literal to them. My favorite comment came from my daughter when I read "Mr. Bear" to an audience. She came up afterward and said, "Mr. Bear is kind of an asshole."

Indeed.

MR. BEAR

JIM WATCHED AS the plane filled up. It was a pretty tightly stacked flight, but last time, coming into Houston, he had watched as every seat filled except for the one on his left and the one on his right. He had hit the jackpot that time, no row mates. That made it comfortable, having all that knee and elbow room.

He had the middle seat again, an empty seat to his left and one to his right. He sat there hoping there would be the amazing repeat of the time before.

A couple of big guys, sweating and puffing, were moving down the aisle, and he thought, Yep, they'll be the ones. Probably one of them on either side. Shit, he'd settle for just having one seat filled, the one by the window, so he could get out on the aisle side. Easy to go to the bathroom that way, stretch your legs.

The big guys passed him by. He saw a lovely young woman carrying a straw hat making her way down the center. He thought, Someone has got to sit by me, maybe it'll be her. He could perhaps strike up a conversation. He might even find she's going where he's going, doesn't have a boyfriend. Wishful thinking, but it was a better thing to think about than big guys on either side of him, hemming him in like the center of a sandwich.

But no, she passed him by as well. He looked up at her, hoping she'd look his way. Maybe he could get a smile at least. That would be nice.

Course, he was a married man, so that was no way to think.

But he was thinking it.

She didn't look and she didn't smile.

Jim sighed, waited. The line was moving past him. There was only one customer left: a shirtless bear in dungarees and work boots, carrying a hat. The bear looked peeved, or tired, or both.

Oh, shit, thought Jim. Bears, they've got to stink. All that damn fur. He passes me by, I'm going to have a seat free to myself on either side. He doesn't, well, I've got to ride next to him for several hours.

But the bear stopped in his row, pointed at the window seat. "That's my seat."

"Sure," Jim said, and moved out of the middle seat and out into the aisle, let the bear in. The bear settled in by the window and fastened his seatbelt and rested his hat on his knee. Jim slid back into the middle seat. He could feel the heat off the bear's big, hairy arm. And there was a smell. Nothing nasty or ripe. Just a kind of musty odor, like an old fur coat hung too long in a closet, dried blood left in a carpet, a whiff of cigarette smoke and charred wood.

Jim watched the aisle again. No one else. He could hear them closing the door. He unfastened his seatbelt and moved to the seat closest to the aisle. The bear turned and looked at him. "You care I put my hat in the middle seat?"

"Not at all," Jim said.

"I get tired of keeping up with it. Thinking of taking it out of the wardrobe equation."

Suddenly it snapped. Jim knew the bear. Had seen him on TV. He was a famous environmentalist. Well, that was something. Had to sit by a musty bear, helped if he was famous. Maybe there would be something to talk about.

"Hey," the bear said, "I ask you something, and I don't want it to sound rude, but . . . can I?"

"Sure."

"I got a feeling, just from a look you gave me, you recognized me."

"I did."

"Well, I don't want to be too rude, sort of leave a fart hanging in the air, though, I might . . . deer carcass. Never agrees. But, I really don't want to talk about me or what I do or who I am . . . and let me just be completely honest. I was so good at what I do. . . . Well, I am good. Let me rephrase that. I was really as successful as people think, you believe I'd be riding coach? After all my years of service to the forest, it's like asking your best girl to ride bitch like she was the local poke. So, I don't want to talk about it."

"I never intended to ask," Jim said. That was a lie, but it seemed like the right thing to say.

"Good. That's good," said the bear, and leaned back in his seat and put the hat on his head and pulled it down over his eyes.

For a moment Jim thought the bear had gone to sleep, but no, the bear spoke again. "Now that we've got that out of the way, you want to talk, we can talk. Don't want to, don't have to, but we can talk, just don't want to talk about the job and me and the television ads, all that shit. You know what I'd like to talk about?"

"What's that?"

"Poontang. All the guys talk about pussy, but me, I'm a bear, so it makes guys uncomfortable, don't want to bring it up. Let me tell you something man, I get plenty, and I don't just mean bear stuff. Guy like me, that celebrity thing going and all, I can line them up outside the old motel room, knock 'em off like shooting ducks from a blind. Blondes, redheads, brunettes, bald, you name it, I can bang it."

This made Jim uncomfortable. He couldn't remember the last time he'd had sex with his wife and here was a smelly bear with a goofy hat knocking it off like there was no tomorrow. He said, "Aren't we talking about your celebrity after all? I mean, in a way?"

"Shit. You're right. Okay. Something else. Maybe nothing. Maybe we just sit. Tell you what, I'm going to read a magazine, but you think of something you want to talk about, you go ahead. I'm listening."

Jim got a magazine out of the pouch in front of him and read a little, even came across an ad with the bear's picture in it, but he didn't want to bring that up. He put the magazine back and thought about the book he had in the overhead, in his bag, but it was the usual thriller, so he didn't feel like bothering with it.

After a while the flight attendant came by. She was a nice-looking woman who looked even nicer because of her suit, way she carried herself, the air of authority. She asked if they'd like drinks.

Jim ordered a diet soda, which was free, but the bear pulled out a bill and bought a mixed drink, a bloody mary. They both got peanuts. When the flight attendant handed the bear his drink, the bear said, "Honey, we land, you're not doing anything, I could maybe show you my wild side, find yours."

The bear grinned, showed some very ugly teeth.

The flight attendant leaned over Jim, close to the bear, said, "I'd rather rub dirt in my ass than do anything with you."

This statement hung in the air like backed-up methane for a moment, then the flight attendant smiled, moved back and stood in the aisle, looked right at Jim, said, "If you need anything else, let me know," and she was gone.

The bear had let down his dining tray and he had the drink in its plastic cup in his hand. The bloody mary looked very bloody. The bear drank it in one big gulp. He said, "Flight drinks. You could have taken a used Tampax and dipped it in rubbing alcohol and it would taste the same."

Jim didn't say anything. The bear said, "She must be a lesbian. Got to be. Don't you think?"

The way the bear turned and looked at him, Jim thought it was wise to agree. "Could be."

The bear crushed the plastic cup. "No could be. Is. Tell me you agree. Say *is*."

"Is," Jim said, and his legs trembled slightly.

"That's right, boy. Now whistle up that lesbian bitch, get her back over here. I want another drink."

When they landed in Denver the bear was pretty liquored up. He walked down the ramp crooked and his hat was cocked at an odd angle that suggested it would fall at any moment. But it didn't.

The plane had arrived late and this meant Jim had missed his connecting flight due to a raging snowstorm. The next flight was in the morning and it was packed. He'd have to wait until tomorrow, mid-afternoon, just to see if a flight was available. He called his wife on his cell phone, told her, and then rang off feeling depressed and tired and wishing he could stay home and never fly again.

Jim went to the bar, thinking he might have a nightcap, catch a taxi to the hotel, and there was the bear, sitting on a stool next to a blonde with breasts so big, they were resting on the bar in front of her. The bear, his hat still angled oddly on his head, was chatting her up.

Jim went behind them on his way to a table. He heard the bear say, "Shid, darlin', you dun't know whad yer missin'. 'Ere's wimen all o'er 'is world would lige to do it wid a bear."

"I'm not that drunk, yet," the blonde said, "and I don't think they have enough liquor here to make me that drunk." She got up and walked off.

Jim sat down at a table with his back to the bar. He didn't want the bear to recognize him, but he wanted a drink. And then he could smell the bear. The big beast was right behind him. He turned slightly. The bear was standing there, dripping saliva onto his furry chest thick as sea foam.

"Eh, buddy, 'ow you doin'?" The bear's words were so slurred, it took Jim a moment to understand.

"Oh," he said. "Not so good. Flight to Seattle is delayed until tomorrow."

"Me, too," the bear said, and plopped down in a chair at the table so hard the chair wobbled and Jim heard a cracking sound that made him half expect to see the chair explode and the bear go tumbling to the floor. "See me wid dat gal? Wus dryin' to roun' me ub sum, ya know."

"No luck?"

"Les'bin. The're eberyware."

Jim decided he needed to get out of this pretty quick. "Well, you know, I don't think I'm going to wait on that drink. Got to get a hotel room, get ready for tomorrow."

"Naw, dunt do 'at. Er, led me buy ya a drank. Miz. You in dem tidht panss."

So the waitress came over and the bear ordered some drinks for them both. Jim kept trying to leave, but, no go. Before he knew it, he was almost as hammered as the bear.

Finally, the bear, just two breaths short of a complete slur, said, "Eber thang 'ere is den times duh prize. Leds go ta a real bar." He paused. "Daby Crogett killed a bar." And then the bear broke into insane laughter.

"Wen e wus ony tree . . . three. Always subone gad ta shood sub bar subware. Cum on, eds go. I know dis town ligh duh bag ob muh 'and."

They closed down a midtown bar. Jim remembered that pretty well. And then Jim remembered something about the bear saying they ought to have some companionship, and then things got muddled. He awoke in a little motel room, discovered the air was full of the smell of moldy bear fur, alcohol farts, a coppery aroma, and sweaty perfume.

Sitting up in bed, Jim was astonished to find a very plump girl with short blond hair next to him in bed. She was lying face down, one long, bladder-like tit sticking out from under her chest, the nipple pierced with a ring that looked like a washer.

Jim rolled out of bed and stood up beside it. He was nude and sticky. "Shit," he said. He observed the hump under the sheet some more, the washer in the tit. And then, as his eyes adjusted, he looked across the room and saw another bed, and he could see on the bed post the bear's hat, and then the bear, lying on the bed without his pants. There was another lump under the blanket. One delicate foot stuck out from under the blanket near the end of the bed, a gold chain around the ankle. The bear was snoring softly. There were clothes all over the floor, a pair of panties large enough to be used as a sling for the wounded leg of a hippopotamus was dangling from the light fixture. That would belong to his date.

Except for his shoes and socks, Jim found his clothes and put them on and sat in a chair at a rickety table and put his head in his hands. He repeated softly over and over, "Shit, shit, shit."

With his hands on his face, he discovered they had a foul smell about them, somewhere between workingman sweat and a tuna net. He was hit with a sudden revelation that made him feel ill. He slipped into the bathroom and showered and redressed; this time he put on his socks and shoes. When he came out the light was on over the table and the bear was sitting there, wearing his clothes, even his hat.

"Damn, man," the bear said, his drunk gone, "that was some time we had. I think. But, I got to tell you, man, you got the ugly one."

Jim sat down at the table, feeling as if he had just been hit by a car. "I don't remember anything."

"Hope you remembered she stunk. That's how I tracked them down, on a corner. I could smell her a block away. I kind of like that, myself. You know, the smell. Bears, you know how it is. But, I seen her, and I thought, goddamn, she'd have to sneak up on a glass of water, so I took the other one. You said you didn't care."

"Oh, god," Jim said.

"The fun is in the doing, not the remembering. Trust me, some things aren't worth remembering."

"My wife will kill me."

"Not if you don't tell her."

"I've never done anything like this before."

"Now you've started. The fat one, I bet she drank twelve beers before she pissed herself."

"Oh, Jesus."

"Come on, let's get out of here. I gave the whores the last of my money. And I gave them yours."

"What?"

"I asked you. You said you didn't mind."

"I said I don't remember a thing. I need that money."

"I know that. So do I."

The bear got up and went over to his bed and picked up the whore's purse and rummaged through it, took out the money. He then found the other whore's purse on the floor, opened it up and took out money.

Jim staggered to his feet. He didn't like this, not even a little bit. But he needed his money back. Was it theft if you paid for services you didn't remember?

Probably. But. . . .

As Jim stood, in the table light he saw that on the bear's bed was a lot of red paint, and then he saw it wasn't paint, saw too that the whore's head was missing. Jim let out a gasp and staggered a little.

The bear looked at him. The expression on his face was oddly sheepish.

"Thought we might get out of here without you seeing that. Sometimes, especially if I've been drinking, and I'm hungry, I revert to my basic nature. If it's any consolation, I don't remember doing that."

"No. No. It's no consolation at all."

At this moment, the fat whore rolled over in bed and sat up and the covers dropped down from her, and the bear, moving very quickly, got over there and with a big swipe of his paw sent a spray of blood and a rattle of teeth flying across the room, against the wall. The whore fell back, half her face clawed away.

"Oh, Jesus. Oh, my god."

"This killing I remember," the bear said. "Now come on, we got to wipe everything down before we leave, and we don't have all night."

They walked the streets in blowing snow, and even though it was cold, Jim felt as if he were in some kind of fever dream. The bear trudged along beside him, said, "I had one of the whores pay for the room in cash. They never even saw us at the desk. Wiped down the prints in the room, anything we might have touched. I'm an expert at it. We're cool. Did that 'cause I know how these things can turn out. I've had it go bad before. Employers have got me out of a few scrapes, you know. I give them that. You okay? You look a little peaked."

"I . . . I. . . ."

The bear ignored him, rattled on. "You now, I'm sure you can tell by now, I'm not really all that good with the ladies. On the plane, I was laying the bullshit on. . . . Damn, I got all this fur, but that don't mean I'm not cold. I ought to have like a winter uniform, you know? A jacket, with a big collar that I can turn up. Oh, by the way. I borrowed your cell phone to call out for pizza last night, but before I could, I dropped it and stepped on the motherfucker. Can you believe that? Squashed like a clamshell. I got it in my pocket. Have to throw it away. Okay. Let me be truthful. I had it in my back pocket and I sat my fat ass on it. That's the thing. . . . You a little hungry? Shit. I'm hungry. I'm cold."

That was the only comment for a few blocks, then the bear said, "Fuck this," and veered toward a car parked with several others at the curb. The bear reached in his pocket and took out a little packet, opened it. The street-lights revealed a series of shiny lockpick tools. He went to work on the car door with a tool that he unfolded and slid down the side of the car window until he could pull the lock. He opened the door, said, "Get inside." The bear flipped a switch that unlocked the doors, and Jim, as if he was obeying the commands of a hypnotist, walked around to the other side and got in.

The bear was bent under the dash with his tools, and in a moment, the car roared to life. The bear sat in the seat and closed the door, said, "Seatbelts. Ain't nobody rides in my car, they don't wear seatbelts."

Jim thought, It's not your car. But he didn't say anything. He couldn't. His heart was in his mouth. He put on his seatbelt.

They tooled along the snowy Denver streets and out of town and the bear said, "We're leaving this place, going to my stomping grounds. Yellowstone Park. Know some back trails. Got a pass. We'll be safe there. We can hang. I got a cabin. It'll be all right."

"I . . . I . . ." Jim said, but he couldn't find the rest of the sentence.

"Look in the glovebox, see there's anything there. Maybe some prescription medicine of some kind. I could use a jolt."

"I . . ." Jim said, and then his voice died and he opened the glovebox. There was a gun inside. Lazily, Jim reached for it.

The bear leaned over and took it from him. "You don't act like a guy been around guns much. Better let me have that." The bear, while driving, managed with one hand to pop out the clip and slide it back in. "A full load. Wonder he's got a gun permit. You know, I do. 'Course, not for this gun. But, beggars can't be choosers, now can they?"

"No. No. Guess not," Jim said, having thought for a moment that he would have the gun, that he could turn the tables, at least make the bear turn back toward Denver, let him out downtown.

"See any gum in there?" the bear said. "Maybe he's got some gum. After that whore's head, I feel like my mouth has a pair of shitty shorts in it. Anything in there?"

Jim shook his head. "Nothing."

"Well, shit," the bear said.

The car roared on through the snowy night, the windshield wipers beating time, throwing snow wads left and right like drunk children tossing cotton balls.

The heater was on. It was warm. Jim felt a second wave of the alcohol blues; it wrapped around him like a warm blanket, and without really meaning to, he slept.

"I should be hibernating," the bear said, as if Jim were listening. "That's why I'm so goddamn grumpy. The work. No hibernation. Paid poon and cheap liquor. That's no way to live."

The bear was a good driver in treacherous weather. He drove on through the night and made good time.

When Jim awoke it was just light and the light was red and it came through the window and filled the car like blood-stained streams of heavenly piss.

Jim turned his head. The bear had his hat cocked back on his head and he looked tired. He turned his head slightly toward Jim, showed some teeth at the corner of his mouth, then glared back at the snowy road.

"We got a ways to go yet, but we're almost to Yellowstone. You been asleep two days."

"Two days."

"Yeah. I stopped for gas once, and you woke up once and you took a piss."

"I did."

"Yeah. But you went right back to sleep."

"Good grief. I've never been that drunk in my life."

"Probably the pills you popped."

"What?"

"Pills. You took them with the alcohol, when we were with the whores."

"Oh, hell."

"It's all right. Ever' now and again you got to cut the tiger loose, you know. Don't worry. I got a cabin. That's where we're going. Don't worry. I'll take care of you. I mean, hell, what are friends for?"

The bear didn't actually have a cabin, he had a fire tower, and it rose up high into the sky overlooking very tall trees. They had to climb a ladder up there, and the bear, sticking the automatic in his belt, sent Jim up first, said, "Got to watch those rungs. They get wet, iced over, your hand can slip. Forest ranger I knew slipped right near the top. We had to dig what was left of him out of the ground. One of his legs went missing. I found it about a month later. It was cold when he fell so it kept pretty good. Wasn't bad, had it with some beans. Waste not, want not. Go on, man. Climb."

Inside the fire tower it was very nice, though cold. The bear turned on the electric heater and it wasn't long before the place was toasty.

The bear said, "There's food in the fridge. Shitter is over there. I'll sleep in my bed, and you sleep on the couch. This'll be great. We can hang. I got all kinds of movies, and as you can see, that TV is big enough for a drive-in theater. We ain't got no bitches, but hell, they're just trouble anyway. We'll just pull each other's wieners."

Jim said, "What now?"

"I don't stutter, boy. It ain't so bad. You just grease a fellow up and go to work."

"I don't know."

"Nah, you'll like it."

As night neared, the light that came through the tower's wrap-around windows darkened and died, and Jim could already imagine grease on his hands.

But by then, the bear had wetted his whistle pretty good, drinking straight from a big bottle of Jack Daniel's. He wasn't as wiped out as before, not stumbling drunk, and his tongue still worked, but fortunately the greased-weenie pull had slipped from the bear's mind. He sat on the couch with his bottle and Jim sat on the other end, and the bear said, "Once upon a goddamn time the bears roamed these forests and we were the biggest, baddest, meanest motherfuckers in the woods. That's no shit. You know that?"

Jim nodded.

"But, along come civilization. We had fires before that, I'm sure. You know, natural stuff. Lightning. Too dry. Natural combustion. But when man arrived, it was doo-doo time for the bears and everything else. I mean, don't take me wrong. I like a good meal and a beer," he held up the bottle, "and some Jack, and hanging out in this warm tower, but something has been sapped out of me. Some sort of savage beast that was in me has been tapped and run off into the ground. . . . I was an orphan. Did you know that?"

"I've heard the stories," Jim said.

"Yeah, well, who hasn't? It was a big fire. I was young. Some arsonists. Damn fire raged through the forest and I got separated from my mom. Dad, he'd run off. But, you know, no biggie. That's how bears do. Well, anyway, I climbed a tree like a numbnuts cause my feet got burned, and I just clung and clung to that tree. And then I seen her, my mother. She was on fire. She ran this way and that, back and forth, and I'm yelling, 'Mama,' but she's not paying attention, had her own concerns. And pretty soon she goes down and the fire licks her all over and her fur is gone and there ain't nothing but a blackened hunk of smoking bear crap left. You know what it is to see a thing like that, me being a cub?"

"I can't imagine."

"No, you can't. You can't. No one can. I had a big fall, too. I don't really remember it, but it left a knot on the back of my head, just over the right ear. . . . Come here. Feel that."

Jim dutifully complied.

The bear said, "Not too hard now. That knot, that's like my Achilles heel. I'm weak there. Got to make sure I don't bump my head too good. That's no thing to live with and that's why I'm not too fond of arsonists. There are several of them, what's left of them, buried not far from here. I roam these forests and I'll tell you, I don't just report them. Now and again, I'm not doing that. Just take care of business myself. Let me tell you, slick, there's a bunch of them that'll never squat over a commode again. They're out there, their gnawed bones buried deep. You know what it's like to be on duty all the time, not to be able to hibernate, just nap? It makes a bear testy. Want a cigar?"

"Beg your pardon?"

"A cigar. I know it's funny coming from me, and after what I just told you, but, we'll be careful here in my little nest."

Jim didn't answer. The bear got up and came back with two fat, black cigars. He had boxed matches with him. He gave Jim a cigar and Jim put it in his mouth, and the bear said, "Puff gently."

Jim did and the bear lit the end with a wooden match. The bear lit his own cigar. He tossed the box of matches to Jim. "If it goes out, you can light up again. Thing about a cigar is you take your time, just enjoy it, don't get into it like a whore sucking a dick. It's done casual. Pucker your mouth like you're kissing a baby."

Jim puffed on the cigar but didn't inhale. The action of it made him feel high, and not too good, a little sick even. They sat and smoked. After a long while, the bear got up and opened one of the windows, said, "Come here."

Jim went. The woods were alive with sounds: crickets, night birds, howling.

"That's as it should be. Born in the forest, living there, taking game there, dying there, becoming one with the soil. But look at me. What the fuck have I become? I'm like a goddamn circus bear."

"You do a lot of good."

"For who though? The best good I've done was catching those arsonists that are buried out there. That was some good. I'll be straight with you, Jim. I'm happy you're going to be living here. I need a buddy, and, well, tag, you're it."

"Buddy."

"You heard me. Oh, the door, it's locked, and you can't work the lock from inside, 'cause it's keyed, and I got the key. So don't think about going anywhere."

"That's not very buddy-like," Jim said.

The bear studied Jim for a long moment, and Jim felt himself going weak. It was as if he could see the bear's psychosis move from one eye to another, like it was changing rooms. "But, you're still my buddy, aren't you, Jim?"

Jim nodded.

"Well, I'm sort of bushed, so I think I'll turn in early. Tomorrow night we'll catch up on that weenie pull."

When the bear went to the bedroom and lay down, Jim lay on the couch with the blanket and pillow the bear had left for him, and listened. The bear had left the bedroom door open, and after a while he could hear the bear snoring like a lumberjack working a saw on a log.

Jim got up and eased around the tower and found that he could open windows, but there was nowhere to go from there except straight down, and that was one booger of a drop. Jim thought of how easily the bear had killed the whore and how he admitted to killing others, and then he thought about tomorrow night's weenie pull, and he became even more nervous.

After an hour of walking about and looking, he realized there was no way out. He thought about the key but had no idea where the bear kept it. He feared if he went in the bear's room to look, he could startle the bear and that might result in getting his head chewed off. He decided to let it go. For now. Ultimately, pulling a greased bear weenie couldn't be as bad as being headless.

Jim went back to the couch, pulled the blanket over him, and almost slept.

Next morning, Jim, who thought he would never sleep, had finally drifted off, and what awoke him was not a noise, but the smell of food cooking. Waffles.

Jim sat up slowly. A faint pink light was coming through the window. The kitchenette area of the tower was open to view, part of the bigger room, and the bear was in there wearing an apron and a big chef hat. The bear turned and saw him. The apron had a slogan on it: If Mama Ain't Happy, Ain't Nobody Happy.

The bear spotted him, gave Jim a big-fanged, wet smile. "Hey, brother, how are you? Come on in here and sit your big ass down and have one of Mr. Bear's waffles. It's so good you'll want to slap your mama."

Jim went into the kitchenette, sat at the table where the bear instructed. The bear seemed in a light and cheery mood. Coffee was on the table, a plate stacked with waffles, big strips of bacon, pats of butter, and a bottle of syrup in a plastic bear modeled after Mr. Bear himself.

"Now you wrap your lips around some of this stuff, see what you think."

While Jim ate, the bear regaled him with all manner of stories about his life, and most were in fact interesting, but all Jim could think about was the bear biting the head off of that hooker, and then slashing the other with a strike of his mighty paw. As Jim ate, the tasty waffles with thick syrup became wads of blood and flesh in his mouth, and he felt as if he were eating of Mr. Bear's wine and wafer, his symbolic blood and flesh, and it made Jim's skin crawl.

All it would take to end up like the whores was to make a misstep. Say something wrong. Perhaps a misinterpreted look. A hesitation at tonight's weenie pull. . . . Oh, damn, Jim thought. The weenie pull.

"What I thought we'd do is we'd go for a drive, dump the car. There's a ravine I know where we can run it off, and no one will see it again. Won't even know it's missing. Excuse me while I go to the shitter. I think I just got word there's been a waffle delivery called."

The bear laughed at his own joke and left the room. Jim ate a bit more of the waffle and all the bacon. He didn't want the bear to think he wasn't grateful. The beast was psychotic. Anything could set him off.

Jim got up and washed his hands at the sink, and just as he was passing into the living room, he saw the gun they had found in the car lying on a big fluffy chair. Part of it, the barrel, had slipped into the crack in the cushions. Maybe the bear had forgotten all about it, or at least didn't have it at the forefront of his mind. That was it. He'd been drunker than a Shriners' convention. He probably didn't even remember having the gun.

Jim eased over and picked up the weapon and put it under his shirt, in the small of his back. He hoped he would know how to use it. He had seen them used before. If he could get up close enough—

"Now, that was some delivery. That motherfucker probably came with a fortune cookie and six-pack of Coke. I feel ten pounds lighter. You ready, Jimbo?"

In the early morning the forests were dark and beautiful and there was a slight mist and with the window of the car rolled down, it was cool and damp and the world seemed newborn. But all Jim could think about was performing a greased-weenie pull and then getting his head chewed off.

Jim said, "You get rid of the car, how do we get back?"

The bear laughed. "Just like a citizen. We walk, of course."

"We've gone quite a distance."

"It'll do you good. Blow out the soot. You'll like it. Great scenery. I'm gonna show you the graves where I buried what was left of them fellows, the arsonists."

"That's all right," Jim said. "I don't need to see that."

"I want you to. It's not like I can show everyone, but my bestest bud, that's a different matter, now ain't it?"

"Well, I don't . . ." Jim said.

"We're going to see it."

"Sure. Okay."

Jim had a sudden revelation. Maybe there never was going to be a weenie pull, and as joyful as that perception was, the alternative was worse. The bear was going to get rid of him. Didn't want to do it in his tower. You don't shit where you eat . . . well, the bear might. But the idea was you kept your place clean of problems. This wasn't just a trip to dump the car—this was a death ride. The bear was going to kill him and leave him where the arsonists were. Jim felt his butthole clench on the car seat.

They drove up higher and the woods grew thicker and the road turned off and onto a trail. The car bumped along for some miles until the trees overwhelmed everything but the trail, and the tree limbs were so thickly connected they acted as a kind of canopy overhead. They drove in deep shadow and there were spots where the shadows were broken by light and the light played across the trail in speckles and spots and birds shot across their view like feathered bullets, and twice there were deer in sight, bounding into the forest and disappearing like wraiths as the car passed.

They came to a curve and then a sharp rise and the bear drove up the rise. The trail played out, and still he drove. He came to a spot, near the peak of the hill, where the sun broke through, stopped the car and got out. Jim got out. They walked to the highest rise of the hill, and where they stood was a clean wide swath in the trees. Weeds and grass grew there. The grass was tall and mostly yellow but brown in places.

"Spring comes," the bear said. "There will be flowers, all along that path, on up to this hill, bursting all over it. This is my forest, Jim. All the dry world used to be a forest, or nearly was, but man has cut most of it down and that's done things to all of us and I don't think in the long run much of it is good. Before man, things had a balance, know what I mean? But man. . . . Oh, boy. He sucks. Like that fire that burned me. Arson. Just for the fun of it. Burned down my goddamn home, Jim. I was just a cub. Little. My mother dying like that . . . I always feel two to three berries short of a pie."

"I'm sorry."

"Aren't they all? Sorry. Boy, that sure makes it better, don't it. Shit." The bear paused and looked over the swath of meadow. He said, "Even with there having been snow, it's dry, and when it's dry, someone starts a fire, it'll burn. The snow don't mean a thing after it melts and the thirsty ground sucks it up, considering it's mostly been dry all year. That one little snow, it ain't nothing more than whipped cream on dry cake." The bear pointed down the hill. "That swath there, it would burn like gasoline on a shag carpet. I keep an eye out for those things. I try to keep this forest safe. It's a thankless and continuous job. . . . Sometimes, I have to leave, get a bit of recreation . . . like the motel room . . . time with a friend."

"I see."

"Do you? The graves I told you about. They're just down the hill. You see, they were bad people, but sometimes, even good people end up down there, if they know things they shouldn't, and there have been a few."

"Oh," Jim said, as if he had no idea what the bear was talking about.

"I don't make friends easily, and I may seem a little insincere. Species problems, all that. Sometimes, even people I like, well . . . it doesn't turn out so well for them. Know what I'm saying?"

"I . . . I don't think so."

"I think you do. That motel room back there, those whores. I been at this for years. I'm not a serial killer or anything. Ones I kill deserve it. The people I work for, they know how I am. They protect me. How's it gonna be an icon goes to jail? That's what I am. A fuckin' icon. So, I kinda get a free ride, someone goes missing, you know. Guys in black, ones got the helicopters and the black cars. They clean up after me. They're my homies, know what I'm saying?"

"Not exactly."

"Let me nutshell it for you: I'm pretty much immune to prosecution. But you, well . . . kind of a loose end. There's a patch down there with your name on it, Jimbo. I put a shovel in the car early this morning while you were sleeping. It isn't personal, Jim. I like you. I do. I know that's cold comfort, but that's how it is."

The bear paused, took off his hat and removed a small cigar from the inside hat band and struck a match and took a puff, said, "Thing is though, I can't get to liking someone too good, cause—"

The snapping sound made the bear straighten up. He was still holding his hat in his paw, and he dropped it. He almost made a turn to look at Jim, who was now standing right by him holding the automatic to the bump on the bear's noggin'. The bear's legs went out. He stumbled and fell forward and went sliding down the hill on his face and chest, a bullet nestled snuggling in his brain.

Jim took a deep breath. He went down the hill and turned the bear's head using both hands, took a good look at him. He thought the bear didn't really look like any of the cartoon versions of him, and when he was on TV he didn't look so old. Of course, he had never looked dead before. The eyes had already gone flat and he could see his dim reflection in one of them. The bear's cigar was flattened against his mouth, like a coiled worm. Jim found the bear's box of matches and was careful to use a handkerchief from the bear's pants pocket to handle it. He struck the match and set the dry grass on fire, then stuck the match between the bear's claws on his left paw. The fire gnawed patiently at the grass, whipping up enthusiasm as the wind rose. Jim wiped down the automatic with his shirt tail and put it in the bear's right paw using the handkerchief, and pushed the bear's claw through the trigger guard, and closed the bear's paw around the weapon so it looked like he had shot himself.

Jim went back up the hill. The fire licked at the grass and caught some more wind and grew wilder, and then the bear got caught up in it as well, chewing his fur and cackling over his flesh like a crazed hag. The fire licked its way down the hill, and then the wind changed and Jim saw the fire climbing up toward him.

He got in the car and started and found a place where he could back it around. It took some work, and by the time he managed it onto the narrow trail, he could see the fire in the mirror, waving its red head in his direction.

Jim drove down the hill, trying to remember the route. Behind him, the fire rose up into the trees as if it were a giant red bird spreading its wings.

"Dumb bear," he said aloud, "ain't gonna be no weenie pull now, is there?" and he drove on until the fire was a just a small bright spot in the rearview mirror, and then it was gone and there was just the tall, dark forest that the fire had yet to find.

"The Job" came to me in a flash. I have always been an Elvis fan and have found professional impersonators interesting. So, this is what you do with your whole life? Could be worse things. Anyway, I was thinking about hitmen and Elvis for some reason, and this jumped out in a flash. It was in a bizarre Western anthology. I can't say I justified this story well enough to be included as Western-related, but I was co-editor, so it went in. It has been quite popular. Reprinted a lot and made into a short film with an actual Elvis impersonator. He was a thinner version of Elvis. The early Elvis, where in the story he is an older version. I have since seen him on TV a few times. My son Keith and I have walk-on parts in the film. I'm a school principal, and Keith is a student. Keith went with me to most of the film adaptations of my work as well as a stage play I wrote. In the long run, it was important. He has written or co-written screenplays since, and a couple were made into films.

THE JOB

For Pat LoBrutto

BOWER PULLED THE sun visor down and looked in the mirror there and said, "You know, hadn't been for the travel, I'd have done all right. I could even shake my ass like him. I tell you, it drove the women wild. You should have seen 'em."

"Don't shake it for me," Kelly said. "I don't want to see it. Things I got to do are tough enough without having to see that."

Bower pushed the visor back. The light turned green. Kelly put the gas to the car and they went up and over a hill and turned right on Melroy.

"Guess maybe you do look like him," Kelly said. "During his fatter days, when he was on the drugs and the peanut butter."

"Yeah, but these pocks on my cheeks messes it up some. When I was on stage, I had makeup on 'em. I looked okay then."

They stopped at a stop sign and Kelly got out a cigarette and pushed in the lighter.

"A nigger nearly tail-ended me here once," Kelly said. "Just come barreling down on me." He took the lighter and lit his smoke. "Scared the piss out of me. I got him out of his car and popped him some. I bet he was one careful nigger from then on." He pulled away from the stop sign and cruised.

"You done one like this before? I know you've done it, but like this?"

"Not just like this. But I done some things might surprise you. You getting nervous on me?"

"I'm all right. You know, thing made me quit the Elvis imitating was travel, 'cause one night on the road I was staying in this cheap motel, and it wasn't heated too good. I'd had those kinds of rooms before, and I always carried couple of space heaters in the trunk of the car with the rest of my junk, you know. I got them plugged in, and I was still cold, so I pulled the mattress on the floor by the heaters. I woke up and was on fire. I had been so worn out I'd gone to sleep in my Elvis outfit. That was the end of my best white jumpsuit, you know, like he wore with the gold glitter and all. I must have been funny on fire like that, hopping around the room beating it out. When I got that suit off I was burned like the way you get when you been out in the sun too long."

"You gonna be able to do this?"

"Did I say I couldn't?"

"You're nervous. I can tell way you talk."

"A little. I always get nervous before I go on stage too, but I always come through. Crowd came to see Elvis, by god, they got Elvis. I used to sign autographs with his name. People wanted it like that. They wanted to pretend, see."

"Women mostly?"

"Uh-huh."

"What were they, say, fifty-five?"

"They were all ages. Some of them were pretty young."

"Ever fuck any of 'em?"

"Sure, I got plenty. Sing a little 'Love Me Tender' to them in the bedroom and they'd do whatever I wanted."

"Was it the old ones you was fucking?"

"I didn't fuck no real old ones, no. Whose idea is it to do things this way, anyhow?"

"Boss, of course. You think he lets me plan this stuff? He don't want them chinks muscling in on the shrimping and all."

"I don't know, we fought for these guys. It seems a little funny."

"Reason we lost the war over there is not being able to tell one chink from another and all of them being the way they are. I think we should have nuked the whole goddamned place. Went over there when it cooled down and stopped glowing, put in a fucking Disneyland or something."

They were moving out of the city now, picking up speed.

"I don't see why we don't just whack this guy outright and not do it this way," Bower said. "This seems kind of funny."

"No one's asking you. You come on a job, you do it. Boss wants some chink to suffer, so he's gonna suffer. Not like he didn't get some warnings or nothing. Boss wants him to take it hard."

"Maybe this isn't a smart thing on account of it may not bother chinks like it'd bother us. They're different about stuff like this, all the things they've seen."

"It'll bother him," Kelly said. "And if it don't, that ain't our problem. We got a job to do and we're gonna do it. Whatever comes after comes after. Boss wants us to do different next time, we do different. Whatever he wants, we do it. He's the one paying."

They were out of the city now and to the left of the highway they could see the glint of the sea through a line of scrubby trees.

"How're we gonna know?" Bower said. "One chink looks like another."

"I got a photograph. This one's got a burn scar on the face. Everything's timed. Boss has been planning this. He had some of the guys watch and take notes. It's all set up."

"Why us?"

"Me because I've done some things before. You because he wants to see what you're made of. I'm kind of here as your nursemaid."

"I don't need anybody to see that I do what I'm supposed to do."

They drove past a lot of boats pulled up to a dock. They drove into a small town called Wilborn. They turned a corner at Catlow Street.

"It's down here a ways," Kelly said. "You got your knife? You left your knife and brought your comb, I'm gonna whack you."

Bower got the knife out of his pocket. "Thing's got a lot of blades, some utility stuff. Even a comb."

"Christ, you're gonna do it with a Boy Scout knife?"

"Utility knife. The blade I want is plenty sharp, you'll see. Why couldn't we use a gun? That wouldn't be as messy. A lot easier."

"Boss wants it messy. He wants the chink to think about it some. He wants them to pack their stuff on their boats and sail back to chink land. Either that, or they can pay their percentages like everyone else. He lets the chinks get away with things, everyone'll want to get away with things."

They pulled over to the curb. Down the street was a school. Bower looked at his watch.

"Maybe if it was a nigger," Bower said.

"Chink, nigger, what's the difference?"

They could hear a bell ringing. After five minutes they saw kids going out to the curb to get on the buses parked there. A few kids came down the sidewalk toward them. One of them was a Vietnamese girl about eight years old. The left side of her face was scarred.

"Won't they remember me?" Bower said.

"Kids? Naw. Nobody knows you around here. Get rid of that Elvis look and you'll be okay."

"It don't seem right. In front of these kids and all. I think we ought to whack her father."

"No one's paying you to think, Elvis. Do what you're supposed to do. I have to do it and you'll wish you had."

Bower opened the utility knife and got out of the car. He held the knife by his leg and walked around front, leaned on the hood just as the Vietnamese girl came up. He said, "Hey, kid, come here a minute." His voice got thick. "Elvis wants to show you something."

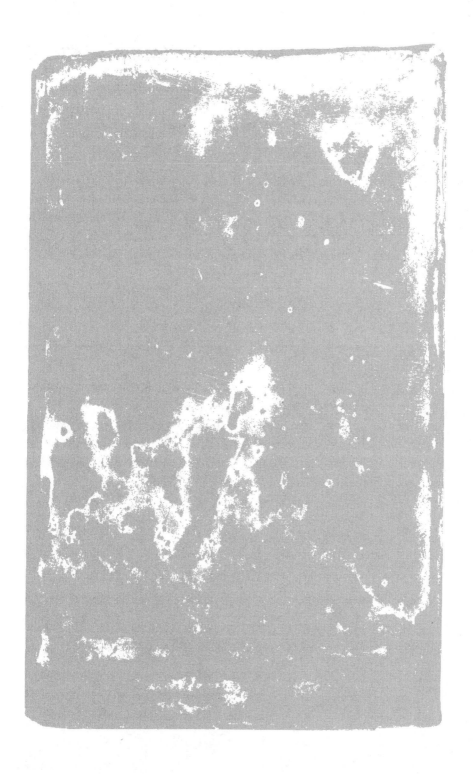

Gary Phillips is to blame for this one. He edited a really cool anthology of Black Pulp stories and asked me to contribute. I thought of a Dime Detective *or* Black Mask *story concept, or at least those magazines created for me. I tried to imagine a more modern version of one of those on modern newsstands, which actually don't really exist much anymore. But imagining an alternate universe where I could weld the forties and the present together for a nasty little tale was my driving inspiration. I decided I'd write from a criminal's point of view. An immoral man on a mission to save himself struck me as perfect. The story really just told itself. Once I pictured Six-Finger Jack, it fell together. I like to think it was sufficiently pulpy. I know it was well received, and if Gary were to need me again, I'd jump in line to write a story for him.*

SIX-FINGER JACK

JACK HAD SIX fingers. That's how Big O, that big, fat, white, straw-hatted son-of-a-bitch, was supposed to know he was dead. Maybe, by some real weird luck, a man could kill some other black man with six fingers, cut off his hand and bring it in and claim it belonged to Jack, but not likely. So he put the word out: whoever killed Jack and cut off his paw and brought it back was gonna get one hundred thousand dollars and a lot of goodwill.

I went out there after Jack just like a lot of other fellas, and one woman I knew of, Lean Mama Tootin', who was known for shotgun shootin' and ice-pick work. She went out there too.

But the thing I had on them was I was screwing Jack's old lady. Jack didn't know it of course. Jack was a bad dude, and it wouldn't have been smart to let him know my bucket was in his well. Nope. Wouldn't have been smart for me or for Jack's old lady. He'd known that before he had to make a run for it, might have been good to not sleep, 'cause he might show up and be most unpleasant. I can be unpleasant too, but I prefer when I'm on the stalk, not when I'm being stalked. It sets the dynamics all different.

You see, I'm a philosophical kind of guy.

Thing was, though, I'd been laying the pipeline to his lady for about six weeks, because Jack had been on the run ever since he'd tried to muscle in on Big O's whores and take over that business, found out he couldn't. That wasn't enough, he took up with Big O's old lady like it didn't matter none, but it did. Rumor was, Big O put the old lady under about three feet of concrete out by his lake boat stalls, put her in the hole while she was alive, hands tied behind her back, lookin' up at that concrete mixer truck dripping out the goo, right on top of her naked self.

Jack hears this little tidbit of information, he quit foolin' around and made with the jack rabbit, took off lickity-split, so fast he almost left a vapor trail. It's one thing to fight one man, or two, but to fight a whole organization, not so easy. Especially if that organization belonged to Big O.

Loodie, Jack's personal woman, was a hot-flash number who liked to have her ashes hauled, and me, I'm a tall, lean fellow with good smile and a willing attitude. Loodie was ready to lose Jack because he had a bad temper and a bit of a smell. He was short on baths and long on cologne. Smell-good juice on top of his stinky smell, she said, made a kind of funk that would make a skunk roll over dead and cause a wild hyena to leave the body where it lay.

She, on the other hand, was like sweet wet sin dipped in coffee and sugar with a dash of cinnamon; God's own mistress with a surly attitude, which goes to show even God likes a little bit of the devil now and then.

She'd been asked about Jack by them who wanted to know. Bad folks with guns, and a need for dough. But she lied, said she didn't know where he was. Everyone believed her because she talked so bad about Jack. Said stuff about his habits, about how he beat her, how bad he was in bed, and how he stunk. It was convincin' stuff to everyone.

But me.

I knew that woman was a liar, because I knew her whole family, and they was the sort like my daddy used to say would rather climb a tree and lie than stand on the ground and tell the truth and be given free flowers. Lies flowed through their veins as surely as blood.

She told me about Jack one night while we were in bed, right after we had toted the water to the mountain. We're laying there lookin' at the ceilin', like there's gonna be manna from heaven, watchin' the defective light from the church across the way flash in and out and bounce along the wall, and she says in that burnt toast voice of hers, "You split that money, I'll tell you where he is?"

"You wanna split it?"

"Naw, I'm thinkin' maybe you could keep half and I could give the other half to the cat."

"You don't got a cat."

"Well, I got another kind of cat, and that cat is one you like to pet."

"You're right there," I said. "Tellin' me where he is, that's okay, but I still got to do the ground work. Hasslin' with that dude ain't no easy matter, that's what I'm tryin' to tell you. So, me doin' what I'm gonna have to do, that's gonna be dangerous as trying to play with a daddy lion's balls. So, that makes me worth more than half, and you less than half."

"You're gonna shoot him when he ain't lookin', and you know it."

"I still got to take the chance."

She reached over to the nightstand, nabbed up a pack, shook out a cigarette, lit it with a cheap lighter, took a deep drag, coughed out a puff, said, "Split, or nothin'."

"Hell, honey, you know I'm funnin'," I said. "I'll split it right in half with you."

I was lyin' through my teeth. She may have figured such, but she figured with me she at least had a possibility, even if it was as thin as the edge of playin' card.

She said, "He's done gone deep East Texas. He's over in Marvel Creek. Drove over there in his big black Cadillac that he had a chop shop turn blue."

"So he drove over in a blue Caddy, not a black," I said. "I mean, if it was black, and he had it painted blue, it ain't black no more. It's blue."

"Aren't you one for the details, and at a time like this," she said, and used her foot to rub my leg. "But, technically, baby, you are so correct."

That night Loodie laid me out a map written in pencil on a brown paper sack, made me swear I was gonna split the money with her again. I told her what she wanted to hear. Next mornin', I started over to Marvel Creek.

Now, technically, Jack was in a place outside of the town, along the Sabine River, back in the bottom land where the woods was still thick, down a little trail that wound around and around, to a cabin Loodie said was about the size of a postage stamp, provided the stamp had been scissor trimmed.

I oiled my automatic, put on gloves, went to the store and bought a hatchet, cruised out early, made Marvel Creek in about an hour and fifteen, went glidin' over the Sabine River bridge. I took a gander at the water, which was dirty brown and up high on account of rain. I had grown up along that river, over near a place called Big Sandy. It was a place of hot sand and tall pines and no opportunity.

It wasn't a world I missed none.

I stopped at a little diner in Marvel Creek and had me a hamburger. There was a little white girl behind the counter with hair blonde as sunlight, and we made some goo-goo eyes at one another. Had I not been on a mission, I might have found out when she got off work, seen if me and her could get a drink and find a motel and try and make the beast with two backs.

Instead I finished up, got me a tall Styrofoam cup of coffee to go. I drove over to a food store and went in and bought a huge jar of pickles, a bag of cookies and a bottle of water. I put the pickles on the floorboard between the backseat and the front. It was a huge jar and it fit snugly. I laid the bag with the cookies and the water on the backseat.

The bottoms weren't far, about twenty minutes, but the roads were kind of tricky. Some of them were little more than mud and a suggestion. Others were slick and shiny like snot on a water glass.

I drove carefully and sucked on my coffee. I went down a pretty wide road that became narrow, then took another road that wound off into the deeper woods. Drove until I found what I thought was the side road that led to the cabin. It was really a glorified path. Sun hardened, not very wide, bordered on one side by trees, and on the other side by marshy land that would suck the shoes off your feet, or bog up a car tire until you had to pull a gun and shoot the engine like a dying horse.

I stopped in the road and held Loodie's hand-drawn map, checked it, looked up. There was a curve went around and between the trees and the marsh. There were tire tracks in it. Pretty fresh. At the bend in the curve was a little wooden bridge with no railings.

So far Loodie's map was on the money.

I finished off my coffee, got out and took a pee behind the car and watched some big white-water birds flying over. When I was growing up over in Big Sandy I used to see that kind of thing all the time, not to mention all manner of wildlife, and for a moment I felt nostalgic. That lasted about as long as it took me to stick my dick back in my pants and zipper up.

I got my hatchet out of the trunk and laid it on the front passenger seat as I got back in the car. I pulled out my automatic and checked it over, popped out the clip and slid it back in. I always liked the sound it made when it snapped into place. I looked at myself in the mirror, like maybe I was goin' on a date. Thought maybe if things fucked up, it might be the last time I got a good look at myself. I put the car in gear, wheeled around the curve and over the bridge, going at a slow pace, the map on the seat beside me, held in place by the hatchet.

I came to a wide patch, like on the map, and pulled off the road. Some-one had dumped their garbage at the end of the spot where it ended close to the trees. There were broken-up plastic bags spilling cans and paper, and there was an old bald tire leaning against a tree, as if taking a break before rolling on its way.

I got out and walked around the bend, looked down the road. There was a broad pond of water to the left, leaked there by the dirty Sabine. On the right, next to the woods, was a log cabin. Small, but well-made and kind of cool lookin'. Loodie said it was on property Jack's parents had owned.

Twenty acres or so. Cabin had a chimney chuggin' smoke. Out front was a big blue Cadillac El Dorado, the tires and sides splashed with mud. It was parked up close to the cabin. I could see through the Cadillac's win-dows, and they lined up with a window in the cabin. I moved to the side of the road, stepped in behind some trees, and studied the place carefully.

There weren't any wires runnin' to the cabin. There was a kind of lean-to shed off the back. Loodie told me that was where Jack kept the genera-tor that gave the joint electricity. Mostly the cabin was heated by the fire-wood piled against the shed, and lots of blankets come late at night. Had a gas stove with a nice-sized tank. I could just imagine Jack in there with Loodie, his six fingers on her sweet chocolate skin. It made me want to kill him all the more, even though I knew Loodie was the kind of girl made a minx look virginal. You gave your heart to that woman, she'd eat it.

I went back to the car and got my gun-cleaning goods out of the glove box, and took out the clip, and cleaned my pistol and reloaded it. It was unnecessary, because the gun was as clean as a model's ass, but I liked to be sure.

I patted the hatchet on the seat like it was a dog.

I sat there and waited, thought about what I was gonna do with one hundred thousand dollars. You planned to kill someone and cut off their hand, you had to think about stuff like that, and a lot.

Considering on it, I decided I wasn't gonna get foolish and buy a car. One I had got me around and it looked all right enough. I wasn't gonna spend it on Loodie or some other split tail in a big-time way. I was gonna use it carefully. I might get some new clothes and put some money down on a place instead of rentin'. Fact was, I might move to Houston.

If I lived close to the bone and picked up the odd bounty job now and again, just stuff I wanted to do, like bits that didn't involve me having to deal with some goon big enough to pull off one of my legs and beat me with it, I could live safer, and better. Could have some stretches where I didn't have to do a damn thing but take it easy, all on account of that one-hundred-thousand-dollar nest egg.

Course, Jack wasn't gonna bend over and grease up for me. He wasn't like that. He could be a problem.

I got a paperback out of the glove box and read for a while. I couldn't get my mind to stick to it. The sky turned gray. My light was goin'. I put the paperback in the glove box with the gun-cleaning kit. It started to rain. I watched it splat on the windshield. Thunder knocked at the sky. Lighting licked a crooked path against the clouds and passed away.

I thought about all manner of different ways of pullin' this off, and finally came up with somethin', decided it was good enough, because all I needed was a little edge.

The rain was hard and wild. It made me think Jack wasn't gonna be comin' outside. I felt safe enough for the moment. I tilted the seat back and lay there with the gun in my hand, my arm folded across my chest, and dozed for a while with the rain pounding the roof.

It was fresh night when I awoke. I waited about an hour, picked up the hatchet, and got out of the car. It was still raining, and the rain was cold. I pulled my coat tight around me, stuck the hatchet through my belt and went to the back of the car and unlocked the trunk. I got the jack handle out of there, stuck it in my belt opposite the hatchet, started walking around the curve.

The cabin had a faint light shining through the window that in turn shone through the lined-up windows of the car. As I walked, I saw a shape, like a huge bullet with arms, move in front of the glass. That size made me lose a step briefly, but I gathered up my courage, kept going.

When I got to the back of the cabin, I carefully climbed on the pile of firewood, made my way to the top of the lean-to. It sloped down off the main roof of the cabin, so it didn't take too much work to get up there, except that hatchet and tire iron gave me a bit of trouble in my belt and my gloves made my grip a little slippery.

On top of the cabin, I didn't stand up and walk, but instead carefully made my way on hands and knees toward the front of the place.

When I got there, I leaned over the edge and took a look. The cabin door was about three feet below me. I made my way to the edge so I was overlooking the Cadillac. A knock on the door wouldn't bring Jack out. Even he was too smart for that, but that Cadillac, he loved it. Bought a new one every year. I pulled out the tire iron, laid down on the roof, looking over the edge, cocked my arm back and threw the iron at the windshield. It made a hell of a crash, cracking the glass so that it looked like a spider web, setting off the car alarm.

I pulled my gun and waited. I heard the cabin door open, heard the thumping of Jack's big feet. He came around there mad as a hornet. He was wearing a long-sleeved white shirt with the sleeves rolled up. He hadn't had time to notice the cold. But the best thing was it didn't look like he had a gun on him.

I aimed and shot him. I think I hit him somewhere on top of the shoulder, but I wasn't sure. But I hit him. He did a kind of bend at the knees, twisted his body, then snapped back into shape and looked up.

"You," he said.

I shot him again, and it had about the same impact. Jack was on the hood of his car and then on the roof, and then he jumped. That big bastard could jump, could probably dunk a basketball and grab the rim. He hit with both hands on the edge of the roof, started pulling himself up. I was up now, and I stuck the gun in his face, and pulled the trigger.

And, let me tell you how the gas went out of me. I had cleaned that gun and cleaned that gun, and now . . . it jammed. First time ever. But it was a time that mattered.

Jack lifted himself onto the roof, and then he was on me, snatching the gun away and flinging it into the dark. I couldn't believe it. What the hell was he made of? Even in the wet night, I could see that much of his white shirt had turned dark with blood.

We circled each other for a moment. I tried to decide what to do next, and then he was on me. I remembered the hatchet, but it was too late. We were going back off the roof and onto the lean-to, rolling down that. We hit the stacked firewood and it went in all directions and we splattered to the ground.

I lost my breath. Jack kept his. He grabbed me by my coat collar and lifted me and flung me around and against the side of the lean-to. I hit on my back and came down on my butt.

Jack grabbed up a piece of firewood. It looked to me that that piece of wood had a lot of heft. He came at me. I made myself stand. I pulled the hatchet free. As he came and struck down with the wood, I sidestepped and swung the hatchet.

The sound the hatchet made as it caught the top of his head was a little like what you might expect if a strong man took hold of a piece of cardboard and ripped it.

I hit him so hard his knees bent and hot blood jumped out of his head and hit my face. The hatchet came loose of my hands, stayed in his skull.

His knees straightened. I thought, What is this motherfucker, Rasputin?

He grabbed me and started to lift me again. His mouth was partially open and his teeth looked like machinery cogs to me.

The rain was washing the blood on his head down his face in murky rivers. He stunk like roadkill.

And then his expression changed. It seemed as if he had just realized he had a hatchet in his head. He let go, turned, started walking off, taking hold of the hatchet with both hands, trying to pull it loose. I picked up a piece of firewood and followed after him. I went up behind him and hit him in the back of the head as hard as I could. It was like hitting an elephant in the ass with a twig. He turned and looked at me. The look on his face was so strange, I almost felt sorry for him.

He went down on one knee, and I hauled back and hit him with the firewood, hitting the top of the hatchet. He vibrated, and his neck twisted to one side, and then his head snapped back in line.

He said, "Gonna need some new pigs," and then fell out. Pigs?

He was lying face forward with the stock of the hatchet holding his head slightly off the ground. I dropped the firewood and rolled him over on his back, which only took about as much work as trying to roll his Cadillac. I pulled the hatchet out of his head. I had to put my foot on his neck to do it.

I picked up the firewood I had dropped, put it on the ground beside him, and stretched his arm out until I had the hand with the six fingers positioned across it. I got down on my knees and lifted the hatchet, hit as hard as I could. It took me three whacks, but I cut his hand loose.

I put the bloody hand in my coat pocket and dug through his pants for his car keys, didn't come across them. I went inside the cabin and found them on the table. I drove the Cadillac to the back where Jack lay, pulled him into the backseat, almost having a hernia in the process. I put the hatchet in there with him.

I drove the El Dorado over close to the pond and rolled all the windows down and put it in neutral. I got out of the car, went to the back of it and started shoving. My feet slipped in the mud, but finally I gained traction. The car went forward and slipped into the water, but the back end of it hung on the bank.

Damn.

I pushed and I pushed, and finally I got it moving, and it went in, and with the windows down, it sunk pretty fast.

I went back to the cabin and looked around. I found some candles. I turned off the light, and I went and turned off the generator. I went back inside and lit about three of the big fat candles and stuck them in drinking glasses and watched them burn for a moment. I went over to the stove and turned on the gas. I let it run a few seconds, looked around the cabin.

Nothing there I needed.

I left, closed the door behind me. When the gas filled the room enough, those candles would set the air on fire, the whole place would blow. I don't know exactly why I did it, except maybe I just didn't like Jack. Didn't like that he had a Cadillac and a cabin and some land, and for a while there, he had Loodie. Because of all that, I had done all I could do that could be done to him. I even had his six-fingered hand in my pocket.

By the time I got back to the car, I was feeling weak. Jack had worked me over pretty good, and now that the adrenaline had started to ease out of me, I was feeling it. I took off my jacket and opened the jar of pickles in the floorboard, pulled out a few of them and threw them away. I ate one, and had my bottle of water with it and some cookies.

I took Jack's hand and put it in the big pickle jar. I sat in the front seat, and was overcome with a feeling of nausea. I didn't know if it was the pickle or what I had done, or both. I opened the car door and threw up. I felt cold and damp from the rain. I started the car and turned on the heater. I cranked back my seat and closed my eyes. I had to rest before I left, had to. All of me seemed to be running out through the soles of my feet.

I slept until the cabin blew. The sound of the gas generator and stove going up with a one-two boom snapped me awake.

I got out of the car and walked around the curve. The cabin was nothing more than a square dark shape inside an envelope of fire. The fire wavered up high and grew narrow at the top like a cone. The fire crackled like someone wadding up cellophane.

I doubted, out here, anyone heard the explosion, and no one could see the flames. Wet as it was, I figured the fire wouldn't go any farther than the cabin. By morning, even with the rain still coming down, that place would be smoked down to the mineral rights.

I drove out of there, and pretty soon the heater was too hot, and I turned it off. It was as if my body was as on fire as the cabin. I rolled down the window and let in some cool air. I felt strange. Not good, not bad. I had bounty hunted for years, and I had done a bit of head-whopping before, but this was my first murder.

I had really hated Jack and I had hardly known him.

It was the woman that made me hate him. The woman I was gonna cheat out of some money. But a hundred thousand dollars is a whole lot of money, honey.

When I got home, the automatic garage opener lifted the door and I wheeled in and closed the place up. I went inside and took off my clothes and showered carefully and looked in the mirror. There was a knot on my head that looked as if you might need mountaineering equipment to scale it. I got some ice and put it in a sock and pressed it to my head while I sat on the toilet lid and thought about things. If any thoughts actually came to me, I don't remember them well.

I dressed, bunched up my murder clothes, and put them in a black plastic garbage bag.

In the garage, I removed the pickle jar and cleaned the car. I opened the jar and looked at the hand. It looked like a black crab in there amongst the pickles. I studied it for a long time until it started to look like one hundred thousand dollars.

I couldn't wait until morning, and after a while I drove toward Big O's place. Now, you would think a man with the money he's got would live in a mansion, but he didn't. He lived in three double-wide mobile homes that had been lined together by screened-in porches. I had been inside once, when I had done Big O a very small favor, and had never been inside since. But one of those homes was nothing but one big space, no rooms, and it was Big O's lounge. He hung in there with some ladies and some bodyguards. He had two main guys: Be Bop Lewis, who was a skinny white guy who always acted as if someone was sneaking up on him, and a black guy named Lou Boo (keep in mind, I didn't name them) who thought he was way cool and smooth as velvet.

The rain had followed me from the bottom land, on into Tyler, to the outskirts, and on the far side. It was way early morning, and I figured on waking Big O up and dragging his ass out of bed and showing him them six fingers and getting me one hundred thousand dollars, a pat on the head, and hell, he might ask Be Bop to give me a hand job, on account of I had done so well.

More I thought about it, more I thought he might not be as happy to see me as I thought. A man like Big O liked his sleep, so I pulled into a motel not too far from where I had to go to see Big O, the big jar of pickles and one black six-fingered hand beside my bed, the automatic under my pillow.

I dreamed Jack was driving the Cadillac out of that pond. I saw the lights first and then the car. Jack was steering with his nub laid against the wheel, and his face behind the glass was a black mass without eyes or smile or features of any kind.

It was a bad dream and it woke me up. I washed my face, went back to bed, slept this time until late morning. I got up and put back on my same clothes, loaded up my pickle jar and left out of there. I thought about the axe in Jack's head, his hand chopped off and in the pickle jar, and regret moved through me like shit through a goose and was gone.

I drove out to Big O's place.

By the time I arrived at the property, which was surrounded by a barbed-wire fence, and had driven over a cattle guard, I could see there were men in a white pickup coming my way. Two in the front and three in the bed in the back, and they had some heavy-duty fire power. Parked behind them, up by the double-wides, were the cement trucks and dump trucks and backhoes and graders that were part of the business Big O claimed to operate. Construction. But his real business was a bit of this, and a little of that, construction being little more than the surface paint.

I stopped and rolled down my window and waited. Outside the rain had burned off and it was an unseasonably hot day, sticky as honey on the fingers.

When they drove up beside my window, the three guys in the bed pointed their weapons at me. The driver was none other than one of the two men I recognized from before. Be Bop. His skin was so pale and thin, I could almost see the skull beneath it.

"Well, now," he said. "I know you."

I agreed he did. I smiled like me and him was best friends. I said, "I got some good news for Big O about Six-Finger Jack."

"Six-Finger Jack, huh," Be Bop said. "Get out of the car."

I got out. Be Bop got out and frisked me. I had nothing sharp or anything full of bullets. He asked if there was anything in the car. I told him no. He had one of the men in the back of the pickup search it anyway. The man came back, said, "Ain't got no gun, just a big jar of pickles."

"Pickles," Be Bop said. "You a man loves pickles?"

"Not exactly," I said.

"Follow us on up," Be Bop said.

We drove on up to the trio of double-wides. There had been some work done since I had last been here, and there was a frame of boards laid out for a foundation, and out to the side there was a big hole that looked as if it was going to be a swimming pool.

I got out of the car and leaned on it and looked things over. Be Bop and his men got out of the truck. Be Bop came over. "He buildin' a house on that foundation?" I asked.

"Naw, he's gonna put an extension on one of the trailers. I think he's gonna put in a pool room and maybe some gamin' stuff. Swimmin' pool over there. Come on."

I got my jar of pickles out of the backseat, and Be Bop said, "Now wait a minute. Your pickles got to go with you?"

I set the jar down and screwed off the lid and stepped back. Be Bop looked inside. When he lifted his head, he said, "Well, now."

Next thing I know I'm in the big trailer, the one that's got nothin' but the couch, some chairs and stands for drinks, a TV set about the size of a downtown theater. It's on, and there's sports goin'. I glance at it and see it's an old basketball game that was played a year back, but they're watchin' it, Big O and a few of his boys, includin' Lou Boo, the black guy I've seen before. This time, there aren't any women there.

Be Bop came inside with me, but the rest of the pickup posse didn't.

They were still protecting the perimeter. It seemed silly, but truth was, there was lots of people wanted to kill Big O.

No one said a thing to me for a full five minutes. They were waitin' for a big score in the game, somethin' they had seen before. When the shot came, they all cheered. I thought only Big O sounded sincere.

I didn't look at the game. I couldn't take my eyes off Big O. He wasn't wearin' his cowboy hat. His head had only a few hairs left on it, like worms working their way over the face of the moon. His skin was white and lumpy like cold oatmeal. He was wearin' a brown pair of stretch overalls. When the fat moved, the material moved with him, which was a good idea, 'cause

it looked as if Big O had packed on about one hundred extra pounds since I saw him last.

He was sitting in a motorized scooter, had his tree trunk legs stretched out in front of him on a leg lift. His stomach flowed up and fell forward and over his sides, like four hundred pounds of bagged mercury. I could hear him wheezing across the room. His right foot was missing. There was a nub there and his stretch pants had been sewn up at the end. On the stand, near his right elbow was a tall bottle of malt liquor and a greasy box of fried chicken.

His men sat on the couch to his left. The couch was unusually long and there were six men on it, like pigeons in a row. They all had guns in shoulder holsters. The scene made Big O looked like a whale on vacation with a male harem of sucker fish to attend him.

Big O spoke to me, his voice sounded small coming from that big body. "Been a long time since I seen you last."

I nodded.

"I had a foot then."

I nodded again.

"The diabetes. Had to cut it off. Dr. Jacobs says I need more exercise, but, hey, glandular problems, so what you gonna do? Packs the weight on. But still, I got to go there every Thursday mornin'. Next time, he might tell me the other foot's got to go. But you know, that's not so bad. This chair, it can really get you around. Motorized you know."

Be Bop, who was still by me, said, "He's got somethin' for you, Big O."

"Chucky," Big O said, "cut off the game."

Chucky was one of the men on the couch, a white guy. He got up and found a remote control and cut off the game. He took it with him back to the couch, sat down.

"Come on up," Big O said.

I carried my jar of pickles up there, got a whiff of him that made my memory of Jack's stink seem mild. Big O smelled like dried urine, sweat, and death. I had to fight my gag reflex.

I set the jar down and twisted off the lid and reached inside the blood-stained pickle juice, and brought out Jack's dripping hand. Big O said, "Give me that."

I gave it to him. He turned it around and around in front of him. Pickle juice dripped off of the hand and into his lap. He started to laugh. His fat vibrated, and then he coughed. "That there is somethin'."

He held the hand up above his head. Well, he lifted it to about shoulder height. Probably the most he had moved in a while. He said, "Boys, do you see this? Do you see the humanity in this?"

I thought, Humanity?

"This hand tried to take my money and stuck its finger up my old lady's ass . . . maybe all six. Look at it now."

His boys all laughed. It was like the best goddamn joke ever told, way they yucked it up.

"Well now," Big O said, "that motherfucker won't be touchin' nothin', won't be handlin' nobody's money, not even his own, and we got this dude to thank."

Way Big O looked at me then made me a little choked up. I thought there might even be a tear in his eye. "Oh," he said. "I loved that woman. God, I did. But I had to cut her loose. She hadn't fucked around, me and her might have gotten married, and all this—" he waved Jack's hand around, "would have been hers to share. But no. She couldn't keep her pants on. It's a sad situation. And though I can't bring her back, this here hand, it gives me some kind of happiness. I want you to know that."

"I'm glad I could have been of assistance," I said.

"That's good. That's good. Put this back in the pickle jar, will you?"

I took the hand and dropped it in the pickle jar.

Big O looked at me, and I looked at him. After a long moment, he said, "Well, thanks."

I said, "You're welcome."

We kept looking at one another. I cleared my throat. Big O shifted a little in his chair. Not much, but a little.

"Seems to me," I said, "there was a bounty on Jack. Some money."

"Oh," Big O said. "That's right, there was."

"He was quite a problem."

"Was he now. . . . Yeah, well, I can see the knot on your head. You ought to buy that thing its own cap. Somethin' nice."

Everyone on the couch laughed. I laughed too. I said, "Yeah, it's big.

And, I had some money, like say, one hundred thousand dollars, I'd maybe put out ten or twenty for a nice designer cap."

I was smilin', waiting for my laugh, but nothin' came. I glanced at Be Bop. He was lookin' off like maybe he heard his mother callin' somewhere in the distance.

Big O said, "Now that Jack's dead, I got to tell you, I've sort of lost the fever."

"Lost the fever?" I said.

"He was alive, I was all worked up. Now that he's dead, I got to consider, is he really worth one hundred thousand dollars?"

"Wait a minute, that was the deal. That's the deal you spread all over."

"I've heard those rumors," Big O said.

"Rumors?"

"Oh, you can't believe everything you hear. You just can't." I stood there stunned.

Big O said, "But I want you to know, I'm grateful. You want a Coke, a beer before you go?"

"No. I want the goddamn money you promised."

That had come out of my mouth like vomit. It surprised even me.

Everyone in the room was silent.

Big O breathed heavy, said, "Here's the deal, friend. You take your jar of pickles, and Jack's six fingers, and you carry them away. Cause if you don't, if you want to keep askin' me for money I don't want to pay, your head is gonna be in that jar, but not before I have it shoved up your ass. You savvy?"

It took me a moment, but I said, "Yeah. I savvy."

Lying in bed with Loodie, not being able to do the deed, I said, "I'm gonna get that fat sonofabitch. He promised me money. I fought Jack with a piece of firewood and a hatchet. I fell off a roof. I slept in my car in the cold. I was nearly killed."

"That sucks," Loodie said.

"Sucks? You got snookered too. You was gonna get fifty thousand, now you're gonna get dick."

"Actually, tonight, I'm not even gettin' that."

"Sorry, baby. I'm just so mad. . . . Every Thursday mornin', Big O, he goes to a doctor's appointment at Dr. Jacobs. I can get him there."

"He has his men, you know."

"Yeah. But when he goes in the office, maybe he don't. And maybe I check it out this Thursday, find out when he goes in, and next Thursday, I maybe go inside and wait on him."

"How would you do that?"

"I'm thinkin' on it, baby."

"I don't think it's such a good idea."

"You lost fifty grand, and so did I, so blowin' a hole in his head is as close as we'll get to satisfaction."

So Thursday mornin', I'm goin' in the garage to go and check things out, and when I get in the car, before I can open up the garage and back out, a head raises up in the back seat, and a gun barrel, like a wet kiss, pushes against the side of my neck.

I can see him in the mirror. It's Lou Boo. He says, "You got to go where I tell you, else I shoot a hole in you."

I said, "Loodie."

"Yeah, she come to us right away."

"Come on, man. I was just mad. I wasn't gonna do nothin'."

"So here it is Thursday mornin', and now you're tellin' me you wasn't goin' nowhere."

"I was gonna go out and get some breakfast. Really."

"Don't believe you."

"Shit," I said.

"Yeah, shit," Lou Boo said.

"How'd you get in here without me knowin'?"

"I'm like a fuckin' ninja . . . and the door slides up you pull it from the bottom."

"Really?"

"Yeah, really."

"Come on, Lou Boo, give a brother a break. You know how it is."

Lou Boo laughed a little. "Ah, man. Don't play the brother card. I'm what you might call one of them social progressives. I don't see color, even if it's the same as mine. Let's go, my man."

It was high morning and cool when we arrived. I drove my car right up to where the pool was dug out, way Lou Boo told me. There was a cement mixer truck parked nearby for cementing the pool. We stopped and Lou Boo told me to leave it in neutral. I did. I got out and walked with him to where Big O was sitting in his motorized scooter with Loodie on his lap. His boys were all around him. Be Bop pointed his finger at me and dropped his thumb.

"My man," Be Bop said.

When I was standing in front of Big O, he said, "Now, I want you to understand, you wouldn't be here had you not decided to kill me. I can't have that, now can I?"

I didn't say anything.

I looked at Loodie, she shrugged.

"I figured you owed me money," I said.

"Yeah," Big O said. "I know. You see, Loodie, she comes and tells me she's gonna make a deal with you to kill Jack and make you think you made a deal with her. That way, the deal I made was with her, not you. You followin' me on this, swivel dick? Then, you come up with this idea to kill me at the doctor's office. Loodie, she came right to me."

"So," I said, "you're gettin' Loodie out of the deal, and she's gettin' one hundred thousand."

"That sounds about right, yeah," Big O said.

I thought about that. Her straddlin' that fat bastard in his scooter. I shook my head, glared at her, said, "Damn, girl."

She didn't look right at me.

Big O said, "Loodie, you go on in the house there, and amuse yourself. Get a beer, or somethin'. Watch a little TV. Do your nails. Whatever."

Loodie started walking toward the trailers. When she was inside, Big O said, "Hell, boy. I know how she is, and I know what she is. It's gonna be white gravy on sweet chocolate bread for me. And when I get tired of it, she gonna find a hole out here next to you. I got me all kind of room here. I ain't usin' the lake boat stalls no more. That's risky. Here is good. Though I'm gonna have to dig another spot for a pool, but that's how it is. Ain't no big thing, really."

"She used me," I said. "She's the one led me to this."

"No doubt, boy. But you got to understand. She come to me and made the deal before you did anything. I got to honor that."

"I could just go on," I said. "I could forget all about it. I was just mad. I wouldn't never bother you. Hell, I can move. I can go out of state."

"I know that," he said, "but, I got this rule, and it's simple. You threaten to kill me, I got to have you taken care of. Ain't that my rule, boys?"

There was a lot of agreement.

Lou Boo was last. He said, "Yep, that's the way you do it, boss." Big O said, "Lou Boo, put him in the car, will you?"

Lou Boo put the gun to the back of my head, said, "Get on your knees."

"Fuck you," I said, but he hit me hard behind the head. Next thing I know I'm on my knees, and he's got my hands behind my back, and has fastened a plastic tie over my wrists.

"Get in the car," Lou Boo said.

I fought him all the way, but Be Bop came out and kicked me in the nuts a couple of times, hard enough I threw up, and then they dragged me to the car and shoved me inside behind the wheel and rolled down the windows and closed the door.

They went behind the car then and pushed. The car wobbled, then fell, straight down, hit so hard the air bag blew out and knocked the shit out of me. I couldn't move with it the way it was, my hands bound behind my back, the car on its nose, its back wheels against the side of the hole. It looked like I was tryin' to drive to hell. I was stunned and bleeding. The bag had knocked a tooth out. I heard the sound of a motor above me, a little motor. The scooter.

I could hear Big O up there. "If you hear me, want you to know I'm having one of the boys bring the cement truck around. We're gonna fill this hole with cement, and put, I don't know, a tennis court or somethin' on top of it. But the thing I want you to know is this is what happens when someone fucks with Big O."

"You stink," I said. "And you're fat. And you're ugly."

He couldn't hear me. I was mostly talking into the air bag.

I heard the scooter go away, followed by the sound of a truck and a beeping as it backed up. Next, I heard the churning of the cement in the big mixer that was on the back of it. Then the cement slid down and pounded on the roof and started to slide over the windshield. I closed my eyes and held my breath, and then I felt the cold wet cement touch my elbow as it came through the open window. I thought about some way out, but there was nothing there, and I knew that within moments there wouldn't be anything left for me to think about at all.

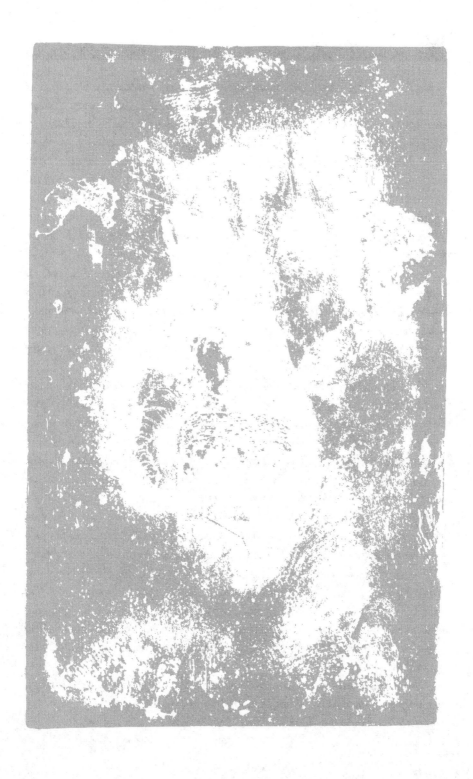

When I was young, Charles Whitman climbed up in the tower at the University of Texas with a lot of guns and started shooting people for no discernible reason. He was an Eagle Scout, crack shot, all around good ol' American apple-cheeked boy. Later, he had gunpowder on those apple cheeks. He shot a pregnant woman, killing her unborn child, along with her boyfriend, not to mention a lot more people on campus. There was some real bravery that day as the cops and a civilian made their way up to the tower to kill him, to stop the slaughter. They achieved their mission. It was later found out that he had killed his mother and wife, or perhaps she was his girlfriend, I forget, before putting together a trunk full of guns and hauling them upstairs to the tower, killing or wounding folks he met along the way. I watched it unfold on TV.

Some years later, Kinky Friedman wrote a song about there being a rumor of a tumor at the base of his brain. I believe the song was called "The Ballad of Charles Whitman." The song was inspired by the fact that his actions were so rare at that time, some experts tried to explain them by suggesting a tumor. As for the shooting, I don't know if I saw it when it happened, or later that day on the news, but I remember the puffs of gunpowder from the tower.

Years later, when I briefly attended the University of Texas, I went up in the tower and looked out. It would have been a perfect sniper's nest. Walking around campus, I was shown marks in the steps and walls where bullets had struck. I think they were just that. Looked like it. A weird thing. Whitley Streiber once claimed to have been there, and he told the story in great detail. Later, it was determined he wasn't there. To explain it, he said he was kidnapped by aliens and the false memory was placed there. Damn, man. Something else about the tower.

While I was going to school there, a young woman climbed up to the tower, took off her shoes, placed them neatly on the ledge, stepped up on the ledge, and jumped. That morning I was at class, and when I walked by the tower, they were hosing down the bushes. I found out what had happened when I arrived at the place where I was living, and wondered later if what they were hosing down was the blood from that poor girl, for that's what she was. A girl. I don't know what caused her to jump, but for some reason, she felt she needed to end her life. Barricades were erected to prevent something like that from happening again. I don't know if you can even go up to the top of the tower anymore.

This all stuck with me, and when I was asked to write a story for an anthology, this story came to mind. I think I was trying, at least fictionally, to explain why Charles Whitman would do such a thing. Are the shadows real? You decide.

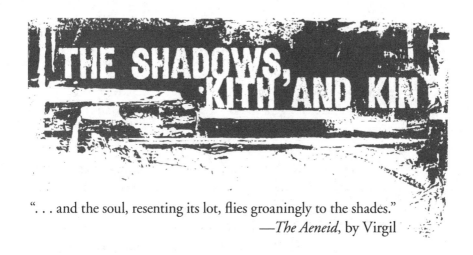

THE SHADOWS, KITH, AND KIN

"... and the soul, resenting its lot, flies groaningly to the shades."
—*The Aeneid*, by Virgil

THERE ARE NO leaves left on the trees, and the limbs are weighted with ice and bending low.

Many of them have broken and fallen across the drive. Beyond the drive, down where it and the road meet, where the bar ditch is, there is a brown savage run of water.

It is early afternoon, but already it is growing dark, and the fifth week of the storm raves on.

I have never seen such a storm of wind and ice and rain, not here in the South, and only once before have I been in a cold storm bad enough to force me to lock myself tight in my home.

So many things were different then, during that first storm.

No better. But different.

On this day while I sit by my window, looking out at what the great, white, wet storm has done to my world, I feel at first confused, and finally elated.

The storm. The ice. The rain. All of it. It's the sign I was waiting for.

I thought for a moment of my wife, her hair so blonde it was almost white as the ice that hung in the trees, and I thought of her parents, white-headed too, but white with age, not dye, and of our little dog Constance, not white at all, but all brown and black with traces of tan; a rat terrier mixed with all other blends of dog you might imagine.

I thought of all of them. I looked at my watch. There wasn't really any reason to. I had no place to go, and no way to go if I did. Besides, the battery in my watch had been dead for almost a month.

Once, when I was a boy, just before night fall, I was out hunting with my father, out where the bayou water gets deep and runs between the twisted trunks and low hanging limbs of water-loving trees; out there where the frogs bleat and jump and the sun don't hardly shine.

We were hunting for hogs. Then out of the brush came a man, running. He was dressed in striped clothes and he had on very thin shoes. He saw us and the dogs that were gathered about us, blue-ticks, long-eared and dripping spit from their jaws; he turned and broke and ran with a scream.

A few minutes later, the Sheriff and three of his deputies came beating their way through the brush, their shirts stained with sweat, their faces red with heat.

My father watched all of this with a kind of hard-edged cool, and the Sheriff, a man Dad knew, said, "There's a man escaped off the chain gang, Hirem. He run through here. Did you see him?"

My father said that we had, and the Sheriff said, "Will those dogs track him?"

"I want them to, they will," my father said, and he called the dogs over to where the convict had been, where his footprints in the mud were filling slowly with water, and he pushed the dogs' heads down toward these shoe prints one at a time, and said, "Sic him," and away the hounds went.

We ran after them then, me and my dad and all these fat cops who huffed and puffed out long before we did, and finally we came upon the man, tired, leaning against a tree with one hand, his other holding his business while he urinated on the bark. He had been defeated some time back, and now he was waiting for rescue, probably thinking it would have been best to have not run at all.

But the dogs, they had decided by private conference that this man was as good as any hog, and they came down on him like heat-seeking missiles. Hit him hard, knocked him down. I turned to my father, who could call them up and make them stop, no matter what the situation, but he did not call.

The dogs tore at the man, and I wanted to turn away, but did not. I looked at my father and his eyes were alight and his lips dripped spit; he reminded me of the hounds.

The dogs ripped and growled and savaged, and then the fat Sheriff and his fat deputies stumbled into view, and when one of the deputies saw what had been done to the man, he doubled over and let go of whatever grease-fried goodness he had poked into his mouth earlier that day.

The Sheriff and the other deputy stopped and stared, and the Sheriff said, "My God," and turned away, and the deputy said, "Stop them, Hirem. Stop them. They done done it to him. Stop them."

My father called the dogs back, their muzzles dark and dripping. They sat in a row behind him, like sentries. The man, or what had been a man, the convict, lay all about the base of the tree, as did the rags that had once been his clothes.

Later, we learned the convict had been on the chain gang for cashing hot checks.

Time keeps on slipping, slipping. . . . Wasn't that a song?

As day comes I sleep, then awake when night arrives. The sky has cleared and the moon has come out, and it is merely cold now. Pulling on my coat, I go out on the porch and sniff the air, and the air is like a meat slicer to the brain, so sharp it gives me a headache. I have never known cold like that.

I can see the yard close up. Ice has sheened all over my world, all across the ground, up in the trees. The sky is like a black velvet backdrop, the stars like sharp shards of blue ice clinging to it. I leave the porch light on, go inside, return to my chair by the window, burp. The air is filled with the aroma of my last meal, canned ravioli, eaten cold.

I take off my coat and hang it on the back of the chair.

Has it happened yet, or is it yet to happen?

Time, it just keeps on slippin', slippin', yeah it do.

I nod in the chair, and when I snap awake from a deep nod, there is snow blowing across the yard and the moon is gone and there is only the porch light to brighten it up.

But, in spite of the cold, I know they are out there.

The cold, the heat, nothing bothers them.

They are out there.

They came to me first on a dark night several months back, with no snow and no rain and no cold, but a dark night without clouds and plenty of heat in the air, a real humid night, sticky like dirty undershorts. I awoke and sat up in bed and the yard light was shining thinly through our window. I turned to look at my wife lying there beside me, her very blonde hair silver in that light. I looked at her for a long time, then got up and went into the living room. Our little dog, who made his bed by the front door, came over and sniffed me, and I bent to pet him. He took to this for a minute, then found his spot by the door again, laid down.

Finally I turned out the yard light and went out on the porch. In my underwear. No one could see me, not with all our trees, and if they could see me, I didn't care.

I sat in a deck chair and looked at the night, and thought about the job I didn't have and how my wife had been talking of divorce, and how my in-laws resented our living with them, and I thought too of how every time I did a thing I failed, and dramatically at that. I felt strange and empty and lost.

While I watched the night, the darkness split apart and some of it came up on the porch, walking. Heavy steps full of all the world's shadow.

I was frightened, but I didn't move. Couldn't move. The shadow, which looked like a tar-covered human-shape, trudged heavily across the porch until it stood over me, looking down.

When I looked up, trembling, I saw there was no face, just darkness, thick as chocolate custard.

It bent low and placed hand shapes on the sides of my chair and brought its faceless face close to mine, breathed on me; a hot languid breath that made me ill.

"You are almost one of us," it said, then turned, and slowly moved along the porch and down the steps and right back into the shadows. The darkness, thick as a wall, thinned and split, and absorbed my visitor; then the shadows rustled away in all directions like startled bats. I heard a dry crackling leaf sound amongst the trees.

My God, I thought. There had been a crowd of them.

Out there.

Waiting.

Watching.

Shadows.

And one of them had spoken to me.

Lying in bed later that night, I held up my hand and found that what intrigued me most were not the fingers, but the darkness between them. It was a thin darkness, made weak by light, but it was darkness and it seemed more a part of me than the flesh.

I turned and looked at my sleeping wife.

I said, "I am one of them. Almost."

I remember all this as I sit in my chair and the storm rages outside, blowing snow and swirling little twirls of water that in turn become ice. I remember all this, holding up my hand again to look.

The shadows between my fingers are no longer thin.

They are dark.

They have connection to flesh.

They are me.

Four flashes. Four snaps.

The deed is done.

I wait in the chair by the window.

No one comes.

As I suspected.

The shadows were right.

You see, they come to me nightly now. They never enter the house. Perhaps they cannot.

But out on the porch, there they gather. More than one now. And they flutter tight around me and I can smell them, and it is a smell like nothing I have smelled before. It is dark and empty and mildewed and old and dead and dry.

It smells like home.

Who are the shadows?

They are all of those who are like me.

They are the empty congregation. The faceless ones. The failures.

The sad empty folk who wander through life and walk beside you and never get so much as a glance; nerds like me who live inside their heads and imagine winning the lottery and scoring the girls and walking tall. But instead, we stand short and bald and angry, our hands in our pockets, holding not money, but our limp balls.

Real life is a drudge.

No one but another loser like myself can understand that.

Except for the shadows, for they are the ones like me. They are the losers and the lost, and they understand and they never do judge.

They are of my flesh, or, to be more precise, I am of their shadow.

They accept me for who I am.

They know what must be done, and gradually they reveal it to me.

The shadows.

I am one of them.

Well, almost.

My wife, my in-laws, every human being who walks this earth, underrates me.

There are things I can do.

I can play computer games, and I can win them. I have created my own characters. They are unlike humans. They are better than humans. They are the potential that is inside me and will never be.

Oh, and I can do some other things as well. I didn't mention all the things I can do well. In spite of what my family thinks of me, I can do a number of things that they don't appreciate, but should.

I can make a very good chocolate milk shake.

My wife knows this, and if she could, she would admit that I do. She used to say so. Now she does not. She has closed up to me. Internally. Externally.

Battened down hatches, inwardly and outwardly.

Below. In her fine little galley, that hatch is tightly sealed.

But there is another thing I do well.

I can really shoot a gun.

My father, between beatings, he taught me that. It was the only time we were happy together. When we held the guns.

Down in the basement I have a trunk.

Inside the trunk are guns.

Lots of them.

Rifles and shotguns and revolvers and automatics.

I have collected them over the years.

One of the rifles belongs to my father-in-law.

There is lots of ammunition.

Sometimes, during the day, if I can't sleep, while my wife is at work and my in-laws are about their retirement—golf—I sit down there and clean the guns and load them and repack them in the crate. I do it carefully, slowly, like foreplay. And when I finish my hands smell like gun oil. I rub my hands against my face and under my nose, the odor of the oil like some kind of musk.

But now, with the ice and the cold and the dark, with us frozen in and with no place to go, I clean them at night. Not during the day while they are gone.

I clean them at night.

In the dark.

After I visit with the shadows.

My friends.

All the dark ones, gathered from all over the world, past and present. Gathered out there in my yard—my wife's parents' yard—waiting on me. Waiting for me to be one with them, waiting on me to join them.

The only club that has ever wanted me.

They are many of those shadows, and I know who they are now. I know it on the day I take the duct tape and use it to seal the doors to my wife's bedroom, to my parents-in-law's bedroom.

The dog is with my wife.

I can no longer sleep in our bed.

My wife, like the others, has begun to smell.

The tape keeps some of the stench out.

I pour cologne all over the carpet.

It helps.

Some.

How it happened. I'll line it out:

One night I went out and sat and the shadows came up on the porch in such numbers there was only darkness around me and in me, and I was like something scared, but somehow happy, down deep in a big black sack held by hands that love me.

Yet, simultaneously, I was free.

I could feel them touching me, breathing on me. And I knew, then, it was time.

Down in the basement, I opened the trunk, took out a well-oiled weapon, a hunting rifle. I went upstairs and did it quick. My wife first. She never awoke. Beneath her head, on the pillow, in the moonlight, there was a spreading blossom the color of gun oil.

My father-in-law heard the shot, met me at their bedroom door, pulling on his robe. One shot. Then another for my mother-in-law who sat up in bed, her face hidden in shadow—but a different shadow. Not one of my shadow friends, but one made purely by an absence of light, and not an absence of being.

The dog bit me.

I guess it was the noise.

I shot the dog too.

I didn't want him to be lonely.

Who would care for him?

I pulled my father-in-law into his bed with his wife and pulled the covers to their chins. My wife is tucked in too, the covers over her head. I put our little dog, Constance, beside her.

How long ago was the good deed done?

I can't tell.

I think, strangely, of my father-in-law. He always wore a hat. He thought it strange that men no longer wore hats. When he was growing up in the forties and fifties, men wore hats.

He told me that many times.

He wore hats. Men wore hats, and it was odd to him that they no longer did, and to him the men without hats were manless.

He looked at me then. Hatless. Looked me up and down. Not only was I hatless in his eyes, I was manless.

Manless?

Is that a word?

The wind howls and the night is bright and the shadows twist and the moon gives them light to dance by.

They are many and they are one, and I am almost one of them.

One day I could not sleep and sat up all day. I had taken to the couch at first, in the living room, but in time the stench from behind the taped doors seeped out and it was strong. I made a pallet in the kitchen and pulled all the curtains tight and slept the day away, rose at night and roamed and watched the shadows from the windows or out on the porch. The stench was less then, at night, and out on the porch I couldn't smell it at all.

The phone has rang many times and there are messages from relatives. Asking about the storm. If we are okay.

I consider calling to tell them we are.

But I have no voice for anyone anymore. My vocal cords are hollow and my body is full of dark.

The storm has blown away and in a small matter of time people will come to find out how we are doing. It is daybreak and no car could possibly get up our long drive, not way out here in the country like we are. But the ice is starting to melt.

Can't sleep.

Can't eat.

Thirsty all the time.

Have masturbated till I hurt.

Strange, but by nightfall the ice started to slip away and all the whiteness was gone and the air, though chill, was not as cold, and the shadows gathered on the welcome mat, and now they have slipped inside, like envelopes pushed beneath the bottom of the door.

They join me.

They comfort me.

I oil my guns.

Late night, early morning, depends on how you look at it. But the guns are well-oiled and there is no ice anywhere. The night is as clear as my mind is now.

I pull the trunk upstairs and drag it out on the porch toward the truck. It's heavy, but I manage it into the back of the pickup. Then I remember there's a dolly in the garage.

My father-in-law's dolly.

"This damn dolly will move anything," he used to say. "Anything."

I get the dolly, load it up, stick in a few tools from the garage, start the truck and roll on out.

I flunked out of college.

Couldn't pass the test.

I'm supposed to be smart.

My mother told me when I was young that I was a genius.

There had been tests.

But I couldn't seem to finish anything.

Dropped out of high school. Took the G.E.D. eventually. Didn't score high there either, but did pass. Barely.

What kind of genius is that?

Finally got into college, four years later than everyone else.

Couldn't cut it. Just couldn't hold anything in my head. Too stuffed up there, as if Kleenex had been packed inside.

My history teacher, he told me, "Son, perhaps you should consider a trade."

I drive along campus. My mind is clear, like the night. The campus clock tower is very sharp against the darkness, lit up at the top and all around. A giant phallus punching up at the moon.

It is easy to drive right up to the tower and unload the gun trunk onto the dolly.

My father-in-law was right.

This dolly is amazing.

And my head, so clear. No Kleenex.

And the shadows, thick and plenty, are with me.

Rolling the dolly, a crowbar from the collection of tools stuffed in my belt, I proceed to the front of the tower. I'm wearing a jumpsuit. Gray. Workman's uniform. For a while I worked for the janitorial department on campus. My attempt at a trade.

They fired me for reading in the janitor's closet.

But I still have the jumpsuit.

The foyer is open, but the elevators are locked.

I pull the dolly upstairs.

It is a chore, a bump at a time, but the dolly straps hold the trunk and I can hear the guns rattling inside, like they want to get out.

By the time I reach the top I'm sweating, feeling weak. I have no idea how long it has taken, but some time I'm sure. The shadows have been with me, encouraging me.

Thank you, I tell them.

The door at the top of the clock tower is locked.

I take out my burglar's key. The crowbar. Go to work.

It's easy.

On the other side of the door I use the dolly itself to push up under the door handle, and it freezes the door. It'll take some work to shake that loose.

There's one more flight inside the tower.

I have to drag the trunk of guns.

Hard work. The rope handle on the crate snaps and the guns slide all the way back down.

I push them up.

I almost think I can't make it. The trunk is so heavy. So many guns. And all that sweet ammunition.

Finally, to the top, shoving with my shoulder, bending my legs all the way.

The door up there is not locked, the one that leads outside to the runway around the clock tower.

I walk out, leaving the trunk. I walk all around the tower and look down at all the small things there.

Soon the light will come, and so will the people.

Turning, I look up at the huge clock hands. Four o'clock.

I hope time does not slip. I do not want to find myself at home by the window, looking out.

The shadows.

They flutter.

They twist.

The runway is full of them, thick as all the world's lost ones. Thick as all the world's hopeless. Thick, thick, thick, and thicker yet to be. When I join them.

There is one fine spot at the corner of the tower runway. That is where I should begin.

I place a rifle there, the one I used to put my family and dog asleep.

I place rifles all around the tower.

I will probably run from one station to the other.

The shadows make suggestions.

All good, of course.

I put a revolver in my belt.

I put a shotgun near the entrance to the runway, hidden behind the edge of the tower, in a little outcrop of artful bricks. It tucks in there nicely.

There are huge flower pots stuffed with ferns all about the runway. I stick pistols in the pots.

When I finish, I look at the clock again.

An hour has passed.

Back home in my chair, looking out the window at the dying night. Back home in my chair, the smell of my family growing familiar, like a shirt worn too many days in a row.

Like the one I have on. Like the thick coat I wear.

I look out the window and it is not the window, but the little split in the runway barrier. There are splits all around the runway wall.

I turn to study the place I have chosen and find myself looking out my window at home, and as I stare, the window melts and so does the house.

The smell.

That does not go with the window and the house.

The smell stays with me.

The shadows are way too close. I am nearly smothered. I can hardly breathe.

Light cracks along the top of the tower and falls through the campus trees and runs along the ground like spilt warm honey.

I clutch my coat together, pull it tight. It is very cold. I can hardly feel my legs.

I get up and walk about the runway twice, checking on all my guns.

Well oiled. Fully loaded.

Full of hot lead announcements.

Telegram. You're dead.

Back at my spot, the one from which I will begin, I can see movement. The day has started. I poke the rifle through the break in the barrier and bead down on a tall man walking across campus.

I could take him easy.

But I do not.

Wait, say the shadows. Wait until the little world below is full.

The hands on the clock are loud when they move, they sound like the machinery I can hear in my head. Creaking and clanking and moving along.

The air has turned surprisingly warm.

I feel so hot in my jacket.

I take it off.

I am sweating.

The day has come but the shadows stay with me.

True friends are like that. They don't desert you.

It's nice to have true friends.

It's nice to have with me the ones who love me.

It's nice to not be judged.

It's nice to know I know what to do and the shadows know too, and we are all the better for it.

The campus is alive.

People swim across the concrete walks like minnows in the narrows.

Minnows everywhere in their new sharp clothes, ready to take their tests and do their papers and meet each other so they might screw. All of them, with futures.

But I am the future-stealing machine.

I remember once, when I was a child, I went fishing with minnows. Stuck them on the hooks and dropped them in the wet. When the day was done, I had caught nothing. I violated the fisherman's code. I did not pour the remaining minnows into the water to give them their freedom. I poured them on the ground.

And stomped them.

I was in control.

A young, beautiful girl, probably eighteen, tall like a model, walking like a dream, is moving across the campus. The light is on her hair and it looks very blonde, like my wife's.

I draw a bead.

The shadows gather. They whisper. They touch. They show me their faces. They have faces now.

Simple faces.

Like mine.

I trace my eye down the length of the barrel.

Without me really knowing it, the gun snaps sharp in the morning light.

The young woman falls amidst a burst of what looks like plum jelly.

The minnows flutter. The minnows flee.

But there are so many, and they are panicked. Like they have been poured on the ground to squirm and gasp in the dry.

I began to fire. Shot after shot after shot.

Each snap of the rifle a stomp of my foot.

Down they go.

Squashed.

I have no hat, father-in-law, and I am full of manliness.

The day goes up hot.

Who would have thunk?

I have moved from one end of the tower to the other.

I have dropped many of them.

The cops have come.

I have dropped many of them.

I hear noise in the tower.

I think they have shook the dolly loose.

The door to the runway bursts open.

A lady cop steps through. My first shot takes her in the throat. But she snaps one off at about the same time. A revolver shot. It hits next to me where I crouch low against the runway wall.

Another cop comes through the door. I fire and miss.

My first miss.

He fires. I feel something hot inside my shoulder.

I find that I am slipping down, my back against the runway wall. I can't hold the rifle. I try to drag the pistol from my belt, but can't. My arm is dead. The other one, well, it's no good either.

The shot has cut something apart inside of me. The strings to my limbs. My puppet won't work.

Another cop has appeared. He has a shotgun. He leans over me. His teeth are gritted and his eyes are wet.

And just as he fires, the shadows say:

Now, you are one of us.

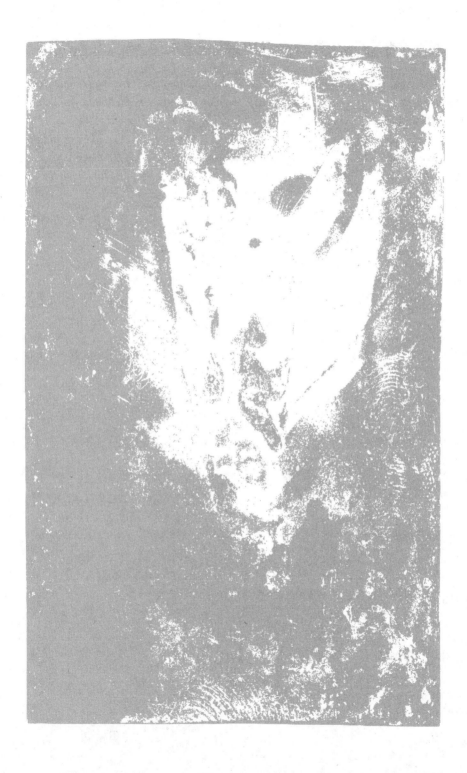

"The Ears" was for an Otto Penzler anthology. Supposed to be a really short story, and it is. It came to me instantly. I can't begin to tell you where it came from, how it developed. My subconscious had it waiting for me when I got up in the morning, and I wrote it in one setting, revised slightly, and sent it off. I think it originally appeared as "The Ear," but it was always supposed to be titled "The Ears."

THE EARS

It WAS A third date. The first date had been dinner and a movie and a kiss goodnight, dropped off at her door, that sort of thing. The second, they ended up in a hotel room. Tonight, she was at his place, had driven over. They were going to have dinner at his house, then go to a movie. All very casual. Nothing highly romantic. She liked that. It made her comfortable; two lovers who were starting to know each other well enough not to do anything fancy.

When she got there, he let her in before she could knock, like he had been watching. The place was lit up and she could hear the TV going and could smell cooking. He was wearing one of those novelty aprons that said KISS THE COOK.

"This is it," Jim said, waving his arm at the interior of the house. It was nice. Nothing fantastic, but nice. He was neat for a guy, especially a traveling salesman that went all over the states and didn't stay home much.

"You wore the earrings?" he said.

"You asked me to. You like them that much?"

"Liked them when I bought them for you," he said.

"Date three, thought they might get a little old," she said.

"Not yet. You want a drink?"

"Sure," she said, and followed him into the kitchen. The TV prattled on in the other room. He poured her a drink.

"You know," she said, "we could stay here tonight."

Jim was at the stove, stirring spaghetti in a pot of boiling water. He turned and looked at her. "You want to?"

"You got some movies?" she said.

"Yeah, or we can order one off the TV."

"Let's do that, and then let's go to bed. You can fix me dinner tonight and breakfast in the morning."

"That sounds fine," he said, smiling that killer smile he had. "That sounds really nice."

"I hoped you'd think so," she said. "Bathroom?"

"Down the hall, around the corner to the left."

She walked down the hall and turned the corner, opened the door to the left. She had missed the bathroom. It was the bedroom. She started out, saw a dresser drawer slightly open. He was neat, but not that neat. She, on the other hand, had a thing about open doors and drawers. She slipped over quickly, started to push it shut, saw what was blocking it. An ear.

Taking a deep breath, she thought, surely not. Sliding the drawer open she got a better look. There was a string running through the ear. She pulled it out of the drawer. There were a number of dried ears on it. They had a faint smell, a combination of decay and the smell of pickles; they had been in some kind of preservative, but the flesh was still losing the battle. Something sparkled on one of them.

"It's from the war," he said.

She turned, gasping. He was standing in the doorway, his head hung, looking silly in that apron.

"I'm sorry," she said, because she didn't know what else to say.

"My brother, he was in Afghanistan. Brought it home with him. This will sound odd, but when he died, I didn't know what to do with it. I kept it. Thought I had it put away better. I should throw it away."

"It's pretty awful," she said, lowering the ears back into the drawer, pushing it shut.

"Forgive me for having it, for keeping it."

"He died in the war?"

"Cancer. Came home from the war with his collection, those ears. Come on, forget it. I'll throw them out."

She went back to the kitchen and later they ate dinner. When he went into the den to pick a movie she slipped out the front door and drove home, trying to remember if she had told him where she lived, then thinking, even if she hadn't, these days it wasn't so hard to find out. Easy really.

In her house, sitting in the dark with a fresh drink, she felt stupid to have fallen for Jim so quickly, to not know him as well as she should have. Guy like that wasn't a guy she wanted to know any more about.

She finished her drink and went to bed.

In the middle of the night she was startled awake, sat up in bed, her face covered in a cold sweat.

She remembered Jim said on their first date he was an only child, but tonight he said he had a brother, said the ears were from Afghan warriors. Several thoughts hit her like a barrage of arrows. She hadn't just awakened. She had heard something moving in the house; that's what brought her awake with her mind full of thoughts and questions. That sound was what woke her up. And in that moment she realized that she remembered all those ears were small and one of them had something shiny on it. She knew now what it was. She had only glimpsed it, but now she knew. A woman's earring. Not too unlike those she had worn tonight.

Something banged lightly in the other room, and then her bedroom door opened.

I don't exactly remember how this one came about, but I do remember I was asked for a story for The Strand, *or perhaps I just sent it to the editor. But I had fun writing it. I was in a kind of Christmas crime mood, and one thing deliciously fit into the other without me trying too hard. I kind of had the old* Manhunt Magazine *in mind when I wrote it. I also wanted to do something twisty. I like the way it came out.*

SANTA AT THE CAFÉ

WHEN SANTA CAME into the café, he had the fake beard pulled off his chin and it hung down on his chest. He had his Santa hat folded and stuck through the big black belt around his waist. His hair was red, so it was a sharp contrast to the rest of his outfit.

No one took much notice of him, as the city was full of Santas this time of year, but the middle-aged man behind the counter, a big guy wearing a food-stained white shirt, lifted his hand and waved.

Santa waved back. It was their usual greeting.

Santa took a seat at a booth in the rear, sat down with a sigh and took a look around. The place was packed, as it always was this time of night, and with it being Christmas Eve, and with many eateries shutting down early tonight, it was a natural gathering spot. He felt lucky to have found an empty booth. There were still dishes left on it from the last customer.

A young woman, who looked as if she might be one cup of coffee short of her hair starting to crawl, came over and sat down across from him. She said, "Do you mind?"

He did mind. Or he would have normally, but she wasn't bad-looking. She was thin-faced and nicely built with eyes that drooped slightly, as if she might drop off to sleep at any moment. She had a wide mouth full of nice teeth. She had on blue jeans and a sweater and a heavy coat. She had a huge cloth purse with a long shoulder strap.

She said, "There are only a few seats."

"Sure," he said. "Sure, go ahead."

She took off her coat and sat down.

"You work the department store?" she asked.

"Yeah. I got off a few minutes ago."

"Don't see many thin, red-headed Santas," she said.

"Well, at the store, I got this pillow, you see, and I put it under the suit. I finish for the night, I put the pillow back. It don't belong to me, it belongs to the store. The suit, that's mine though. I do this every Christmas. You can make pretty good, you work it right."

"Yeah, how's that?"

"I do it for a couple weeks before Christmas, and if there are enough kids sitting on my lap, and they feel like they're bringing in some business, they like to toss a little extra my way. I mean, you can't live on what I make, but it's a nice enough slice of cheese."

While they talked, a man came over and gathered up the dishes, came back with a rag and wiped their table, and was gone as swiftly and silently as he had come.

The waitress, wearing a striped uniform the colors of a candy cane, arrived. She walked like her feet hurt and there was nothing to go home to.

She wore a bright green sprig of plastic mistletoe on her blouse. For all the Christmas spirit she showed, it might as well have been poison ivy.

The young woman ordered coffee. Santa ordered steak and eggs and a side of wheat toast and a glass of milk.

When the waitress left, Santa said, "You ought to eat something, kid. You look like maybe you been holding back on that a bit."

"Just cutting calories."

He studied her for a moment.

"Okay," she said, withering under his gaze. "I'm short on money. I'm not doing so good lately."

"Let me help you out. I'll buy you something."

"I'm fine. Thanks. But I'm fine."

"Really. Let me. No obligations."

"None," she said.

"None," he said.

"I don't want you to think I'm trying to work you, that that's why I sat here."

"I don't think that," he said, and then he thought, you know, maybe that's exactly what she did.

But he didn't care.

Santa caught the waitress's eye and called her over. She came with less enthusiasm than before, which wasn't something Santa thought she could do, and took the woman's order, and went away.

"What's your name?" asked Santa.

"Mary. What's yours?"

"Hell, tonight, just call me Santa. I'm buying you a late dinner. Or early breakfast, whatever you want to call it."

They talked a little, and Santa liked the talk. The food came, and when it did he removed the beard and folded it up and pushed it into his belt on the opposite side of his Santa hat.

While they were eating, he saw that the crowd was thinning. That's the way it was. Business hit hard, and then went away. He had taken note the last two weeks. Every night after work he'd come here to eat and watch the crowd. It was entertaining.

He and the young woman finished eating, and Santa looked up and saw a nervous young man come in. Very nervous. He had sweat beads on his forehead the size of witch warts. He sat down and shifted in his seat and touched something inside his coat. The waitress came over and the man ordered.

Santa kept his eye on him. He had seen the type before. Fact was, the nervous man made him nervous. The young woman noticed the nervous man as well.

"He don't seem right," she said.

"No. No he doesn't."

"Place like this," she said, "it'll fool you. There's lots of money made here. For a greasy spoon it maybe makes as much as Bloomingdale's."

"I doubt that," said Santa.

"All right, that's an exaggeration, but you got to think, way customers come and go, it does all right."

"I figure you're right."

After awhile, the customers thinned. There were half a dozen people left. A few came and went, picking up coffee, but that was it. Santa looked at his watch. 2 a.m.

"You got a home to go to?" the young woman asked Santa.

"Yeah, but I been there before."

"No wife?"

"No dog. No cat. Not much of anything but four walls and a pretty good couch to sleep on."

"No bed?"

"No bed."

"What do you do when you're not Santa?"

"These days, I don't do much of anything. I lost my job a while back."

"What did you do?"

"Short-order cook. . . . Hell, look there."

She turned to look, the nervous man was up and he pulled a gun out from under his coat just as the waitress was approaching his booth. For no reason at all, he struck out and hit her on the side of the neck, dropped her and the coffee pot she was carrying to the floor. The pot was hard plastic and it rolled, spilling coffee all over the place. The waitress lay on the floor, not moving.

The man pointed the gun at the man behind the counter. "Give me the money. All of it."

"Hey now," said the man behind the counter, "you don't want to do this."

"Yeah," said the nervous man, "I do."

"All right, take it easy." The counter man looked at Santa, like maybe he had some magic that would help. Santa didn't move. The girl didn't move. The well-dressed man at the bar turned slightly on his stool.

The nervous man pointed his gun at the well-dressed man. "I say don't move, that means you too. You too over there, Santa and the chick. Freeze up."

Everyone was still, except the counter man. He started unloading the money from the register, sticking it in a to-go sack. "Come on," said the nervous man, shaking a little. "Hurry. Don't try and hold back."

"Ain't my money," said the counter man. "You can have it. I don't want to get shot over money."

The counter man was stuffing the money in a big take-away sack. There was a lot of it.

When he was almost finished with the stuffing, the nervous man came closer to the counter. The well-dressed man hardly seemed to move, but move he did, and there was a gun in his hand and he said, "Now hold up. I'm a cop."

The nervous man didn't hold up. He turned with his gun and the cop fired his. The nervous man staggered and sat down on the floor, got part of the way up, then staggered and fell over one of the tables at a booth. He bled on the table and the blood ran down into the coffee the waitress had dropped.

The well-dressed man got up and leaned slightly over the counter, said, "Actually, I ain't no cop. I want the money."

"Not a cop?" said the counter man.

"Naw. But I thought it might stop him. I didn't want to kill nobody. Just planned on the money."

The counter man gave him the bag and the man who was not a cop walked briskly out the door and left.

Cops came, and Santa and the young woman and the counter man gave their statements, told how two crooks had got into it, and how one of them was dead and the other had walked away with about two thousand dollars in a to-go bag.

It took about an hour for the interviews, then the dead man's body was carried away, and the waitress, who had come to with a headache, told the man behind the counter she quit. She went out and got a taxi. The man behind the counter got a mop and a bucket and pushed it out to wipe up the blood and coffee.

Santa and the young woman were still there. The counter man told them they could have free coffee.

"I'm gonna close it," said the counter man, when they had their Styrofoam cups of coffee.

Santa and the young woman went out. "That was some night," she said.

"Yeah," Santa said. "Some night."

She caught a cab after a long wait with Santa standing beside her at the curb. Santa opened the door and watched her get in and saw the taxi drive off. Santa sighed. She was one fine-looking girl. A little skinny, but fine just the same.

Santa went back to the diner and tugged on the door. It was locked. He knocked.

The counter man came over and let him in and locked the door. "Damn," said the counter man. "How about that?"

"Yeah," said Santa. "How about it?"

"Makes it easier, don't it?"

"Yeah, easier."

"Come on," said the counter man. They went back behind the counter and into a little office. The counter man moved a bad still-life painting on the wall and there was a safe behind it.

As he turned the dial, the counter man said, "This way, no one will be looking for you or thinking of me. It's better this way, way things worked out."

"It's one hell of a coincidence."

"I was worried. I figured you took the money at gunpoint, they might think I had something to do with it."

"You do."

The counter man talked while he turned the dials on the safe. "I know. But this way, you don't even have to be a fake robber. We just split it. It works out good, man. I told the police the robber got all we had. All of it. I didn't mention the safe. Boss asks, I'll tell him it was all out. I hadn't put it in the safe yet. Meant to, but got swamped. But I put it in all right. It was safe. All the guy got was the till. You and me, we're gonna split twenty thousand dollars tonight, and the cops, they're looking for a well-dressed man who pretended to be a cop and got away with a few thousand. They think he got it all. It's sweet."

"Yeah," Santa said, "that's sweet all right."

They split the money and the counter man put his in a take-away bag, and Santa put his inside his Santa suit. It just made him look a little fat.

They went out of the café and the counter man locked the door. Walking around the corner, the counter man said, "You parked in the same lot?"

"No. I didn't come by car."

"No?"

"No," said Santa. And then the counter man got it. They were at a dark intersection near an alley. No one was in the alley. Santa pulled a gun from one of his big pockets and pointed it at the counter man.

"Come on, man," said the counter man. "You and me, we been friends since you was a fry cook, back over at the Junction Café."

"I knew you from there," Santa said. "But friends, not so much."

"For god's sake," the counter man, said, "it's Christmas Eve."

"Merry Christmas, then," Santa said, and shot the counter man in the head with his little pistol. It hardly made more than a pop.

Santa picked up the dropped take-away bag and put it inside his suit. Now he really looked like Santa. He put on the beard and the hat and shoved the pistol in his pocket.

He walked smartly back toward the café. He had to pass it on his way to the subway. When he was almost there, he realized there was someone pacing him on the sidewalk across the street. It was dark back where he had been, but now as he neared the café there was light. He could see who was there. Walking on the opposite side of the street was the young woman.

He stopped and turned and looked at her as she crossed the street.

"I decided I didn't want to go home," she said. "You think maybe you could show me your place?"

"My couch?" he said.

"Sure, I can stand it if you can."

"You just been waiting on me?"

"I drove down a piece, changed my mind and walked back. I thought I might catch you."

"That was a long shot."

"Yep. But here you are."

Santa smiled. It was some night. Money, a profitable dissolution of a partnership, and now this fine-looking dame. "All right," he said.

She patted his belly.

"You put on weight since I seen you last, what, thirty minutes ago?"

"I got a takeout order with me. Something for tomorrow."

"Under your coat?"

"Yeah, under my coat."

She smiled, and he smiled, and then he quit smiling. She had a gun in her hand. It came out of her big purse as smooth as a samurai drawing a sword.

"I got to say it, just got to let you know that I know your type," she said, "'cause I'm the same type. I saw you watching the counter man count that money. I could see it in your eyes, what you had planned, though I didn't know the counter man was in on it. That was something else. There I was, thinking how I can hang in there until everyone leaves, because, you see, I got plans myself. Then that nervous man came in, and the other guy, the well-dressed fellow, that was some coincidence. When all that happened, I was glad to leave. As I was driving away in the taxi, I looked back, saw you go back to the diner. I thought that was suspicious, 'cause you see, I'm the suspicious type. I had the taxi stop. I walked back and hid in the shadows. Saw the two of you come out. I followed, carefully. I'm like a cat, I want to be. I saw you shoot the counter man, take his share. Guess what, it all fell together then, what went on. Now, I'm gonna take both your shares. That's what I call a real Christmas surprise and one hell of a present for me. I mean, come on, you're Santa. You got to want me to have a good Christmas, right?"

"Now, wait a minute," Santa said, easing his hand toward his pocket for the gun.

He didn't make it. A bullet parted his beard and hit him in the neck and he went back and leaned against the diner wall.

She popped him again. This time in the head. Santa sat down hard. His hat fell off.

She opened up his coat and got the money. It was a lot of money. She put the gun away, stuffed the money that was loose inside his suit into her huge cloth purse. She picked up the to-go bag. Someone saw it, it could be a bag of sandwiches, a bag of doughnuts. It could be most anything.

"Merry Christmas," she said to Santa's corpse, and crossed the street and started toward the lights and the subway, and a short ride home.

"I Tell You It's Love" was written for a one-shot magazine that Lewis Shiner put together. I had been reading a lot about all manner of perverse things for research, and this was leftover material that I shaped into something dark and short. It was an exploration of this mindset, which I do not in the least understand. But, like most of us, the dark mysteries of the human mind fascinate me.

I TELL YOU IT'S LOVE

THE BEAUTIFUL WOMAN had no eyes, just sparklers of light where they should have been—or so it seemed in the candlelight. Her lips, so warm and inviting, so wickedly wild and suggestive of strange pleasures, held yet a hint of disaster, as if they might be fat, red things skillfully molded from dried blood.

"Hit me," she said.

That is my earliest memory of her; a doll for my beating, a doll for my love.

I laid it on her with that black silk whip, slapping it across her shoulders and back, listening to the whisper of it as it rode down, delighting in the flat, pretty sound of it striking her flesh.

She did not bleed, which was a disappointment. The whip was too soft, too flexible, too difficult to strike hard with.

"Hurt me," she said softly. I went to where she knelt. Her arms were outstretched, crucifixion style, and bound to the walls on either side with strong silk cord the color and texture of the whip in my hand.

I slapped her. "Like it?" I asked. She nodded and I slapped her again . . . and again. A one-two rhythm, slow and melodic, time and again.

"Like it?" I repeated, and she moaned. "Yeah, oh yeah."

Later, after she was untied and had tidied up the blood from her lips and nose, we made brutal love; me with my thumbs bending the flesh of her throat, she with her nails entrenched in my back. She said to me when we were finished, "Let's do someone."

That's how we got started. Thinking back now, once again I say I'm glad for fate; glad for Gloria; glad for the memory of the crying sounds, the dripping blood, and the long, sharp knives that murmured through flesh like a lover's whisper cutting the dark.

Yeah, I like to think back to when I walked hands in pockets down the dark wharves in search of that special place where there were said to be special women with special pleasures for a special man like me.

I walked on until I met a sailor leaning against a wall smoking a cigarette, and he says when I ask about the place, "Oh, yeah, I like that sort of pleasure myself. Two blocks down, turn right, there between the warehouses, down the far end. You'll see the light." And he points and I walk on, faster.

Finding it, paying for it, meeting Gloria was the goal of my dreams. I was more than a customer to that sassy, dark mamma with the sparkler eyes. I was the link to fit her link. We made two strong, solid bonds in a strange, cosmic chain. You could feel the energy flowing through us; feel the iron of our wills. Ours was a mating made happily in hell.

So time went by and I hated the days and lived for the nights when I whipped her, slapped her, scratched her, and she did the same to me. Then one night she said, "It's not enough. Just not enough anymore. Your blood is sweet and your pain is fine, but I want to see death like you see a movie, taste it like licorice, smell it like flowers, touch it like cold, hard stone."

I laughed, saying, "I draw the line at dying for you." I took her by the throat, fastened my grip until her breathing was a whistle, and her eyes protruded like bloated corpse bellies.

"That's not what I mean," she managed. And then came the statement that brings us back to what started it all. "Let's do someone."

I laughed and let her go.

"You know what I mean?" she said. "You know what I'm saying."

"I know what you said. I know what you mean." I smiled. "I know very well."

"You've done it before, haven't you?"

"Once," I said, "in a shipyard, not that long ago."

"Tell me about it. God, tell me about it."

"It was dark and I had come off ship after six months out, a long six months with the men, the ship, and the sea. So I'm walking down this dark alley, enjoying the night like I do, looking for a place with the dark ways, our kind of ways, baby, and I came upon this old wino lying in a doorway, cuddling a bottle to his face as if it were a lady's loving hand."

"What did you do?"

"I kicked him," I said, and Gloria's smile was a beauty to behold.

"Go on," she said.

"God, how I kicked him. Kicked him in the face until there was no nose, no lips, no eyes. Only red mush dangling from shrapneled bone; looked like a melon that had been dropped from on high, down into a mass of broken white pottery chips. I touched his face and tasted it with my tongue and my lips."

"Ohh," she signed, and her eyes half closed. "Did he scream?"

"Once. Only once. I kicked him too hard, too fast, too soon. I hammered his head with the toes of my shoes, hammered until my cuffs were wet and sticking to my ankles."

"Oh, God," she said, clinging to me. "Let's do it, let's do it."

We did. First time was a drizzly night and we caught an old woman out. She was a lot of fun until we got the knives out and then she went quick. There was that crippled kid next, lured him from the theater downtown, and how we did that was a stroke of genius. You'll find his wheelchair not far from where you found the van and the other stuff.

But no matter. You know what we did, about the kinds of tools we had, about how we hung that crippled kid on that meat hook in my van until the flies clustered around the doors thick as grapes.

And of course, there was the little girl. It was a brilliant idea of Gloria's to get the kid's tricycle into the act. The things she did with those spokes. Ah, but that woman was a connoisseur of pain.

There were two others, each quite fine, but not as nice as the last. Then came the night Gloria looked at me and said, "It's not enough. Just won't do."

I smiled. "No way, baby. I still won't die for you."

"No," she gasped, and took my arm. "You miss my drift. It's the pain I need, not just the watching. I can't live through them, can't feel it in me. Don't you see, it would be the ultimate."

I looked at her, wondering did I have it right?

"Do you love me?"

"I do," I said.

"To know that I would spend the last of my life with you, that my last memories would be the pleasure on your face, the feelings of pain, the excitement, the thrill, the terror."

Then I understood, and understood good. Right there in the car I grabbed her, took her by the throat and cracked her head against the windshield, pressed her back, choked, released, choked, made it linger. By this time I was quite a pro. She coughed, choked, smiled. Her eyes swung from fear to love. God, it was wonderful and beautiful and the finest experience we had ever shared.

When she finally lay still there in the seat, I was trembling, happier than I had ever been. Gloria looked fine, her eyes rolled up, her lips stretched in a rictus smile.

I kept her like that at my place for days, kept her in my bed until the neighbors started to complain about the smell.

I've been talking to this guy and he's got some ideas. Says he thinks I'm one of the future generation, and the fact of that scares him all to hell. A social mutation, he says. Man's primitive nature at the height of the primal scream.

Dog shit, we're all the same, so don't look at me like I'm some kind of freak. What does he do come Monday night? He's watching the football game, or the races or boxing matches, waiting for a car to overturn or for some guy to be carried out of the ring with nothing but mush left for brains. Oh, yeah, he and I are similar, quite alike. You see, it's in us all. A low-pitch melody not often heard, but there just the same. In me it peaks and thuds, like drums and brass and strings. Don't fear it. Let it go. Give in to the beat and amplify. I tell you, it's love of the finest kind.

So I've said my piece and I'll just add this: when they fasten my arms and ankles down and tighten the cap, I hope I feel the pain and delight in it before my brain sizzles to bacon, and may I smell the frying of my very own flesh. . . .

Supernatural private detective story. I've done more than one. This one is the one where I really tried to ring the bells of the classic private eye, and perhaps toss in a bit of the tone of the old Night Stalker *TV show. It plays with the private-eye tropes of the fifties a lot, and there's a whiff, a supernatural, sulfurous whiff of the old supernatural detective stories by a variety of authors. Like Manly Wade Wellman, William Hope Hodgson, Algernon Blackwood, although all of his seemed to have a religious theme at their base, if memory serves me. I've always been taken with the supernatural detective, even though I'm not a believer in the supernatural. But it's a cool combination.*

DEAD SISTER

I HAD MY office window open, and the October wind was making my hair ruffle. I was turned sideways and had my feet up, cooling my heels on the edge of my desk, noticing my socks. Once the pattern on the socks had been clocks, now the designs were so thin and colorless, I could damn near see my ankles through them.

I was looking out the window, watching the town square from where I sat, three floors up, which was as high as anything went in Mud Creek. It seemed pretty busy down there for a town of only eight thousand. Even a couple of dogs were looking industrious, as if they were in a hurry to get somewhere and do something important. Chase a cat, bite a mailman, or bury a bone.

Me, I wasn't working right then, and hadn't in a while. For me, 1958 had not been a banner year.

I was about to get a bottle of cheap whisky out of my desk drawer, when there was a knock on the door. I could see my name spelled backwards on the pebbled glass, and beyond that a shadow that had a nice overall shape.

I said, "Come on in, the water's fine."

A blonde woman wearing a little blue pill hat came in. She was the kind of dame if she walked real fast she might set the walls on fire. She sat down in the client chair and crossed her legs and let her cool blue dress slide up so I could see her knees. She was wearing stockings so sheer, she might as well have not had any on. She lifted her head and stared at me with eyes that would make a monk set fire to his Bible.

She was carrying a cute little purse that might hold a compact, a couple of quarters and a pencil. She let it rest on her lap, laid her hand on it like it was a pet cat.

"Mr. Taylor? I was wondering if you could check on something for me?" she said.

"If it's on your person, no charge."

She smiled at me. "I heard you thought you were funny."

"Not really, but I try the stuff out anyway. See how this one works for you. I get fifty a day plus expenses."

"You might have to do some rough stuff."

"How rough?" I said.

"I don't know. I really don't know what's going on at all, but I think it may be someone who's not quite right."

"Did you talk to the police?" I asked.

She nodded. "They checked, watched for three nights. But nobody showed. Soon as they quit, it started over again."

"Where did they watch, and what did they watch?"

"The graveyard. They were watching a grave. I could swear someone was digging it up at night."

"You saw this?"

"If I saw it, I'd be sure, wouldn't I?"

"You got me there," I said.

"My sister, Susan. She died of something unexpected. Eighteen. Beautiful. One morning she's feeling ill, and then the night comes, and she's feeling worse, and the next day she's dead. Just like that. She was buried in the Sweet Pine Cemetery, and I go each morning on my way to work to bring flowers to her grave. The ground never settled. I got the impression it was being worked over at night. That someone was digging there. That they were digging up my sister, or trying to."

"That's an odd thing to think."

"The dirt was always disturbed," she said. "The flowers from the day before were buried under the dirt. It didn't seem right."

"So, you want me to check the place out, see if that's what's going on?"

"The police were so noisy and so obvious I doubt they got a true view of things. No one would try with them there. They thought I was crazy. What I need is someone who can be discreet. I would go myself, but I might need someone with some muscle."

"Yeah, you're too nice a piece of chicken to be wandering a graveyard. It would be asking for trouble. Your sister's name is Susan. What's yours?"

"Oh, I didn't tell you, did I? It's Cathy. Cathy Carter. Can you start right away?"

"Soon as the money hits my palm."

I probably didn't need a .38 revolver to handle a grave robber, but you never know. So, I brought it with me.

My plan was if there was someone actually there, to put the gun on him and make him lie down, tie him up, and haul him to the police. If he was digging up somebody's sister, the county cops downtown might not let him make it to trial. He might end up with a warning shot in the back of the head. That happened, I could probably get over it.

Course, it could be more than one. That's why the .38.

My take, though, was it was all hooey. Not that Cathy Carter didn't believe it. She did. But my guess was the whole business was nothing more than her grieving imagination, or a dog or an armadillo digging around at night.

I decided to go out there and look at the place during the day. See if I thought there was any kind of monkey business going on.

Sweet Pine isn't a pauper graveyard on the whole, but a lot of paupers are buried there, on the back, low end near Coats Creek. Actually on the other side of the graveyard fence. Even in death, they couldn't get inside with the regular people. Outsiders to the end.

There've been graves there since the Civil War. A recent flood had washed away a lot of headstones and broke the ground open and pushed some rotten bones and broken coffins around. It was all covered up in a heap with a dozer after that; sons and daughters, mothers and fathers, grandmas and grandpas, massed together in one big ditch for their final rest.

The fresher graves on the higher ground inside the cemetery fence were fine. That's where Susan was buried.

I parked at the gate, which was a black ornamental thing with fence tops like spear heads. The fence was six feet high and went all around the cemetery. The front was a large open area with a horseshoe sign over it that read in metal curlicues SWEET PINE CEMETERY.

That was just in case you thought the headstones were for show.

Inside, I went where Cathy told me Susan was buried, and found her grave easy enough. There was a stone marker with her name on it, and the dates of birth and death. The ground did look fresh dug. I bent down and looked close. There were scratches in the dirt, but they didn't look like shovel work. There were a bunch of cigarette butts heel-mashed into the ground near the grave.

I went over to a huge shade tree nearby and leaned on it, pulled out a stick of gum and chewed. It was comfortable under the tree, with the day being cool to begin with, and the shadow of the limbs lying on the ground like spilled night. I chewed the gum and looked at the grave for a long time. I looked around and decided if there was anything to what Cathy had said, then the cops wouldn't have seen it, or rather they would have discouraged any kind of grave-bothering soul from entering the cemetery in the first place. Those cigarette butts were the tipoff. My guess was they belonged to the cops, and they had stood not six feet from the grave, smoking, watching. Probably, like me, figuring it was all a pipe dream. Only thing was, I planned to give Cathy her whole dollar.

I drove back to the office and sat around there for a few hours, and then I went home and changed into some old duds, left my hat, grabbed a burger at Dairy Queen, and hustled my car back over to the cemetery.

I drove by it and parked my heap about a half mile from the graveyard under a hickory nut tree well off the main road and hoped no one would bother it.

I walked back to the cemetery and stood under the tree near Susan's grave and looked up at it. There was a low limb and I got hold of that and pulled myself up, and then climbed higher. The oak had very few leaves, but the limbs were big, and I found a place where there was a naturally scooped-out spot in the wood and laid down on that. It wasn't comfortable, but I lay there anyway and chewed some gum, and waited for the sun to set. That wouldn't be long this time of year. By five-thirty or six the sun was gone and the night was up.

Night came and I lay on the limb until my chest hurt. I got up and climbed higher, found a place where I could stand on a limb and wedge my ass in a fork in the tree. From there I had a good look at the grave.

The dark was gathered around me like a blanket. To see me, you'd have to be looking for me. I took the gum out of my mouth and stuck it to the tree, and leaned back so that I was nestled firmly in the narrow fork. It was almost like an easy chair.

I could see the lights of the town from there, and I watched those for awhile, and watched the headlights of cars in the distance. It was kind of hypnotic. Then I watched lightning bugs. A few mosquitoes came to visit, but it was a little cool for them, so they weren't too bad.

I touched my coat pocket to make sure my .38 was in place, and it was.

I had five shots. I didn't figure I would need to shoot anyone, and if I did, I doubted it would take more than five shots.

I added up the hours I had invested in the case, my expenses, which were lunch and a few packs of chewing gum. This wasn't the big score I was looking for, and I was beginning to feel silly, sitting in a tree waiting on someone to come along and dig around a grave. I wanted to check my watch, but I couldn't see the hands well enough, and though I had a little flashlight in my pocket, I didn't want any light to give me away.

I'll admit I wasn't much of a sentry. After awhile, I dozed. What woke me was a scratching sound. When I came awake I nearly fell out of the tree, not knowing where I was. By the time I had it figured the sound was really loud. It was coming from the direction of the grave.

When I looked down I saw an animal digging at the grave, and then I realized it wasn't a dog at all. I had only thought it was. It was a man in a long black jacket. He was bent over the grave and he was digging with his hands like a dog. He wasn't throwing the dirt far, just mounding it up.

While I had napped like a squirrel in a nest, he had dug all the way down to the coffin.

I pulled the gun from my pocket and yelled, "Hey, you down there. Leave that grave alone."

The man wheeled then, looked up, and when he did, I got a glimpse of his face in the moonlight. It wasn't a good glimpse, but it was enough to nearly cause me to fall out of the tree. The face was as white as a nun's ass and the eyes were way too bright, even if he was looking up into the moonlight; those eyes looked the way coyote eyes look staring out of the woods.

He hissed at me, and went back to his work, which was now popping the lid off the coffin like it was a cardboard box. It snapped free, and he reached inside and pulled out the body of a girl. Her hair was undone and it was long and blonde and fell over the dirty white slip she was wearing. He pulled her out of there before I could get down from the tree with the gun. The air was full of the stink of death. Susan's body, I guessed.

By the time I hit the ground, he had the body thrown over his shoulder, and he was running across the graveyard, between the stones, like a goddamn deer. I ran after him with my gun, yelling for him to stop. He was really moving. I saw him jump one of the tall upright gravestones like it was lying down and land so light he seemed like a crepe paper floating down.

Now that he was running, not crouching and digging like a dog, I could tell more about his body type. He was a long, skinny guy with stringy white hair and the long black coat that spread out around him like the wings of a roach. The girl bounced across his shoulder as though she was nothing more than a bag of dry laundry.

I chased him to the back fence, puffing all the way, and then he did something that couldn't be done. He sprang and leaped over that spear-tipped fence with Susan's body thrown over his shoulder, hit the ground running and darted down to the creek, jumped it, and ran off between the trees and into the shadows and out of my sight.

That fence was easily six feet high.

I started to drive over to Cathy's place. I had her address. But I didn't know what to say. I didn't go there, and I didn't go home, which was a dingy apartment. I went to the office, which was slightly better, and got the bottle out of the drawer, along with my glass, and poured myself a shot of my medicine. It wasn't a cure, but it was better than nothing. I liked it so much I poured another.

I went to the window with my fresh filled glass and looked out. The night looked like the night and the moon looked like the moon and the street looked like the street. I held my hand up in front of me. Nope. That was my hand and it had a glass of cheap whisky in it. I wasn't dreaming, and to the best of my knowledge I wasn't crazy.

I finished off the drink. I thought I should have taken a shot at him. But I didn't because of Susan's body. She wouldn't mind a bullet in the head, but I didn't want to have to explain that to her sister if I accidentally hit her.

I laid down on the couch for a little while, and the whisky helped me sleep, but when I came awake, and turned on the light and looked at my watch, it was just then midnight.

I got my hat and my gun and my car keys off the desk, went down to my car and drove back to the cemetery.

I didn't park down from the place this time. I drove through the horse-shoe opening and drove down as close as I could get to the grave. I got out and looked around, hoping I wouldn't see the man in the long coat, and hoping in another way I would.

I got my gun from my pocket and held it down by my side, and walked over to the grave. It was covered up, patted down. The air still held that stench as before. Less of it, but it still lingered, and I had this odd feeling it wasn't the stink of Susan's body after all. It was that man. It was his stink.

I felt sure of it, but there was no reasoning as to why I thought that. Call it instinct. I looked down at the grave. It was closed up.

The hair on the back of my neck stood up like I had been shot with a quiver full of little arrows.

Looking every which way as I went, I made it back to the car and got inside and locked all the doors and started it up and drove back to town and over to Cathy's place.

We were in her little front room sitting on the couch. There was coffee in cups on saucers sitting on the coffee table. I sipped mine and tried to do it so my hand didn't shake.

"So now you believe me," she said.

"But I don't know anyone else will. We tell the cops this, we'll both be in the booby hatch."

"He took her body?"

I nodded.

"Weren't you supposed to stop him?"

"I actually didn't think that was going to come up. But I couldn't stop him. He didn't look like much, but he was fast, and to leap like that, he had to be strong. He carried your sister's body like it was nothing."

"My heavens, what could he want with her?"

I had an idea, considering she only had on a slip. That meant he'd been there before, undressed her, and put her back without her burial clothes. But Cathy, she was on the same page.

"Now someone has her body," she said, "and they're doing who knows what to her . . . oh, Jesus. This is like a nightmare. Listen, you've got to take me out there."

"You don't want to do that," I said.

"Yes I do, Mr. Taylor. That's exactly what I want to do. And if you won't do it, I'll go anyway."

She started to cry and leaned into me. I held her. I figured part of it was real and part of it was like the way she showed me her legs; she'd had practice getting her way with men.

I drove her over there.

It was just about daybreak when we arrived. I drove through the gate and parked near the grave again. I saw that fellow, even if he was carrying two dead blondes on his shoulders, I was going to take a shot at him. Maybe two. That didn't work, I was going to try and run over him with my car.

Cathy stood over the grave. There was still a faint aroma of the stink from before.

Cathy said, "So he came back and filled it in while you were at your office, doing what did you say—having a drink?"

"Two actually."

"If you hadn't done that, he would have come back and you would have seen him."

"No reason for me to think he'd come back. I just came to look again to make sure I wasn't crazy."

As the sun came up, we walked across the cemetery, me tracing the path the man had taken as he ran. When I got to the fence, I looked to see if there was anything he could have jumped up on or used as a springboard to get over. There wasn't.

We went back to the car and I drove us around on the right side near the back of the cemetery. I had to park well before we got to the creek. It was muddy back there where the creek had rose, and there were boot prints in the mud from the flooding. The flood had made everything a bog.

I looked at the fence. Six feet tall, and he had landed some ten feet from the fence on this side. That wasn't possible, but I had seen him do it, and now I was looking at what had to be his boot tracks.

I followed the prints down to the creek, where he had jumped across.

It was all I could do to stay on my feet, as it was such a slick path to follow, but he had gone over it as surefootedly as a goat.

Cathy came with me. I told her to go back, but she wouldn't listen. We walked along the edge of the creek until we found a narrow spot, and I helped her cross over. The tracks played out when the mud played out. As we went up a little rise, the trees thickened even more and the land became drier. Finally we came to a nearly open clearing. There were a few trees growing there, and they were growing up close to an old sawmill. One side of it had fallen down, and there was an ancient pile of blackened sawdust mounded up on the other where it had been dumped from the mill and rotted by the weather.

We went inside. The floorboards creaked, and the whole place, large as it was, shifted as we walked.

"Come on," I said. "Before we fall all the way to hell."

On the way back, as we crossed the creek, I saw something snagged on a little limb. I bent over and looked at it. It stank of that smell I had smelled in the graveyard. I got out my handkerchief and folded the handkerchief around it and put it in my pocket.

Back in the car, driving to town, Cathy said, "It isn't just some kook, is it?"

"Some kook couldn't have jumped a fence like that, especially with a body thrown over its shoulder. It couldn't have gone across that mud and over that creek like it did. It has to be something else."

"What does *something else* mean?" Cathy said.

"I don't know," I said.

We parked out near the edge of town and I took the handkerchief out and unfolded it. The smell was intense.

"Throw it away," Cathy said.

"I will, but first, you tell me what it is."

She leaned over, wrinkled her pretty nose. "It's a piece of cloth with meat on it."

"Rotting flesh," I said. "The cloth goes with the man's jacket; the man I saw with Susan's body. Nobody has flesh like this if they're alive."

"Could it be from Susan?" she asked.

"Anything is possible, but this is stuck to the inside of the cloth. I think it came off him."

In town I bought a shovel at the hardware store, and then we drove back to the cemetery. I parked so that I thought the car might block what I was doing a little, and I told Cathy to keep watch. It was broad daylight and I hoped I looked like a grave digger and not a grave robber.

She said, "You're going to dig up the grave?"

"Dang tootin'," I said, and I went at it.

Cathy didn't like it much, but she didn't stop me. She was as curious as I was. It didn't take long because the dirt was soft, the digging was easy. I got down to the coffin, scraped the dirt off, and opened it with the tip of the shovel. It was a heavy lid, and it was hard to do. It made me think of how easily the man in the coat had lifted it.

Susan was in there. She looked very fresh and she didn't smell. There was only that musty smell you get from slightly damp earth. She had on the slip, and the rest of her clothes were folded under her head. Her shoes were arranged at her feet.

"Jesus," Cathy said. "She looks so alive. So fair. But why would someone dig her up, and then bring her back?"

"I'm not sure, but I think the best thing to do is go see my mother."

My mother is the town librarian. She's one of those that believes in astrology, ESP, little green men from Mars, ghosts, a balanced budget, you name it. And she knows about that stuff. I grew up with it, and it never appealed to me. Like my dad, I was a hard-headed realist. And at some point, my mother had been too much for him. They separated. He lives in Hoboken with a showgirl, far from East Texas. He's been there so long he might as well be a Yankee himself.

The library was nearly empty, and as always, quiet as God's own secrets. My mother ran a tight ship. Mom saw me when I came in and frowned. She's no bigger than a minute with over-dyed hair and an expression on her face like she's just eaten a sour persimmon.

I waved at her, and she waved at me to follow her to the back, where her office was.

In the back, she made Cathy sit at a table near the religious literature, and took me into her office, which was only a little larger than a janitor's closet, and closed the door. She sat behind her cluttered desk, and I sat in front of it.

"So, you must need money," she said.

"When have I asked you for any?"

"Never, but since I haven't seen you in a month of Sundays, and you live across town, I figured it had to be money. If it's for that floozy out there, to buy her something, forget it. She looks cheap."

"I don't even know her that well," I said. She gave me a narrow-eyed look.

"No. It's not like that. She's a client."

"I bet she is."

"Listen, Mom, I'm going to jump right in. I have a situation. It has to do with the kind of things you know about."

"That would be a long list."

I nodded. "But this one is a very specialized thing." And then I told her the story.

She sat silent for a while, processing the information. "Cauldwell Hogston," she said.

"Beg pardon?"

"The old graveyard, behind the fence. The one they don't use anymore. He was buried there. Fact is he was hanged in the graveyard from a tree limb. About where the old sawmill is now."

"There are graves there?" I asked.

"Well, there were. The flood washed up a bunch of them. Hogston was one of the ones buried there, in an unmarked grave. Here, it's in one of the books about the growth of the city, written in 1940."

She got up and pulled a dusty-looking book off one of her shelves. The walls were lined with them, and these were her personal collection. She put the book on her desk, sat back down and started thumbing through the volume, then paused.

"Oh, what the heck. I know it by heart." She closed the book and sat back down in her chair and said, "Cauldwell Hogston was a grave robber. He stole bodies."

"To sell to science?"

"No. To have . . . well, you know."

"No. I don't know."

"He had relations with the bodies."

"That's nasty," I said.

"I'll say. He would take them and put them in his house and pose them and sketch them. Young women. Old women. Just as long as they were women."

"Why?"

"Before daybreak, he would put them back. It was a kind of ritual. But he got caught and he got hung, right there in the graveyard. Preacher cursed him. Later they found his notebooks in his house, and his drawings of the dead women. Mostly nudes."

"But Mom, I think I saw him. Or someone like him."

"It could be him," she said.

"You really think so?"

"I do. You used to laugh at my knowledge, thought I was a fool. What do you think now?"

"I think I'm confused. How could he come out of the grave after all these many years and start doing the things he did before? Could it be someone else? Someone imitating him?"

"Unlikely."

"But he's dead."

"What we're talking about here, it's a different kind of dead. He's a ghoul. Not in the normal use of the term. He's a real ghoul. Back when he was caught, and that would be during the Great Depression, no one questioned that sort of thing. This town was settled by people from the old lands. They knew about ghouls. Ghouls are mentioned as far back as One Thousand and One Nights. And that's just their first-known mention. They love the dead. They gain power from the dead."

"How can you gain power from something that's dead?"

"Some experts believe we die in stages, and that when we are dead to this world, the brain is still functioning on a plain somewhere between life and death. There's a gradual release of the soul."

"How do you know all this?"

"Books. Try them sometime. The brain dies slowly, and a ghoul takes that slow dying, that gradual release of soul, and feasts on it."

"He eats their flesh?"

"There are different kinds of ghouls. Some eat flesh. Some only attack men, and some are like Hogston. The corpses of women are his prey."

"But how did he become a ghoul?"

"Anyone who has an unholy interest in the dead, no matter what religion, no matter if they have no religion, if they are killed violently, they may well become a ghoul. Hogston was certainly a prime candidate. He stole women's bodies and sketched them, and he did other things. We're talking about, you know—"

"Sex?"

"If you can call it that with dead bodies. By this method he thought he could gain their souls and their youth. Being an old man, he wanted to live forever. Course, there were some spells involved, and some horrible stuff he had to drink, made from herbs and body parts. Sex with the bodies causes the remains of their souls to rise to the surface, and he absorbs them through his own body. That's why he keeps coming back to a body until it's drained. It all came out when he was caught replacing the body of Mary Lawrence in her grave. I went to school with her, so I remember all this very well. Anyway, when they caught him, he told them everything, and then there were his notebooks and sketches. He was quite proud of what he had done."

"But why put the bodies back? And, Susan, she looked like she was just sleeping. She looked fresh."

"He returned the bodies before morning because for the black magic to work, they must lie at night in the resting place made for them by their loved ones. Once a ghoul begins to take the soul from a body, it will stay fresh until he's finished, as long as he returns it to its grave before morning. When he drains the last of its soul, the body decays. What he gets out of all this, besides immortality, are powers he didn't have as a man."

"Like being strong and able to jump a six-foot fence flat-footed," I said.

"Things like that, yes."

"But they hung the old man," I said. "How in hell could he be around now?"

"They did more than hang him. They buried him in a deep grave filled with wet cement and allowed it to dry. That was a mistake. They should have completely destroyed the body. Still, that would have held him, except the flood opened the graves, and a bulldozer was sent in to push the old bones away. In the process, it must have broken open the cement and let him out."

"What's to be done?" I said.

"You have to stop it."

"Me?"

"I'm too old. The cops won't believe this. So it's up to you. You don't stop him, another woman dies, he'll take her body. It could be me. He doesn't care I'm old."

"How would I stop him?"

"That part might prove to be difficult. First, you'll need an axe, and you'll need some fire. . . ."

With Cathy riding with me, we went by the hardware store and bought an axe and a file to sharpen it up good. I got a can of paint thinner and a new lighter and a can of lighter fluid. I went home and got my twelve-gauge double barrel. I got a handful of shotgun shells. I explained to Cathy what I had to do.

"According to Mom, the ghoul doesn't feel pain much. But, they can be destroyed if you chop their head off, and then you got to burn the head. If you don't, it either grows a new head, or body out of the head, or some such thing. She was a little vague. All I know is she says it's a way to kill mummies, ghouls, vampires, and assorted monsters."

"My guess is she hasn't tried any of this," Cathy said.

"No, she hasn't. But she's well schooled in these matters. I always thought she was full of it, but turns out, she isn't. Who knew?"

"And if it doesn't work?"

"Look for my remains."

"I'm going with you," she said.

"No you're not."

"Do you really think you can stop me? It's my sister. I hired you."

"Then let me do my job."

"I just have your word for all this."

"There you are. I wouldn't tromp around in the dark based on my word."

"I'm going."

"It could get ugly."

"Once again, it's my sister. You don't get to choose for me."

I parked my car across the road from the cemetery under a willow. As it grew dark, shadows would hide it reasonably well. This is where Cathy was to sit. I, on the other hand, would go around to the rear where the ghoul would most likely come en route to Susan's grave.

Sitting in my jalopy talking, the sun starting to drop, I said, "I'll try and stop him before he gets to the grave. But, if he comes from some other angle, another route, hit the horn and I'll come running."

"There's the problem of the six-foot fence," Cathy said.

"I may have to run around the graveyard fence, but I'll still come. You can keep honking the horn and turn on the lights and drive through the cemetery gate. But whatever you do, don't get out of the car."

I handed her my shotgun.

"Ever shot one of these?" I said.

"Daddy was a bird hunter. So, yes."

"Good. Just in case it comes to it."

"Will it kill him?"

"Mom says no, but it beats harsh language."

I grabbed my canvas shoulder bag and axe and got out of the car and started walking. I made it around the fence and to the rear of the grave-yard, near the creek and the mud, about fifteen minutes before dark.

I got behind a wide pine and waited. I didn't know if I was in the right place, but if his grave had been near the sawmill this seemed like a likely spot. I got a piece of chewing gum and went to work on it.

The sun was setting.

I hoisted the axe in my hand, to test the weight. Heavy. I'd have to swing it pretty good to manage decapitation. I thought about that. Decapitation. What if it was just some nut, and not a ghoul?

Well, what the hell. He was still creepy.

I put the axe-head on the ground and leaned on the axe handle. I guess about an hour passed before I heard something crack.

I looked out toward the creek where I had seen him jump with Susan's body. I didn't see anything but dark. I felt my skin prick, and I had a sick feeling in my stomach.

I heard another cracking. It wasn't near the creek.

It wasn't in front of me at all.

It was behind me.

I wheeled, and then I saw the ghoul. He hadn't actually seen me, but he was moving behind me at a run, and boy could he run. He was heading straight for the cemetery fence.

I started after him, but I was too far behind and too slow. I slipped on the mud and fell. When I looked up, it was just in time to see the ghoul make a leap. For a moment, he seemed pinned against the moon, like a curious broach on a golden breast. His long white hair trailed behind him and his coat was flying wide. He had easily leaped ten feet high.

He came down in the cemetery as light as a feather. By the time I was off my ass and had my feet under me, he was running across the cemetery toward Susan's grave.

I ran around the edge of the fence, carrying the axe, the bag slung over my shoulder. As I ran, I saw him, moving fast. He was leaping gravestones again.

Before I reached the end of the fence, I heard my horn go off, and saw lights come on. The car was moving. As I turned the corner of the fence, I could see the lights had pinned the ghoul for a moment, and the car was coming fast. The ghoul threw up its arm and the car hit him and knocked him back about twenty feet.

The ghoul got up as if nothing had happened. Its movements were puppet-like, as if he were being pulled by invisible strings.

Cathy, ignoring everything I told her, got out of the car. She had the shotgun.

The ghoul ignored her, and ran toward Susan's grave, started digging as if Cathy wasn't there. As I came through the cemetery opening, and past my car, Cathy cut down on the thing with the shotgun. Both barrels.

It was a hell of a roar, and dust and cloth and flesh flew up from the thing. The blast knocked it down. It popped up like a Jack-in-the-Box and hissed like a cornered possum. It lunged at Cathy. She swung the shotgun by the barrel, hit the ghoul upside the head.

I was at Cathy's side now, and without thinking I dropped the axe and the bag fell off my shoulder. Before the ghoul could reach her, I tackled the thing.

It was easy. There was nothing to Cauldwell Hogston. It was like grabbing a hollow reed. But the reed was surprisingly strong. Next thing I knew I was being thrown into the windshield of my car, and then Cathy was thrown on top of me.

When I had enough of my senses back I tried to sit up. My back hurt. The back of my head ached, but otherwise, I seemed to be all in one piece.

The ghoul was digging furiously at the grave with its hands, throwing dirt like a dog searching for a bone. He was already deep into the earth.

Still stunned, I jumped off the car and grabbed the canvas bag and pulled the lighter fluid and the lighter out of it. I got as close as I dared, and sprayed a stream of lighter fluid at the creature. It soaked the back of its head. Hogston wheeled to look at me. I sprayed the stuff in his eyes and onto his chest, drenching him. He swatted at the fluid as I squeezed the can.

I dropped the can. I had the lighter, and I was going to pop the top and hit the thumb wheel, when the next thing I knew the ghoul leaped at me and grabbed me and threw me at the cemetery fence. I hit hard against it and lay there stunned.

When I looked up, the ghoul was dragging the coffin from the grave, and without bothering to open it this time, threw it over its shoulder and took off running.

I scrambled to my feet, found the lighter, stuffed it in the canvas bag, and swung the bag over my shoulder and picked up the axe. I yelled for Cathy to get in the car. She was still dazed, but managed to get in the car.

Sliding behind the wheel, I gave her the axe and the bag, turned the key, popped the clutch, and backed out of the cemetery. I whipped onto the road, jerked the gear into position, and tore down the road.

"He's over there!" Cathy said. "See!"

I glimpsed the ghoul running toward the creek with the coffin. "I see," I said. "But I think I know where he's going."

The sawmill road was good for a short distance, but then the trees grew in close and the road was grown up with small brush. I had to stop the car. We started rushing along on foot. Cathy carried the canvas bag. I carried the axe.

"What's in the bag?" she said.

"More lighter fluid."

Trees dipped their limbs around us, and when an owl hooted, then fluttered through the pines, I nearly crapped my pants.

Eventually, the road played out, and there were only trees. We pushed through some limbs, scratching ourselves in the process, and finally broke out into a partial clearing. The sawmill was in the center of it, with its sagging roof and missing wall and trees growing up through and alongside it. The moonlight fell over it and colored it like thin yellow paint.

"You're sure he's here," Cathy said.

"I'm not sure of much of anything anymore," I said. "But, his grave was near here. It's about the only thing he can call home now."

When we reached the sawmill, we took deep breaths, as if on cue, and went inside. The boards creaked under our feet. I looked toward a flight of open stairs and saw the ghoul moving up those as swift and silent as a rat. The coffin was on his shoulder, held there as if it were nothing more than a shoebox.

I darted toward the stairway, and the minute my foot hit them, they creaked and swayed.

"Stay back," I said, and Cathy actually listened to me. At least for a moment.

I climbed on up, and then there was a crack, and my foot went through. I felt a pain like an elephant had stepped on my leg. I nearly dropped the axe.

"Taylor," Cathy yelled. "Are you all right?"

"Good as it gets," I said.

Pulling my leg out, I limped up the rest of the steps with the axe, turned left at the top of the stairs—the direction I had seen it take. I guess I was probably thirty feet high by then.

I walked along the wooden walkway. To my right were walls and doorways without doors, and to my left was a sharp drop to the rotten floor below. I hobbled along for a few feet, glanced through one of the doorways. The floor on the other side was gone. Beyond that door was a long drop.

I looked down at Cathy.

She pointed at the door on the far end. "He went in there," she said.

Girding my loins, I came to the doorway and looked in. The roof of the room was broken open, and the floor was filled with moonlight. On the floor was the coffin, and the slip Susan had worn was on the edge of the coffin, along with the ghoul's rotten black coat.

Cauldwell Hogston was in the coffin on top of her.

I rushed toward him, just as his naked ass rose up, a bony thing that made him look like some sad concentration camp survivor. As his butt came down, I brought the axe downward with all my might.

It caught him on the back of the neck, but the results were not as I expected. The axe cut a dry notch, but up he leaped, as if levitating, grabbed my axe handle, and would have had me, had his pants not been around his ankles. It caused him to fall. I staggered back through the doorway, and now he was out of his pants and on his feet, revealing that though he was emaciated, one part of him was not.

Backpedaling, I stumbled onto the landing. He sprang forward, grabbed my throat. His hands were like a combination of vise and ice tongs; they bit into my flesh and took my air. Up close, his breath was rancid as roadkill. His teeth were black and jagged and the flesh hung from the bones of his face like cheap curtains. The way he had me, I couldn't swing the axe and not hit myself.

In the next moment, the momentum of his rush carried us backwards, along the little walkway, and then, out into empty space.

Falling didn't take any time. When I hit the ground my air was knocked out of me, and the boards of the floor sagged.

The ghoul was straddling me, choking me.

And then I heard a click, a snap. I looked. Cathy had gotten the lighter from the bag. She tossed it.

The lighter hit the ghoul, and the fluid I had soaked him with flared. His head flamed and he jumped off of me, and headed straight for Cathy.

I got up as quickly as I could, which was sort of like asking a dead hippo to roll over. On my feet, lumbering forward, finding that I still held the axe in my hand, I saw that the thing's head was flaming like a match, and yet, it had gripped Cathy by the throat and was lifting her off the ground.

I swung the axe from behind, caught its left leg just above the knee. The blade I had sharpened so severely did its work. It literally cut the ghoul off at the knee, and he dropped, letting go of Cathy. She moved back quickly, holding her throat, gasping for air.

The burning thing lay on its side. I brought the axe down on its neck.

It took me two more chops before its rotten, burning head came loose. I chopped at the head, sending the wreckage of flaming skull in all directions.

I faltered a few steps, looked at Cathy, said, "You know, when you lit him up, I was under him."

"Sorry."

And then I saw her eyes go wide. I turned.

The headless, one-legged corpse was crawling toward us, swift as a lizard. It grabbed my ankle.

I slammed the axe down, took off the hand at the wrist, then kicked it loose of my leg. That put me in a chopping frenzy. I brought the axe down time after time, snapping that dry stick of a creature into thousands of pieces.

By the time I finished that, I could hardly stand. I had to lean on the axe. Cathy took my arm, said, "Taylor."

Looking up, I saw the fire from the ghoul had spread out in front of us and the rotten lumber and old sawdust had caught like paper. The canvas bag with the lighter fluid in it caught too, and within a second, it blew, causing us to fall back.

The only way out was up the stairs, and in the long run, that would only prolong the roasting. Considering the alternative, however, we were both for prolonging our fiery death instead of embracing it.

Cathy helped me up the stairs, because by now my ankle had swollen up until it was only slightly smaller than a Civil War cannon. I used the axe like a cane. The fire licked the steps behind us, climbed up after us, as if playing tag.

When we made the upper landing, we went through the door where Susan's body lay. I looked in the coffin. She was nude, looking a lot rougher than before. Perhaps the ghoul had gotten the last of her, or without him to keep her percolating with his magic she had gone for the last roundup; passed on over into true solid death. I hoped in the end, her soul had been hers, and not that monster's.

I let go of Cathy, and using the axe for support, made it to the window. The dark sawdust was piled deep below.

Stumbling back to the coffin, I dropped the axe, got hold of the edge, and said, "Push."

Cathy did just that. The coffin scraped across the floor. Smoke wafted up through cracks, and it was growing hot. Flame licked up now and then, as if searching for us.

We pushed the coffin and Susan out the window. She fell free of the box and hit the sawdust. We jumped after her.

When we were on the pile, spitting sawdust, trying to work our way down the side of it, the sawmill wall started to fall. We rolled down the side of the piled sawdust and hit the ground.

The burning wall hit the sawdust. The mound was high enough we were protected from it. We crawled out from under it and managed to get about fifty feet away before we looked back.

The sawmill, the sawdust pile, and poor Susan's body, and anything that was left of Cauldwell Hogston was now nothing more than a raging mountain of sizzling, cracking flames.

I did this for a gaming company that wanted to do an anthology of hard-boiled stories. I think mine was almost too hard-boiled for them. But it's a favorite of mine, dealing with lost treasure, quirky characters, and screwed-up situations, with a bit of coincidence thrown in for seasoning. I think they edited it slightly, if I remember correctly, and it pissed me off. It was a small thing, but it mattered to me, and I corrected it. Being edited isn't necessarily a problem, but editing without permission is.

BOOTY AND THE BEAST

"Where do you keep the sugar?" Mulroy said, as he pulled open cabinet doors and scrounged about.

"Go to hell," Standers said.

"That's no way to talk," Mulroy said. "I'm a guest in your house. A guest isn't supposed to be treated that way. All I asked was where's the sugar?"

"And I said go to hell. And you're not a guest."

Mulroy, who was standing in the kitchen part of the mobile home, stopped and stared at Standers in the living room. He had tied Standers's hands together and stretched them out so he could loop the remainder of the lamp cord around a doorknob. He had removed Standers's boots and tied his feet with a sheet, wrapped them several times. The door Standers was bound to was the front door of the trailer and it was open. Standers was tied so that he was sitting with his back against the door, his arms stretched and strained above him. Mulroy thought he ought to have done it a little neater, a little less painful, then he got to thinking about what he was going to do and decided it didn't matter, and if it did, tough.

"You got any syrup or honey?"

This time Standers didn't answer at all.

Mulroy neatly closed the cabinet doors and checked the refrigerator. He found a large plastic see-through bear nearly full of syrup. He squeezed the bear and shot some of the syrup on his finger and tasted it. Maple.

"This'll do. You know, I had time, I'd fix me up some pancakes and use this. I taste this, it makes me think pancakes. They got like an IHOP in town?"

Standers didn't answer.

Mulroy strolled over to Standers and set the plastic bear on the floor and took off his cowboy hat and nice Western jacket. He tossed the hat on the couch and carefully hung his jacket on the back of a chair. The pistol in the holster under his arm dangled like a malignancy.

Mulroy took a moment to look out the open door at the sun-parched grass and the fire-ant hills in the yard. Here was a bad place for a mobile home. For a house. For anything. No neighbors. No trees, just lots of land with stumps. Mulroy figured the trees had been cut down for pulp money. Mulroy knew that's what he'd have done.

Because there were no trees, the mobile home was hot, even with the air conditioner going. And having the front door open didn't help much, way it was sucking out what cool air there was.

Mulroy watched as a mockingbird alit in the grass. It appeared on the verge of heat stroke. It made one sad sound, then went silent. Way, way out, Mulroy could hear cars on the highway, beyond the thin line of pine trees.

Mulroy reached down and unbuckled Standers's pants. He tugged down the pants and underwear, exposing Standers. He got hold of the bear and squeezed some of the syrup onto Standers's privates.

Standers said, "Whatcha doin', fixin' breakfast?"

"Oh ho," Mulroy said. "I am cut to the quick. Listen here. No use talkin' tough. This isn't personal. It's business. I'm going to do what I got to do, so you might as well not take it personal. I don't have anything against you."

"Yeah, well, great. I feel a hell of a lot better."

Mulroy eased down to Standers's feet, where his toes were exposed. He put the syrup on Standers's toes. He squirted some on Standers's head.

Mulroy went outside then. The mockingbird flew away. Mulroy walked around and looked at the fire-ant hills. Fire ants were a bitch. They were tenacious bastards, and when they stung you, it was some kind of sting.

There were some people so allergic to the little critters, one bite would make them go toes up. And if there were enough of them, and they were biting on you, it could be Goodbye City no matter if you were allergic or not. It was nasty poison.

Mulroy reached in his back pocket, pulled out a half-used sack of Red Man, opened it, pinched some out and put it in his mouth. He chewed a while, then spit on one of the ant hills. Agitated ants boiled out of the hill and spread in his direction. He walked off a way and used the toe of his boot to stir up another hill, then another. He squirted syrup from the bear on one of the hills and ran a thin, dribbling stream of syrup back to the mobile home, up the steps, across the floor and directed the stream across Standers's thigh and onto his love apples. He said, "A fire ant hurts worse than a regular ant, but it isn't any different when it comes to sweets. He likes them. They like them. There're thousands of ants out there. Maybe millions. Who the hell knows? I mean, how you gonna count mad ants, way they're running around?"

For the first time since Mulroy first surprised Standers—pretending to be a Bible salesman, then giving him an overhand right, followed by a left uppercut to the chin—he saw true concern on Standers's face.

Mulroy said, "They hurt they bite you on the arm, leg, foot, something like that. But they get on your general, crawl between your toes, where it's soft, or nip your face around the lips, eyes and nose, it's some kind of painful. Or so I figure. You can tell me in a minute."

Suddenly, Mulroy cocked his head. He heard a car coming along the long road that wound up to the trailer. He went and looked out the door, came back, sat down on the couch and chewed his tobacco.

A few moments later the car parked behind Mulroy's car. A door slammed, a young slim woman in a short tight dress with hair the color of fire ants came through the door and looked first at Mulroy, then Standers. She pivoted on her high heels and waved her little handbag at Standers, said, "Hey, honey. What's that on your schlong?"

"Syrup," Mulroy said, got up, pushed past the woman and spat a stream of tobacco into the yard.

"Bitch," Standers said.

"The biggest," she said. Then to Mulroy: "Syrup on his tallywhacker?"

Mulroy stood in the doorway and nodded toward the yard. "The ants."

The woman looked outside, said, "I get it. Very imaginative." She eyed the plastic bear where Mulroy had placed it on the arm of the couch. "Oh, that little bear is the cutest."

"You like it," Mulroy said. "Take it with you." Then to Standers he said, "You think maybe now you want to talk to us?"

Standers considered, decided either way he was screwed. He didn't tell, he was going to suffer, then die. Maybe he told what they wanted, he'd just die. He could make that part of the deal, and hope they kept their side of the bargain. Not that there was any reason they should. Still, Mulroy, he might do it. As for Babe, he couldn't trust her any kind of way.

Nonetheless, looking at her now, she was certainly beautiful. And his worm's-eye view right up her dress was exceptional, considering Babe didn't wear panties and was a natural redhead.

"I was you," Mulroy said, "I'd start talking. Where's the loot?"

Standers took a deep breath. If he'd only kept his mouth shut, hadn't tried to impress Babe, he wouldn't be in this mess.

During World War II his dad had been assigned to guard Nazi treasure in Germany. His dad had confiscated a portion of the treasure, millions of dollars' worth, and shipped it home to East Texas. A number of religious icons had been included in the theft, like a decorated box that was supposed to contain a hair from the Virgin Mary's head.

Standers's father had seen all this as spoils of war, not theft. When he returned home, much of the treasure was split up between relatives or sold. After the war the Germans had raised a stink and the U.S. government ended up making Standers's dad return what was left. The Germans offered to pay his father a price for it to keep things mellow. A flat million, a fraction of what it was worth.

Divided among family members, that million was long gone. But there was something else. Standers's dad hadn't given up all the treasure. There were still a few unreturned items; gold bars and the so-called hair of the Virgin Mary.

Early last year the Germans raised yet another stink about items still missing. It had been in the papers and Standers's family had been named, and since he was the last of his family line, it was assumed he might know where this treasure was. Reporters came out. He told them he didn't know anything about any treasure. He laughed about how if he had treasure, he wouldn't be living in a trailer in a cow pasture. The reporters believed him, or so it seemed from the way it read in the papers.

A month later he met Babe, in a store parking lot. She was changing a tire and just couldn't handle it, and would he help her. He had, and while he did the work, he got to look up the line of her leg and find out she wore nothing underneath the short dresses she preferred. And she knew how to talk him up and lead him on. She was a silver-tongued, long-legged slut with heaven between her legs. He should have known better.

One night, after making love, Babe mentioned the stuff in the papers, and Standers, still high on flesh friction, feeling like a big man, admitted he had a large share of the money socked away in a foreign bank, and the rest, some gold bars, and the box containing the hair from the Virgin Mary, hidden away here in East Texas.

The relationship continued, but Standers began to worry when Babe kept coming back to the booty. She wanted to know where it was. She didn't ask straight out; she danced around matters; he didn't talk. He'd been stupid enough, no use compounding the matter. She was after the money, and not him, and he felt like a jackass. He doubled up on the sex for a while, then sent her away.

This morning, posing as a Bible salesman, Mulroy had shown up, clocked him, tied him up, introduced himself and tried to get him to tell the whereabouts of the loot. When Babe came through the door, it all clicked in place.

"I got a question," Standers said.

"So do we," Mulroy said. "Where's the spoils? We don't even want the money you got in a foreign bank. Well, we want it, but that might be too much trouble. We'll settle for the other. What did you tell Babe it was? Gold bars and a cunt hair off the Virgin Mary?"

"I just want to know," Standers continued, "were you and Babe working together from the start?"

Mulroy laughed. "She was on her own, but when she couldn't get what she wanted from you, she needed someone to provide some muscle."

"So you're just another one she's conned," Standers said.

"No," Mulroy said, "you were conned. I'm a business partner. I'm not up for being conned. You wouldn't do that to me, would you, Babe?"

Babe smiled.

"Yeah, well, I guess you would," Mulroy said. "But I ain't gonna let you. You see, I know she's on the con. Knew it from the start. You didn't. Conning the marks is what I do for a living."

"It was all bullshit," Standers said. "I just told her that to sound big. She gets you in bed, she makes your dick think it's the president. I was tryin' to keep that pussy comin', is all. I had money, you think I'd be living like this?"

"If you were smart, you would," Mulroy said.

"I'm not smart," Standers said. "I sell cars. And that's it."

"Man," Mulroy said, "you tell that so good I almost believe it. Almost. Shit, I bet you could sell me an old Ford with a flat tire and missing transmission. Almost. Hey, let's do it like this. You give the location of the stuff, and we let you go, and we even send you a little of the money. You know, ten thousand dollars. Isn't much, but it beats what you might get. I think that's a pretty good deal, all things considered."

"Yeah, I'll wait at the mailbox for the ten thousand," Standers said.

"That's a pretty hard one to believe, isn't it?" Mulroy said. "But you can't blame me for tryin'. Hell, I got to go to the can. Watch him, Babe."

When Mulroy left the room, Standers said, "Nice, deal, huh? You and him get the loot, split it fifty-fifty."

Babe didn't say anything. She went over and sat on the couch.

"I can do you a better deal than he can," Standers said. "Get rid of him, and I'll show you the loot and split it fifty-fifty."

"What's better about that?" Babe said.

"I know where it is," Standers said. "It'd go real easy."

"I got time to go less easy, I want to take it," she said.

"Yeah," Standers said. "But why take it? Sooner you get it, sooner we spend it."

Mulroy came back into the room. Babe picked the plastic bear off the couch arm and went over to the refrigerator and opened it. She put the bear inside and got out a soft drink and pulled the tab on the can. "Man, I'm hungry," she said, then swigged the drink.

"What?" Mulroy said.

"Hungry," Babe said. "You know. I'd like to eat. You hungry?"

"Yeah," Mulroy said. "I was thinking about pancakes, but I kinda got other things on my mind here. We finish this, we'll eat. Besides, there's food here."

"Yeah, you want to eat this slop?" Babe said. "Go get us a pizza."

"A pizza?" Mulroy said. "You want I should get a pizza? We're fixin' to torture a guy with fire ants, maybe cut him up a little, set him on fire, whatever comes to mind that's fun, and you want me to drive out and get a fuckin' pizza? Honey, you need to stop lettin' men dick you in the ear. It's startin' to mess up your brain. Drink your soda pop."

"Canadian bacon, and none of those little fishies," Babe said. "Lots of cheese, and get the thick chewy crust."

"You got to be out of your beautiful red head."

"It'll take a while anyway," Babe said. "I don't think a couple of ant bites'll make him cave. And I'd rather not get tacky with cuttin' and burnin', we can avoid it. Whatever we do, it'll take some time, and I don't want to do it on an empty stomach. I'm tellin' you, I'm seriously and grown-up hungry here."

"You don't know fire ants, Babe," Mulroy said. "It ain't gonna take long at all."

"It's like, what, fifteen minutes into town?" Babe said, sipping her drink. "I could use a *pizza*. That's what I want. What's the big deal?"

Mulroy scratched the back of his neck, looked out the doorway. The ants were at the steps, following the trail of syrup.

"They'll be on him before I get back," he said.

"So," Babe said, "I've heard a grown man scream before. He tells me somethin', you get back, we'll go, eat the pizza on the way."

Mulroy used a finger to clear the tobacco out of his cheek. He flipped it into the yard. He said, "All right. I guess I could eat." Mulroy put on his coat and hat and smiled at Babe and went out.

When Mulroy's car was way out on the drive, near the highway, Babe opened her purse and took out a small .38 and pointed it at Standers. "I figure this will make you a more balanced kind of partner. You remember that. You mess with me, I'll shoot your dick off."

"All right," Standers said.

Babe put the revolver in her other hand, got a flick-blade knife out of her purse, used it to cut the sheets around Standers's ankles. She cut the lamp cord off his wrist.

Standers stood, and without pulling his pants up, hopped to the sink. He got the hand towel off the rack and wet it and used it to clean the syrup off his privates, his feet and head. He pulled up his pants, got his socks, sat on the couch and put his boots back on.

"We got to hurry," Babe said. "Mulroy, he's got a temper. I seen him shoot a dog once for peeing on one of his hub caps."

"Let me get my car keys," Standers said.

"We'll take my car," she said. "You'll drive."

They went outside and she gave him the keys and they drove off.

As they drove onto the highway, Mulroy, who was parked behind a swathe of trees, poked a new wad of tobacco into his mouth and massaged it with his teeth.

Babe had sold out immediately, like he thought she would. Doing it this way, having them lead him to the treasure, was a hell of a lot better than sitting around in a hot trailer watching fire ants crawl on a man's balls. And this way he didn't have to watch his back all the time. That Babe, what a kidder. She was so greedy, she thought he'd fall for that lame pizza gag. She'd been winning too long; she wasn't thinking enough moves ahead anymore.

Mulroy rode well back of them, putting his car behind other cars when he could. He figured his other advantage was they weren't expecting him. He thought about the treasure and what he could do with it while he drove.

Until Babe came along, he had been a private detective, doing nickel and dime divorces out of Tyler; taking pictures of people doing the naked horizontal mambo. It wasn't a lot of fun. And the little cons he pulled on the side, clever as they were, were bullshit money, hand to mouth.

He made the score he wanted from all this, he'd go down to Mexico, buy him a place with a pool, rent some women. One for each day of the week, and each one with a different sexual skill, and maybe a couple who could cook. He was damn sure tired of his own cooking. He wanted to eat a lot and get fat and lay around and poke the señoritas. This all fell through, he thought he might try and be an evangelist or some kind of politician or a lawman with a regular check.

Standers drove for a couple of hours, through three or four towns, and Mulroy followed. Eventually, Standers pulled off the highway, onto a blacktop. Mulroy gave him time to get ahead, then took the road too. With no cars to put between them and himself, Mulroy cruised along careful like. Finally, he saw Standers way up ahead on a straight stretch.

Standers veered off the road and into the woods.

Mulroy pulled to the side of the road and waited a minute, then followed. The road in the woods was a narrow dirt one, and Mulroy had only gone a little way when he stopped his car and got out and started walking. He had a hunch the road was a short one, and he didn't want to surprise them too early.

Standers drove down the road until it dead-ended at some woods and a load of trash someone had dumped. He got out and Babe got out. Babe was still holding her gun.

"You're tellin' me it's hidden under the trash?" she said. "You better not be jackin' with me, honey."

"It's not under the trash. Come on."

They went into the woods and walked along awhile, came to an old white house with a bad roof. It was surrounded by vines and trees and the porch was falling down.

"You keep a treasure here?" she said.

Standers went up on the porch, got a key out of his pocket and unlocked the door. Inside, pigeons fluttered and went out holes in the windows and the roof. A snake darted into a hole in the floor. There were spiders and spider webs everywhere. The floor was dotted with rat turds.

Standers went carefully across the floor and into a bedroom. Babe followed, holding her revolver at the ready. The room was better kept than the rest of the house. She could see where boards had been replaced in the floor. The ceiling was good here. There were no windows, just plyboard over the spots where they ought to be. There was a dust-covered desk, a bed with ratty covers, and an armchair covered in a faded flower print.

Standers got down on his hands and knees, reached under the bed and tugged diligently at a large suitcase.

"It's under the bed?" Babe said.

Standers opened the suitcase. There was a crowbar in it. He got the crowbar out. Babe said, "Watch yourself. I don't want you should try and hit me. It could mess up my makeup."

Standers carried the crowbar to the closet, opened it. The closet was sound. There was a groove in the floor. Standers fitted the end of the crowbar into the groove and lifted. The flooring came up. Standers pulled the trap door out of the closet and put it on the floor.

Babe came over for a look, careful to keep an eye on Standers and a tight grip on the gun. Where the floor had been was a large metal-lined box. Standers opened the box so she could see what was inside.

What she saw inside made her breath snap out. Gold bars and a shiny wooden box about the size of a box of cigars.

"That's what's got the hair in it?" she asked.

"That's what they say. Inside is another box with some glass in it. You can look through the glass and see the hair. Box was made by the Catholic Church to hold the hair. For all I know it's an armpit hair off one of the popes. Who's to say? But it's worth money."

"How much money?"

"It depends on who you're dealing with. A million. Two to three million. Twenty-five million."

"Let's deal with that last guy."

"The fence won't give money like that. We could sell the gold bars, use that to finance a trip to Germany. There're people there would pay plenty for the box."

"A goddamn hair," Babe said. "Can you picture that?"

"Yeah, I can picture that." Babe and Standers turned as Mulroy spoke, stepped into the room cocking his revolver with one hand, pushing his hat back with the other.

Mulroy said, "Put the gun down, Babe, or I part your hair about two inches above your nose."

Babe smiled at him, lowered her gun. "See," she said. "I got him to take me here, no trouble. Now we can take the treasure."

Mulroy smiled. "You are some kind of kidder. I never thought you'd let me have fifty percent anyway. I was gonna do you in from the start. Same as you were with me. Drop the gun, Babe."

Babe dropped the revolver. "You got me all wrong," she said.

"No I don't," Mulroy said.

"I guess you didn't go for pizza," Standers said.

"No, but I tell you what," Mulroy said. "I'm pretty hungry right now, so let's get this over with. I'll make it short and sweet. A bullet through the head for you, Standers. A couple more just to make sure you aren't gonna be some kind of living cabbage. As for you, Babe. There's a bed here, and I figure I might as well get all the treasure I can get. Look at it this way. It's the last nice thing you can do for anybody, so you might as well make it nice. If nothing else, be selfish and enjoy it."

"Well," Standers said, looking down at Babe's revolver on the floor. "You might as well take the gun."

Standers stepped out from behind Babe and kicked her gun toward Mulroy, and no sooner had he done that, than he threw the crowbar.

Mulroy looked down at the revolver sliding his way, then looked up. As he did, the crowbar hit him directly on the bridge of the nose and dropped him. He fell unconscious with his back against the wall.

Soon as Mulroy fell, Babe reached for her revolver. Standers kicked her legs out from under her, but she scuttled like a crab and got hold of it and shot in Standers's direction. The shot missed, but it stopped Standers.

Babe got up, pulled her dress down and smiled. "Looks like I'm ahead."

She turned suddenly and shot the unconscious Mulroy behind the ear.

Mulroy's hat, which had maintained its position on his head, came off as he nodded forward. A wad of tobacco rolled over his lip and landed in his lap. Blood ran down his cheek and onto his nice Western coat.

Babe smiled again, spoke to Standers. "Now I just got you. And I need you to carry those bars out of here."

Standers said. "Why should I help?"

"'Cause I'll let you go."

Standers snorted.

"All right then, because I'll shoot you in the knees and leave you here if you don't. That way, you go slow. Help me, I'll make it quick."

"Damn, that's a tough choice."

"Let's you and me finish up in a way you don't have to suffer, baby cakes."

Standers nodded, said, "You promise to make it quick?"

"Honey, it'll happen so fast you won't know it happened."

"I can't take the strain," Standers said. He pointed to the room adjacent to the bedroom. "There's a wheelbarrow in there. It's the way I haul stuff out. I get that, we can make a few trips, get it over with. I don't like to think about dying for a long time. Let's just get it done."

"Fine with me," Babe said.

Standers started toward the other room. Babe said, "Hold on."

She bent down and got Mulroy's gun. Now she had one in either hand. She waved Standers back against the wall and peeked in the room he had indicated. There was a wheelbarrow in there.

"All right, let's do it," she said.

Standers stepped quickly inside, and as Babe started to enter the room, he said sharply, "Don't step there!"

Babe held her foot in mid-air, and Standers slapped her closest gun arm down and grabbed it, slid behind her and pinned her other arm. He slid his hands down and took the guns from her. He used his knee to shove her forward. She stumbled and the floor cracked and she went through and spun and there was another crack, but it wasn't the floor. She screamed and moaned something awful. After a moment, she stopped bellowing and turned to Standers, she opened her mouth to speak, but nothing came out.

Standers said, "What's the matter? Kind of run out of lies? There ain't nothing you can say would interest me. It's just a shame to have to kill a good-lookin' piece like you."

"Please," she said, but Standers shot her in the face with Mulroy's gun and she fell backwards, her broken leg still in the gap in the floor. Her other leg flew up and came down and her heel hit the floor with a slap. Her dress hiked up and exposed her privates.

"Not a bad way to remember you," Standers said. "It's the only part of you that wasn't a cheat."

Standers took the box containing the hair out of the closet, put the closet back in shape, got the wheelbarrow and used it to haul Babe, her purse, and the guns out of there and through the woods to a pond his relatives had built fifty years ago.

He dumped Babe beside the pond, went back for Mulroy and dumped him beside her. He got Mulroy's car keys out of his pocket and Babe's keys out of her purse.

Standers walked back to Babe's car and drove it to the edge of the pond, rolled down the windows a little, put her and Mulroy in the back seat with her purse and the guns, then he put the car in neutral. He pushed it off in the water. It was a deep, dirty pond. The car went down quick.

Standers waited at the shack until almost dark, then took the box containing the hair, walked back, found Mulroy's car and drove it out of there. He stopped the car beside a dirt road about a mile from his house and wiped it clean with a handkerchief he found in the front seat. He got the box out of the car and walked back to his trailer.

It was dark when he got there. The door was still open. He went inside, locked up and set the box with the hair on the counter beside the sink. He opened the box and took out the smaller box and studied the hair through the smeary glass.

He thought to himself, What if this is the Virgin Mary's hair? It could even be an ass hair, but if it's the Virgin Mary's. Well, it's the Virgin Mary's. And what if it's a dog hair? It'll still sell for the same. It was time to get rid of it. He would book a flight to Germany tomorrow, search out the right people, sell it, sock what he got from it away in his foreign bank account, come back and fence the gold bars and sell all his land, except for the chunk with the house and pond on it. He'd fill the pond in himself with a rented backhoe and dozer, plant some trees on top of it, let it set while he lived abroad.

Simple, but a good plan, he thought.

Standers drank a glass of water and took the box and lay down on the couch snuggling it. He was exhausted. Fear of death did that to a fella. He closed his eyes and went to sleep immediately.

A short time later he awoke in pain. His whole body ached. He leaped up, dropping the box. He began to slap at his legs and chest, tear at his clothes.

Jesus. The fire ants! His entire body was covered with the bastards.

Standers felt queasy. My God, he thought. I'm having a reaction. I'm allergic to the little shits.

He got his pants and underwear peeled down to his ankles, but he couldn't get them over his boots. He began to hop about the room. He hit the light switch and saw the ants all over the place. They had followed the stream of syrup, and then they had found him on the couch and gone after him.

Standers screamed and slapped, hopped over and grabbed the box from the floor and jerked open the front door. He held the box in one hand and tugged at his pants with the other, but as he was going down the steps, he tripped, fell forward and landed on his head and lay there with his head and knees holding him up. He tried to stand, but couldn't. He realized he had broken his neck, and from the waist down he was paralyzed.

Oh God, he thought. The ants. Then he thought, Well, at least I can't feel them, but he found he could feel them on his face. His face still had sensation.

It's temporary, the paralysis will pass, he told himself, but it didn't. The ants began to climb into his hair and swarm over his lips. He batted at them with his eyelashes and blew at them with his mouth, but it didn't do any good. They swarmed him. He tried to scream, but with his neck bent the way it was, his throat constricted somewhat, he couldn't make a good noise. And when he opened his mouth the furious little ants swarmed in and bit his tongue, which swelled instantly.

Oh Jesus, he thought. Jesus and the Virgin Mary.

But Jesus wasn't listening. Neither was the Virgin Mary.

The night grew darker and the ants grew more intense, but Standers was dead long before morning.

About 10 A.M. a car drove up in Standers's drive and a fat man in a cheap blue suit with a suitcase full of Bibles got out; a real Bible salesman with a craving for drink.

The Bible salesman, whose name was Bill Longstreet, had his mind on business. He needed to sell a couple of moderate-priced Bibles so he could get a drink. He'd spent his last money in Beaumont, Texas, on a double, and now he needed another.

Longstreet strolled around his car, whistling, trying to put up a happy Christian front. Then he saw Standers in the front yard supported by his head and knees, his ass exposed, his entire body swarming with ants. The corpse was swollen up and spotted with bites. Standers's neck was twisted so that Longstreet could see the right side of his face, and his right eye was nothing more than an ant cavern, and the lips were eaten away and the nostrils were a tunnel for the ants. They were coming in one side, and going out the other.

Longstreet dropped his sample case, staggered back to his car, climbed on the hood and just sat there and looked for a long time.

Finally, he got over it. He looked about and saw no one other than the dead man. The door to the trailer was open. Longstreet got off the car. Watching for ants, he went as close as he had courage and yelled toward the open door a few times.

No one came out.

Longstreet licked his lips, eased over to Standers, and moving quickly, stomping his feet, he reached in Standers's back pocket and pulled out his wallet.

Longstreet rushed back to his car and got up on the hood. He looked in the wallet. There were two ten-dollar bills and a couple of ones. He took the money, folded it neatly and put it in his coat pocket. He tossed the wallet back at Standers, got down off the car and got his case and put it on the back seat. He got behind the wheel, was about to drive off, when he saw the little box near Standers's swollen hand.

Longstreet sat for a moment, then got out, ran over, grabbed the box, and ran back to the car, beating the ants off as he went. He got behind the wheel, opened the box and found another box with a little crude glass window fashioned into it. There was something small and dark and squiggly behind the glass. He wondered what it was.

He knew a junk store bought stuff like this. He might get a couple bucks from the lady who ran it. He tossed it in the back seat, cranked up the car and drove into town and had a drink.

He had two drinks. Then three. It was nearly dark by the time he came out of the bar and wobbled out to his car. He started it up and drove out onto the highway right in front of a speeding semi.

The truck hit Longstreet's car and turned it into a horseshoe and sent it spinning across the road, into a telephone pole. The car ricocheted off the pole, back onto the road and the semi, which was slamming hard on its brakes, clipped it again. This time Longstreet and his car went through a barbed-wire fence and spun about in a pasture and stopped near a startled bull.

The bull looked in the open car window and sniffed and went away. The semi driver parked and got out and ran over and looked in the window himself.

Longstreet's brains were all over the car and his face had lost a lot of definition. His mouth was dripping bloody teeth. He had fallen with his head against an open Bible. Later, when he was hauled off, the Bible had to go with him. Blood had plastered it to the side of his head, and when the ambulance arrived, the blood had clotted and the Bible was even better attached; way it was on there, you would have thought it was some kind of bizarre growth Longstreet had been born with. Doctors at the hospital wouldn't mess with it. What was the point. Fucker was dead and they didn't know him.

At the funeral home they hosed his head down with warm water and yanked the Bible off his face and threw it away.

Later on, well after the funeral, Longstreet's widow inherited what was left of Longstreet's car, which she gave to the junkyard. She burned the Bibles and all of Longstreet's clothes. The box with the little box in it she opened and examined. She couldn't figure what was behind the glass.

She used a screwdriver to get the glass off, tweezers to pinch out the hair.

She held the hair in the light, twisted it this way and that. She couldn't make out what it was. A bug leg, maybe. She tossed the hair in the commode and flushed it. She put the little box in the big box and threw it in the trash.

Later yet, she collected quite a bit of insurance money from Longstreet's death. She bought herself a new car and some see-through panties and used the rest to finance her lover's plans to open a used-car lot in downtown Beaumont, but it didn't work out. He used the money to finance himself and she never saw him again.

This was part of my novel The Nightrunners. *When I wrote it, I was really excited. The publishers less so. Oh, they seemed to think I had done something cool, but they weren't cool enough to publish it. At least not at first. It went out a lot. And remember, back then there were a lot of publishers. In the process of marketing it, I pulled several pieces from it; some I used literally, like this one—or for the most part as it was in the book—and the others inspired other stories that I wrote and sold. Among them were stories like "God of the Razor,"* Something Lumber This Way Comes, *a children's book, no less, and an adult version of the same titled "The Shaggy House," a title William F. Nolan gave it. It's one of my more powerful pieces. It kind of makes my skin crawl. That was the point.*

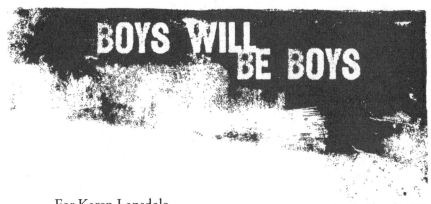

BOYS WILL BE BOYS

For Karen Lansdale

I.

NOT SO LONG ago, about a year back, a very rotten kid named Clyde Edson walked the earth. He was street-mean and full of savvy and he knew what he wanted and got it any way he wanted.

He lived in a big, evil house on a dying, gray street in Galveston, Texas, and he collected to him, like an old lady who brings in cats half-starved and near-eaten with mange, the human refuse and the young discards of a sick society.

He molded them. He breathed life into them. He made them feel they belonged. They were his creations, but he did not love them. They were just things to be toyed with until the paint wore thin and the batteries ran down, then out they went.

And this is the way it was until he met Brian Blackwood.

Things got worse after that.

2.

Guy had a black leather jacket and dark hair combed back virgin-ass tight, slicked down with enough grease to lube a bone-dry Buick; came down the hall walking slow, head up, ice-blue eyes working like acid on everyone in sight; had the hall nearly to himself, plenty of room for his slow-stroll swagger. The other high school kids were shouldering the wall, shedding out of his path like frenzied snakes shedding out of their skins.

You could see this Clyde was bad news. Hung in time. Fifties-looking. Out of step. But who's going to say, "Hey, dude, you look funny"?

Tough, this guy. Hide like the jacket he wore. No books under his arm, nothing at all. Just cool.

Brian was standing at the water fountain first time he saw Clyde, and immediately he was attracted to him. Not in a sexual way. He wasn't funny. But in the manner metal shavings are attracted to a magnet—can't do a thing about it, just got to go to it and cling.

Brian knew who Clyde was, but this was the first time he'd ever been close enough to feel the heat. Before, the guy'd been a tough greaser in a leather jacket who spent most of his time expelled from school. Nothing more.

But now he saw for the first time that the guy had something; something that up close shone like a well-boned razor in the noonday sun.

Cool. He had that.

Class. He had that.

A difference. He had that.

He was a walking power plant.

Name was Clyde. Ol' mean, weird, don't-fuck-with-me Clyde.

"You looking at something?" Clyde growled.

Brian just stood there, one hand resting on the water fountain.

After a while he said innocently, "You."

"That right?"

"Uh-huh."

"Staring at me?"

"I guess."

"I see."

And then Clyde was on Brian, had him by the hair, jerking his head down, driving a knee into his face. Brian went back seeing constellations. Got kicked in the ribs then. Hit in the eye as he leaned forward from that. Clyde was making a regular bop bag out of him.

He hit Clyde back, aimed a nose-shot through a swirling haze of colored dots.

And it hurt so good. Like when he made that fat pig Betty Sue Flowers fingernail his back until he bled; thrust up her hips until his cock ached and the rotten-fish smell of her filled his brain. . . . Only this hurt better. Ten times better.

Clyde wasn't expecting that. This guy was coming back like he liked it. Clyde dug that.

He kicked Brian in the nuts, grabbed him by the hair and slammed his forehead against the kid's nose. Made him bleed good, but didn't get a good enough lick in to break it.

Brian went down, grabbed Clyde's ankle, bit it.

Clyde yowled, dragged Brian around the hall.

The students watched, fascinated. Some wanted to laugh at what was happening, but none dared.

Clyde used his free foot to kick Brian in the face. That made Brian let go . . . for a moment. He dove at Clyde, slammed the top of his head into Clyde's bread basket, carried him back against the wall crying loudly, "Motherfucker!"

Then the principal came, separated them, screamed at them, and Clyde hit the principal and the principal went down and now Clyde and Brian were both standing up, together, *kicking the goddamned shit out of the goddamned principal in the middle of the goddamned hall.* Side by side they stood. Kicking. One. Two. One. Two. Left leg. Right leg. Feet moving together like the legs of a scurrying centipede. . . .

3.

They got some heat slapped on them for that; juvenile-court action. It was a bad scene.

Brian's mother sat at a long table with his lawyer and whined like a blender on whip.

Good old mom. She was actually good for something. She had told the judge, "He's a good boy, your honor. Never got in any trouble before. Probably wouldn't have gotten into this, but he's got no father at home to be an example," and so forth.

If it hadn't been to his advantage, he'd have been disgusted. As it was, he sat in his place with his nice clean suit and tried to look ashamed and a little surprised at what he had done. And in a way he was surprised.

He looked over at Clyde. He hadn't bothered with a suit. He had his jacket and jeans on. He was cleaning his fingernails with a fingernail clipper.

When Mrs. Blackwood finished, Judge Lowry yawned. It was going to be one of those days. He thought, The dockets are full, this Blackwood kid has no priors, looks clean-cut enough, and this other little shit has a book full . . . yet, he is a kid, and I feel big-hearted. Or, to put this into perspective, there's enough of a backlog without adding this silly case to it.

If I let the Blackwood kid go, it'll look like favoritism because he's clean-cut and this is his first time—and that is good for something. Yet, if I don't let the Edson kid go too, then I'm saying the same crime is not as bad when it's committed by a clean-cut kid with a whining momma.

All right, he thought. We'll keep it simple. Let them both go, but give it all some window dressing.

And it was window dressing, nothing more. Brian was put on light probation, and Clyde, already on probation, was given the order to report to his probation officer more frequently, and that was the end of that.

Piece of cake.

The school expelled them for the rest of the term, but that was no mean thing. They were back on the streets before the day was out.

For the moment, Clyde went his way and Brian went his.

But the bond was formed.

4.

A week later, mid-October.

Brian Blackwood sat in his room, his head full of pleasant but overwhelming emotions. He got a pen and loose-leaf notebook out of his desk drawer, began to write savagely.

I've never kept a journal before, and I don't know if I'll continue to keep one after tonight, but the stuff that's going on inside of me is boiling up something awful and I feel if I don't get it out I'm going to explode and there isn't going to be anything left of me but blood and shit stains on the goddamned wall.

In school I read about this writer who said he was like that, and if he could write down what was bothering him, what was pushing his skull from the inside, he could find relief, so I'm going to try that and hope for the best, because I've got to tell somebody, and I sure as hell can't tell Mommy-dear this, not that I can really tell her anything, but I've got to let this out of me and I only wish I could write faster, put it down as fast as I think.

This guy, Clyde Edson, he's really different and he's changed my life and I can feel it, I know it, it's down in my guts, squirming around like some kind of cancer, eating at me from the inside out, changing me into something new and fresh.

Being around Clyde is like being next to pure power, yeah, like that. Energy comes off of him in waves that nearly knock you down, and it's almost as if I'm absorbing that energy, and like maybe Clyde is sucking something out of me, something he can use, and the thought of that, of me giving Clyde something, whatever it is, makes me feel strong and whole. I mean, being around Clyde is like touching evil, or like that sappy Star Wars *shit about being seduced by the Dark Side of the Force, or some such fucking malarkey. But you see, this seduction by the Dark Side, it's a damn good fuck, a real jism-spurter, kind that makes your eyes bug, your back pop and your asshole pucker.*

Maybe I don't understand this yet, but I think it's sort of like this guy I read about once, this philosopher whose name I can't remember, but who said something about becoming a Superman. Not the guy with the cape. I'm not talking comic book, do-gooder crap here, I'm talking the real palooka. Can't remember just what he said, but from memory of what I read, and from the way I feel now, I figure that Clyde and I are two of the chosen, the Supermen of now, this moment, mutants for the future. I see it sort of like this: Man was once a wild animal type that made right by the size of his muscles and not by no bullshit government and laws. Time came when he had to become civilized to survive all the other hardnoses, but now that time has passed 'cause most of the hardnoses have died off and there isn't anything left but a bunch of fucking pussies who couldn't find their ass with a road map or figure how to wipe it without a blueprint. But you see, the mutations are happening again. New survivors are being born, and instead of that muck scientists say we crawled out of in the first place, we're crawling out of this mess the pussies have created with all their human rights shit and laws to protect the weak. Only this time, it isn't like before. Man might have crawled out of that slime to escape the sharks of the sea back then, but this time it's the goddamned sharks that are crawling out and we're mean sonofabitches with razor-sharp teeth and hides like fresh-dug gravel. And most different of all, there's a single-mindness about us that just won't let up.

I don't know if I'm saying this right, it's not all clear in my head and it's hard to put into words, but I can feel it, goddamnit, I can feel it. Time has come when we've become too civilized, overpopulated, so evolution has taken care of that, it's created a social mutation—Supermen like Clyde and me.

Clyde, he's the raw stuff, sewer sludge. He gets what he wants because he doesn't let anything stand in the way of what he wants, nothing. God, the conversations we had the last couple of days. . . . See now, lost my train of thought. . . . Oh yeah, the social mutations.

You see, I thought I was some kind of fucking freak all this time. But what it is, I'm just new, different. I mean, from as far back as I can remember, I've been different. I just don't react the way other people do, and I didn't understand why. Crying over dead puppies and shit like that. Big fucking deal. Dog's dead, he's dead. What the fuck do I care? It's the fucking dog that's dead, not me, so why should I be upset?

I mean, I remember this little girl next door that had this kitten when we were kids. She was always cooing and petting that little mangy bastard. And one day my dad—that was before he got tired of the Old Lady's whining and ran off, and good riddance, I say—sent me out to mow the yard. He had this thing about the yard being mowed, and he had this thing about me doing it. Well, I'm out there mowing it, and there's that kitten, wandering around in our yard. Now, I was sick of that kitten, Mr. Journal, so I picked it up and petted it, went to the garage and got myself a trowel. I went out in the front yard and dug a nice deep hole and put that kitten in it, all except the head, I left that sticking up. I patted the dirt around its neck real tight, then I went back and got the lawn mower, started it and began pushing it toward that little fucking cat. I could see its head twisting and it started moving its mouth—meowing, but I couldn't hear it, though I wish I could have—and I pushed the mower slow-like toward it, watching the grass chute from time to time, making sure the grass was really coming out of there in thick green blasts, and then I'd look up and see that kitten. When I got a few feet from it, I noticed that I was on a hard. I mean, I had a pecker you could have used for a cold chisel.

When I was three feet away, I starved to push that thing at a trot, and when I hit that cat, what a sound, and I had my eye peeled on that mower chute, and for a moment there was green and then there was red with green and hunks of ragged, gray fur spewing out, twisting onto the lawn.

Far as I knew, no one ever knew what I did. I just covered up the stump of the cat's neck real good and went on about my business. Later that evening when I was finishing up, the little shit next door came home and I could hear her calling out, "Kitty, kitty, kitty," it was all I could do not to fall down behind the mower laughing. But I kept a straight face, and when she came over and asked if I'd seen Morris—can you get that, Morris?—I said, "No, I'm sorry, I haven't," and she doesn't even get back to her house before she's crying and calling for that little fucking cat again.

Ah, but so much for amusing sidelights, Mr. Journal. I guess the point I'm trying to make is people get themselves tied up and concerned with the damnedest things, dogs and cats, stuff like that. I've yet to come across a dog or cat with a good, solid idea.

God, it feels good to say what I want to say for a change, and to have someone like Clyde who not only understands, but agrees, sees things the same way. Feels good to realize why all the Boy Scout good deed shit never made me feel diddlyshit. Understand now why the good grades and being called smart never thrilled me either. Was all bullshit, that's why. We Supermen don't go for that petty stuff, doesn't mean dick to us. Got no conscience 'cause a conscience isn't anything but a bullshit tool to make you a goddamned pussy, a candy-ass coward. We do what we want, as we please, when we want. I got this feeling that there are more and more like Clyde and me, and in just a little more time, we new ones will rule. And those who are born like us won't feel so out of step, because they'll know by then that the way they feel is okay, and that this is a dog-eat-dog world full of fucking red, raw meat, and there won't be any bullshit, pussy talk from them, they'll just go out and find that meat and eat it.

These new ones aren't going to be like the rest of the turds who have a clock to tell them when to get up in the morning, a boss that tells them what to do all day and a wife to nag them into doing it to keep her happy lest she cut off the pussy supply. No, no more of that. That old dog ain't going to hunt no more. From then on it'll be every man for himself, take what you want, take the pussy you want, whatever. What a world that would be, a world where every sonofabitch on the block is as mean as a junkyard dog. Every day would be an adventure, a constant battle of muscle and wits.

Oh man, the doors that Clyde has opened for me. He's something else. Just a few days ago I felt like I was some kind of freak hiding out in this world, then along comes Clyde and I find out that the freaks are plentiful, but the purely sane, like Clyde and me, are far and few—least right now. Oh yeah, that Clyde . . . it's not because he's so smart, either. Least not in a book-learned sense. The thing that impresses me about him is the fact that he's so raw and ready to bite, to just take life in his teeth and shake that motherfucker until the shit comes out.

Me and Clyde are like two halves of a whole. I'm blond and fair, intelligent, and he's dark, short and muscular, just able to read. I'm his gears and he's my oil, the stuff that makes me run right. We give to each other. . . . What we give is . . . Christ, this will sound screwy, Mr. Journal, but the closest I can come to describing it is psychic energy. We feed off each other.

Jesus Fucking H. Christ, starting to ramble. But feel better. That writer's idea must be working because I feel drained. Getting this out is like having been constipated for seventeen years of my life, and suddenly I've taken a laxative and I've just shit the biggest turd that can be shit by man, bear or elephant, and it feels so goddamned good, I want to yell to the skies.

Hell, I've had it. Feel like I been on an all-night fuck with a nympho on Spanish fly. Little later Clyde's supposed to come by, and I'm going out the window, going with him to see The House. He's told me about it, and it sounds really fine. He says he's going to show me some things I've never seen before. Hope so.

Damn, it's like waiting to be blessed with some sort of crazy, magical power or something. Like being given the ability to strike people with leprosy or wish some starlet up all naked and squirming on the rack and you with a dick as long and hard and hot as a heated poker, and her looking up at you and yelling for you to stick it to her before she cums just looking at you. Something like that, anyway.

Well, won't be long now and Clyde will be here. Guess I need to go sit over by the window, Mr. Journal, so I won't miss him. If Mom finds me missing after a while, things could get a little sticky, but I doubt she'll report her only, loving son to the parole board. Would be tacky. I always just tell her I'll be moving out just as soon as I can get me a job, and that shuts her up. Christ, she acts like she's in love with me or something, isn't natural.

Enough of this journal shit. Bring on the magic, Clyde.

5.

Two midnight shadows seemed to blow across the yard of the Blackwood home. Finally, those shadows broke out of the overlapping darkness of the trees, hit the moonlight and exploded into two teenagers. Clyde and Brian, running fast and hard. Their heels beat a quick, sharp rhythm on the sidewalk, like the too-fast ticking of clocks; timepieces from the Dark Side, knocking on toward a gruesome destiny.

After a moment the running stopped. Doors slammed. A car growled angrily. Lights burst on, and the black '66 sailed away from the curb. It sliced down the quiet street like a razor being sliced down a vein, cruised between dark houses where only an occasional light burned behind a window like a fearful gold eye gazing through a contact lens.

A low-slung, yellow dog making its nightly trashcan route crossed the street, fell into the Chevy's headlights.

The car whipped for the dog, but the animal was fast and lucky and only got its tail brushed before making the curb.

A car door flew open in a last attempt to bump the dog, but the dog was too far off the street. The car bounced up on the curb briefly, then lurched back onto the pavement.

The dog was gone now, blending into the darkness of a tree-shadowed yard.

The door slammed and the motor roared loudly. The car moved rapidly off into the night, and from its open windows, carried by the wind, came the high wild sound of youthful laughter.

6.

The House, as Clyde called it, was just below Stoker Street, just past where it intersected King, not quite book-ended between the two streets, but nearby, on a more narrow one. And there it waited.

Almost reverently, like a hearse that has arrived to pick up the dead, the black '66 Chevy entered the drive, parked.

Clyde and Brian got out, stood looking up at The House for a moment, considering it as two monks would a shrine.

Brian felt a sensation of trembling excitement, and although he would not admit it, a tinge of fear.

The House was big, old, gray and ugly. It looked gothic, out of step with the rest of the block. Like something out of Poe or Hawthorne. It crouched like a falsely obedient dog. Upstairs two windows showed light, seemed like cold, rectangular eyes considering prey.

The moon was bright enough that Brian could see the dead grass in the yard, the dead grass in all the yards down the block. It was the time of year for dead grass, but to Brian's way of thinking, this grass looked browner, deader. It was hard to imagine it ever being alive, ever standing up tall and bright and green.

The odd thing about The House was the way it seemed to command the entire block. It was not as large as it first appeared—though it was large—and the homes about it were newer and more attractive. They had been built when people still cared about the things they lived in, before the era of glass and plastic and builders who pocketed the money that should have been used on foundation and structure. Some of the houses stood a story above the gothic nightmare, but somehow they had taken on a rundown, anemic look, as if the old gray house was in fact some sort of alien vampire that could impersonate a house by day, but late at night it would turn its head with a wood-grain creak, look out of its cold, rectangle eyes and suddenly stand to reveal thick peasant-girl legs and feet beneath its firm wooden skin, and then it would start to stalk slowly and crazily down the street, the front door opening to reveal long, hollow, woodscrew teeth, and it would pick a house and latch onto it, fold back its rubbery front porch lips and burrow its many fangs into its brick or wood and suck out the architectural grace and all the love its builders had put into it. Then, as it turned to leave, bloated, satiated, the grass would die beneath its steps and it would creep and creak back down the street to find its place, and it would sigh deeply, contentedly, as it settled once more, and the energy and grace of the newer houses, the loved houses, would bubble inside its chest. Then it would sleep, digest, and wait.

"Let's go in," Clyde said.

The walk was made of thick white stones. They were cracked and weather swollen. Some of them had partially tumbled out of the ground dragging behind a wad of dirt and grass roots that made them look like abscessed teeth that had fallen from some giant's rotten gums.

Avoiding the precarious stepping-stones, they mounted the porch, squeaked the screen and groaned the door open. Darkness seemed to crawl in there. They stepped inside.

"Hold it," Clyde said. He reached and hit the wall switch.

Darkness went away, but the light wasn't much. The overhead fixture was coated with dust and it gave the room a speckled look, like sunshine through camouflage netting.

There was a high staircase to their left and it wound up to a dangerous-looking landing where the railing dangled out of line and looked ready to fall. Beneath the stairs, and to the far right of the room, were many doors. Above, behind the landing, were others, a half dozen in a soldier row. Light slithered from beneath the crack of one.

"Well?" Clyde said.

"I sort of expect Dracula to come down those stairs any moment."

Clyde smiled. "He's down here with you, buddy. Right here."

"What nice teeth you have."

"Uh-huh, real nice. How about a tour?"

"Lead on."

"The basement first?"

"Whatever."

"All right, the basement then. Come on."

Above them, from the lighted room, came the sound of a girl giggling, then silence.

"Girls?" Brian asked.

"More about that later."

They crossed the room and went to a narrow doorway with a recessed door. Clyde opened it. It was dark and foul-smelling down there, the odor held you like an embrace.

Brian could see the first three stair steps clearly, three more in shadow, the hint of one more, then nothing.

"Come on," Clyde said.

Clyde didn't bother with the light, if there was one. He stepped on the first step and started down.

Brian watched as Clyde was consumed by darkness. Cold air washed up and over him. He followed.

At the border of light and shadow, Brian turned to look behind him. There was only a rectangle of light to see, and that light seemed almost reluctant to enter the basement, as if it were too fearful.

Brian turned back, stepped into the veil of darkness, felt his way carefully with toe and heel along the wooden path. He half-expected the stairs to withdraw with a jerk and pull him into some creature's mouth, like a toad tongue that had speared a stupid fly. It certainly smelled bad enough down there to be a creature's mouth.

Brian was standing beside Clyde now. He stopped, heard Clyde fumble in his leather jacket for something. There was a short, sharp sound like a single cricket-click, and a match jumped to life, waved its yellow-red head around, cast the youngsters' shadows on the wall, made them look like monstrous Siamese twins, or some kind of two-headed, four-armed beast. Water was right at their feet. Another step and they would have been in it. A bead of sweat trickled from Brian's hair, ran down his nose and fell off. He realized that Clyde was testing him.

"Basements aren't worth a shit around this part of the country," Clyde said, "except for a few things they're not intended for."

"Like what?"

"You'll find out in plenty of time. Besides, how do I know I can trust you?"

That hurt Brian, but he didn't say anything. The first rule of being a Superman was to be above that sort of thing. You had to be strong, cool. Clyde would respect that sort of thing.

Clyde nodded at the water. "That's from last month's storm."

"Nice place if you raise catfish."

"Yeah."

The match went out. And somehow, Brian could sense Clyde's hand behind him, in a position to shove, considering it. Brian swallowed quietly, said very coolly, "Now what?"

After a long moment, Brian sensed Clyde's hand slip away, heard it crinkle into the pocket of his leather jacket. Clyde said, "Let's go back, unless you want to swim a little. Want to do that?"

"Didn't bring my trunks. Wouldn't want you to see my wee-wee."

Clyde laughed. "What's the matter, embarrassed at only having an inch?"

"Naw, was afraid you'd think it was some kind of big water snake and you'd try to cut it."

"How'd you know I had a knife?"

"Just figures."

"Maybe I like you."

"Big shit." But it was a big shit to Brian, and he was glad for the compliment, though he wasn't about to let on.

Clyde's jacket crinkled. Another match flared. "Easy turning," Clyde said, "these stairs are narrow, maybe rotten."

Brian turned briskly, started up ahead of Clyde.

"Easy, I said."

Brian stopped. He was just at the edge of the light. He turned, smiled down. He didn't know if Clyde could see his smile in the match light or not, but he hoped he could feel it. He decided to try a little ploy of his own.

"Easy, hell," he said. "Didn't you bring me down here just to see if I'd panic? To see if those creaky stairs and that water and you putting a hand behind me would scare me?"

Clyde's match went out. Brian could no longer see him clearly. That made him nervous.

"Guess that was the idea," Clyde said from the darkness.

Another match smacked to life.

"Thought so."

Brian turned, started up, stepping firmly, but not hurriedly. The stairs rocked beneath his feet.

It felt good to step into the room's speckled light. Brian sighed softly, took a deep breath. It was a musty breath, but it beat the sour, rotten smell of the basement. He leaned against the wall, waited.

After what seemed like a long time, Clyde stepped out of the basement and closed the door. He turned to look at Brian, smiled.

(What nice teeth you have.)

"You'll do," Clyde said softly. "You'll do." Now came the grand tour. Clyde led Brian through rooms stuffed with trash, full of the smell of piss, sweat, sex and dung, through empty rooms, cold and hollow as the inside of a petrified god's heart.

Rooms. So many rooms.

Finally the downstairs tour was finished and it was time to climb the stairs and find out what was waiting behind those doors, to look into the room filled with light.

They paused at the base of the stairs. Brian laid a hand on Clyde's shoulder.

"How in hell did you come by all this?" he asked.

Clyde smiled.

"Is it yours?" Brian asked.

"All mine," Clyde said. "Got it easy. Everything I do comes easy. One day I decided to move in and I did."

"How did you—"

"Hang on, listen: You see, this was once a fancy apartment house. Had a lot of old folks as customers, sort of an old fossil box. I needed a place to stay, was living on the streets then. I liked it here, but didn't have any money.

"So I found the caretaker. Place had a full-time one then. Guy with a crippled leg.

"I say to this gimp, I'm moving into the basement—wasn't full of water then—and if he don't like it, I'll push his face in for him. Told him if he called the cops I'd get him on account of I'm a juvenile and I've been in and out of kiddie court so many times I got a lunch card. Told him I knew about his kids, how pretty that little daughter of his was, how pretty I thought she'd look on the end of my dick. Told him I'd put her there and spin her around on it like a top. I'd done my homework on the old fart, knew all about him, about his little girl and little boy.

"So, I scared him good. He didn't want any trouble and he let me and the cunt I was banging then move in."

A spark moved in Clyde's eyes. "About the cunt, just so you know I play hardball, she isn't around anymore. She and the brat she was going to have are taking an extended swimming lesson."

"You threw her in the bay?"

Clyde tossed his head at the basement.

"Ah," Brian said, and he felt an erection, a real blue-veiner. Something warm moved from the tips of his toes to the base of his skull, foamed inside his brain. It was as if his bladder had backed up and filled his body with urine. Old Clyde had actually killed somebody and had no remorse, was in fact proud. Brian liked that. It meant Clyde was as much of a Superman as he expected. And since Clyde admitted the murder to him, he knew he trusted him, considered him a comrade, a fellow Superman.

"What happened next?" Brian asked. It was all he could do not to lick his lips.

"Me and the cunt moved in. Couple guys I knew wanted to come too, bring their cunts along. I let them. Before long there's about a half dozen of us living in the goddamned basement. We got the caretaker to see we got fed, and he did it too on account of he was a weenie, and we kept reminding him how much we like little-girl pussy. I got to where I could describe what we wanted to do to her real good.

"Anyway, that went on for a while, then one day he doesn't show up with the grub. Found out later that he'd packed up the dumpling wife, the two ankle-biters and split. So I say to the guys—by the way, don't ask no cunt nothing, they got opinions on everything and not a bit of it's worth stringy dogshit, unless you want to know the best way to put a tampon in or what color goes well with blue—so, I say to the guys, this ain't no way to live, and we start a little storm trooper campaign. Scared piss out of some of the old folks, roughed up an old lady, nailed her dog to the door by its ears."

"Didn't the cops come around?"

"Yeah. They came and got us on complaints, told us to stay out. But what could they do? No one had seen us do a damn thing except those complaining, and it was just our word against theirs. They made us move out though.

"So we went and had a little talk with the manager, made a few threats, got a room out of the deal and started paying rent. By this time we had the cunts hustling for us, bouncing tail on the streets and bringing in a few bucks. Once we start paying rent, what can they say? But we keep up the stormtrooper campaign, just enough to keep it scary around here. Before long the manager quit and all the old folks hiked."

"What about the owner?"

"He came around. We paid the rent and he let us stay. He's a slumlord anyway. It was the old folks kept the place up. After they left, it got pretty trashy, and this guy wasn't going to put out a cent on the place. He was glad to take our money and run. We were paying him more than all the old codgers together. The pussy business was really raking in the coins. And besides, he don't want to make us mad, know what I mean?"

"Some setup."

"It's sweet all right. Like being a juvenile. The courts are all fucked up on that one. They don't know what to do with us, so they usually just say the hell with us. It's easier to let us go than to hassle with us. After you're eighteen life isn't worth living. That's when the rules start to apply to us too. Right now we're just misguided kids who'll straighten out in time."

"I hear that."

"Good. Let's go upstairs. Got some people I want you to meet."

"Yeah?"

"A girl I want you to fuck."

"Yeah?"

"Yeah. Got this one cunt that's something else. Thirteen years old, a runaway or something. Picked her up off the street about a month ago. Totally wiped out in the brain department, not that a cunt's got that much brain to begin with, but this one is a clean slate. But, man, does she have tits. They're big as footballs. She's as good a fuck as a grown woman."

"This going to cost me?"

"You kidding? You get what you want, no charge—money anyway."

"What's that mean?"

"I want your soul, not your money."

Brian grinned. "So what are you, the devil? Thought you were Dracula."

"I'm both of them."

"Do I have to sign something in blood?"

Clyde laughed hysterically. "Sure, that's a good one. Blood. Write something in fucking blood. I like you, Brian, I really do."

So Brian saw the dark rooms upstairs, and finally the one with the light and the people.

The room stank. There was a mattress on the floor and there was a nude girl on the mattress and there was a nude boy on the girl and the girl was not moving but the boy was moving a lot.

On the other side of the mattress a naked blonde girl squatted next to a naked boy. The girl had enormous breasts and dark brown eyes. The boy was stocky and square-jawed. They lifted their heads as Clyde and Brian came in, and Brian could see they were stoned to the max. The two smiled at them in unison, as if they had but one set of facial muscles between them.

The boy riding the girl grunted, once, real loud. After a moment he rolled off her smiling, his penis half-hard, dripping.

The girl on the mattress still did not move. She lay with her eyes closed and her arms by her sides.

"This is Looney Tunes," Clyde said, pointing to the boy who had just rolled off the girl. "This is Stone," he said, pointing to the stocky boy. "If he talks, I've never heard it." He did not introduce either girl. "This is all we got around here right now, cream of the crop."

The girl on the mattress still had not moved.

The one called Looney Tunes laughed once in a while, for no apparent reason.

Clyde said, "Go ahead and tend to your rat killing, me and Brian got plans." Then he snapped his fingers and pointed to the nude girl with the big breasts and the silly smile.

She stood up, wavering a bit. With ten pounds and something to truly smile about, she might have been pretty. She looked like she needed a bath.

Clyde held out his hand. She came around the mattress and took it. He put an arm around her waist.

The one called Stone crawled on top of the girl on the mattress.

She still did not move.

Brian could see now that her eyes were actually only half-closed and her eyeballs were partly visible. They looked as cool and expressionless as marbles.

Stone took hold of his sudden erection and put it in her.

She still did not move.

Stone began to grunt.

Looney Tunes laughed.

She still did not move.

"Come on," Clyde said to Brian, "the next room."

So they went out of there, the big-eyed girl sandwiched between them.

There was a small mattress in the closet in the next room, and Clyde, feeling his way around in the dark with experienced ease, pulled it out. He said, "Keeping in practice for when I quit paying the light bill, learning to be a bat."

"I see," Brian said. The girl leaned against him. She muttered something once, but it made no sense. She was so high on nose candy and cheap wine she didn't know where she was or who she was. She smelled like mildewed laundry.

After Clyde had tossed the mattress on the floor, he took his clothes off, called them over. The girl leaned on Brian all the way across the room.

When they were standing in front of Clyde, he said, "This is the big-titted thirteen-year-old I told you about. Looks older, don't she?" But he didn't wait for Brian to answer. He said loudly to the girl, "Come here."

She crawled on the mattress. Brian took his clothes off. They all lay down together. The mattress smelled of dirt, wine and sweat.

And that night Brian and Clyde had the thirteen-year-old, and later, when Brian tried to think back on the moment, he would not be able to remember her face, only that she was blonde, had massive breasts and dark eyes like pools of fresh-perked coffee, pools that went down and down into her head like wet tunnels to eternity.

She was so high they could have poked her with knives and she would not have felt it. She was just responding in automaton fashion. Clyde had it in her ass and Brian had it in her mouth, and they were pumping in unison, the smell of their exertion mingling with hers, filling the room.

The girl was slobbering and choking on Brian's penis and he was ramming it harder and harder into her mouth, and he could feel her teeth scraping his flesh, making his cock bleed, and it seemed to him that he was extending all the way down her throat, all the way through her, and that the head of his penis was touching Clyde's and Clyde's penis was like the finger of God giving life to the clay form of Adam, and that he was Adam, and he was receiving that spark from the Holy On High, and for

the power and the glory he was grateful; made him think of the Frankenstein monster and how it must have felt when its creator threw the switch
and drove the power of the storm through its body and above the roll of
the thunder and the crackling flash of lighting Dr. Frankenstein yelled at
the top of his lungs, *"It's alive!"*

Then he and Clyde came in white-hot-atomic-blast unison and in Brian's mind it was the explosive ending of the old world and the Big Bang
creation of the new.

Only the sound of panting now, the pleasant sensation of his organ
draining into the blonde's mouth.

Clyde reached out and touched Brian's hand, squeezed his fingers, and
Clyde's touch was as cold and clammy as the hand of death.

Clyde drove Brian home. Brian stole silently into the house and climbed
the stairs. Once in his room he went to the window to look out. He could
hear Clyde's '66 Chevy in the distance, and though it was a bright night
and he could see real far, he could not see as far as Clyde had gone.

And later:

Back at The House the girl Clyde and Brian had shared would start
to wail and fight invisible harpies in her head, and Clyde would take her
to the basement for a little swim. The body of the girl on the mattress
would follow suit. Neither managed much swimming; and there would
be a series of unprecedented robberies that night all over the city; and in
a little quiet house near Galveston Bay, an Eagle Scout and honor student
would kill his father and rape his mother; and an on-duty policeman with
a fine family and plenty of promotion to look forward to would pull over
to the curb on a dark street and put his service revolver in his mouth and
pull the trigger, coating the back windshield with brains, blood and clinging skull shrapnel; and a nice meek housewife in a comfortable house by
Sea-Arama would take a carving knife to her husband's neck while he
slept; would tell police later that it was because he said he didn't like the
way she'd made the roast that night, which was ridiculous since he'd liked
it fixed exactly that same way the week before.

All in all, it was a strange night in Galveston, Texas. A lot of dogs howled.

This one came to me in a flash and was written in a flash, and I think to say any more about it might ruin it. It's short, but a definite favorite of mine.

BILLIE SUE

About a week before the house next door sold to the young couple, Billie Sue and I broke up. It was painful and my choice. Some stupid argument we'd had, but I tried to tell myself I had made the right decision.

And in the light of day it seemed I had. But come night when the darkness set in and the king-size bed was like a great raft on which I floated, I missed Billie Sue. I missed her being next to me, holding her. The comfort she had afforded me had been greater than I imagined, and now that she was gone, I felt empty, as if I had been drained from head to toe and that my body was a husk and nothing more.

But the kids next door changed that. For a time.

I was off for the summer. I teach math during the high school term, and since Billie Sue and I had broken up, I had begun to wish that I had signed on to teach summer school. It would have been some kind of diversion. Something to fill my days with besides thinking of Billie Sue.

About the second day the kids moved in, the boy was out mowing their yard, and I watched him from the window for a while, then made up some lemonade and took it out on the patio and went over and stood by where he was mowing.

He stopped and killed the engine and smiled at me. He was a nice-looking kid, if a little bony. He had very blond hair and was shirtless and was just starting to get hair on his chest. It looked like down, and the thought of that made me feel ill at ease, because, bizarrely enough, the downlike hair made me think of Billie Sue, how soft she was, and that in turn made me think of the empty house and the empty bed and the nights that went on and on.

"Hey," the boy said. "You're our neighbor?"

"That's right. Kevin Pierce."

"Jim Howel. Glad to meet you." We shook hands. I judged him to be about twenty. Half my age.

"Come on and meet my wife," he said. "You married?"

"No," I said, but I felt strange saying it. It wasn't that Billie Sue and I were married, but it had seemed like it. The way I felt about her, a marriage license wasn't necessary. But now she was gone, and the fact that we had never officially been hitched meant nothing.

I walked with him to the front door, and about the time we got there, a young woman, his wife, of course, opened the screen and looked out. She wore a tight green halter top that exposed a beautiful brown belly and a belly button that looked as if it had been made for licking. She had on white shorts and thongs. Her black hair was tied back, and some of it had slipped out of the tie and was falling over her forehead and around her ears, and it looked soft and sensual. In fact, she was quite the looker.

It wasn't that her face was all that perfect, but it was soft and filled with big brown eyes, and she had those kind of lips that look as if they've been bruised and swollen. But not too much. Just enough to make you want to put your lips on them, to maybe soothe the pain.

"Oh, hi," she said.

"Hi," I said.

Jim introduced us. Her name was Sharon.

"I've got some lemonade next door, if you two would like to come over and share it," I said. "Just made it."

"Well, yeah," said Jim. "I'd like that. I'm hot as a pistol."

"I guess so," said the girl, and I saw Jim throw her a look. A sort of, hey, don't be rude kind of look. If she saw the look, she gave no sign of it.

As we walked over to my house, I said, "You folks been married long?"

"Not long," Jim said. "How long, honey?"

"Eighteen months."

"Well, congratulations," I said. "Newlyweds."

We sat out on the patio and drank the lemonade, and Jim did most of the talking. He wanted to be a lawyer, and Sharon was working at some café in town putting him through. He tried to talk like he was really complimenting her, and I think he was, but I could tell Sharon wasn't feeling complimented. There was something about her silence that said a lot. It said, Look what I've got myself into. Married this chatterbox who wants to be a lawyer and can't make a dollar 'cause he's got to study, so I've got to work, and law school isn't any hop, skip, and a jump. We're talking years of tips and pinches on the ass, and is this guy worth it anyhow?

She said all that and more without so much as opening her mouth.

When we finished off the lemonade, Jim got up and said he had to finish the lawn.

"I'll sit here a while," Sharon said. "You go on and mow."

Jim looked at her, then he looked at me and made a smile. "Sure," he said to her. "We'll eat some lunch after a while."

"I ate already," she said. "Get you a sandwich, something out of the box."

"Sure," he said, and went back to mow.

As he went, I noticed his back was red from the sun. I said, "You ought to tell him to get some lotion on. Look at his back."

She swiveled in her chair and looked, turned back to me, said, "He'll find out soon enough he ought to wear lotion. You got anything stronger than lemonade?"

I went in the house, got a couple of beers and a bottle of Jack Daniel's, and some glasses. We drank the beers out on the veranda, then, as it turned hotter, we came inside and sat on the couch and drank the whiskey. While Jim's mower droned on, we talked about this and that, but not really about anything. You know what I mean. Just small talk that's so small it's hardly talk.

After about an hour, I finally decided what we were really talking about, and I put my hand out and touched her hand on the couch and she didn't move it.

"Maybe you ought to go on back."

"You want me to?"

"That's the problem, I don't want you to."

"I just met you."

"I know. That's another reason you ought to go back to your husband."

"He's a boring son of a bitch. You know that. I thought he was all right when we met. Good-looking and all, but he's as dull as a cheap china plate, and twice as shallow. I'm nineteen years old. I don't want to work in any goddamn café for years while he gets a job where he can wear a suit and get people divorces. I want to get my divorce now."

She slid over and we kissed. She was soft and pliant, and there were things about her that were better than Billie Sue, and for a moment I didn't think of Billie Sue at all. I kissed her for a long time and touched her, and finally the mower stopped.

"Goddamn it," she said. "That figures."

She touched me again, and in the right place. She got up and retied her halter top, which I had just managed to loosen.

"I'm sorry," I said. "I let this get out of hand."

"Hell, I'm the one sorry it didn't get completely out of hand. But it will. We're neighbors."

I tried to avoid Sharon after that, and managed to do so for a couple days. I even thought about trying to patch things up with Billie Sue, but just couldn't. My goddamn pride.

On the fourth night after they'd moved in, I woke up to the sound of dishes breaking. I got out of bed and went into the living room and looked out the window at my neighbor's house, the source of the noise. It was Sharon yelling and tossing things that had awakened me. The yelling went on for a time. I got a beer out of the box and sat down with a chair pulled up at the window and watched. There was a light on in their living room window, and now and then their shadows would go across the light, then move away.

Finally I heard the front door slam, and Jim went out, got in their car and drove away. He hadn't so much as departed when Sharon came out of the house and started across the yard toward my place.

I moved the chair back to its position and sat down on the couch and waited. She knocked on the door. Hard. I let her knock for a while, then I got up and answered the door. I was in my underwear when I answered, but of course, I didn't care. She was in a short black nightie, no shoes, and she didn't care either.

I let her in. She said, "We had a fight. I hope the son of a bitch doesn't come back."

She took hold of me then, and we kissed, and then we made our way to the bedroom, and it was sweet, the way she loved me, and finally, near morning, we fell asleep.

When I awoke it was to Jim's voice. In our haste, we had left the front door open, and I guess he'd seen the writing on the wall all along, and now he was in the house, standing over the bed yelling.

Sharon sat up in bed, and the sheet fell off her naked breast and she yelled back. I sat up amazed, more than embarrassed. I had to learn to lock my doors, no matter what.

This yelling went on for a time, lots of cussing, then Jim grabbed her by the wrist and jerked her out of the bed and onto the floor.

I jumped up then and hit him, hit him hard enough to knock him down. He sat up and opened his mouth and a tooth fell out.

"Oh my God, Jim," Sharon said. She slid across the floor and took his head in her hands and kissed his cheek. "Oh, baby, are you all right?"

"Yeah, I'm all right," he said.

I couldn't believe it. "What the hell?" I said.

"You didn't have to hit him," Sharon said. "You're older, stronger. You hurt him."

I started to argue, but by that time Jim was up and Sharon had her arm around him. She said, "I'm sorry, baby, I'm so sorry. Let's go home."

Sharon pulled on her nightie, and away they went. I picked up the panties she'd left and put them over my head, trying to look as foolish as I felt. They smelled good though.

Dumb asshole, I said to myself. How many times have they done this? There are strange people in this world. Some get their kicks from wearing leather, being tied down and pissed on, you name it, but this pair has a simpler method of courtship. They fight with each other, break up, then

Sharon flirts and sleeps around until Jim discovers her, then they yell at each other and he forgives her, and he's all excited to think she's been in bed with another man, and she's all excited to have been there, and they're both turned on and happy.

Whatever. I didn't want any part of it.

That night I decided to make up with Billie Sue. I got my shovel out of the garage and went out and dug her up from under the rose bushes. I got her out of there and brushed the dirt off and carried her inside. I washed her yellow body off in the sink. I fondled her bill and told her I was sorry. I was so sorry I began to cry. I just couldn't help myself. I told her I'd never bury her in the dirt again.

I filled the bathtub with water and put Billie Sue in there and watched her float. I turned her in the water so that she could watch me undress. I stripped off my clothes slowly and got in the tub with her. She floated and bobbed toward me, and I picked her up and squeezed her and dirt puffed from the noisemaker in her beak and the sound she made was not quite a squeak or a quack.

I laughed. I squeezed her hard, the way she likes it, the way she's always liked it since the first time my mother gave her to me when I was a child. I squeezed her many times. I floated her in the tub with me, moved her around my erection, which stuck up out of the water like a stick in a pond, and I knew then what I should have always known.

Billie Sue was the love of my life.

Perhaps we were not too unlike that silly couple next door. We fought too. We fought often. We had broken up before. I had buried her under the rose bushes before, though never for this long. But now, holding her, squeezing her hard, listening to her quack, I knew never again. I began to laugh and laugh and laugh at what she was saying. She could be like that when she wanted. So funny. So forgiving.

Oh, Billie Sue. Billie Sue. My little rubber duckie poo.

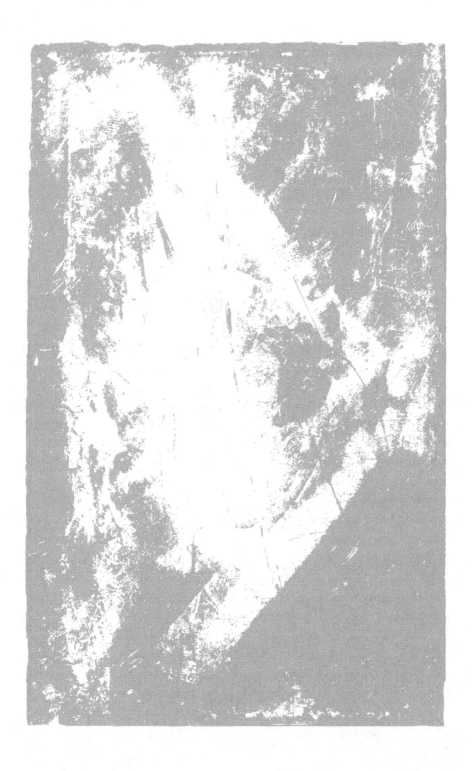

"The Phone Woman" is based on a series of weird and true events. "The Phone Woman" was real and really did come to our house in much the way described here. Keith, my son, and my wife, Karen, and I had a similar event happen with her in the house, and she did come back. The rest, of course, I made up. But it's something that's sort of haunted me for years. It struck me, if she had come to the wrong house, and I heard rumors that she eventually did, it might have worked out worse than it did in real life. I hope things came out better for her in time, though I'm not optimistic.

THE PHONE WOMAN

JOURNAL ENTRIES
A WEEK TO REMEMBER . . .

After this, my little white-page friend, you shall have greater security, kept under not only lock and key, but you will have a hiding place. If I were truly as smart as I sometimes think I am, I wouldn't write this down. I know better. But, I am compelled.

Compulsion. It comes out of nowhere and owns us all. We put a suit and tie and hat on the primitive part of our brain and call it manners and civilization, but ultimately, it's just a suit and tie and a hat. The primitive brain is still primitive, and it compels, pulses to the same dark beat that made our less civilized ancestors and the primordial ooze before them throb to simple, savage rhythms of sex, death, and destruction.

Our nerves call out to us to touch and taste life, and without our suits of civilization, we can do that immediately. Take what we need if we've muscle enough. Will enough. But all dressed up in the trappings of civilization, we're forced to find our thrills vicariously. And eventually, that is not enough. Controlling our impulses that way is like having someone eat your food for you. No taste. No texture. No nourishment. Pitiful business.

Without catering to the needs of our primitive brains, without feeding impulses, trying instead to get what we need through books and films and the lives of the more adventurous, we cease to live. We wither. We bore ourselves and others. We die. And are glad of it.

Whatcha gonna do, huh?

Saturday Morning, June 10th, through Saturday 17th:
I haven't written in a while, so I'll cover a few days, beginning with a week ago today.

It was one of those mornings when I woke up on the wrong side of the bed, feeling a little out of sorts, mad at the wife over something I've forgotten and she probably hasn't forgotten, and we grumbled down the hall, into the kitchen, and there's our dog, a Siberian Husky—my wife always refers to him as a Suburban Husky because of his pampered lifestyle, though any resemblance to where we live and suburbia requires a great deal of faith— and he's smiling at us, and then we see why he's smiling. Two reasons: (1) He's happy to see us. (2) He feels a little guilty.

He has reason to feel guilty. Not far behind him, next to the kitchen table, was a pile of shit. I'm not talking your casual little whoopsie-doo, and I'm not talking your inconvenient pile, and I'm not talking six to eight turds the size of large bananas. I'm talking a certified, pure-dee, god-damn prize-winning SHIT. There were enough dog turds there to shovel out in a pickup truck and dump on the lawn and let dry so you could use them to build an adobe hut big enough to keep your tools in and have room to house your cat in the winter.

And right beside this sterling deposit, was a lake of piss wide enough and deep enough to go rowing on.

I had visions of a Siberian Husky hat and slippers, or possibly a nice throw rug for the bedroom, a necklace of dog claws and teeth; maybe cut that smile right out of his face and frame it. But the dog-lover in me took over, and I put him outside in his pen where he cooled his dewclaws for a while. Then I spent about a half-hour cleaning up dog shit while my wife spent the same amount of time keeping our two-year-old son, Kevin, known to me as Fruit of My Loins, out of the shit.

Yep, Oh Great White Page of a Diary, he was up now. It always works that way. In times of greatest stress, in times of greatest need for contemplation or privacy, like when you're trying to get that morning piece off the Old Lady, the kid shows up, and suddenly it's as if you've been deposited inside an ant farm and the ants are crawling and stinging. By the time I finished cleaning up the mess, it was time for breakfast, and I got to tell you, I didn't want anything that looked like link sausage that morning.

So Janet and I ate, hoping that what we smelled while eating was the aroma of disinfectant and not the stench of shit wearing a coat of disinfectant, and we watched the kid spill his milk eighty-leben times and throw food and drop stuff on the floor, and me and the wife we're fussing at each other more and more, about whatever it was we were mad about that morning—a little item intensified by our dog's deposits—and by the time we're through eating our meal, and Janet leaves me with Fruit of My Loins and his View-Master and goes out to the laundry room to do what the room is named for—probably went out there to beat the laundry clean with rocks or bricks, pretending shirts and pants were my head—I'm beginning to think things couldn't get worse. About that time the earth passes through the tail of a comet or something, some kind of dimensional gate is opened, and the world goes weird.

There's a knock at the door.

At first I thought it was a bird pecking on the glass, it was that soft. Then it came again and I went to the front door and opened it, and there stood a woman about five feet tall wearing a long, wool coat, and untied, flared-at-the-ankles shoes, and a ski cap decorated with a silver pin. The wool ski cap was pulled down so tight over her ears her face was pale. Keep in mind that it was probably eighty degrees that morning, and the temperature was rising steadily, and she was dressed like she was on her way to plant the flag at the summit of Everest. Her age was hard to guess. Had that kind of face. She could have been twenty-two or forty-two.

She said, "Can I use your phone, mister? I got an important call to make."

Well, I didn't see any ready-to-leap companions hiding in the shrubbery, and I figured if she got out of line I could handle her, so I said, "Yeah, sure. Be my guest," and let her in.

The phone was in the kitchen, on the wall, and I pointed it out to her, and me and Fruit of My Loins went back to doing what we were doing, which was looking at the View-Master. We switched from Goofy to Winnie the Pooh, the one about Tigger in the tree, and it was my turn to look at it, and I couldn't help but hear that my guest's conversation with her mother was becoming stressful—I knew it was her mother because she addressed her by that title—and suddenly Fruit of My Loins yelled, "Wook, Daddy, wook."

I turned and "wooked," and what do I see but what appears to be some rare tribal dance, possibly something having originated in higher altitudes where the lack of oxygen to the brain causes wilder abandon with the dance steps. This gal was all over the place. Fred Astaire with a hot coat hanger up his ass couldn't have been any brisker. I've never seen anything like it. Then, in mid-do-si-do, she did a leap like cheerleaders do, one of those things where they kick their legs out to the side, open up like a nutcracker and kick the palms of their hands, then she hit the floor on her ass, spun, and wheeled as if on a swivel into the hallway and went out of sight. Then there came a sound from in there like someone on speed beating the bongos. She hadn't dropped the phone either. The wire was stretched tight around the corner and was vibrating like a big fish was on the line.

I dashed over there and saw she was lying crosswise in the hallway, bamming her head against the wall, clutching at the phone with one hand and pulling her dress up over her waist with the other, and she was making horrible sounds and rolling her eyes, and I immediately thought: this is it, she's gonna die. Then I saw she wasn't dying, just thrashing, and I decided it was an epileptic fit.

I got down and took the phone away from her, took hold of her jaw, got her tongue straight without getting bit, stretched her out on the floor away from the wall, picked up the phone and told her mama, who was still fussing about something or another, that things weren't so good, hung up on her in mid-sentence and called the ambulance.

I ran out to the laundry room, told Janet a strange woman was in our hallway puffing her dress over her head and that an ambulance was coming. Janet, bless her heart, has become quite accustomed to weird events following me around, and she went outside to direct the ambulance, like one of those people at the airport with light sticks. I went back to the woman and watched her thrash awhile, trying to make sure she didn't choke to death, or injure herself, and Fruit of My Loins kept clutching my leg and asking me what was wrong. I didn't know what to tell him.

After what seemed a couple of months and a long holiday, the ambulance showed up with a whoop of siren, and I finally decided the lady was doing as good as she was going to do, so I went outside. On either side of my walk were all these people. It's like Bradbury's story "The Crowd." The one where when there's an accident all these strange people show up out of nowhere and stand around and watch.

I'd never seen but two of these people before in my life, and I've been living in this neighborhood for years.

One lady immediately wanted to go inside and pray for the woman, who she somehow knew, but Janet whispered to me that there wasn't enough room for our guest in there, let alone this other woman and her buddy, God, so I didn't let her in.

All the other folks are just a jabbering, and about all sorts of things. One woman said to another, "Mildred, how you been?"

"I been good. They took my kids away from me this morning, though. I hate that. How you been?"

"Them hogs breeding yet?" one man says to another, and the other goes into not only that they're breeding, but he tells how much fun they're having at it.

Then here comes the ambulance boys with a stretcher. One of the guys knew me somehow, and he stopped and said, "You're that writer, aren't you?"

I admitted it.

"I always wanted to write. I got some ideas that's make a good book and a movie. I'll tell you about 'em. I got good ideas, I just can't write them down. I could tell them to you and you could write them up and we could split the money."

"Could we talk about this later?" I said. "There's a lady in there thrashing in my hallway."

So they went in with the stretcher, and after a few minutes the guy I talked to came out and said, "We can't get her out of there and turned through the door. We may have to take your back door out."

That made no sense to me at all. They brought the stretcher through and now they were telling me they couldn't carry it out. But I was too addled to argue and told them to do what they had to do.

Well, they managed her out the back door without having to remodel our home after all, and when they came around the edge of the house I heard the guy I'd talked to go, "Ahhh, damn, I'd known it was her I wouldn't have come."

I thought they were going to set her and the stretcher down right there, but they went out to the ambulance and jerked open the door and tossed her and the stretcher inside like they were tossing a dead body over a cliff. You could hear the stretcher strike the back of the ambulance and bounce forward and slide back again.

I had to ask: "You know her?"

"Dark enough in the house there, I couldn't tell at first. But when we got outside, I seen who it was. She does this all the time, but not over on this side of town in a while. She don't take her medicine on purpose so she'll have fits when she gets stressed, or she fakes them, like this time. Way she gets attention. Sometimes she hangs herself, cuts off her air. Likes the way it feels. Sexual or something. She's damn near died half-dozen times. Between you and me, wish she'd go on and do it and save me some trips."

And the ambulance driver and his assistant were out of there. No lights. No siren.

Well, the two people standing in the yard that we knew were still there when I turned around, but the others, like mythical creatures, were gone, turned to smoke, dissolved, become one with the universe, whatever. The two people we knew, elderly neighbors, said they knew the woman, who by this time I had come to think of as the Phone Woman.

"She goes around doing that," the old man said. "She stays with her mamma who lives on the other side of town, but they get in fights on account of the girl likes to hang herself sometimes for entertainment. Never quite makes it over the ridge, you know, but gets her mother worked up. They say her mother used to do that too, hang herself, when she was a girl. She outgrew it. I guess the girl there . . . you know I don't even know her name . . . must have seen her mamma do that when she was little, and it kind of caught on. She has that 'lepsy stuff too, you know, thrashing around and all, biting on her tongue?"

I said I knew and had seen a demonstration of it this morning.

"Anyway," he continued, "they get in fights and she comes over here and tries to stay with some relatives that live up the street there, but they don't cotton much to her hanging herself to things. She broke down their clothesline post last year. Good thing it was old, or she'd been dead. Wasn't nobody home that time. I hear tell they sometimes go off and leave her there and leave rope and wire and stuff laying around, sort of hoping, you know. But except for that time with the clothesline, she usually does her hanging when someone's around. Or she goes in to use the phone at houses and does what she did here."

"She's nutty as a fruitcake," said the old woman. "She goes back on behind here to where that little trailer park is, knocks on doors where the wet backs live, about twenty to a can, and they ain't got no phone, and she knows it. She's gotten raped couple times doing that, and it ain't just them Mex's that have got to her. White folks, niggers. She tries to pick who she thinks will do what she wants. She wants to be raped. It's like the hanging. She gets some kind of attention out of it, some kind of living. 'Course, I ain't saying she chose you cause you're that kind of person."

I assured her I understood.

The old couple went home then, and another lady came up, and sure enough, I hadn't seen her before either, and she said, "Did that crazy ole girl come over here and ask to use the phone, then fall down on you and flop?"

"Yes, ma'am."

"Does that all the time."

Then this woman went around the corner of the house and was gone, and I never saw her again. In fact, with the exception of the elderly neighbors and the Phone Woman, I never saw any of those people again and never knew where they came from. Next day there was a soft knock on the door. It was the Phone Woman again. She asked to use the phone.

I told her we had taken it out.

She went away and I saw her several times that day. She'd come up our street about once every half hour, wearing that same coat and hat and those sad shoes, and I guess it must have been a hundred and ten out there. I watched her from the window. In fact I couldn't get any writing done because I was watching for her. Thinking about her lying there on the floor, pulling her dress up, flopping. I thought too of her hanging herself now and then, like she was some kind of suit on a hanger.

Anyway, the day passed and I tried to forget about her, then the other night, Monday probably, I went out on the porch to smoke one of my rare cigars (about four to six a year), and I saw someone coming down the dark street, and from the way that someone walked, I knew it was her, the Phone Woman.

She went on by the house and stopped down the road a piece and looked up and I looked where she was looking, and through the trees I could see what she saw. The moon.

We both looked at it a while, and she finally walked on, slow, with her head down, and I put my cigar out well before it was finished and went inside and brushed my teeth and took off my clothes and tried to go to sleep. Instead, I lay there for a long time and thought about her, walking those dark streets, maybe thinking about her mom, or a lost love, or a phone, or sex in the form of rape because it was some kind of human connection, about hanging herself because it was attention and it gave her a sexual high . . . and then again, maybe I'm full of shit and she wasn't thinking about any of these things.

Then it struck me suddenly, as I lay there in bed beside my wife, in my quiet house, my son sleeping with his teddy bear in the room across the way, that maybe she was the one in touch with the world, with life, and that I was the one gone stale from civilization. Perhaps life had been civilized right out of me.

The times I had truly felt alive, in touch with my nerve centers, were in times of violence or extreme stress. Where I had grown up, in Mud Creek, violence simmered underneath everyday life like lava cooking beneath a thin crust of earth, ready at any time to explode and spew. I had been in fights, been cut by knives. I once had a job bouncing drunks. I had been a bodyguard in my earlier years, had illegally carried a .38. On one occasion, due to a dispute the day before while protecting my employer, who sometimes dealt with a bad crowd, a man I had insulted and hit with my fists pulled a gun on me, and I had been forced to pull mine. The both of us ended up with guns in our faces, looking into each other's eyes, knowing full well our lives hung by a thread and the snap of a trigger.

I had killed no one, and had avoided being shot. The Mexican standoff ended with us both backing away and running off, but there had been that moment when I knew it could be all over in a flash. Out of the picture in a blaze of glory. No old folks' home for me. No drool running down my chin and some young nurse wiping my ass, thinking how repulsive and old I was, wishing for quitting time so she could roll up with some young stud some place sweet and cozy, open her legs to him with a smile and a sigh, and later a passionate scream, while in the meantime, back at the old folks' ranch, I lay in the bed with a dead dick and an oxygen mask strapped to my face.

Something about the Phone Woman had clicked with me. I understood her suddenly. I understood then that the lava that had boiled beneath the civilized facade of my brain was no longer boiling. It might be bubbling way down low, but it wasn't boiling, and the realization of that went all over me and I felt sad, very, very sad. I had dug a grave and crawled into it and was slowly pulling the dirt in after me. I had a home. I had a wife. I had a son. Dirt clods all. Dirt clods filling in my grave while life simmered somewhere down deep and useless within me.

I lay there for a long time with tears on my cheeks before exhaustion took over and I slept in a dark world of dormant passion.

Couple days went by, and one night after Fruit of My Loins and Janet were in bed, I went out on the front porch to sit and look at the stars and think about what I'm working on—a novella that isn't going well—and what do I see but the Phone Woman, coming down the road again, walking past the house, stopping once more to look at the moon.

I didn't go in this time, but sat there waiting, and she went on up the street and turned right and went out of sight. I walked across the yard and went out to the center of the street and watched her back going away from me, mixing into the shadow of the trees and houses along the street, and I followed.

I don't know what I wanted to see, but I wanted to see something, and I found for some reason that I was thinking of her lying there on the floor in my hallway, her dress up, the mound of her sex, as they say in porno novels, pushing up at me. The thought gave me an erection, and I was conscious of how silly this was, how unattractive this woman was to me, how odd she looked, and then another thought came to me: I was a snob. I didn't want to feel sexual towards anyone ugly or smelly in a winter coat in the dead of summer.

But the night was cool and the shadows were thick, and they made me feel all right, romantic maybe, or so I told myself.

I moved through a neighbor's backyard where a dog barked at me a couple of times and shut up. I reached the street across the way and looked for the Phone Woman, but didn't see her.

I took a flyer, and walked on down the street toward the trailer park where those poor illegal aliens were stuffed in like sardines by their unscrupulous employers, and I saw a shadow move among shadows, and then there was a split in the trees that provided the shadows, and I saw her, the Phone Woman. She was standing in a yard under a great oak, and not far from her was a trailer. A pathetic air conditioner hummed in one of its windows.

She stopped and looked up through that split in the trees above, and I knew she was trying to find the moon again, that she had staked out spots that she traveled to at night; spots where she stood and looked at the moon or the stars or the pure and sweet black eternity between them.

Like the time before, I looked up too, took in the moon, and it was beautiful, as gold as if it were a great glob of honey. The wind moved my hair, and it seemed solid and purposeful, like a lover's soft touch, like the beginning of foreplay. I breathed deep and tasted the fragrance of the night, and my lungs felt full and strong and young.

I looked back at the woman and saw she was reaching out her hand to the moon. No, a low limb. She touched it with her fingertips. She raised her other hand, and in it was a short, thick rope. She tossed the rope over the limb and made a loop and pulled it taut to the limb. Then she tied a loop to the other end, quickly, expertly, and put that around her neck.

Of course, I knew what she was going to do. But I didn't move. I could have stopped her, I knew, but what was the point? Death was the siren she had called on many a time, and finally, she had heard it sing.

She jumped and pulled her legs under her and the limb took her jump and held her. Her head twisted to the left and she spun about on the rope and the moonlight caught the silver pin on her ski cap and it threw out a cool beacon of silver light, and as she spun, it hit me once, twice, three times.

On the third spin her mouth went wide and her tongue went out and her legs dropped down and hit the ground and she dangled there, unconscious.

I unrooted my feet and walked over there, looking about as I went.

I didn't see anyone. No lights went on in the trailer.

I moved up close to her. Her eyes were open. Her tongue was out.

She was swinging a little. Her knees were bent and the toes and tops of her silly shoes dragged the ground. I walked around and around her, an erection pushing at my pants. I observed her closely, tried to see what death looked like.

She coughed. A little choking cough. Her eyes shifted toward me. Her chest heaved. She was beginning to breathe. She made a feeble effort to get her feet under her, to raise her hands to the rope around her neck.

She was back from the dead.

I went to her, I took her hands, gently pulled them from her throat, let them go. I looked into her eyes. I saw the moon there. She shifted so that her legs held her weight better. Her hands went to her dress. She pulled it up to her waist. She wore no panties. Her bush was like a nest built between the boughs of a snow-white elm.

I remembered the day she came into the house. Everything since then, leading up to this moment, seemed like a kind of perverse mating ritual. I put my hand to her throat. I took hold of the rope with my other hand and jerked it so that her knees straightened, then I eased behind her, put my forearm against the rope around her throat, and I began to tighten my hold until she made a soft noise, like a virgin taking a man for the first time. She didn't lift her hands. She continued to tug her dress up. She was trembling from lack of oxygen. I pressed myself against her buttocks, moved my hips rhythmically, my hard-on bound by my underwear and pants. I tightened the pressure on her throat.

And choked her.

And choked her.

She gave up what was left of her life with a shiver and a thrusting of her pelvis, and finally she jammed her buttocks back into me and I felt myself ejaculate, thick and hot and rich as shaving foam.

Her hands fell to her side. I loosened the pressure on her throat but clung to her for a while, getting my breath and my strength back. When I felt strong enough, I let her go. She swung out and around on the rope and her knees bent and her head cocked up to stare blindly at the gap in the trees above, at the honey-golden moon.

I left her there and went back to the house and slipped into the bedroom and took off my clothes. I removed my wet underwear carefully and wiped them out with toilet paper and flushed the paper down the toilet. I put the underwear in the clothes hamper. I put on fresh and climbed into bed and rubbed my hands over my wife's buttocks until she moaned and woke up. I rolled her on her stomach and mounted her and made love to her. Hard, violent love, my forearm around her throat, not squeezing, but thinking about the Phone Woman, the sound she had made when I choked her from behind, the way her buttocks had thrust back into me at the end. I closed my eyes until the sound that Janet made was the sound the Phone Woman made and I could visualize her there in the moonlight, swinging by the rope.

When it was over, I held Janet and she kissed me and joked about my arm around her throat, about how it seemed I had wanted to choke her. We laughed a little. She went to sleep. I let go of her and moved to my side of the bed and looked at the ceiling and thought about the Phone Woman. I tried to feel guilt. I could not. She had wanted it. She had tried for it many times. I had helped her do what she had never been able to manage. And I had felt alive again. Doing something on the edge. Taking a risk.

Well, journal, here's the question: Am I a sociopath?

No. I love my wife. I love my child. I even love my Suburban Husky.

I have never hunted and fished, because I thought I didn't like to kill. But there are those who want to die. It is their one moment of life; to totter on the brink between light and darkness, to take the final, dark rush down a corridor of black, hot pain.

So, Oh Great White Pages, should I feel guilt, some inner torment, a fear that I am at heart a cold-blooded murderer?

I think not.

I gave the sweet gift of truly being alive to a woman who wanted someone to participate in her moment of joy. Death ended that, but without the threat of it, her moment would have been nothing. A stage rehearsal for a high school play in street clothes.

Nor do I feel fear. The law will never suspect me. There's no reason to.

The Phone Woman had a record of near suicides. It would never occur to anyone to think she had died by anyone's hand other than her own.

I felt content, in touch again with the lava beneath the primal crust. I have allowed it to boil up and burst through and flow, and now it has gone down once more. But it's no longer a distant memory. It throbs and rolls and laps just below, ready to jump and give me life. Are there others out there like me? Or better yet, others for me, like the Phone Woman?

Most certainly.

And now I will recognize them. The Phone Woman has taught me that. She came into my life on a silly morning and brought me adventure, took me away from the grind, and then she brought me more, much, much more. She helped me recognize the fine but perfect line between desire and murder; let me know that there are happy victims and loving executioners.

I will know the happy victims now when I see them, know who needs to be satisfied. I will give them their desire, while they give me mine.

This last part with the Phone Woman happened last night and I am recording it now, while it is fresh, as Janet sleeps. I think of Janet in there and I have a hard time imagining her face. I want her, but I want her to be the Phone Woman, or someone like her.

I can feel the urge rising up in me again. The urge to give someone that tremendous double-edged surge of life and death.

It's like they say about sex. Once you get it, you got to have it on a regular basis. But it isn't sex I want. It's something like it, only sweeter.

I'll wrap this up. I'm tired. Thinking that I'll have to wake Janet and take the edge off my need, imagine that she and I are going to do more than fornicate; that she wants to take that special plunge and that she wants me to shove her.

But she doesn't want that. I'd know. I have to find that in my dreams, when I nestle down into the happy depths of the primitive brain.

At least until I find someone like the Phone Woman, again, that is.

Someone with whom I can commit the finest of adultery.

And until that search proves fruitful and I have something special to report, dear diary, I say, good night.

"Dirt Devils" is based on my interest in the Great Depression. My parents were older when I was born. My brother is nearly seventeen years older than me. They had seen hard times, and frankly, when I was born, times were for them only marginally better. I also had over the years read a lot about the great crime sprees by people like Bonnie and Clyde, whom my dad knew, at least in passing, Dillinger, Pretty Boy Floyd, Machine Gun Kelly, and so on. I took a less glamorous view.

DIRT DEVILS

The FORD CAME into town full of men and wrapped in a cloud of dust and through the dust the late afternoon sun looked like a cheap lamp shining through wraps of gauze. The cloud glided for a great distance, slowed when the car stopped moving forward, spun and finally faded out and down on all sides until the car could clearly be seen coated in a sheet of white powder. It took a moment to realize that beneath the grime the car was as black as tar. The wind that had been blowing stopped and shifted and the dust wound itself up into a big dust devil that twirled and gritted its way down the rutted street and tore out between two wind-squeaked abandoned buildings toward a gray tree line in the distance.

Outside of the car there wasn't much of the town to see, just a few ramshackle buildings wiped clean by the sandstorms that chewed wood and scraped paint and bleached the color out of clothes hung on wash lines. The dust was everywhere, coating windows and porch steps and rooftops. Sometimes, in just the right light, the dust looked like snow and one half expected polar bears and bewildered Eskimos to appear.

The infernal sand seeped under cracks no matter how well blocked or rag stuffed, and it crept into closed cars and through nailed-down windows. The world belonged to sand.

The street was slightly less sandy in spots since tire wheels and foot-steps kept it worn down, but you had to stay in the ruts if you drove a car, and the Ford had done just that before parking in front of a little store with a single gas pump with the gas visible in a big dust-covered bulb on top.

The car parked and a man on the passenger side got out. He had a hat in his hand and he put it on. He wore a nice blue suit and fine black shoes and he looked almost clean, the dust having only touched his out-fit and hat like glitter tossed at him by The Great Depression Fairy. He leaned left and then leaned right, stretching himself. The other doors opened and three men got out. They all wore suits. One of the men wearing a brown pinstripe suit and two-tone shoes came over and put his foot on the back of the car and wiped at his shoes with a handker-chief that he refolded and put in his inside coat pocket. He said to the man in the blue suit, "You want I should get some Co-Colas or some-thin', Ralph?"

"Yeah, that'll be all right. But don't come back with all manner of shit like you do. We ain't havin' a picnic. Get some drinks, a few things to nibble on, and that's it."

As the man in the pinstripe suit went into the store, an old man came out to the pump. He looked as if he had once been wadded and was now starting to slowly unfold. His hair was as white as the sand and floated when he walked. "I help you fellas?"

"Yeah," said Ralph. "Fill 'er up."

The old man took the hose and removed the car's gas cap and started filling the tank. He looked at the car window, and then he looked away and looked back at the store. He swallowed once, hard, like he had an apple hung in his throat.

Ralph leaned against the car and took off his hat and ran his hand through his oiled hair and put it back on. He stared at the old man a long time. "Much hunting around here?" he asked the old man.

"Lot of hunting, but not much catching. Depression must be gettin' better though, only seen one man chasin' a rabbit the other day." It was a tired joke, but Ralph grinned.

"This used to be a town," the old man said. "Wasn't never nothing much, but it was a town. Now most of the folks done moved off and what's here is worn out and gritted over. Hell, you get up in the morning you find sand in the crack of your ass."

Ralph nodded. "Everything's gritted over, and just about everybody too. I think I'm gonna go to California."

"Lots done have. But there ain't no work out there."

"My kind of work, I can find something."

The old man hesitated, and when he asked the question, it was like the words were sneaking out of the corner of his mouth: "What do you do?"

"I work with banks."

"Oh," the old man said. "Well, banking didn't do so good either."

"I work a special division."

"I see. . . . Well, it's gonna be another bad night with lots of wind and plenty of dust."

"How can you tell?"

"'Cause it always is. And when it ain't, I can tell before it comes about. I can sniff it. I used to farm some before the winds came, before the dust. Then I bought this and it ain't no better than farming because people 'round here are farmers and they ain't got no money 'cause they ain't got no farms so I ain't got no money. I don't make hardly nothin'."

"Nothin', huh?"

"What you're givin' me for this here gas and the like, that's all I've made all day."

"That does sound like a problem."

"Tell me about it."

"So if I was to rob you, I'd just be keepin' my own money."

"You would. . . . You boys staying in town long?"

"Where's to stay?"

"You got that right. Thirty, forty more feet, you're out of town. There ain't nothing here and ain't nobody got nothin'."

"That right?"

"Nothing to be had."

Ralph said, "My daddy, he had a store like this in Kansas. He ain't got nothin' now. He got droughted out and blown out. He died last spring. You remind me somethin' of him."

The other two men who had been loitering on the other side of the car came around to join Ralph and the old man, and when Ralph said what he said about his old man, one of the men, brown-suited, glanced at Ralph, then glanced away.

"Me, I'm just hanging in by the skin of my teeth, and I just got a half dozen of 'em left." The old man smiled at Ralph so he would know it was true. "I'm just about done here."

"You a Bible reader?" Ralph asked the old man.

"Every day."

"I figured that much. My old man was a Bible reader. He could quote chapter and verse."

"I can quote some chapters and some verses."

"You done any preachin'?"

"No. I don't preach."

"My old man did. He ran a store and preached and had too many children. I was the last of 'em."

The old man looked at the tank. "You was bone dry, son, but I about got you filled now."

In the store the man in the brown suit with pinstripes, whose name was Emory, saw a little Negro boy sitting on a stool wearing a thick cloth cap that looked as if it had been used to catch baseballs. The boy had a little pocketknife and was whittlin' on a stick without much energy.

Emory looked at the boy. The boy latched his eyes on Emory.

"What you lookin' at, boy?"

"Nuthin'."

"Nuthin', sir."

"Yes, suh."

Emory wandered around the store and found some candies and some canned peaches. He got some Co-Colas out of the ice box and set them dripping wet on the counter with the canned peaches and the candies.

Emory turned and looked at the boy.

"You help out here, nigger?"

"Just a little."

"Well, why don't you do just a little? Get over here behind the counter and get me some of them long cigars there, and a couple packs of smokes."

"I don't do that kind of thing," the boy said. "That there is Mr. Grady's job. I just run errands and such. I ain't supposed to go behind the counter."

"Yeah. I guess that make sense. And them errands. What's a nigger get for that kind of work?"

"A nickel sometimes."

"Per errand?"

"Naw, suh. Per day."

"That's a little better. There's white men workin' in the fields ain't making a dollar a day."

"Yes, suh. They's colored men too."

"Yeah. Well, how hard are they workin'?"

"They workin' plenty hard."

"Say they are," Emory said, and took a hard look at the boy. The boy's eyes were still locked on his and the boy had his hands on his knees. The boy's face was kind of stiff like he was thinking hard on something but one eye sagged slightly to the left and there was a scar above and below it. He had one large foot and a very worn-looking oversized shoe about the size of a cinder block.

"What happened to your eye?"

"I had a saw jump back on me. I was cuttin' some wood and it got stuck and I yanked and it come back on me. I can still see though."

"I can tell that. What's wrong with your foot?"

"It's a club foot."

"What club does it belong to?"

"What's that?"

"You ain't so smart, are you?"

"Smart enough, I reckon."

"So, with that foot, you don't really run errands, you walk 'em."

The boy finally quit looking at Emory.

"Ain't that right," Emory said when the boy didn't answer.

"I s'pose so," the boy said. "That a gun you got under your coat?"

"You a nosey little nigger, ain't ya? Yeah, that's a gun. You know what I call it?"

The boy shook his head.

"My nigger shooter. You know what I shoot with it?"

The boy jumped up. It caused the stool to turn over. The boy dropped the stick and the pocketknife and moved as fast as his foot would allow toward the door, turned and went right along the side of the store, giving Emory a glance at him through the dusty glass, and then there was just wall and the boy was gone from view.

Emory laughed. "Bet that's the fastest he ever run," he said aloud. "Bet that's some kind of club-footed nigger record."

The old man was topping off the pump as the boy ran by and around the edge of the building and out of sight. By the time the old man called out "Joshua," it was too late and from the way the boy was moving, unlikely to stop anyway.

"What the hell has got into him?" the old man said.

"Ain't no way to figure a colored boy," Ralph said.

"He's all right," the old man said. "He's a good boy."

The other two men were standing next to the pump, and Ralph looked at them. He said, "John, why don't you and Billy go in there and see you can help Emory?"

"He don't need no help," Billy said. He was a small man in an oversized black suit and no hat and he had enough hair for himself and a small dog, all of it greasy and nested on top of his head, the sides of his skull shaved to the skin over the ears so that he gave the impression of some large leafy vegetable ready to be pulled from the ground.

"Well," Ralph said, "you go help him anyway."

The old man was hanging up the gas nozzle. He said, "That's gonna be a dollar."

"Damn," Ralph said. "You run some of that out on the ground?"

"Things gone up," the old man said. "In this town, we got to charge off of what the suppliers charge us. You know that, your daddy owned a store."

Ralph pondered that. He buttoned and unbuttoned his coat. "Yeah, I know it. Just don't like it. Hell, I'm gonna go in the store too. A minute out of this sun ain't gonna hurt me, that's for sure."

Ralph and the old man went into the store side by side until they came to the door, and Ralph let the old man go in first.

The old man went behind the counter and Ralph said, "You sure look a lot like my old man."

"Don't reckon I'm him, though," the old man said, and showed his scattered teeth again, but the smile waved a bit, like the lips might fall off.

"No," Ralph said. "You ain't him, that's for sure. He's good and dead."

"Well, I'm almost dead," the old man said. "Here until God calls me."

"He don't call some," Ralph said. "Some he yanks."

The old man didn't know what to say to that. Ralph noticed that there were pops of sweat on the old man's forehead.

"You look hot," Ralph said.

"I ain't so hot," the old man said.

"You sweatin' good," Billy said.

"Ain't nobody talkin' to you," Ralph said. "Go on over there and sit on that stool and shut up."

Billy didn't pick up and sit on the stool, but he went quiet.

"I guess maybe I am a little hot," the old man said, straightening the items on the counter. "We got the gas, and we got these goods. Canned peaches, some candies, and Co-Colas. That's be about a dollar fifty for all that, and then the gas."

"That dollar tank of gas," Ralph said.

"Yes, sir. That'll be two-fifty."

"You got all manner of stuff, didn't you, Emory?" Ralph said. "I told you not to get all that stuff."

"I got carried away," Emory said, and turned to the old man. "You give any stamps or any kind of shit like that with a purchase?"

The men had gathered together near the counter, except for Billy, who was standing off to the side with hurt feelings and some of his hair in his eyes.

The old man shook his head. "No. Nothing like that."

"That don't seem right," Emory said. "Some stores do that."

"Do they?" the old man said.

"Some give dishes," Emory said.

"Shut up," Ralph said. "You wouldn't know what to do with a dish you had it. You'd shit in a bowl and sling the plates. Just get things together and let's go."

The old man was sacking up the groceries, but he left the Co-Colas on the counter. "You gonna carry those separate?" he asked.

"That'll be all right," Ralph said. "You even got hands like my old man. That's somethin'."

"Yes, sir," the old man said, "I s'pose it is."

Ralph looked around and saw that the others were staring at him. When he looked at them they looked away. Ralph turned back to the old man.

"You got a phone here?"

"No. No phone."

Ralph nodded. "Total it. I'm goin' on out to the car. Emory, you or John take care of it."

Ralph walked around to the front of the car and got out his cigarettes and pulled one loose of the pack with his lips, put the pack away and lit up with a wooden kitchen match he struck on the bottom of his shoe. As he smoked, he looked through the front window of the car. He walked around to the side of the car and looked in. The tommy gun he had told Billy to put up lay on the backseat in plain view.

He walked around to the other side of the car where the gas pump was and looked in through the side window. You could see it real good from that angle, about where the old man stood to put the gas in.

He walked back around to the front of the car and started to lean against it but saw it was covered in dust, so didn't. He just stood there smoking and thinking.

After a bit, there was a sharp snapping sound from inside the store. Ralph tossed the cigarette and went inside. Emory was putting away his gun.

"What you done?" Ralph said, and he walked to the edge of the counter and took a look. The old man lay on the floor. His eyes were open and his head was turned toward Ralph. The old man had one arm propped on his elbow, and his hand stuck up in the air and his fingers were spread like he was waving hello. On his forehead was what looked like a cherry blossom and it grew darker and the petals fell off and splashed down the old man's face and dripped on the floor in red explosions and then a pool of the same spread out at the back of his head and coated the floor thick as spilled paint.

Ralph turned and looked at Emory. "Why'd you do that?"

"You told me to," Emory said.

Ralph came out from behind the counter and hit Emory hard enough with the flat of his hand to knock Emory's hat off. "I meant pay the man, not shoot him." Emory put a hand to the side of his face.

"We all thought that it's what you wanted," Billy said, and Ralph turned and kicked Billy in the balls. Billy went to his knees.

"I didn't say kill nobody."

"You know he seen that gun in the car," Emory said, backing up. "We all knowed it. We was twenty feet down the road, he was gonna go somewhere and find a phone."

Ralph looked at John. John held both hands up. "Hey, I didn't say to do nothing. It was over before I knew it was happening."

Emory picked up his hat. Billy lay on the floor with his hands between his legs. John didn't move. Ralph took a deep breath, said, "You think nobody noticed a gun shot? You think that little nigger ain't gonna remember you, 'cause I know you run him out. Grab that shit and let's go. And help that retard Billy up."

John drove and Ralph set up front on the passenger side. Billy was behind him, and across from Billy was Emory, his hands still tucked between his legs, holding what made him a gentleman.

"I thought you meant kill him, Ralph," Emory said. "I figured on account of what you said, him like your father and all, and considering what you—"

"Shut up! Shut the hell up!"

Emory shut up.

Ralph said to John, "You better find some back roads. I know some out this way, but it's been awhile. There's one that a car can travel on down by the river."

They took the road when Ralph pointed it out. It wound down amongst some ragged cottonwood trees. The trees had few leaves and what leaves it had were brown with sand stripping and the limbs were covered in sand the color of cigarette ash. The car dipped over a rise and there were some rare green trees below that hadn't been stripped. The trees stood by the river where it was low down and the wind was cut by the hills. The river was thin on water and there were drifts of sand all around it. They drove down there and turned along the edge of the river and went that way awhile till Ralph told John to stop.

They got out and Ralph went over by the bank and looked at the remains of the river. Emory came over. He said, "I didn't mean to make you mad. I thought you wanted me to do what I did."

Ralph didn't say anything. Emory unbuttoned his fly and started peeing in the water. "I just thought it was one way and it was another," he said while he peed. "I didn't understand."

Ralph reached inside his coat. He didn't do it fast, just with certainty. He turned and had a .45 in his hand. He shot Emory in the mouth when he turned his head toward him, while he was trying to explain something. Emory's head went back so hard it seemed as if it would fly off his neck and parts of it went down the bank and a piece slid into the chalky-colored water and the water turned rusty. Emory lay on his side, still holding his pecker with his right hand. He was still peeing, but in a dribble, and he had clenched himself so hard between thumb and forefinger it looked like he was trying to pinch it off.

"Goddamn!" Billy said. "Goddamn."

He came over and went down the bank and bent over Emory and looked at what was left of his head and saw pieces of Emory's skull on the ground and in the dark water. "Goddamn. You killed him."

"I should think so," Ralph said.

Billy stood up straight and looked at Ralph, who had the gun down by his side. "Wasn't no cause for that. He did what he thought you wanted on account of you saying he looked like your old man. Goddamn it, Ralph."

Ralph lifted the .45 a little and John came over and put his hand on Ralph's arm, said, "It's all right, Ralph. You done done it. Billy ain't thinking. He and Emory were cousins. He don't know how things are. He's grieving. You understand that. We all been there."

"Double cousins," Billy said. "Goddamn it."

"Shut up, Billy," John said, and he kept his hand on Ralph's arm.

Billy looked at Ralph's face, and some of his spirit drained away. Billy said, "All right. All right."

"Why don't you put the gun up?" John asked Ralph.

Ralph slowly put the gun in the shoulder holster under his coat. "That fellow looked so much like my old man."

"I know," John said.

"He had the same hands."

"I know."

"Emory shouldn't have done that. Now the town will turn out. They'll have the law all over us. That little nigger will remember Emory's face."

"That won't be a problem. He ain't got a face no more. I don't think he seen the rest of us that good."

"It don't matter," Ralph said, taking off his hat.

"They'll know who we are."

"They got to catch us first," John said.

Ralph took off his hat and ran his hand through his oily hair. There was dust on his fingers and some of it came off in his hair. He put the hat back on. "Goddamn, Emory. Goddamn him." He looked over at Billy.

Billy was sitting on the bank looking at Emory's body. Flies had already collected on it.

Ralph started over that way. John touched his arm, but Ralph gently pulled it away. Ralph stood over Billy. "You get to thinking what you ought not, it could go bad for you."

Billy turned his head and looked up at Ralph. "Only thing I'm thinking is my cousin's dead."

"And he ain't comin' back. No matter how much you look at him or shake him, he ain't gonna come around and his head ain't gonna go back together. And I want you to know, I don't feel bad for doin' it. I tell you to do somethin', you don't figure what I mean, you got to know what I mean, not guess. I run this outfit."

Billy ran his hands over his knees, lifting his fingers so that they stood up like white tarantulas. "Yeah. Yeah."

"Give me your gun," Ralph said.

Billy looked at him so hard his eyes teared up. "I'm over it," he said.

"Give me your gun."

Billy reached inside his coat and took hold of a .38 revolver and pulled it out and when he did, Ralph pulled out his .45. "I'll just hold it for you," Ralph said. "While you grieve."

Billy gave Ralph the .38. It was small enough Ralph put it in his coat pocket. "Sometimes, we're upset, we do things we shouldn't."

"That's what you did," Billy said.

"It wasn't something I shouldn't have done. I don't feel bad at all. Ain't no one kills no one unless I say so."

Billy seemed about to say something but didn't.

Ralph said, "Build up a fire. I don't think anyone will see the smoke much down here, and we'll just have it for a while."

"Why?" Billy said.

"We'll get right on it," John said, came over and took hold of Billy's arm and pulled him up and pushed him toward the woods. He called back to Ralph, "We'll get some wood right away."

While they were gathering wood, Billy said, "He killed him for nothing. He killed him while he was holding his dick in his hand. He didn't have to do that, didn't have to kill him that way."

"He killed him because the old man reminded him of his old man. He'd be just as dead if he hadn't been holding his dick."

"His old man. . . . That can't be it. You know what he done."

"I know, but there ain't no way to figure it straight, because what he did wasn't straight. It's just his way."

"Just his way? Jesus. That was my cousin."

"Yeah, and he ain't gonna get no deader, and he ain't gonna get alive not even a little bit, so you got to let it go. I've had to let a lot of things go. Drop it."

"I don't know I want to keep doing this."

"We split up the money, then we can go the ways we want. But you don't want to make Ralph nervous. You make him nervous, only so much I'm gonna do. Me, I plan to make Thanksgiving at home this year.

I don't want to end up on the creek bank with part of me in the water and flies all over me. So I'm doin' the last of what I'm doin' for you, you savvy, because I'm more worried about me and I want my share of money. Look at it this way, more money split three ways than four. That's a thing to think about. You savvy?"

"More split two ways than three," Billy said.

"I wouldn't think that. You think that, you'll think yourself into the dirt with your head blown off."

They stacked up the wood like Ralph said and then they sat on a hill above the bank for a while and then Ralph said, "John, you go look in the turtle hull and get out the hose and the jug there, siphon out a bit of gas. Maybe about half a jug full. And bring me back a can of them peaches."

"Sure," John said, and got up to go do it.

Billy made to get up too, but Ralph said, "You stay here and keep me company."

Billy sat back down. Ralph said, "Listen here, now, boy. Your cousin talked too much and didn't listen to me good. John should have stopped him. He should have known better. You're just a dumb kid. But you ain't gonna get to be any older or any smarter you don't start payin' attention. You get me?"

"Yeah," Billy said.

"I don't think you get me."

"I do."

"Not really."

"No. I do."

"We'll see. You go down there and get your cousin, don't have to bring up his brains and stuff, just drag his body up here and you put him face down on that pile of sticks you got together, and then you fold his hands up so that they're under his face."

"Why would I do that?"

"See there, boy, you don't get me. You don't understand a thing I tell you and you always got a question. Now, I told you to go down there and get him."

Billy got up and went down the bank. Ralph didn't move. He lipped out a cigarette and lit it with one of his kitchen matches. After a while, Billy come up the hill tugging at Emory by the heels. He got the body over by the sticks about the time John come back with the clear jug half full of gasoline and the can of peaches. He gave Ralph the peaches.

"Take that gasoline," Ralph said, "and put about half on that pile of sticks, sprinkle it around, and pour the rest on Emory's hands and face. That way, ain't nobody gonna recognize him and he ain't gonna have no fingerprints. Take off his clothes first."

Billy had quit pulling on Emory. He said, "They'll know who we are anyway. You said yourself that little nigger seen us. And Emory hasn't got much of a face left."

"We're just making it harder for them," Ralph said.

"I think you're just making it meaner," Billy said. "I think you're teaching me a lesson."

Ralph turned his head to one side curiously. "That what you think? You think you ain't already got a hole God's gonna put you in? A slot."

"That ain't your call?" Billy said.

"It sure was with Emory. I helped God fit him to his slot. I sent him where he was goin' and I didn't choose his place, just his time, and that there, it was preordained, my old man taught me that. And the place Emory went, I don't figure him nor any of us is going to a place we'd like to go, do you?"

"Ain't mine to think about."

"Oh, Billy, sure it is."

"Not if it's done planned."

"Billy," John said. "I'll help you."

"I ain't gonna put him on that fire."

"You don't, it'll still get done," Ralph said, "and maybe I get John to siphon out some more gas, get some more sticks. You get where the wind is blowing on that?"

Billy was breathing heavy. John said, "Billy, let's just do it. Okay?" Billy looked at John. John's face was pleading. "All right," Billy said. Billy and John got hold of Emory and rolled him over. They took off his clothes except for his shorts, which were full of shit. Billy got a stick and worked Emory's dick back into the slit in his underwear. John started to pour gasoline on Emory's open-eyed face. The top of Emory's head looked like it had been worked open with a dull can opener.

"No," Ralph said. "Have Billy do that." John handed Billy the jug. Billy looked at John, but there was no help there. He took the jug and poured gas on Emory's head.

"Now put him face down on the sticks and put his hands under his head," Ralph said. He had used his pocketknife to open the can of peaches and he was poking them with the knife and gobbling them down, some of the peach juice running down his chin.

Billy and John did as they were asked and then Ralph gave John a kitchen match. John set the sticks on fire. The stench of Emory's burning body filled the air.

"Let's go," Billy said. "I don't want to see this, smell it neither."

"No," Ralph said, eating more peaches, "you just find you a seat. We'll kinder pretend we're at the movies."

The three of them sat on the hill but Billy sat with his face away from the fire. The fire licked at Emory and pretty soon the head and hands were burned up and so were the feet and parts of the rest of his body.

"Close enough," Ralph said. He had long finished the peaches and had tossed the can down the bank toward the water, but it didn't go that far. "Spread them sticks out and kill the fire so we don't burn half the county down. What's left of him won't matter. Dogs and such will have them a cooked meal tonight."

When they went out to the car, Ralph fell back and said to John, "Any kind of noise goes off, you just hold steady, you hear?"

"Yeah," John said, and then he walked briskly away from Ralph toward the driver's side. Billy was about to get in the backseat when Ralph said, "You sit up front, Billy."

Billy turned and looked at Ralph. He studied him for a long hard moment. He said, "That's okay. I don't mind the back."

"You sit up front," Ralph said.

"You always ride up front," Billy said.

"Not today."

"I don't mind."

"You sit in my seat."

Ralph sat behind Billy in the back, and John drove. They drove out of the trail and out of the woods and onto the main road. It was starting to get dark. John pulled on the lights.

John glanced at Billy. Billy's face was beaded up with sweat. "I been thinking," Billy said. "Everything you was talking about was right, Ralph. I was just upset."

"Yeah," Ralph said.

"Yeah. I mean, I wasn't thinking."

Billy turned halfway around and put his arm on the seat. Ralph was looking right at him. In the early evening he was only slightly better defined than a shadow. He had his hat pulled down tight.

"Turn around, Billy," Ralph said.

Billy turned. He looked at John. John said, "I done told you."

Billy said, "He's my cousin, so of course I was upset. I ain't gonna say nothing about it to no one. Not even his mama."

"That's good," Ralph said, and reached in his pocket and took Billy's revolver out of it and rested it on his knee, his hand resting gently on top of it like a man caressing a pet.

"You know we all done done the sins that's gonna send us to hell," Ralph said. "It's just a matter of when now, but we're all goin'. There ain't a thing we can do to change things. For some of us when it comes, it'll come quick and with a pop."

"Sure we can," Billy said. "We can all do better."

"I don't think so," Ralph said.

"It's like you said, I ain't nothin' but a kid. I ain't thinkin' things through. But I'll get better. We all thought you wanted that old man done."

"Leave me out of this," John said. "I ain't part of that we."

Billy was talking fast. "You sayin' he looked like your daddy, and us knowing what you did."

"Don't mention my old man again," Ralph said. "Ever."

"Sure," Billy said. "Sure. But I've learned my lesson. I've learned a lot."

"Sure you have," Ralph said, and then there was a long silence, and then Billy heard the revolver cock.

"Drive-In Date" was my way to sort of piss on the idea that serial killers were masterminds. I don't mind that in fiction to some extent, and some of them are bright, but a lot of them are more lucky than bright. My guys could only exist by accident, what people call good luck. They are horrible, shallow, misogynistic for sure, but there's a human side as well. Just not a particularly comfortable one. I guess I kind of had Henry Lee Lucas and Otis Toole in mind when I wrote this, but only as a catalyst. This was a one-act, Grand Guignol play as well. Me and Del Close and Neal Barrett Jr. and others were once asked for dark plays for a night of Grand Guignol. I got paid for my play, and things sounded set, but as we neared the event, plans folded. Neal Barrett Jr. said I ruined it for everyone because of my super-dark play. In a phone call, Del Close said he felt much the same. They were kidding, of course. Or at least I think they were.

DRIVE-IN DATE

THE LINE INTO the Starlite Drive-In that night was short. Monday nights were like that. Dave and Merle paid their money at the ticket house and Dave drove the Ford to a spot up near the front where there were only a few cars. He parked in a space with no one directly on either side. On the left, the first car was four speakers away, on the right, six speakers.

Dave said, "I like to be up close so it all looks bigger than life. You don't mind do you?"

"You ask me that every time," Merle said. "You don't never ask me that when we're driving in, you ask when we're parked."

"You don't like it, we can move."

"No, I like it. I'm just saying, you don't really care if I like it. You just ask."

"Politeness isn't a crime."

"No, but you ought to mean it."

"I said we can move."

"Hell no, stay where you are. I'm just saying when you ask me what I like, you could mean it."

"You're a testy motherfucker tonight. I thought coming to see a monster picture would cheer you up."

"You're the one likes 'em, and that's why you come. It wasn't for me, so don't talk like it was. I don't believe in monsters, so I can't enjoy what I'm seeing. I like something that's real. Cop movies. Things like that."

"I tell you, Merle, there's just no satisfying you, man. You'll feel better when they cut the lot lights and the movie starts. We can get our date then."

"I don't know that makes me feel better."

"You done quit liking pussy?"

"Watch your mouth. I didn't say that. You know I like pussy. I like pussy fine."

"Whoa. Aren't we fussy? Way you talk, you're trying to convince me. Maybe it's buttholes you like."

"Goddamnit, don't start on the buttholes."

Dave laughed and got out a cigarette and lipped it. "I know you did that one ole gal in the butt that night." Dave reached up and tapped the rearview mirror. "I seen you in the mirror here."

"You didn't see nothing," Merle said.

"I seen you get in her butthole. I seen that much."

"What the hell you doing watching? It ain't good enough for you by yourself, so you got to watch someone else get theirs?"

"I don't mind watching."

"Yeah, well, I bet you don't. You're like one of those fucking perverts."

Dave snickered, popped his lighter and lit his cigarette. The lot lights went out. The big lights at the top of the drive-in screen went black. Dave rolled down the window and pulled the speaker in and fastened it to the door. He slapped at a mosquito on his neck.

"Won't be long now," Dave said.

"I don't know if I feel up to it tonight."

"You don't like the first feature, the second's some kind of mystery. It might be like a cop show."

"I don't mean the movies."

"The girl?"

"Yeah. I'm in a funny mood."

Dave smoked for a moment. "Merle, this is kind of a touchy subject, but you been having trouble, you know, getting a bone to keep, I'll tell you, that happens. It's happened to me. Once."

"I'm not having trouble with my dick, okay?"

"If you are, it's no disgrace. It'll happen to a man from time to time."

"My tool is all right. It works. No problem."

"Then what's the beef?"

"I don't know. It's a mood. I feel like I'm going through a kind of, I don't know . . . mid-life crisis or something."

"Mood, huh? Let me tell you, when she's stretched out on that back seat, you'll be all right, crisis or no crisis. Hell, get her butthole if you want it, I don't care."

"Don't start on me."

"Who's starting? I'm telling you, you want her butthole, her ear, her goddamn nostril, that's your business. Me, I'll stick to the right hole, though."

"Think I don't know a snide remark when you make it?"

"I hope you do, or I wouldn't make it. You don't know I'm making one, what's the fun of making it?" Dave reached over and slapped Merle playfully on the arm. "Lighten up, boy. Let's see a movie, get some pussy. Hey, you feel better if I went and got us some corn and stuff. . . . That'd do you better, wouldn't it?"

Merle hesitated. "I guess."

"Back in a jiffy."

Dave got out of the car.

Fifteen minutes and Dave was back. He had a cardboard box that held two bags of popcorn and some tall drinks. He set the box on top of the car, opened the door, then got the box and slid inside. He put the box on the seat between them.

"How much I owe you?" Merle said.

"Not a thing. You get it next time. . . . Think how much more expensive this would be, we had to pay for her to eat too."

"A couple or three dollars. So what? That gonna break us?"

"No, but it's beer money. You think about it."

Merle sat and thought about it.

The big white drive-in screen was turned whiter by the projector light, then there was a flicker and images moved on the screen: Ads for the concession. Coming attractions.

Dave got his popcorn, started eating. He said, "I'm getting kind of horny thinking about her. You see the legs on that bitch?"

"Course I seen the legs. You don't know from legs. A woman's got legs is all you care, and you might not care about that. Couple of stumps would be all the same to you."

"No, I don't care for any stumps. Got to be feet on one end, pussy on the other. That's legs enough. But this one, she's got some good ones. Hell, you're bound to've noticed how good they were."

"I noticed. You saying I'm queer or something? I noticed. I noticed she's got an ankle bracelet on the right leg and she wears about a size ten shoe. Biggest goddamn feet I've ever seen on a woman."

"Now, it comes out. You wanted to pick the date, not me?"

"I never did care for a woman with big feet. You got a good-looking woman all over and you get down to them feet and they look like something goes on either side of a water plane . . . well, it ruins things."

"She ain't ruined. Way she looks, big feet or not, she ain't ruined. Besides, you don't fuck the feet . . . well, maybe you do. Right after the butthole."

"You gonna push one time too much, Dave. One time too much."

"I'm just kidding, man. Lighten up. You don't ever lighten up. Don't we deserve some fun after working like niggers all day?"

Merle sighed. "You got to use that nigger stuff? I don't like it. It makes you sound ignorant. Will, he's colored and I like him. He's done me all right. Man like that, he don't deserve to be called nigger."

"He's all right at the plant, but you go by his house and ask for a loan."

"I don't want to borrow nothing from him. I'm just saying people ought to get their due, no matter what color they are. *Nigger* is an ugly word."

"You like *boogie* better, Martin Luther? How about *coon* or *shine*? I was always kind of fond of *burrhead* or *wooly*, myself."

"There's just no talking to you, is there?"

"Hell, you like niggers so much, next date we set up, we'll make it a nigger. Shit, I'd fuck a nigger. It's all pink on the inside, ain't that what you've heard?"

"You're a bigot is what you are."

"If that means I'm not wanting to buddy up to coons, then, yeah, that's what I am." Dave thumped his cigarette butt out the window. "You got to learn to lighten up, Merle. You don't, you'll die. My uncle, he couldn't never lighten up. Gave him a spastic colon, all that tension. He swelled up until he couldn't wear his pants. Had to get some stretch pants, one of those running suits, just so he could have on clothes. He eventually got so bad they had to go in and operate. You can bet he wished he didn't do all that worrying now. It didn't get him a thing but sick. He didn't get a better life on account of that worry, now did he? Still lives over in that apartment where he's been living, on account of he got so sick from worry he couldn't work. They're about to throw him out of there, and him a grown man and sixty years old. Lost his good job, his wife—which he ought to know is a good thing—and now he's doing little odd shit here and there to make ends meet. Going down to catch the day work truck with the winos and niggers—excuse me. Afro-Americans, colored folks, whatever you prefer.

"Before he got to worrying over nothing, he had him some serious savings and was about ready to put some money down on a couple of acres and a good double-wide."

"I was planning on buying me a double-wide, that'd make me worry. Them old trailers ain't worth a shit. Comes a tornado, or just a good wind, and you can find those fuckers at the bottom of the Gulf of Mexico, next to the regular trailers. Tornado will take a double-wide easy as any of the others."

Dave shook his head. "You go from one thing to the other, don't you? I know what a tornado can do. It can take a house, too. Your house. That don't matter. I'm not talking about mobile homes here, Merle. I'm talking about living. It's a thing you better attend to. You're forty goddamn years old. Your life's half over. . . . I know that's a cold thing to say, but there you have it. It's out of my mouth. I'm forty this next birthday, so I'm not just putting the doom on you. It's a thing every man's got to face. Getting over the hill. Before I die, I'd like to think I did something fun with my life. It's the little things that count. I want to enjoy things, not worry them away. Hear what I'm saying, Merle?"

"Hard not to, being in the goddamn car with you."

"Look here. Way we work, we deserve to lighten up a little. You haul your ashes first. That'll take some edge off."

"Well. . . ."

"Naw, go on."

"All right . . . but one thing."

"What?"

"Don't do me no more butthole jokes, okay? One friend to another, Dave, no more butthole jokes."

"It bothers you that bad, okay. Deal."

Merle climbed over the seat and got on his knees in the floorboard. He took hold of the back seat and pulled. It was rigged with a hinge. It folded down. He got on top of the folded-down seat and bent and looked into the exposed trunk. The young woman's face was turned toward him, half of her cheek was hidden by the spare tire. There was a smudge of grease on her nose.

"We should have put a blanket back here," Merle said. "Wrapped her in that. I don't like 'em dirty."

"She's got pants on," Dave said. "You take them off, the part that counts won't be dirty."

"That part's always dirty. They pee and bleed out of it, don't they? Hell, hot as it is back here, she's already starting to smell."

"Oh, bullshit." Dave turned and looked over the seat at Merle. "You can't get pleased, can you? She ain't stinking. She didn't even shit her pants when she checked out. And she ain't been dead long enough to smell, and you know it. Quit being so goddamn contrary." Dave turned back around and shook out a cigarette and lit it.

"Blow that out the window, damnit," Merle said. "You know that smoke works my allergies."

Dave shook his head and blew smoke out the window. He turned up the speaker. The ads and commercials were over. The movie was starting.

"And don't be looking back here at me neither," Merle said.

Merle rolled the woman out of the trunk, across the seat, onto the floorboard and up against him. He pushed the seat back into place and got hold of the woman and hoisted her onto the back seat. He pushed her

T-shirt over her breasts. He fondled her breasts. They were big and firm and rubbery cold. He unfastened her shorts and pulled them over her shoes and ripped her panties apart at one side. He pushed one of her legs onto the floorboard and gripped her hips and pulled her ass down a little, got it cocked to a position he liked. He unfastened and pulled down his jeans and boxer shorts and got on her.

Dave roamed an eye to the rearview mirror, caught sight of Merle's butt bobbing. He grinned and puffed at his cigarette. After a while, he turned his attention to the movie.

When Merle was finished he looked at the woman's dead eyes. He couldn't see their color in the dark, but he guessed blue. Her hair he could tell was blonde.

"How was it?" Dave asked.

"It was pussy. Hand me the flashlight."

Dave reached over and got the light out of the glove box and handed it over the seat. Merle took it. He put it close to the woman's face and turned it on.

"She's got blue eyes," Merle said.

"I noticed that right off when we grabbed her," Dave said. "I thought then you'd like that, being how you are about blue eyes."

Merle turned off the flashlight, handed it to Dave, pulled up his pants and climbed over the seat. On the screen a worm-like monster was coming out of the sand on a beach.

"This flick isn't half bad," Dave said. "It's kind of funny, really. You don't get too good a look at the monster though. . . . That all the pussy you gonna get?"

"Maybe some later," Merle said.

"You feeling any better?"

"Some."

"Yeah, well, why don't you eat some popcorn while I get me a little. Want a cigarette? You like a cigarette after sex, don't you?"

"All right."

Dave gave Merle a cigarette, lit it.

Merle sucked the smoke in deeply.

"Better?" Dave asked.

"Yeah, I guess."

"Good." Dave thumped his cigarette out the window. "I'm gonna take my turn now. Don't let nothing happen on the movie. Make it wait."

"Sure."

Dave climbed over the seat. Merle tried to watch the movie. After a moment, he quit. He turned and looked out his window. Six speakers down he could see a Chevy rocking.

"Got to be something more to life than this," Merle said without turning to look at Dave.

"I been telling you," Dave said. "This is life, and you better start enjoying. Get you some orientation before it's too late and it's all over but the dirt in the face. . . . Talk to me later. Right now, this is what I want out of life. Little later, I might want a drink."

Merle shook his head.

Dave lifted the woman's leg and hooked her ankle over the front seat. Merle looked at her foot, the ankle bracelet dangling from it. "I bet that damn foot's more a size eleven than a ten," Merle said. "Probably buys her shoes at the ski shop."

Dave hooked her other ankle over the back seat, on the package shelf. "Like I said, it's not the feet I'm interested in."

Merle shook his head again. He rolled down his window and thumped out some ash and turned his attention to the Chevy again. It was still rocking.

Dave shifted into position in the back seat. The Ford began to rock. The foot next to Merle vibrated, made little dead hops.

From the back seat, Dave began to chant: "Give it to me, baby. Give it to me. Am I your Prince, baby? Am I your goddamn King? Take that anaconda, bitch. Take it!"

"For heaven's sake," Merle said.

Five minutes later, Dave climbed into the front seat, said, "Damn. Damn good piece."

"You act like she had something to do with it," Merle said.

"Her pussy, ain't it?"

"We're doing all the work. We could cut a hole in the seat back there and get it that good."

"That ain't true. It ain't the hole does it, and it damn sure ain't the personality, it's how they look. That flesh under you. Young. Firm. Try coming in an ugly or fat woman and you'll see what I mean. You'll have some troubles. Or maybe you won't."

"I don't like 'em old or fat."

"Yeah, well, I don't see the live ones like either one of us all that much. The old ones or the fat ones. Face it, we've got no way with live women. And I don't like the courting. I like to know that I see one I like, I can have her if I can catch her."

Merle reached over and shoved the woman's foot off the seat. It fell heavily to the floorboard. "I'm tired of looking at that slat. Feet like that, they ought to have paper bags over them."

When the second feature was over, they drove to Dave's house and parked out back next to the tall board fence. They killed the lights and sat there for a while, watching, listening.

No movement at the neighbors'.

"You get the gate," Dave said. "I'll get the meat."

"We could just go on and dump her," Merle said. "We could call it a night."

"It's best to be careful. The law can look at sput now and know who it comes from. We got to clean her up some."

Merle got out and opened the gate and Dave got out and opened the trunk and pulled the woman out by the foot and let her fall on her face to the ground. He reached in and got her shorts and put them in the crook of his arm, then bent and ripped her torn panties the rest of the way off and stuffed them in a pocket of her shorts and stuffed the shorts into the front of his pants. He got hold of her ankle and dragged her through the gate.

Merle closed the gate as Dave and the corpse came through. "You got to drag her on her face?" he said.

"She don't care," Dave said.

"I know, but I don't like her messed up."

"We're through with her."

"When we let her off, I want her to be, you know, okay."

"She ain't okay now, Merle. She's dead."

"I don't want her messed up."

Dave shrugged. He crossed her ankle and flipped her on her back and dragged her over next to the house and let go of her next to the water hose. He uncoiled the hose and took the nozzle and inserted it up the woman with a sound like a boot being withdrawn from mud, and turned the water on low.

When he looked up from his work, Merle was coming out of the house with a six-pack of beer. He carried it over to the redwood picnic table and sat down. Dave joined him.

"Have a Lone Star," Merle said.

Dave twisted the top off one. "You're thinking on something. I can tell."

"I was thinking we ought to take them alive," Merle said.

Dave lit a cigarette and looked at him. "We been over this. We take one alive she might scream or get away. We could get caught easy enough."

"We could kill her when we're finished. Way we're doing, we could buy one of those blow-up dolls, put it in the glove box and bring it to the drive-in."

"I've never cottoned to something like that. Even jacking off bothers me. A man ought to have a woman."

"A dead woman?"

"That's the best kind. She's quiet. You haven't got to put up with clothes and makeup jabber, keeping up with the Joneses jabber, getting that promotion jabber. She's not gonna tell you no in the middle of the night. Ain't gonna complain about how you put it to her. One stroke's as good as the next to a dead bitch."

"I kind of like hearing 'em grunt, though. I like being kissed."

"Rape some girl, think she'll want to kiss you?"

"I can make her."

"Dead's better. You don't have to worry yourself about how happy she is. You don't pay for nothing. If you got a live woman, one you're married to even, you're still paying for pussy. If you don't pay in money, you'll pay in pain. They'll smile and coo for a time, but stay out late with the boys, have a little financial stress, they all revert to just what my mamma was. A bitch. She drove my daddy into an early grave, way she nagged, and the old sow lived to be ninety. No wonder women live longer than men. They worry men to death.

"Like my uncle I was talking about. All that worry . . . hell, that was his wife put it on him. Wanting this and wanting that. When he got sick, had that operation and had to dip into his savings, she was out of there. They'd been married thirty years, but things got tough, you could see what those thirty years meant. He didn't even come out of that deal with a place to put his dick at night."

"Ain't all women that way."

"Yeah, they are. They can't help it. I'm not blaming them. It's in them, like germs. In time, they all turn out just the same."

"I'm talking about raping them, though, not marrying them. Getting kissed."

"You're with the kissing again. You been reading *Cosmo* or something? What's this kiss stuff? You get hungry, you eat. You get thirsty, you drink. You get tired, you sleep. You get horny, you kill and fuck. You use them like a product, Merle, then when you get through with the product, you throw out the package. Get a new one when you need it. This way, you always got the young ones, the tan ones, no matter how old or fat or ugly you get. You don't have to see a pretty woman get old, see that tan turn her face to leather. You can keep the world bright and fresh all the time. You listen to me, Merle. It's the best way."

Merle looked at the woman's body. Her head was turned toward him. Her eyes looked to have filled with milk. Water was running out of her and pooling on the grass and starting to spurt from between her legs. Merle looked away from her, said, "Guess I'm just looking for a little romance. I had me a taste of it, you know. It was all right. She could really kiss."

"Yeah, it was all right for a while, then she ran off with a sand nigger."

"Arab, Dave. She ran off with an Arab."

"He was here right now, you'd call him an Arab?"

"I'd kill him."

"There you are. Call him an Arab or a sand nigger. You'd kill him, right?"

Merle nodded.

"Listen," Dave said. "Don't think I don't understand what you're saying. Thing I like about you, Merle, is you aren't like those guys down at the plant, come in do your job, go home, watch a little TV, fall asleep in the chair dreaming about some magazine model 'cause the old lady won't give out, or you don't want to think about her giving out on account of the way she's got ugly. Thing is, Merle, you know you're dissatisfied. That's the first step to knowing there's more to life than the old grind. I appreciate that in you. It's a kind of sensitivity some men don't like to face. Think it makes them weak. It's a strength, is what it is, Merle. Something I wish I had more of."

"That's damn nice of you to say, Dave."

"It's true. Anybody knows you, knows you feel things deeply. And I don't want you to think that I don't appreciate romance, but you get our age, you got to look at things a little straighter. I can't see any romance with an old woman anyway, and a young one, she ain't gonna have me . . . unless it's the way we're doing it now."

Merle glanced at the corpse. Water was spewing up from between her legs like a whale blowing. Her stomach was a fat, white mound.

"We don't get that hose out of her," Merle said, "she's gonna blow the hell up."

"I'll get it," Dave said. He went over and turned off the water and pulled the hose out of her and put his foot on her stomach and began to pump his leg. Water gushed from her and her stomach began to flatten. "She was all right, wasn't she, Merle?"

"'Cept for them feet, she was fine."

They drove out into the pines and pulled off to the side of a little dirt road and parked. They got out and went around to the trunk, and with her legs spread like a wishbone, they dragged her into the brush and dropped her on the edge of an incline coated in blackberry briars.

"Man," Dave said. "Taste that air. This is the prettiest night I can remember."

"It's nice," Merle said.

Dave put a boot to the woman and pushed. She went rolling down the incline in a white moon-licked haze and crashed into the brush at the bottom. Dave pulled her shorts from the front of his pants and tossed them after her.

"Time they find her, the worms will have had some pussy too," Dave said.

They got in the car and Dave started it up and eased down the road.

"Dave?"

"Yeah?"

"You're a good friend," Merle said. "The talk and all, it done me good. Really."

Dave smiled, clapped Merle's shoulder. "Hey, it's all right. I been seeing this coming in you for a time, since the girl before last. . . . You're all right now, though. Right?"

"Well, I'm better."

"That's how you start."

They drove a piece. Merle said, "But I got to admit to you, I still miss being kissed."

Dave laughed. "You and the kiss. You're some piece of work buddy. . . . I got your kiss. Kiss my ass."

Merle grinned. "Way I feel, your ass could kiss back, I just might."

Dave laughed again. They drove out of the woods and onto the highway. The moon was high and bright.

I stayed up all night to write this one, and that's all I remember about it. I think we may have needed money for something for the kids. We often did. I had no fun at all writing it, which is rare for me, but I enjoyed reading it later. I had stopped somewhere on my bookish travels in a diner, and a guy tried to strike up a conversation. It was certainly innocent, no threats of death, or offers like the protagonist has here. But there was something off about the fellow. He said the right things for general conversation, but it all seemed to be piped in from someplace strange and dark. Whatever the case, the conversation didn't stick with me, but it was the impetus for a story. It rested on my mental shelf until I was asked to write a story and the need for money was there, so I wrote. Oftentimes, I've written some of my best stories for financial reasons. I wrote anyway, so it might have come out at another time under more pleasant circumstances. This one, however, due to the strange conversation at the diner, wherever the hell it was, along with the need for dough to pay bills and keep working, inspired this. I will admit, I never wrote better or worse for it, at least not overall, and I sure don't miss those hard times, though it wasn't at that point in my career as hard as it had been, and things kept improving as time went on. Except for that getting old part.

RAINY WEATHER

BRENT WALKED THROUGH some heavy rain and came to a little town called Clark. It was still raining when he got inside the café, and there were only three people there, and one of them was a waitress. He reckoned there was another person out back, in the kitchen, a cook. He could hear pans rattling around back there.

The other two in the café were not sitting together. A big man in a tee-shirt with a gimme cap that Brent figured went along with the 18-wheeler outside, huddled over a large piece of apple pie in a booth with ripped seats, and in another seat was an average-looking man in a brown suit. He had a look on his face like he might be trying desperately to will himself into another dimension. Brent could understand how he felt.

Brent sat on a stool at the counter and studied the blackboard menu on the wall. It made him hungry as hell. But all he had was a couple of dollars, so he decided on coffee.

The waitress, a plump woman who inherited her blondness from a chemical solution, came over and stood behind the counter and asked him what he wanted. He told her, and she bought back some coffee and cream.

He asked for extra cream. He thought if he couldn't afford to eat, the cream would help make his stomach settle better, and the cream was free.

Brent drank the coffee and felt some of the cold from the winter rain go out of him. He sipped the coffee slowly, trying to think what he could do next. Maybe there was a job here in town. If there was a bus station, he could hang out there overnight, and maybe tomorrow find some day work.

He was fed up with that kind of business, but that's about the best he was able to do.

If he ever had a chance to make any real money, it was long passed. If he ever had a chance to make anything of himself, that too was long past.

He had set himself down a road from which he could not return, and he wasn't really sure what kept him going.

He drank the coffee and the waitress poured him a second cup, and the man in the brown suit came over and sat by him. The man had a cup of coffee with him. He sat it on the counter and said, "Mind if I sit here?"

Brent shook his head. The man called the waitress over and she filled both their cups, and the man ordered a bowl of soup. He sat and sipped his coffee until the soup came. He looked at the soup, then he looked at Brent. He said, "You know, I don't know why I ordered this. I don't really want it."

Brent said, "That right?"

"You want it?"

"I don't know."

"Yeah, you take it. I don't want it. It's on me."

"You don't gotta do that."

"I don't, they throw it out."

Brent slid the bowl of soup in front of him and went at it as slowly as he could. It was all he could do not to take hold of the bowl and drink it. He crumbled the crackers that came with it into the soup, then used his spoon and tried not to let his hand shake. The man looked at the jailhouse tattoo on the back of Brent's hand, then looked away, as if he had never looked at all.

"Passing through?" asked the man.

"I guess. I'm looking for work."

"What kind of work do you do?"

"Oh, whatever. I haven't really got any skills, but I'll go at a job hard as I can. I mostly do day labor."

"Yeah. Little down on your luck?"

"I don't know that's your business. Thanks for the soup, but I don't know the soup makes that your business."

"I didn't mean nothing by it. I just thought I might could help you out."

"You saw me here and thought you could help me out?"

The man nodded and sipped his coffee. "Something like that."

"You got work?"

"Maybe. Well, not exactly work. But something I need done. I'll pay you five hundred dollars."

"How many days?"

"You mean how many hours."

Brent said, "Explain yourself."

"I mean what I want you to do, you could do in an hour or two. Maybe three, tops."

"Now? In the rain?"

"Finish your soup, we'll take a little drive, talk about it."

They drove out a ways and Brent began to feel a bit nervous. It occurred to him the man might have been talking about him making the money by some kind of sex act. The thing that worried him most was that he was considering it. Five hundred dollars right now was as good as five million.

They drove down a dirt road and the man pulled over and parked, turned on a little light on the dash, cranked his window down an inch, got a cigarette pack from inside his coat and offered Brent one. Brent passed. The man shook the cigarette out, lit it and puffed. Smoke went up and over the man's head and sucked out the window, as if it were in a hurry and had some important place to go.

Brent thought: Now he lays it on me. Suck my dick or walk.

Brent studied the man. He thought he could go through with it he had to, but he didn't have to. He figured he could take the man, and take his money too. He could throw him out and use the car to go a ways before leaving it somewhere. A plan began to form.

The man said, "I haven't got the five hundred dollars on me."

"What's that?"

"You're thinking what I'm thinking you're thinking, you can save yourself some time. I haven't got any money. Five dollars. I'll give you that. The car has less than a quarter tank worth of gas."

"You don't have five hundred dollars?"

"I got it, but not on me. I got more than five hundred dollars you do this right. And let me tell you something, jumping me won't help anyway. I'm rougher than I look and I've dealt with bad boys before."

Brent took a deep breath. The dude could be lying. He could have money on him. It might be worth finding out.

On the other hand, the guy sounded calm enough to be someone who had indeed dealt with trouble before.

The man said, "I saw that tattoo on your hand. Jailhouse work?"

Brent nodded.

"Shitty work. You do it?"

Brent nodded.

"I don't know what makes a con do it, unless it's boredom. Thing like that, looks like shit and it's bound to hurt doing it. Sticking a pocketknife in your hand, cutting a heart and putting pencil lead in it. Some brain surgery there, pardner."

"You bought me out here to talk about my tattoo?"

"No. I brought you here to talk about my wife. Best goddamn pussy this side of the Atlantic."

"You brought me here to tell me cock dog stories?"

"I brought you here so I could ask you to kill her."

Brent thought about that a while. He had killed a man once during a filling station robbery. It was the reason he had done time, but it had been pretty much an accident. The man had a gun and tried to protect his money, and he and Brent had wrestled and the gun had gone off. For that reason, he hadn't spent as much time in the slammer as he might have.

Brent said, "She's such good pussy, why kill her?"

"Man does not live by pussy alone."

"I'd like to try."

"That's what I used to think. I got hitched with her, I thought I could live on it, but I can't. Tell you what, you like pussy so much, before you kill her, you want to try, go ahead."

"I didn't say I'd kill anyone."

"I think you might. I consider myself a good judge of character. I think you might."

Brent said, "Say I did this thing, how would it go down, and why don't you do it?"

"I want it to look like a burglary. I want to have an alibi."

"All right, but we've been seen together."

"I don't think it matters. I don't live around here. I was passing through on my way home. My wife's murdered, it won't mean anything here. You won't mean anything here. I live a hundred miles away."

"You live a hundred miles away and you're sitting in a shitty café with a rainstorm outside, waiting on some chump."

"I been on a business trip, and on the way home I've sat in a lot of shitty cafés. I been thinking about this, and I saw you—"

"And you saw a loser, huh?"

"Frankly, yes. But it doesn't have to be that way. What you do is I drive you to Freeport. I show you where my house is. I let you out, and you wait until I have time to drive back to town and stop at the Red Barn Restaurant. I got a fellow I'm supposed to see. It's a late business meeting. He's a friend of mine, or he's supposed to be. We'll have a bite, then we'll drive out to the house for a drink and for him to sleep over so we can go fishing the next day. He and I will come in and find Anna dead."

"Me having killed her?"

"That's right."

"You said he's supposed to be a friend. He the guy fucking your wife?"

"Bingo. Another thing. He's a deputy. That'll really put me in the clear, make everything look cozy, 'cause we'll call the medical folks in quick-like. They'll estimate her time of death, and I'm wanting that estimate to be around eleven thirty. I want you to wait until then, do her in. I come in, I'm in the clear. I get some insurance. I'm free of the bitch, and the deputy who is banging my wife is part of my alibi. Ironic, huh?"

"How am I supposed to do this deed? This murder?"

"With a box cutter. I want it to look especially vicious. We keep a box cutter on my desk for opening letters. Or rather my wife does. Right now it's in the glove box. You do the work, you throw the cutter down. I'll identify it, and it'll look like you surprised her and killed her with something available. Make it pretty vicious, you want."

"A box cutter will cut her up all right, but it's not the best murder weapon in the world."

"You may have to strangle her or something, then cut her. I wouldn't be bothered you cut her face up good. I want her cut. Especially her face. And throw stuff around, and I'll say something's missing. I got some things put away so the insurance will have to pay."

"And how do I get away?"

"That's the good part. I'll give you a detailed description of the house as we drive. There's a place in the kitchen. I put it in myself. Anna doesn't know about it. I put it there for no good reason other than I liked the idea. And I guess I been thinking about something like this for a year now."

"But the right guy hadn't come along?"

"That's right. I saw you in that café and I knew I had the right guy. Now listen. You do the job, then you go to where the refrigerator is, you reach behind it and pull forward. It'll roll out on wheels. There's a wall plank there. It's not easy to see, but if you know it's there, you'll find it. It slides sideways. You can grab hold of the refrigerator if you're standing inside. Pull it to you, then slide the panel in. There's room in there to sit down. Fact is, there's a chair in there. And a table. Some dried jerky. Water. A light. A chemical toilet. Stuff like that. Just stay there. Sit quiet. And I'll let you out of there tomorrow and give you your money. I'll see you get someplace safe before I let you out. I got a change of clothes in the back seat there. You can slide back there and put them on. You'll be dry. I'll get rid of your clothes before I get into Freeport."

"How do I know you aren't just setting me up?"

"I could be, but I wouldn't want you to have to talk against me. I can make things work if you just take the money and disappear. And if you try to blackmail me later, I'll just ignore you. Blackmail all you want. It won't do you any good. Between you and me, they're going to believe me.

I've got a good reputation. Thing is, you take the money, and just go, and never let me see you again, and everything will be cozy for both of us."

Brent sat silent for a moment, listening to the rain drum on the roof of the car.

"Make up your mind," the man said, "I have to get going if I'm going to make this work. You say no, I'll take you back to town and we'll say goodbye."

"Make it a thousand."

"Done."

The rain had stopped. Brent was standing in the man's yard looking at a light in the window of the man's house. He didn't even know the bastard's name, and here he was, ready to kill the man's wife for a thousand dollars. He ought to just keep going, but to where? Right now, the idea of the money and hiding somewhere in the warm, dry house was appealing.

Brent went along quietly to the potting shed next to the garden. He watched the light in the window from there. He crept out of the shed and alongside the house and went to the back door. The key was on the sill as the man had said. He felt for the box cutter in his pocket, took it out, unlocked the door and slipped inside.

He climbed the stairs. Light was falling out of a room up there, falling across the hall and down the stairs. Brent went up slowly with the box cutter in his hand.

He went along close to the wall and tried to stay in shadow. He came to the doorway and looked around the edge of it carefully. There was a woman with short, tousled blonde hair sitting in a chair watching television. She had on a short black gown with red and yellow Chinese dragons on it. She had long legs that looked brown and smooth and she had them stretched out in front of her, resting her feet on a stool. The gown was split open and he could see she was wearing very brief black panties and that she was shaved very close. She had one hand to her mouth, and was chewing a nail.

She had pouty red lips.

Brent looked at her and thought about what the man had said. About what a fuck she was. About cutting up her face. She was the kind of woman could make a man crazy, all right.

Brent looked down at the box cutter. He looked at the woman. He would have to settle for the dry clothes and nothing else. He couldn't do it. There was a sound in the room, and Brent looked and saw a man come up behind the woman and bend down and kiss her on top of the head. The man's hands reached inside the gown and found her breast, then he leaned way over her shoulder and slid one hand along her belly until the robe came open all the way. He slid his hand down inside her panties and moved it around. The blonde moaned. Brent saw that the man was wearing a gun and a badge.

Brent thought: What the hell? And at that moment, the man looked up and saw him.

Brent made a run for it, but the man bolted after him. As Brent reached the stairs, the man leaped, tackled him. They both went tumbling down the steps and through the railing. Brent felt the man's hands on him for an instant, then he didn't feel them. The next instant, he found himself at the bottom of the stairs, stunned. He sat up. The deputy had gone through the railing. He was on the floor with his head twisted funny and his ass was in the air.

Brent tried to get up. The woman said. "Don't."

He looked up. She was at the top of stairs, coming down. The robe opened as she came down, and in spite of the situation, he couldn't help but admire the view. She was carrying a small revolver.

She made all the steps and went over to the deputy and bent down and looked at him. She said, "Shit." She took the deputy's pistol, which was still in its holster. The deputy fell over on his side and the light from the open room above hit them and made them look like fractured glass.

The woman studied the dead man for a moment. She seemed about as concerned as if she had seen someone else's potted plant blown over by a high wind.

She turned her attention to Brent. He lay on the floor still. The box cutter had fallen out of his pocket, and it was beside him; her eyes were on that.

She came closer, holding a revolver in either hand. They were pointed at Brent. She paused and took a good look at the box cutter. She said, "Slide that this way. Carefully."

He did. She picked up the box cutter. "This is mine," she said. "I use it to open mail. It's been missing for two days."

Brent didn't say anything.

"How'd you come by it?"

He still didn't say anything.

And then he saw a light shift in her eyes. "He gave it to you," she said. "My husband. He gave it to you, didn't he?"

Brent didn't answer.

"He threatened to cut me with it once. . . . He gave it to you, didn't he?!" She pointed the revolvers at Brent's forehead and cocked back the hammers.

Brent said, "Yes. Yes. Don't shoot. He gave it to me."

"To use on me?"

"Yes."

"Why that shit! That sorry shit! He hired you to kill me, didn't he?"

Brent could see the hall clock behind her. It was eleven o'clock. Her husband would be home in thirty minutes with the deputy.

Or maybe not. This had to be the deputy.

"Tell me what he had in mind," the woman said. "Tell me now, and you best tell it good, or I start shooting."

Brent considered for a moment, then went ahead and told her. He ended with the fact that the husband was supposed to arrive at eleven o'clock.

"He might be here sooner, "Brent said, "He's supposed to meet your deputy in town."

"Wrong deputy," the woman said.

"You screwing the entire police force?"

"Everyone except for the drug dog, and I got my eye on him. Get up."

Brent got up. "Way it's going to work," she said, "is you and I are going to bring the deputy's car around from behind the guest house. We're going to park it in front of the house. You're going to drive it."

"And if I don't?"

"I shoot you."

He drove the car around front and parked it. The woman sat beside him with the gun in her hand. Brent decided he could use a box cutter on this angel-faced devil after all. Fact was, he could beat her head in with a rock and sleep like a baby. She was one conniving bitch.

271

As they got out of the car, she took off the Chinese robe and handed it to him and had him use it to wipe down the seats and dash and steering wheel.

While he worked, he took some looks at her naked breasts and the small black panties and the long brown legs. They looked good in the light from the porch, but he could still cut her and he could still bash her head in with a rock.

When he was finished, she took back the robe and slipped it on while keeping the guns trained on him. She motioned him back inside. As they walked, Brent could smell the air, and it was rich with the smell of damp earth. He figured he would soon be in it, but not smelling it.

Inside, she cut off the porch light and pointed the guns at Brent. Brent said, "What now?"

"I'm going to say I called a deputy I know at his home. I called him there because I heard someone outside, but I didn't want to make a big deal of it. Like all deputies, my husband knows him. It makes sense I might call him. My husband's not available, so I call him. I could have called any of them."

"Even the drug dog if he'd answer the phone."

"That's right. He comes over. You spring on him. You fight. He's killed on the stairs from a fall, and I come down with my gun, and you wrestle it away from me, and about that time my husband comes in and you shoot him, and then, while you're busy doing that, I get my friend Bill's gun, and I shoot you. That way I get rid of hubby, and you. I collect insurance. I'm a wealthy widow. Not bad."

"You don't need to shoot me. I'll help you kill your husband. You let me go, I'll help you."

"I don't think so. Naw. I don't like that plan."

"But he's already here."

"What?"

The woman jerked her head towards the door, and in the instant she did it, just as she realized she had been snookered, Brent jumped at her and grabbed both her wrists and swung her around and onto the floor. But still she didn't let go of the guns. They rolled on the floor, this way and that.

They rolled against a table and overturned it and knocked a lamp off and it burst on Brent's head, and still they rolled.

Finally Brent got on top of her and bent one of her arms back into her face and used her own hand and the gun she was holding to rap her across the mouth. She let go of the gun and it slid away. Brent worked on the other hand and twisted the gun down, and the woman's own finger caused it to go off. She took a shot in the head and lay still.

Brent got off of her.

Shit, it had all gone haywire. He pulled off her Chinese robe, found the box cutter and wiped it off. He got the guns and did the same.

He thought about taking the deputy's car, then decided against it. He'd go across the patch of woods there and on out to the highway and find some house with an average-looking car, and he'd boost it. That beat riding around in a stolen vehicle that stood out like a bull dick on a goat farm.

He went out of there then. Went across the grass and out towards the road. He wondered if his prints were on anything anywhere in the house, then decided he couldn't wonder about that at all. He had to keep moving.

He reached the road and saw car lights through the trees, turning around a curve. He leaped across the road, ready to hunker down in a ditch, and suddenly something leaped at him. He stumbled back and onto the road and into the glow of the headlights. And in that moment, the car's brakes screeched, and in the peripheral glare of the headlights he saw what had leaped at him. A mangy yellow dog. It was standing in the ditch with its teeth bared. He had startled it and it was mad.

But it didn't matter. The car hit him and he went up and high and onto the road, rolled towards the ditch and into it. He could feel his arms were twisted behind him in a funny way, and he was facing the sky, but his stomach was flat in the ditch. He didn't feel any pain. He didn't feel anything. He heard the dog running off through the trees.

A car door slammed, then he heard someone crashing through the tall grass around the ditch. A man bent over him and touched him. The man had a flashlight. He shined it in Brent's face.

The man with the flashlight whispered, "Did you do her? Did you?"

Brent realized it was the husband. He opened his mouth to say something, but nothing came out. He heard another car door slam and heard someone else walking towards them.

"Did you do it?" whispered the man, and his voice was so desperate to know, his hands so nervous, the light swiveled and shone on himself.

It was the man who had hired him. His brown suit coat was hanging open and Brent saw something on the man's shirt that made him laugh. He laughed and coughed a ball of blood onto his chin. He thought: Of course this sonofabitch knew all the deputies, just like the wife said. Of course he did.

Just before Brent lost it and went way down into the darkest pit into which a person can be dropped, he saw the flashlight glint off the badge on the husband's chest. A sheriff's badge, and he saw the other deputy, wearing khakis and boots and a cowboy hat, come around and kneel next to the sheriff.

"Who the fuck is he?" the deputy said.

The sheriff had the flashlight on Brent's face, and he watched as Brent's eyes went blank. Then he felt for a pulse. When he was sure there wasn't one, he said, "I've no idea."

One of my best-known stories. I started with a woman driving at night on a mountain road, and just let the story unfold. Most of mine work that way. It was a delight to write, and it kept surprising me. Later, Don Coscarelli, a hell of a director and friend, with script assistance from Stephen Romano, wrote a script based on it for Showtime's Masters of Horror. *It came out great. I think it's in the top three of the stories filmed, all the stories written by whom the producers deemed "horror masters." Mick Garris was a driving force behind the show, and it should be noted he is one hell of a short-story writer himself. My son, Keith, and I were on the set. I remember loving the opportunity to be there. I also remember Keith eating too much stuff from the craft table and being sick as the proverbial dog and missing a couple of scenes he had wanted to see. But we had fun. Keith has been on a lot of film sets with me, and he's also written scripts that were filmed, and I have been with him on those sets.*

INCIDENT ON AND OFF A MOUNTAIN ROAD

WHEN ELLEN CAME to the moonlit mountain curve, her thoughts, which had been adrift with her problems, grounded, and she was suddenly aware that she was driving much too fast. The sign said CURVE: 30 MPH, and she was doing fifty.

She knew too that slamming on the brakes was the wrong move, so she opted to keep her speed and fight the curve and make it, and she thought she could.

The moonlight was strong, so visibility was high, and she knew her Chevy was in good shape, easy to handle, and she was a good driver.

But as she negotiated the curve a blue Buick seemed to grow out of the ground in front of her. It was parked on the shoulder of the road, at the peak of the curve, its nose sticking out a foot too far, its rear end against the moon-wet, silver railing that separated the curve from a mountainous plunge.

Had she been going an appropriate speed, missing the Buick wouldn't have been a problem, but at her speed she was swinging too far right, directly in line with it, and was forced, after all, to use her brakes. When

277

she did, the back wheels slid and the brakes groaned and the front of the Chevy hit the Buick, and there was a sound like an explosion and then for a dizzy instant she felt as if she were in the tumblers of a dryer.

Through the windshield came: Moonlight. Blackness. Moonlight.

One high bounce and a tight roll, and the Chevy came to rest upright with the engine dead, the right side flush against the railing. Another inch of jump or greater impact against the rail, and the Chevy would have gone over.

Ellen felt a sharp pain in her leg and reached down to discover that during the tumble she had banged it against something, probably the gear shift, and had ripped her stocking and her flesh. Blood was trickling into her shoe. Probing her leg cautiously with the tips of her fingers, she determined the wound wasn't bad and that all other body parts were operative.

She unfastened her seat belt, and as a matter of habit, located her purse and slipped its strap over her shoulder. She got out of the Chevy feeling wobbly, eased around front of it and saw the hood and bumper and roof were crumpled. A wisp of radiator steam hissed from beneath the wadded hood, rose into the moonlight and dissolved.

She turned her attentions to the Buick. Its tail end was now turned to her, and as she edged alongside it, she saw the front left side had been badly damaged. Fearful of what she might see, she glanced inside.

The moonlight shone through the rear windshield bright as a spotlight and revealed no one, but the back seat was slick with something dark and wet and there was plenty of it. A foul scent seeped out of a partially rolled-down back window. It was a hot coppery smell that gnawed at her nostrils and ached her stomach.

God, someone had been hurt. Maybe thrown free of the car, or perhaps they had gotten out and crawled off. But when? She and the Chevy had been airborne for only a moment, and she had gotten out of the vehicle instants after it ceased to roll. Surely she would have seen someone get out of the Buick, and if they had been thrown free by the collision, wouldn't at least one of the Buick's doors be open? If it had whipped back and closed, it seemed unlikely that it would be locked, and all the doors of the Buick were locked, and all the glass was intact, and only on her side was it rolled down, and only a crack. Enough for the smell of the blood to escape, not enough for a person to slip through unless they were thin and flexible as a feather.

On the other side of the Buick, on the ground, between the back door and the railing, there were drag marks and a thick swath of blood, and another swath on the top of the railing; it glowed there in the moonlight as if it were molasses laced with radioactivity.

Ellen moved cautiously to the railing and peered over.

No one lay mangled and bleeding and oozing their guts. The ground was not as precarious there as she expected it. It was pebbly and sloped out gradually and there was a trail going down it. The trail twisted slightly and as it deepened the foliage grew denser on either side of it. Finally it curlicued its way into the dark thicket of a forest below, and from the forest, hot on the wind, came the strong turpentine tang of pines and something less fresh and not as easily identifiable.

Now she saw someone moving down there, floating up from the forest like an apparition; a white face split by silver—braces, perhaps. She could tell from the way this someone moved that it was a man. She watched as he climbed the trail and came within examination range. He seemed to be surveying her as carefully as she was surveying him.

Could this be the driver of the Buick?

As he came nearer Ellen discovered she could not identify the expression he wore. It was neither joy or anger or fear or exhaustion or pain. It was somehow all and none of these.

When he was ten feet away, still looking up, that same odd expression on his face, she could hear him breathing. He was breathing with exertion, but not to the extent she thought him tired or injured. It was the sound of someone who had been about busy work.

She yelled down, "Are you injured?"

He turned his head quizzically, like a dog trying to make sense of a command, and it occurred to Ellen that he might be knocked about in the head enough to be disoriented.

"I'm the one who ran into your car," she said. "Are you all right?"

His expression changed then, and it was most certainly identifiable this time. He was surprised and angry. He came up the trail quickly, took hold of the top railing, his fingers going into the blood there, and vaulted over and onto the gravel.

Ellen stepped back out of his way and watched him from a distance. The guy made her nervous. Even close up, he looked like some kind of spook.

He eyed her briefly, glanced at the Chevy, turned to look at the Buick. "It was my fault," Ellen said.

He didn't reply, but returned his attention to her and continued to cock his head in that curious dog sort of way.

Ellen noticed that one of his shirt sleeves was stained with blood, and that there was blood on the knees of his pants, but he didn't act as if he were hurt in any way. He reached into his pants pocket and pulled out something and made a move with his wrist. Out flicked a lock-blade knife. The thin edge of it sucked up the moonlight and spat it out in a silver spray that fanned wide when he held it before him and jiggled it like a man working a stubborn key into a lock. He advanced toward her, and as he came, his lips split and pulled back at the corners, exposing not braces, but metal-capped teeth that matched the sparkle of his blade.

It occurred to her that she could bolt for the Chevy, but in the same mental flash of lightning, it occurred to her she wouldn't make it.

Ellen threw herself over the railing, and as she leapt, she saw out of the corner of her eye the knife slashing the place she had occupied, catching moonbeams and throwing them away. Then the blade was out of her view and she hit on her stomach and skidded onto the narrow trail, slid downward, feet first. The gravel and roots tore at the front of her dress and ripped through her nylons and gouged her flesh. She cried out in pain and her sliding gained speed. Lifting her chin, she saw that the man was climbing over the railing and coming after her at a stumbling run, the knife held before him like a wand.

Her sliding stopped, and she pushed off with her hands to make it start again, not knowing if this was the thing to do or not, since the trail inclined sharply on her right side, and should she skid only slightly in that direction, she could hurtle off into blackness. But somehow she kept slithering along the trail and even spun around a corner and stopped with her head facing downward, her purse practically in her teeth.

She got up then, without looking back, and began to run into the woods, the purse beating at her side. She moved as far away from the trail as she could, fighting limbs that conspired to hit her across the face or hold her, vines and bushes that tried to tie her feet or trip her.

Behind her, she could hear the man coming after her, breathing heavily now, not really winded, but hurrying. For the first time in months, she was grateful for Bruce and his survivalist insanity. His passion to be in shape and for her to be in shape with him was paying off. All that jogging had given her the lungs of an ox and strengthened her legs and ankles. A line from one of Bruce's survivalist books came to her: Do the unexpected.

She found a trail amongst the pines, and followed it, then abruptly broke from it and went back into the thicket. It was harder going, but she assumed her pursuer would expect her to follow a trail.

The pines became so thick she got down on her hands and knees and began to crawl. It was easier to get through that way. After a moment, she stopped scuttling and eased her back against one of the pines and sat and listened. She felt reasonably well hidden, as the boughs of the pines grew low and drooped to the ground. She took several deep breaths, holding each for a long moment. Gradually, she began breathing normally. Above her, from the direction of the trail, she could hear the man running, coming nearer. She held her breath.

The running paused a couple of times, and she could imagine the man, his strange, pale face turning from side to side, as he tried to determine what had happened to her. The sound of running started again and the man moved on down the trail.

Ellen considered easing out and starting back up the trail, making her way to her car and driving off. Damaged as it was, she felt it would still run, but she was reluctant to leave her hiding place and step into the moonlight. Still, it seemed a better plan than waiting. If she didn't do something, the man could always go back topside himself and wait for her. The woods, covering acres and acres of land below and beyond, would take her days to get through, and without food and water and knowledge of the geography, she might never make it, could end up going in circles for days.

Bruce and his survivalist credos came back to her. She remembered something he had said to one of his self-defense classes, a bunch of rednecks hoping and praying for a commie takeover so they could show their stuff.

He had told them, "Utilize what's at hand. Size up what you have with you and how it can be put to use."

All right, she thought. All right, Brucey, you sonofabitch. I'll see what's at hand.

One thing she knew she had for sure was a little flashlight. It wasn't much, but it would serve for her to check out the contents of her purse. She located it easily, and without withdrawing it from her purse, turned it on and held the open purse close to her face to see what was inside. Before she actually found it, she thought of her nail file kit. Besides the little bottle of nail polish remover, there was an emery board and two metal files. The files were the ticket. They might serve as weapons; they weren't much, but they were something.

She also carried a very small pair of nail scissors, independent of the kit, the points of the scissors being less than a quarter inch. That wouldn't be worth much, but she took note of it and mentally catalogued it.

She found the nail kit, turned off the flash and removed one of the files and returned the rest of the kit to her purse. She held the file tightly, made a little jabbing motion with it. It seemed so light and thin and insignificant.

She had been absently carrying her purse on one shoulder, and now to make sure she didn't lose it, she placed the strap over her neck and slid her arm through.

Clenching the nail file, she moved on hands and knees beneath the pine boughs and poked her head out into the clearing of the trail. She glanced down it first, and there, not ten yards from her, looking up the trail, holding his knife by his side, was the man. The moonlight lay cold on his face and the shadows of the wind-blown boughs fell across him and wavered. It seemed as if she were leaning over a pool and staring down into the water and seeing him at the bottom of it, or perhaps his reflection on the face of the pool.

She realized instantly that he had gone down the trail a ways, became suspicious of her ability to disappear so quickly, and had turned to judge where she might have gone. And, as if in answer to the question, she had poked her head into view.

They remained frozen for a moment, then the man took a step up the trail, and just as he began to run, Ellen went backwards into the pines on her hands and knees.

She had gone less than ten feet when she ran up against a thick limb that lay close to the ground and was preventing her passage. She got down on her belly and squirmed beneath it, and as she was pulling her head under, she saw Moon Face crawling into the thicket, making good time; time made better when he lunged suddenly and covered half the space between them, the knife missing her by fractions.

Ellen jerked back and felt her feet falling away from her. She let go of the file and grabbed out for the limb and it bent way back and down with her weight. It lowered her enough for her feet to touch ground. Relieved, she realized she had fallen into a wash made by erosion, not off the edge of the mountain.

Above her, gathered in shadows and stray strands of moonlight that showed through the pine boughs, was the man. His metal-tipped teeth caught a moonbeam and twinkled. He placed a hand on the limb she held, as if to lower himself, and she let go of it.

The limb whispered away from her and hit him full in the face and knocked him back.

Ellen didn't bother to scrutinize the damage. Turning, she saw that the wash ended in a slope and that the slope was thick with trees growing out like great, feathered spears thrown into the side of the mountain.

She started down, letting the slant carry her, grasping limbs and tree trunks to slow her descent and keep her balance. She could hear the man climbing down and pursuing her, but she didn't bother to turn and look. Below she could see the incline was becoming steeper, and if she continued, it would be almost straight up and down with nothing but the trees for support, and to move from one to the other, she would have to drop, chimpanzee-like, from limb to limb. Not a pleasant thought.

Her only consolation was that the trees to her right, veering back up the mountain, were thick as cancer cells. She took off in that direction, going wide, and began plodding upwards again, trying to regain the concealment of the forest.

She chanced a look behind her before entering the pines, and saw that the man, who she had come to think of as Moon Face, was some distance away.

Weaving through a mass of trees, she integrated herself into the forest, and as she went the limbs began to grow closer to the ground and the trees became so thick they twisted together like pipe cleaners. She got down on her hands and knees and crawled between limbs and around tree trunks and tried to lose herself among them.

To follow her, Moon Face had to do the same thing, and at first she heard him behind her, but after a while, there were only the sounds she was making.

She paused and listened.

Nothing.

Glancing the way she had come, she saw the intertwining limbs she had crawled under mixed with penetrating moonbeams, heard the short bursts of her breath and the beating of her heart, but detected no evidence of Moon Face. She decided the head start she had, all the weaving she had done, the cover of the pines, had confused him, at least temporarily.

It occurred to her that if she had stopped to listen, he might have done the same, and she wondered if he could hear the pounding of her heart. She took a deep breath and held it and let it out slowly through her nose, did it again. She was breathing more normally now, and her heart, though still hammering furiously, felt as if it were back inside her chest where it belonged.

Easing her back against a tree trunk, she sat and listened, watching for that strange face, fearing it might abruptly burst through the limbs and brush, grinning its horrible teeth, or worse, that he might come up behind her, reach around the tree trunk with his knife and finish her in a bloody instant.

She checked and saw that she still had her purse. She opened it and got hold of the file kit by feel and removed the last file, determined to make better use of it than the first. She had no qualms about using it, knew she would, but what good would it do? The man was obviously stronger than she, and crazy as the pattern in a scratch quilt.

Once again, she thought of Bruce. What would he have done in this situation? He would certainly have been the man for the job. He would have relished it. Would probably have challenged old Moon Face to a one-on-one at the edge of the mountain, and even with a nail file, would have been confident that he could take him.

Ellen thought about how much she hated Bruce, and even now, shed of him, that hatred burned bright. How had she gotten mixed up with that dumb, macho bastard in the first place? He had seemed enticing at first. So powerful. Confident. Capable. The survivalist stuff had always seemed a little nutty, but at first no more nutty than an obsession with golf or a strong belief in astrology. Perhaps had she known how serious he was about it, she wouldn't have been attracted to him in the first place.

No. It wouldn't have mattered. She had been captivated by him, by his looks and build and power. She had nothing but her own libido and stupidity to blame. And worse yet, when things turned sour, she had stayed and let them sour even more. There had been good moments, but they were quickly eclipsed by Bruce's determination to be ready for the Big Day, as he referred to it. He knew it was coming, if he was somewhat vague on who was bringing it. But someone would start a war of some sort, a nuclear war, a war in the streets, and only the rugged individualist, well armed and well trained and strong of body and will, would survive beyond the initial attack. Those survivors would then carry out guerrilla warfare, hit-and-run operations, and eventually win back the country from . . . whoever. And if not win it back, at least have some kind of life free of dictatorship.

It was silly. It was every little boy's fantasy. Living by your wits with gun and knife. And owning a woman. She had been the woman. At first Bruce had been kind enough, treated her with respect. He was obviously on the male chauvinist side, but originally it had seemed harmless enough, kind of Old World charming. But when he moved them to the mountains, that charm had turned to domination, and the small crack in his mental state widened until it was a deep, dark gulf.

She was there to keep house and to warm his bed, and any opinions she had contrary to his own were stupid. He read survivalist books constantly and quoted passages to her and suggested she look the books over, be ready to stand tall against the oncoming aggressors.

By the time he had gone completely over the edge, living like a mountain man, ordering her about, his eyes roving from side to side, suspicious of her every move, expecting to hear on his shortwave at any moment World War Three had started, or that race riots were overrunning the U.S., or that a shiny probe packed with extraterrestrial invaders brandishing ray guns had landed on the White House lawn, she was trapped in his cabin in the mountains, with him holding the keys to her Chevy and his Jeep.

For a time she feared he would become paranoid enough to imagine she was one of the "bad guys" and put a .357 round through her chest. But now she was free of him, escaped from all that . . . only to be threatened by another man: a moon-faced, silver-toothed monster with a knife.

She returned once again to the question: what would Bruce do, outside of challenging Moon Face in hand-to-hand combat? Sneaking past him would be the best bet, making it back to the Chevy. To do that Bruce would have used guerrilla techniques. "Take advantage of what's at hand," he always said.

Well, she had looked to see what was at hand, and that turned out to be a couple of fingernail files, one of them lost up the mountain.

Then maybe she wasn't thinking about this in the right way. She might not be able to outfight Moon Face, but perhaps she could outthink him. She had outthought Bruce, and he had considered himself a master of strategy and preparation.

She tried to put herself in Moon Face's head. What was he thinking? For the moment he saw her as his prey, a frightened animal on the run. He might be more cautious because of that trick with the limb, but he'd most likely chalk that one up to accident—which it was for the most part . . . but what if the prey turned on him?

There was a sudden cracking sound, and Ellen crawled a few feet in the direction of the noise, gently moved aside a limb. Some distance away, discerned faintly through a tangle of limbs, she saw light and detected movement, and knew it was Moon Face. The cracking sound must have been him stepping on a limb.

He was standing with his head bent, looking at the ground, flashing a little pocket flashlight, obviously examining the drag path she had made with her hands and knees when she entered into the pine thicket.

She watched as his shape and the light bobbed and twisted through the limbs and tree trunks, coming nearer. She wanted to run, but didn't know where to.

All right, she thought. All right. Take it easy. Think.

She made a quick decision. Removed the scissors from her purse, took off her shoes and slipped off her panty hose and put her shoes on again.

She quickly snipped three long strips of nylon from her damaged panty hose and knotted them together, using the sailor knots Bruce had taught her. She cut more thin strips from the hose—all the while listening for Moon Face's approach—and used all but one of them to fasten her fingernail file, point out, securely to the tapered end of one of the small, flexible pine limbs, then she tied one end of the long nylon strip she had made around the limb, just below the file, and crawled backwards, pulling the limb with her, bending it deep. When she had it back as far as she could manage, she took a death grip on the nylon strip, and using it to keep the limb's position taut, crawled around the trunk of a small pine and curved the nylon strip about it and made a loop knot at the base of a sapling that crossed her knee-drag trail. She used her last strip of nylon to fasten to the loop of the knot, and carefully stretched the remaining length across the trail and tied it to another sapling. If it worked correctly, when he came crawling through the thicket, following her, his hands or knees would hit the strip, pull the loop free, and the limb would fly forward, the file stabbing him, in an eye if she were lucky.

Pausing to look through the boughs again, she saw that Moon Face was on his hands and knees, moving through the thick foliage toward her. Only moments were left.

She shoved pine needles over the strip and moved away on her belly, sliding under the cocked sapling, no longer concerned that she might make noise, in fact hoping noise would bring Moon Face quickly.

Following the upward slope of the hill, she crawled until the trees became thin again and she could stand. She cut two long strips of nylon from her hose with the scissors, and stretched them between two trees about ankle high.

That one would make him mad if it caught him, but the next one would be the corker.

She went up the path, used the rest of the nylon to tie between two saplings, then grabbed hold of a thin, short limb and yanked at it until it cracked, worked it free so there was a point made from the break. She snapped that over her knee to form a point at the opposite end. She made a quick mental measurement, jammed one end of the stick into the soft ground, leaving a point facing up.

At that moment came evidence her first snare had worked—a loud swishing sound as the limb popped forward and a cry of pain. This was followed by a howl as Moon Face crawled out of the thicket and onto the trail. He stood slowly, one hand to his face. He glared up at her, removed his hand. The file had struck him in the cheek; it was covered with blood. Moon Face pointed his blood-covered hand at her and let out an accusing shriek so horrible she retreated rapidly up the trail. Behind her, she could hear Moon Face running.

The trail curved upward and turned abruptly. She followed the curve a ways, looked back as Moon Face tripped over her first strip and hit the ground, came up madder, charged even more violently up the path. But the second strip got him and he fell forward, throwing his hands out. The spike in the trail hit him low in the throat.

She stood transfixed at the top of the trail as he did a push-up and came to one knee and put a hand to his throat. Even from a distance, and with only the moonlight to show it to her, she could see that the wound was dreadful.

Good.

Moon Face looked up, stabbed her with a look, started to rise. Ellen turned and ran. As she made the turns in the trail, the going improved and she theorized that she was rushing up the trail she had originally come down.

This hopeful notion was dispelled when the pines thinned and the trail dropped, then leveled off, then tapered into nothing. Before she could slow up, she discovered she was on a sort of peninsula that jutted out from the mountain and resembled an irregular-shaped diving board from which you could leap off into night-black eternity.

In place of the pines on the sides of the trail were numerous scarecrows on poles, and out on the very tip of the peninsula, somewhat dispelling the diving-board image, was a shack made of sticks and mud and brambles.

After pausing to suck in some deep breaths, Ellen discovered on closer examination that it wasn't scarecrows bordering her path after all. It was people.

Dead people. She could smell them.

There were at least a dozen on either side, placed upright on poles, their feet touching the ground, their knees slightly bent. They were all fully clothed, and in various states of deterioration. Holes had been poked through the backs of their heads to correspond with the hollow sockets of their eyes, and the moonlight came through the holes and shined through the sockets, and Ellen noted, with a warm sort of horror, that one wore a white sundress and . . . plastic shoes, and through its head she could see stars. On the corpse's finger was a wedding ring, and the finger had grown thin and withered and the ring was trapped there by knucklebone alone.

The man next to her was fresher. He too was eyeless and holes had been drilled through the back of his skull, but he still wore glasses and was fleshy. There was a pen and pencil set in his coat pocket. He wore only one shoe.

There was a skeleton in overalls, a wilting cigar stuck between his teeth. A fresh UPS man with his cap at a jaunty angle, the moon through his head, and a clipboard tied to his hand with string. His legs had been positioned in such a way it seemed as if he was walking. A housewife with a crumpled, nearly disintegrated grocery bag under her arm, the contents having long fallen through the worn, wet bottom to heap at her feet in a mass of colorless boxes and broken glass. A withered corpse in a ballerina's tutu and slippers, rotting grapefruits tied to her chest with cord to simulate breasts, her legs arranged in such a way she seemed in mid-dance, up on her toes, about to leap or whirl.

The real horror was the children. One pathetic little boy's corpse, still full of flesh and with only his drilled eyes to show death, had been arranged in such a way that a teddy bear drooped from the crook of his elbow. A toy metal tractor and a plastic truck were at his feet.

There was a little girl wearing a red rubber clown nose and a propeller beanie. A green plastic purse hung from her shoulder by a strap and a doll's legs had been taped to her palm with black electrician's tape. The doll hung upside down, holes drilled through its plastic head so that it matched its owner.

Things began to click. Ellen understood what Moon Face had been doing down here in the first place. He hadn't been in the Buick when she struck it. He was disposing of a body. He was a murderer who brought his victims here and set them up on either side of the pathway, parodying the way they were in life, cutting out their eyes and punching through the backs of their heads to let the world in.

Ellen realized numbly that time was slipping away, and Moon Face was coming, and she had to find the trail up to her car. But when she turned to run, she froze.

Thirty feet away, where the trail met the last of the pines, squatting dead center in it, arms on his knees, one hand loosely holding the knife, was Moon Face. He looked calm, almost happy, in spite of the fact a large swath of dried blood was on his cheek and the wound in his throat was making a faint whistling sound as air escaped it.

He appeared to be gloating, savoring the moment when he would set his knife to work on her eyes, the gray matter behind them, the bone of her skull.

A vision of her corpse propped up next to the child with the teddy bear, or perhaps the skeletal ballerina, came to mind; she could see herself hanging there, the light of the moon falling through her empty head, melting into the path.

Then she felt anger. It boiled inside her. She determined she was not going to allow Moon Face his prize easily. He'd earn it.

Another line from Bruce's books came to her.

Consider your alternatives.

She did, in a flash. And they were grim. She could try charging past Moon Face, or pretend to, then dart into the pines. But it seemed unlikely she could make the trees before he overtook her. She could try going over the side of the trail and climbing down, but it was much too steep there, and she'd fall immediately. She could make for the shack and try and find something she could fight with. The last idea struck her as the correct one, the one Bruce would have pursued. What was his quote? "If you can't effect an escape, fall back and fight with what's available to you."

She hurried to the hut, glancing behind her from time to time to check on Moon Face. He hadn't moved. He was observing her calmly, as if he had all the time in the world.

When she was about to go through the doorless entryway, she looked back at him one last time. He was in the same spot, watching, the knife held limply against his leg. She knew he thought he had her right where he wanted her, and that's exactly what she wanted him to think. A surprise attack was the only chance she had. She just hoped she could find something to surprise him with.

She hastened inside and let out an involuntary rasp of breath.

The place stank, and for good reason. In the center of the little hut was a folding card table and some chairs, and seated in one of the chairs was a woman, the flesh rotting and dripping off her skull like candle wax, her eyes empty and holes in the back of her head. Her arm was resting on the table and her hand was clamped around an open bottle of whiskey. Beside her, also without eyes, suspended in a standing position by wires connected to the roof, was a man. He was a fresh kill. Big, dressed in khaki pants and shirt and work shoes. In one hand a doubled belt was taped, and wires were attached in such a way that his arm was drawn back as if ready to strike. Wires were secured to his lips and pulled tight behind his head so that he was smiling in a ghoulish way. Foil gum wrappers were fixed to his teeth, and the moonlight gleaming through the opening at the top of the hut fell on them and made them resemble Moon Face's metal-tipped choppers.

Ellen felt queasy, but fought the sensation down. She had more to worry about than corpses. She had to prevent herself from becoming one.

She gave the place a quick pan. To her left was a rust-framed rollaway bed with a thin, dirty mattress, and against the far wall was a baby crib, and next to that a camper stove with a small frying pan on it.

She glanced quickly out the door of the hut and saw that Moon Face had moved onto the stretch of trail bordered by the bodies. He was walking very slowly, looking up now and then as if to appreciate the stars.

Her heart pumped another beat.

She moved about the hut, looking for a weapon.

The frying pan.

She grabbed it, and as she did, she saw what was in the crib. What belonged there. A baby. But dead. A few months old. Its skin thin as plastic and stretched tight over pathetic, little rib bones. Eyes gone, holes through its head. Burnt match stubs between blackened toes. It wore a diaper and the stink of feces wafted from it and into her nostrils. A rattle lay at the foot of the crib.

A horrible realization rushed through her. The baby had been alive when taken by this madman, and it had died here, starved and tortured. She gripped the frying pan with such intensity her hand cramped.

Her foot touched something.

She looked down. Large bones were heaped there—discarded mommies and daddies, for it now occurred to her that was who the corpses represented.

Something gleamed amongst the bones. A gold cigarette lighter.

Through the doorway of the hut she saw Moon Face was halfway down the trail. He had paused to nonchalantly adjust the UPS man's clipboard. The geek had made his own community here, his own family, people he could deal with—dead people—and it was obvious he intended for her to be part of his creation.

Ellen considered attacking straight-on with the frying pan when Moon Face came through the doorway, but so far he had proven strong enough to take a file in the cheek and a stick in the throat, and despite the severity of the latter wound, he had kept on coming. Chances were he was strong enough to handle her and her frying pan.

A back-up plan was necessary. Another one of Bruce's pronouncements. She recalled a college friend, Carol, who used to use her bikini panties to launch projectiles at a teddy bear propped on a chair. This graduated to an apple on the bear's head. Eventually, Ellen and her dorm sisters got into the act. Fresh panties with tight elastic and marbles for ammunition were ever ready in a box by the door; the bear and an apple were in constant position. In time, Ellen became the best shot of all. But that was ten years ago. Expertise was long gone, even the occasional shot now and then was no longer taken . . . still. . . .

Ellen replaced the frying pan on the stove, hiked up her dress and pulled her bikini panties down and stepped out of them and picked up the lighter.

She put the lighter in the crotch of the panties and stuck her fingers into the leg loops to form a fork and took hold of the lighter through the panties and pulled it back, assured herself the elastic was strong enough to launch the projectile.

All right. That was a start.

She removed her purse, so Moon Face couldn't grab it and snare her, and tossed it aside. She grabbed the whiskey bottle from the corpse's hand and turned and smashed the bottom of it against the cook stove. Whiskey and glass flew. The result was a jagged weapon she could lunge with. She placed the broken bottle on the stove next to the frying pan.

Outside, Moon Face was strolling toward the hut, like a shy teenager about to call on his date.

There were only moments left. She glanced around the room, hoping insanely at the last second she would find some escape route, but there was none.

Sweat dripped from her forehead and ran into her eye and she blinked it out and half-drew back the panty sling with its golden projectile. She knew her makeshift weapon wasn't powerful enough to do much damage, but it might give her a moment of distraction, a chance to attack him with the bottle. If she went at him straight on with it, she felt certain he would disarm her and make short work of her, but if she could get him off guard. . . .

She lowered her arms, kept her makeshift slingshot in front of her, ready to be cocked and shot.

Moon Face came through the door, ducking as he did, a sour sweat smell entering with him. His neck wound whistled at her like a teapot about to boil. She saw then that he was bigger than she first thought. Tall and broad-shouldered and strong.

He looked at her and there was that peculiar expression again. The moonlight from the hole in the roof hit his eyes and teeth, and it was as if that light was his source of energy. He filled his chest with air and seemed to stand a full two inches taller. He looked at the woman's corpse in the chair, the man's corpse supported on wires, glanced at the playpen.

He smiled at Ellen, squeaked more than spoke, "Bubba's home, Sissie."

I'm not Sissie yet, thought Ellen. Not yet.

Moon Face started to move around the card table and Ellen let out a blood-curdling scream that caused him to bob his head high like a rabbit surprised by headlights. Ellen jerked up the panties and pulled them back and let loose the lighter. It shot out of the panties and fell to the center of the card table with a clunk.

Moon Face looked down at it.

Ellen was temporarily gripped with paralysis, then she stepped forward and kicked the card table as hard as she could. It went into Moon Face, hitting him waist high, startling, but not hurting him.

Now! thought Ellen, grabbing her weapons. Now!

She rushed him, the broken bottle in one hand, the frying pan in the other. She slashed out with the bottle and it struck him in the center of the face and he let out a scream and the glass fractured and a splash of blood burst from him and in that same instant Ellen saw that his nose was cut half in two and she felt a tremendous throb in her hand. The bottle had broken in her palm and cut her.

She ignored the pain and as Moon Face bellowed and lashed out with the knife, cutting the front of her dress but not her flesh, she brought the frying pan around and caught him on the elbow, and the knife went soaring across the room and behind the rollaway bed.

Moon Face froze, glanced in the direction the knife had taken. He seemed empty and confused without it.

Ellen swung the pan again. Moon Face caught her wrist and jerked her around and she lost the pan and was sent hurtling toward the bed, where she collapsed on the mattress. The bed slid down and smashed through the thin wall of sticks and a foot of the bed stuck out into blackness and the great drop below. The bed tottered slightly, and Ellen rolled off of it, directly into the legs of Moon Face. As his knees bent, and he reached for her, she rolled backwards and went under the bed and her hand came to rest on the knife. She grabbed it, rolled back toward Moon Face's feet, reached out quickly and brought the knife down on one of his shoes and drove it in as hard as she could.

A bellow from Moon Face. His foot leaped back and it took the knife with it. Moon Face screamed, "Sissie! You're hurting me!"

Moon Face reached down and pulled the knife out, and Ellen saw his foot come forward, and then he was grabbing the bed and effortlessly jerking it off of her and back, smashing it into the crib, causing the child to topple out of it and roll across the floor, the rattle clattering behind it. He grabbed Ellen by the back of her dress and jerked her up and spun her around to face him, clutched her throat in one hand and held the knife close to her face with the other, as if for inspection; the blade caught the moonlight and winked.

Beyond the knife, she saw his face, pathetic and pained and white. His breath, sharp as the knife, practically wilted her. His neck wound whistled softly. The remnants of his nose dangled wet and red against his upper lip and cheek and his teeth grinned a moonlit, metal good-bye.

It was all over, and she knew it, but then Bruce's words came back to her in a rush: "When it looks as if you're defeated, and there's nothing left, try anything."

She twisted and jabbed out at his eyes with her fingers and caught him solid enough that he thrust her away and stumbled backwards. But only for an instant. He bolted forward, and Ellen stooped and grabbed the dead child by the ankle and struck Moon Face with it as if it were a club. Once in the face, once in the midsection. The rotting child burst into a spray of desiccated flesh and innards and she hurled the leg at Moon Face and then she was circling around the rollaway bed, trying to make the door. Moon Face, at the other end of the bed, saw this, and when she moved for the door, he lunged in that direction, causing her to jump back to the end of the bed. Smiling, he returned to his end, waited for her next attempt.

She lurched for the door again, and Moon Face deep-stepped that way, and when she jerked back, Moon Face jerked back too, but this time Ellen bent and grabbed the end of the bed and hurled herself against it. The bed hit Moon Face in the knees, and as he fell, the bed rolled over him and he let go of the knife and tried to put out his hands to stop the bed's momentum. The impetus of the rollaway carried him across the short length of the dirt floor and his head hit the far wall and the sticks cracked and hurtled out into blackness, and Moon Face followed and the bed followed him, then caught on the edge of the drop and the wheels buried up in the dirt and hung there.

Ellen had shoved so hard she fell face down, and when she looked up, she saw the bed was dangling, shaking, the mattress slipping loose, about to glide off into nothingness.

Moon Face's hands flicked into sight, clawing at the sides of the bed's frame. Ellen gasped. He was going to make it up. The bed's wheels were going to hold.

She pulled a knee under her, cocking herself, then sprang forward, thrusting both palms savagely against the bed. The wheels popped free and the rollaway shot out into the dark emptiness.

Ellen scooted forward on her knees and looked over the edge. There was blackness, a glimpse of the mattress falling free, and a pale object, like a white-washed planet with a great vein of silver in it, jetting through the cold expanse of space. Then the mattress and the face were gone and there was just the darkness and a distant sound like a water balloon exploding.

Ellen sat back and took a breather. When she felt strong again and felt certain her heart wouldn't tear through her chest, she stood up and looked around the room. She thought a long time about what she saw.

She found her purse and panties, went out of the hut and up the trail, and after a few wrong turns, she found the proper trail that wound its way up the mountainside to where her car was parked. When she climbed over the railing, she was exhausted.

Everything was as it was. She wondered if anyone had seen the cars, if anyone had stopped, then decided it didn't matter. There was no one here now, and that's what was important.

She took the keys from her purse and tried the engine. It turned over. That was a relief.

She killed the engine, got out and went around and opened the trunk of the Chevy and looked down at Bruce's body. His face looked like one big bruise, his lips were as large as sausages. It made her happy to look at him.

A new energy came to her. She got him under the arms and pulled him out and managed him over to the rail and grabbed his legs and flipped him over the railing and onto the trail. She got one of his hands and started pulling him down the path, letting the momentum help her. She felt good. She felt strong. First Bruce had tried to dominate her, had threatened her, had thought she was weak because she was a woman, and one night, after slapping her, after raping her, while he slept a drunken sleep, she had pulled the blankets up tight around him and looped rope over and under the bed and used the knots he had taught her, and secured him.

Then she took a stick of stove wood and had beat him until she was so weak she fell to her knees. She hadn't meant to kill him, just punish him for slapping her around, but when she got started she couldn't stop until she was too worn out to go on, and when she was finished, she discovered he was dead.

That didn't disturb her much. The thing then was to get rid of the body somewhere, drive on back to the city and say he had abandoned her and not come back. It was weak, but all she had. Until now.

After several stops for breath, a chance to lie on her back and look up at the stars, Ellen managed Bruce to the hut and got her arms under his and got him seated in one of the empty chairs. She straightened things up as best as she could. She put the larger pieces of the baby back in the crib. She picked Moon Face's knife up off the floor and looked at it and looked at Bruce, his eyes wide open, the moonlight from the roof striking them, showing them to be dull as scratched glass.

Bending over his face, she went to work on his eyes. When she finished with them, she pushed his head forward and used the blade like a drill. She worked until the holes satisfied her. Now if the police found the Buick up there and came down the trail to investigate, and found the trail leading here, saw what was in the shack, Bruce would fit in with the rest of Moon Face's victims. The police would probably conclude Moon Face, sleeping here with his "family," had put his bed too close to the cliff and it had broken through the thin wall and he had tumbled to his death.

She liked it.

She held Bruce's chin, lifted it, examined her work.

"You can be Uncle Brucey," she said, and gave Bruce a pat on the shoulder. "Thanks for all your advice and help, Uncle Brucey. It's what got me through." She gave him another pat.

In recent years, I've written a number of stories for anthologies edited by Lawrence Block, also one of my favorite writers. This one was for an Edward Hopper–inspired anthology of stories. I picked one with a woman usher in a theater. There was something lonely about it. This story popped out. Keith wrote a script based on it, and it's fine, and I was supposed to direct. We came close to having financial backing a couple of times, but it fell apart for different reasons, most recently COVID-19. Perhaps it will still happen. I hope so. I'd like to have my shot at directing a film. I didn't grow up wanting to do that, but in the eighties, John Sayles, who writes stories, books, and scripts that he directs as well as produces, inspired me. Also, Sayles is an actor. An interview he had in Twilight Zone Magazine *truly inspired my interest as a director. So, you got about a million dollars and want to see me direct a film, let me know. Brown paper bag. Mailbox.*

THE PROJECTIONIST

THERE'S SOME THAT think I got it easy on the job, but they don't know there's more to it than plugging in the projector. You got to be there at the right time to change reels, and you got to have it set so it's seamless, so none of the movie gets stuttered, you know. You don't do that right, well, you can cause a reel to flap and there goes the movie right at the good part, or it can get hung up and the bulb will burn it. Then everyone down there starts yelling, and that's not good for business, and it's not good for you, the boss hears about it, and with the racket they make when the picture flubs, he hears all right.

I ain't had that kind of thing happen to me much, two or three times on the flapping, once I got a burn on a film, but it was messed up when we got it. Was packed in wrong and got a twist in it I couldn't see when I pulled it out. That wasn't my fault. Even the boss could see that.

Still, you got to watch it.

It ain't the same kind of hard work as digging a ditch, which I've done, on account of I didn't finish high school. Lacked a little over a year, but I had to drop out on account of some things. Not a lot of opportunities out there if you don't have that diploma.

Anyways, thought I'd go back someday, take a test, get the diploma, but I didn't. Early on, though, I'd take my little bit of earnings and go to the picture show. There was an old man, Bert, working up there, and I knew him because he knew my dad, though not in a real close way. I'd go up there and visit with him. He'd let me in free and I could see the movies from the projection booth. Bert was a really fine guy. He had done some good things for me. I think of him as my guardian angel. He gave me my career.

While I was there, when I'd seen the double feature and it was time for it to start over, he'd show me how the projection was done. So when Bert decided he was going to hang it up, live on his Social Security, I got the job. I was twenty-five. I been at it for five years since then.

One nice thing is I get to watch movies for free, though some of them, once was enough. If I ever have to see *Seven Brides for Seven Brothers* again, I may cry myself into a stupor. I don't like those singing movies much.

Even if you wasn't looking at the picture, you had to hear the words from them over and over, and if the picture was kept over a week, you could pretty much say all the stuff said in the movie like you was a walking record. I tried some of the good lines the guys said to the girls in movies, the pickup lines, but none of them worked for me.

I ain't handsome, but I'm not scary-looking either, but the thing is, I'm not easy with women. I just ain't. I never learned that. My father was quite the ladies' man. Had black, curly hair and sharp features and bright blue eyes. Built up good from a lot of physical work. He made the women swoon. Once he got the one he wanted, he'd grow tired of her, same as he did with my mother, and he was ready to move on. Yeah, he had the knack for getting them in bed and taking a few dollars from them. He was everything they wanted. Until he wasn't.

He always said, "Thing about women, there's one comes of age every day and there's some that ain't of age, but they'll do. All you got to do is flatter them. They eat that shit up. Next thing you know, you got what you really want, and there's new mountains to conquer."

Dad was that kind of fellow.

Bert always said, "Guy like that who can talk a woman out of her panties pretty easy gets to thinking that's what it's all about. That there's nothing else to it. It ought not be like that. Me and Missy, we been married fifty years, and when it got so neither one of us was particularly in a hurry to see the other without drawers, we still wanted to see each other at the breakfast table."

That was Bert's advice on women in a nutshell.

Well, there was another thing. He always said, "Don't sit around trying to figure what she's thinking, 'cause you can't. And when it comes right down to it, she don't know what you're thinking. Just be there for one another."

Thing was, though, I never had anyone to be there for. I think it's how I carry myself. Bert always said, "Stand up, Cartwright. Quit stooping. You ain't no hunchback. Make eye contact, for Christ's sake."

I don't know why I do that, stoop, I mean, but I do. Maybe it's because I'm tall, six-six, and thin as a blade of grass. It's a thing I been trying to watch, but sometimes I feel like I got the weight of memories on my shoulders.

The other night Mr. Lowenstein hired a new usherette. She is something. He has her wear red. Always red. The inside of the theater has a lot of red. Backs of the seats are made out of some kind of red cloth. Some of the seats have gotten kind of greasy over time, young boys with their hair oil pressed into them. The curtains that pull in front of the stage, they're red. I love it when they're pulled, and then they open them so I can play the picture. I like watching them open. It gets to me, excites me in a funny way. I told Bert that once, thinking maybe he'd laugh at me, but he said, "Me too, kid."

They have clowns and jugglers and dog acts and shitty magicians and such on Saturday mornings before the cartoons. They do stuff up there on the stage and the kids go wild, yelling and throwing popcorn and candy.

Now and again, a dog decides to take a dump on the stage, or one of the clowns falls off his bike and does a gainer into the front row, or maybe a juggler misses a toss and hits himself in the head.

Kids like that even better. I think people are kind of strange when you get right down to it, 'cause everything that's funny mostly has to do with being embarrassed or hurt, don't you think?

But this usherette, her name's Sally, and she makes the girls in the movies look like leftover ham and cheese. She is a real beauty. She's younger than me, maybe by six or seven years, got long blonde hair and a face as smooth as a porcelain doll. Except for red dresses the theater gives her to wear, she mostly has some pretty washed-out clothes. She changes at the theater, does her makeup. When she comes out in one of those red dresses with heels on, she lights up the place like Rudolph's nose. Those dresses are provided by Mr. and Mrs. Lowenstein. Mrs. Lowenstein sews them to fit right, and believe me, they do. I don't mean to sound bad by saying it, but Sally is fitted into them so good that if she had a tan, it would break through the cloth, that's how tight they fit.

Mr. Lowenstein, he's sixty-five if he's a day, was standing with me back at the candy counter one time, and I'm getting a hot dog and a drink to take up to the projection booth. That's my lunch and dinner every day 'cause it's free. So this time, right when the theater is opening, just before noon, we see Sally come out of the dressing room across from us, same room the clowns and jugglers and dogs use. She comes out in one of those red dresses and some heels, her blonde hair bouncing on her shoulders, and she smiles at us.

I could feel my legs wilt. When she walked into the auditorium part of the theater to start work, Mr. Lowenstein said, "I think Maude maybe ought to loosen that dress a little."

I didn't say anything to that, but I was thinking, "I hope not."

Every day I'm up in the booth I'm peeking out from up there at Sally. She stands over by the curtains where there are some red bulbs. Not strong light, enough so someone wants to go out to the bathroom, or up to the concession stand, they can find their way without breaking a leg.

Sally, her job is to show people to their seats, which is silly, 'cause they get to sit where they want. She's an added expense at the theater, but the way Mr. and Mrs. Lowenstein saw it, she's a draw for a lot of the teenagers. I figure some of the married men don't mind looking at her either. She is something. It got so I watched her all the time. Just sat up there and looked. Usually, I got bored, I looked down into the back row where there was a lot of boys and girls doing hand work and smacky mouth, but that always seemed like a wrong thing to do, watch them make out, and it seemed wrong that they did it in the theater. Maybe I was just jealous.

It got so I'd peek out at Sally all the time up there, since she had her that spot where she stood every night, that red bulb shining on her, making her blonde hair appear slightly red, her dress brighter yet. I'd got so caught up looking at her, that once, damn if for the first time in a long time, I forgot to change a reel and the picture got all messed up. I had to really hustle to get it going again, all them people down there moaning and complaining and stuff.

Mr. Lowenstein wasn't happy, and he gave me the talk afterward that night. I knew he was right, and I knew it didn't mean nothing. He knew flubs happen. He knew I was good at my work. But he was right. I needed to pay more attention. Still, it was hard to regret looking at Sally.

Right after this talk, things got shifted. Mrs. Lowenstein had long left the ticket stand out front, and had gone home ahead of Mr. Lowenstein. She had her own car, so it was me and him behind the concession counter, and I'm getting my free drink I got coming as part of my job, and Sally came out of the dressing room. She had on a worn, loose, flower-dotted dress, and she saw us and smiled. I like to think it was me she was smiling at. I knew I tried to stand up straight when she looked in my direction.

It was then that two men came in through one of the row of glass doors, and walked over to the stand. Now, I usually lock those doors every night, thirty minutes before the time they came in, but this time I'm messing with the drink, you see, and I hadn't locked the door yet.

After it was locked up, me and Mr. Lowenstein, and sometimes Sally, though she usually left a little ahead of us, would go out the back and Mr. Lowenstein would lock the back door. Every night he'd say, "Need a ride?" And I'd say, "No, I prefer to walk."

If Sally was there when we were, he'd ask her the same thing.

Sally, she walked too. In the other direction. I took a ride once, but Mr. Lowenstein's car stunk so heavily of cigar smoke it made me sick. Dad used to smoke cigars and they smelled just that way, cheap and lingering. That smoke got into your clothes, it took more than one run through the laundry to get the stink out.

Besides, I liked to walk. I even walked home in the rain a couple of times. Mr. Lowenstein argued with me about it, but I told him I liked the rain just fine. I liked coming in out of it, all wet and cold, and then undressing and toweling off, taking a hot shower, and going to bed in my underwear. It's a simple thing, silly maybe, but I liked it.

But this time these guys came in because the door was unlocked when it should have been locked. Doesn't matter. They were the kind of guys that were going to come in eventually.

One of them was like a fireplug in a blue suit. He had a dark hat with the brim pushed back a bit, the kind of style you saw now and then, but it made him look stupid. I figure it wasn't all looks. He had that way about him that tells you he isn't exactly lying in bed at night trying to figure out how electricity works, or for that matter what makes a door swing open. The other guy, he was thinner and smoother. Had on a tan suit and a tan hat and one of his pants legs was bunched up against his ankle like he had a little gun and holster strapped there.

They came over smiling, and the tall one, he looks at Mr. Lowenstein, says, "We work for the Community Protection Board."

"The what?" Mr. Lowenstein said.

"It don't matter," said the short stout one. "All you got to do is be quiet and listen to the service we provide. We make sure you're protected, case someone wants to come in and set fire to the place, rob it, beat someone up. We make sure that don't happen."

"I got insurance," said Mr. Lowenstein. "I been here for years, and I been fine."

"No," said the tall one. "You don't have this kind of insurance. It covers a lot that yours don't. It makes sure certain things don't happen that are otherwise bound to happen."

It was then that me and Lowenstein both got it, knew what they meant.

"Way we see it, you ain't paying your share," said the tall one. "There's people on this block, all these businesses, and we got them paying as of last week, and you're all that's left. You don't pay, you'll be the only holdout."

"Leave me out of it," Mr. Lowenstein said.

The tall one gently shook his head. "That might not be such a good idea, you know. Stuff can go wrong overnight, in a heartbeat. Nice theater like this, you don't want that. Tell you what, Mr. Jew. We're going to go away, but we'll be back next Tuesday, which gives you nearly a week to think about it. But after Tuesday, we don't get, say, one hundred dollars a week, we got to tell you that you haven't got our protection. Without it, things here are surely going to ride a little too far south."

"We'll see you then," said the stout one. "Might want to start putting a few nickels in a jar."

Sally had stopped when they came in. She was standing there listening, maybe ten feet away. The stout one turned and looked at her.

"Sure wouldn't want this little trick to get her worn-out old dress rumpled. And I'm going to tell you, girlie, what you got poured into it is one fine bonbon."

"Don't talk about her like that," Mr. Lowenstein said.

"I talk like I like," said the stout one.

"This is your only warning about circumstances that can happen," said the tall one. "Let's not have any unpleasantness. All you got to do is pay your weekly hundred, things go swimmingly."

"That's right," said the stout one. "Swimmingly."

"Hundred dollars, that's a lot of money," said Mr. Lowenstein.

"Naw," said the stout one. "That's cheap, 'cause what could happen to this place, you, your employees, that fat wife of yours, this nice little girl, the retard there, it could cost a lot more to fix that, and there's some things could happen money can't fix."

They went out then, taking their sweet time about it. Sally came over, said, "What do they mean, Mr. Lowenstein?"

"It's a shakedown, honey," Mr. Lowenstein said. "Don't you worry about it. But tonight, I'm taking you both home."

And he did. I didn't mind. I sat in the backseat behind Sally and looked and smelled her hair through the cigar smoke.

In my little apartment that night I sat and thought about those guys, and they reminded me of my dad quite a bit. Lots of bluster, more than bullies. People who were happily mean. I worried about Mr. and Mrs. Lowenstein, and Sally, of course, and I won't lie to you. I worried about me.

Next day I went to work same as usual, and when I was getting my lunch, my hot dog to take up into the booth, Sally came over and said, "Those men last night. Are they dangerous?"

"I don't know," I said. "I think they could be."

"I need this job," she said. "I don't want to quit, but I'm a little scared."

"I hear you," I said. "I need this job too."

"You're staying?"

"Sure," I said.

"Will you kind of keep a watch on me?" she said.

That was kind of like asking a sparrow to fight a chicken hawk, but I nodded, said, "You bet."

I should have told her to take a hike on out of there and start looking for other employment, because these kinds of things can turn bad. I've seen a bit of it, that badness.

But thing was, I was too selfish. I wanted Sally around. Wanted her to be where I could see her, but another part of me thought about that and knew I might not be able to do a thing to protect her. Good intentions weren't always enough. Bert used to say the road to hell was paved with good intentions.

That night after work, as Sally was starting to walk home, I said, "How about I walk you?"

"I'm the other direction," she said.

"That's all right. I'll walk back after I get you where you need to go."

"All right," she said.

We walked and she said, "You like being a projectionist?"

"Yeah."

"Why?"

"Decent pay, free hot dogs."

She laughed.

"I like it up there in the booth. I get to see all those movies. I like movies."

"Me too."

"It's kind of weird, but I like the private part of it too. I mean, you know, I get a little lonely up there, but not too much. Now and again I've seen a picture enough I'm sick of it, or don't like it, I read some. I'm not a good reader. A book can last me a few months."

"I read magazines and books," she said. "I read *The Good Earth*."

"That's good."

"You've read it?"

"No. But it's good you have. I hear it's good."

"It was all right."

"I guess I prefer picture shows," I said. "Doesn't take as long to get a story. Hour or two and you're done. Another thing I like is being up high like that, in the booth, looking down on folks, and seeing those actors in the movies, me running the reels. It's like I own those people. Like I'm some kind of god up there, and the movies, those actors, and what they do, they don't get to do it unless I make it happen. That sounds odd, don't it?"

"A little," she said.

"I run their lives over and over every week, and then they move on, and for me they don't exist no more, but now I got new people I'm in charge of, you see. They come in canisters. I can't keep them from doing what they do, but without me, they wouldn't be doing nothing. I got to turn them on for them to actually be there."

"That's an interesting perspective," she said.

"Perspective?" I said. "I like that. Like the way you talk."

She seemed embarrassed. "It's just a word."

"Yeah, but you got some words I don't have, or don't use anyway. Don't know how. I'm always scared I'm going to say them wrong, and someone will laugh. I was afraid to say *canister* just then, and I know that one."

"That's okay," she said. "I can't say *aficionado* right. I know I say it wrong, and I don't know how it's actually said. I need to hear someone that knows."

"I don't even know what that word means," I said. "Or how you would come about working it into a sentence."

"I try a little too hard to do that," she said. "I'm taking a few courses on the weekends. They got classes like that over at the college. I've only seen the word in a textbook."

"College, huh?"

"You should sign up. It's fun."

"Costs money, though."

"It's worth it, I can get a better job I get an associate degree. I thought I might get married, but then I thought I'm too young for that. I need to do something, see something before I start wiping baby butts. Besides, the guys I've dated, none of them seem like husband material to me."

"Having a family may not be all that good anyway," I said. "It ain't always."

"I think I'd like it. I think I'd make a good wife. Not now, though. I want to live a little."

Right then I got to thinking maybe a family would be all right. Maybe I could do that with her. But it was just thinking. We passed by the drugstore on Margin Street, and I seen our reflection in the window glass. She looked like some kind of goddess, and me, well, I looked like a few sticks tied together with a hank of hair. Like I said, I don't think I got an ugly face, but I sure knew in that moment, I wasn't in her league. I saw too that the shop was closing down, and there were a couple guys and their girls coming out, arm-in-arm, and they were laughing and smiling.

I seen one of them guys look over at us, see Sally with me, and I could tell he was thinking, "How'd he manage that?" And then they turned and were gone.

We finally came to where she lived, which was a two-story brick building. It wasn't well lit up, but it was brighter than my place. At least there was a streetlight and a light you could see through the door glass into the hallway that led to the stairs.

"I live on the top floor," she said.

"That's good. High up."

"Oh yeah. You said you like being high up, at the theater."

"That's right."

"I look out the window at the people sometimes."

"I watch people too," I said. "It's not as good as the movies, but second or third time one plays, I start to watch people down in the seats, unless the movie is really good. Sometimes I can watch a movie every night and not get tired of it. Nothing is going to happen in it that I don't know about by then, and I like that too. I know who is who and who messes up and how it all ends. Real people. They can't do anything I can figure, not really. I like the movies 'cause I like knowing how it's going to come out."

"That's interesting," Sally said.

I wasn't sure she thought it was really all that interesting, and I wished then I'd talked about the weather, or some such, instead of how I was a god up in the projection booth. I can be such an idiot. That's what Dad always said: "You, son, are a loser and a goddamn idiot."

"All right," I said. "Well, you're here."

"Yes, I am. And thank you."

"Welcome."

We shuffled around there for a moment. She said, "Guess I'll see you tomorrow."

"Sure. I can walk you home again, you want."

"We'll see. Maybe. I mean, it depends. I'm thinking maybe I've blown it all out of proportion."

"Sure. You'll be okay."

I opened the glass door for her and she went inside. She turned at the stairs and looked back at me and smiled. I couldn't tell how real that smile was. Whatever she meant by it, it made me feel kind of small.

I smiled back.

She turned and came back. "It means someone who is a fan, who appreciates."

"How's that?"

"*Aficionado*," she said. "Or however it's supposed to sound."

She smiled and went back inside. I liked that smile better. I watched her through the glass door as she climbed up the stairs.

I showered and looked at my chest in the little medicine cabinet mirror while I dried off. The mirror was cracked, but so was my chest. It was all cracked and wrinkled from where I'd been burned.

I turned off the lights and went to bed.

Next morning I got up and went over to Bert's house. Missy was gone to do shopping, and though I would have been glad to see her normally, right then I was happy she was out.

Bert let me in and poured me some coffee and offered me some toast, and I took it. Sat at his table in their small kitchen and buttered the toast and put some of Missy's fig jam on it. They had about an acre of land out back of the house, and it had a fig tree on it, and they had a little garden out there every spring and part of the summer.

I ate the toast and drank the coffee, and we talked about nothing while I did.

When I finished eating, Bert poured me another cup of coffee, told me to come out and sit on the back porch with him. They had some comfortable chairs out there, and we sat side by side under the porch overhang.

"You want to tell me why you've really come over?" Bert said.

"There's some people come by the theater," I said. "Mooks."

"All right."

"They threatened Mr. Lowenstein, me, and Sally."

"Who's Sally?"

I told him all about her, and everything they'd said, what they looked like.

"I know who they are," he said. "But I don't know them, you understand?"

"Yeah."

"Look, kid. This isn't like in the old days. I'm seventy-four years old. Do I look like a tough guy to you?"

"You're tough enough."

"That time . . . that time there was no way out for you. Now, you got a way out. You quit that job and get another."

"I like it," I said.

"Yeah . . . all right. Yeah. I liked it too. I miss it sometimes, but I like better being home. I like being alive and being home to watch *Gunsmoke*. Me and Missy, we got it all right here. She put up with some stuff, and I don't want her to put up with any of that again."

"I hear you," I said.

"Not that I don't care, kid. Not that I don't bleed for you. But again, I'm seventy-four. I was younger then. And well, it was more immediate, and you being really young . . . you needed the help. You can walk away now. Or tell Lowenstein to pay the money. What I'd do, I'd pay the money."

"No," I said. "I can't."

"Your skin, kid, but I'm telling you, these guys are bad business. There's those two, and there's the three that run that place. Five I think."

"How do you know?"

"I ain't as connected as I once was, back before I started running the projector, but I still know some people and I get word from them now and then. Look, how about this? Let me ask around."

"All right," I said.

I showed a picture that night that I didn't watch, or even remember. I was on time with changing the reels, but I spent all my time watching Sally down there under the red light. She looked nervous, kept looking this way and that.

They said they'd be back next week, and it had only been three days, so I figured for the moment we were fine. I was figuring what to do when next week came.

After the show closed that third night, Lowenstein said, "I'm going to pay them."

"Yeah," I said.

"Yeah. I got a good business here. That's a bite every week, but those guys, I can't do nothing about them. I called the cops next day, and you know what they told me?"

"What?"

"Pay them."

"They said that?"

"Yeah, way I figure it, kid, they have the cops in their pocket. Or at least the right cops. They get money from the businesses, and the cops get a little taste."

I thought that was probably true, things I knew about people.

I walked Sally home again that night, and when I got back to my place, Bert was sitting on the steps. There was a small wooden box on the steps beside him.

"Damn, boy. I was about to give up."

"Sorry. I walked Sally home."

"Good. You got a girl. That's a good thing."

"It's not like that," I said.

"She's the one you told me about, right?"

"Yeah. But it's not like that."

"How is it?"

"Well, it's not like that. I think she wasn't scared, she wouldn't bother with me. I mean she's always nice, but, hell, you know, Bert. There's me, and then there's this doll. Smart. She goes to night classes."

"Does she now?"

"Knows big words."

"How's she look?"

"Very nice."

"Big words and nice, that's fine, kid. You ought to try and touch base with that. You deserve it."

I looked at the box.

"Whatcha got there?"

He patted the box. "You know."

"Yeah. Guess I do."

"Asked around, these guys, they're muscling in on the territory. Giving the cops a bit of their juice. It's not like a big bunch of them. It's five guys, like I heard, way I told you. They think maybe they're going to become big bad business, and you know, they just might."

"All right," I said. "Just five."

"That's still a lot of guys."

"Certainly is. Mr. Lowenstein said he was going to pay them."

"That's good, kid. That's the best way all around. But, I got to tell you, month or two from now, it won't be one hundred dollars, it'll be two. They'll suck the place dry, then end up owning it. That's how they work. They already own the candy store on the corner. They just do a few places at a time till they got everyone in line, but they're growing. Pretty soon, all four blocks there, they'll own them. And then on from there, more blocks. Those kind of guys don't quit."

We were quiet for awhile. Bert stood up.

"I got to go back," he said. "Told Missy I'd only be gone a little while, and I've been gone a long while."

"Did she see the box?"

"No. I was careful about it. What she knows is I had some bad ways before I quit and took to the projector. She don't know about you and me and what happened. She just thinks you're a swell kid. She don't know I got the box. Remember, you don't keep it, or what's in it. You get rid of it. I don't never want to see it again. These guys, they're up the end of the street. The Career Building. Top floor."

"Why's it called that?" I asked.

"No idea. But they ain't so big time they got bodyguards or nothing. They just got themselves and some plans."

I nodded.

"Lowenstein talked to the police," I said.

"Yeah, well, I can tell you without you telling me how that worked out. Keep your head up, kid. And remember, there are other theaters and other girls in other places. Ditch the box and take a hound out of here."

He clapped me on the shoulder as he passed. I turned and watched him hobble along the street, hands in his pockets.

That night I lay down on the bed with my clothes on, still wearing my shoes too. I lay there with the box beside me on the bed.

I remembered how my dad liked to come in with his women when we lived together, how he'd do what he did with them with me laying there nearby, just a kid.

I remembered that it wasn't enough for him, and when they were gone, he'd touch me. He liked to touch me. He said it was all right. It didn't feel all right to me.

One time I said that. That it was not right, that it was odd, and he pushed my chest down on the stove grate and held me there. I screamed and I screamed, but in that place where we lived, no one came. No one cared.

Except Bert. Bert and Missy lived there then. He had just started at the theater, doing the projection, and I'd go up there and talk with him, and one time, he sees me bleeding through my shirt. This was the time I was burned. It scabbed and the scabs busted and bled.

That's how he knew about me. I kind of spilled it all out when he asked how I was hurt. I opened my shirt. You could see the grate marks from the stove as clear as a tattoo.

Bert knew my dad. My dad, Bert said, did some work for certain men in the neighborhood that he knew. Work that involved his fists and sometimes more than that.

I never knew what Dad did until then. I never asked and had never cared. I was happiest when he was gone and I was alone. I liked going to school just to be away from him, but like I said, I had to quit that before I finished.

I told Bert how Dad came in the night he burned me and tried to touch me, and I fought him. I was bigger by then, but I was no match. He held me down and did what he wanted, way he always did. It really hurt that time. He said it would hurt even worse if I fought him next time. Said I'd end up like Doris. That was my mother. I had suspected something bad happened to her, that she didn't just run away like he said, but right then I knew it, and I knew he was the one that did it.

He pushed me into the stove after that. He made me watch him heat it up and when it was hot, he pushed me into it. Said it was a lesson.

I didn't want to whine about what happened, but that time I was in the projection booth with Bert, I told him because I was angry. I felt like there was something wrong with me that my dad wanted to do that to me.

"It ain't you, kid. It's him. He's the one messed up, not you."

"I'm going to kill him," I said.

"He'll turn that around on you," Bert said. "I know who he is and what he is. He's worse than I thought, but he's not someone you can handle, kid. You'll just disappear."

I cried.

Bert put his arm around me, said, "All right, kid. It's going to be okay."

I ended up staying with Bert, which wasn't all that far from where I lived with Dad. Bert had just moved from the apartments where we were to a place around the corner. Word got around where Bert lived and that I was with him. Dad came by with another guy, a short fellow with a shiny bald head. He wasn't the kind of guy that wore a hat. You didn't see that much then, a guy without a hat.

"I've come to pick up my son," Dad said.

Dad was standing outside the door with that bald guy. Bert was holding the door open. He had a .45 automatic in his hand, out of sight behind the door frame. There was a screen between them. I was standing back in the little dump of a living room, out of sight. From the angle I was standing I could see them in the mirror across the way against the wall.

"He don't want to go," Bert said. "He's taking him a kind of vacation."

"I'm his father. He has to go."

"Naw. He don't have to do nothing."

"I could get the police."

"Yeah, you could," Bert said. "You could do that. But, the boy, he's got a story to tell."

"That's what it is, a story."

"You think I think that?"

"I don't care what you think. Tell my son to come out."

"Not today."

"What I'm thinking is we can come in and get him," the bald man said.

"I was thinking you might be thinking that," Bert said. "And I was thinking, you do that, it won't be such a good idea."

"They say you used to be something," the bald man said. "But now you run a projector."

"There's all sorts of people got opinions about me," Bert said.

"You try and take that boy, you're able to talk later, you can form your own opinion, tell people, spread it around."

"All right," Dad said. "You keep him. For now. But he's coming home."

"You get lonely nights?" Bert said.

"It's best you watch your mouth," Dad said. "Best you watch yourself altogether."

"Unless you're going to get tough and eat your way through the screen, you ought to go on now," Bert said.

"You are setting yourself up for a world of hurt," Dad said.

"Am I?" Bert said.

"Guy like you with a nice wife, and a shitty, safe job at the picture show, that could all get stood on its head."

Bert went a little stiff.

"It's never good to threaten me," Bert said.

"What we're doing here," said the bald man, "is giving you chance to make it easy on yourself, or that threat, as you call it, it'll turn into a promise."

"Why wait," Bert said, and brought the .45 around where they could see it. "Come on in."

Bert flipped the latch on the screen with the barrel of the .45.

"I'm giving you an invitation," Bert said.

"We got time," said Dad. "We got time and we got ways, and you have just stepped in the stink, mister."

"We'll see who stinks when it's all over," Bert said.

Dad and the bald man turned and walked away. I went over and stood near the door. I watched them get in a car, the bald man at the wheel. Dad looked out the side window at the house. He saw me. He smiled the way a lion smiles.

So later I was sleeping on the couch, and Missy and Bert were in their room, or so I thought, but I rolled over and there's Bert across the way with a wooden box, and he's taking something out of it and putting it in his coat pockets, and going out the door.

I got up and put on my clothes and went over and looked at the box. It was empty. The bottom of it was packed with cloth. Otherwise, it was empty.

Slipping out the door I went down the drive and looked around the hedges and saw Bert walking brisk-like. I waited until he was pretty far down, and then I followed.

It was a long walk and the wind was high and there was a misty kind of rain. Bert walked fast. He was a younger man then, but no kid, but still, he moved quick.

Bert came to a corner and turned, and when I turned, I didn't see him anymore. I was out of the housing part of town, and there were buildings. I stood there confused for a moment, and then I eased along, and when I got to the far side of the big building, I peeked around it. I saw Bert on one of the little porches off the building, in front of a door. He was under a light. He reached up with something and knocked the bulb out, then he took that something and stuck it in the door. I heard a snick, and a moment later, he was inside and out of sight.

I eased up to the porch, but I couldn't make myself go in. I waited there and listened, and after awhile I heard sounds like someone coughing loudly, and then there was a yell, and then that coughing sound again.

After a moment, the door pushed open and nearly knocked me off the porch. It was Bert.

"Damn, kid. What you doing here?"

"I followed you?"

"I see that."

He took the automatic and held it up and unscrewed the silencer on the end of it. He put the silencer in one coat pocket, the gun in the other.

"Come on, fast. Not running, but don't lollygag neither."

"Did you?"

"Yeah. But not your old man. He's back at the apartments. That's what the bald bastard said when I asked."

"You asked?"

"Yeah. Nicely. And when he told me, I shot him. Couple times. There was another guy there I didn't know about, came out of the toilet. I shot him too. Might as well be straight with you, kid. They're deader than snow in July. Come on, hustle a little."

Stunned is how I felt, but happy too. I mean, those guys back there, they hadn't done nothing to me, not like Dad, but they were on his side. Probably thought I was telling lies. Probably thought a stove burn was something I deserved. Lot of guys thought like that around there. Your father's word was the law. And all those guys, they believed in a strict law. You were either for them, or against them.

We came to the apartment where my dad lived, where I had lived with him. There was a hedge row that was never trimmed that led along both sides of the walk that went up to the apartment house.

Inside, you had to go down the hall and make a turn to the left to get to our place.

Standing in the shadow of the hedge, Bert said, "You sure about this kid? Dead is dead. And he is your father."

"He's nothing to me, Bert. Nothing. He gets me back, he'll just kill me, and you know it. I'm nothing to him, just something to own and use and throw away. Like he did my mother. My mother was all right. I can still remember how she smelled. Then one day she wasn't there, and that's because of him. She's gone. He's here."

"Still, kid, he's your father."

"I'm all right with it."

Bert nodded. He took the gun and silencer out of his coat pockets and screwed the silencer into place. "You sit this one out. Go on home."

"You used to do stuff like this, didn't you, Bert?"

"All the time," he said. "I ain't proud of it. Except for tonight. These guys, your father. I'm all right with that. Maybe it'll make up for some of the other things I done."

"I'm staying with you, Bert."

"You don't want that kid."

"Yeah, I do."

We went along the walk then and when we got to the door, Bert handed me the gun. I held it while he worked the lock and got it open with a
little wedge. He pried the wood loose at the door. I gave him back the gun.
We were inside so quickly and silently, we might as well have been ghosts.

When we got to Dad's door, Bert started with the wedge, but I grabbed
his hand. We had an extra key stuck into the side of the door frame where
it was cracked. You had to be looking for it to know it was there. We kept
some putty over it the color of the wood. I reached around the frame and
took out the putty and pulled out the key. I unlocked the door.

I could feel him in the room. I don't know how else to say that, but I
could feel him. He was sitting in a chair by the bed, smoking a cigarette,
and about the time we saw him, he realized we were in the room.

"It's best you don't call out," Bert said.

Dad clicked the lamp by his chair. He was soaked in light and there
was enough of it he could look out and see us. We stepped closer.

"I guess I should have known you'd come, Bert. I know who you are.
I know what you've done."

"Shouldn't have threatened me," Bert said.

"Guy with me, Amos, he said you did some things some years back, for
some boys he knew. He wasn't in the racket then, just on the outskirts. He
said you were a kind of legend. We saw you the other day, standing in that
doorway, you didn't look so legendary. Yet, here you are."

"Yep," Bert said. "Here I am."

"I'm not going to be all right, I yell or don't yell, am I?"

"Naw, you ain't."

That's when Dad grabbed at the lamp and tried to sling it at Bert, but
the wire was too short and the plug didn't come out of the wall. The lamp
popped out and back when the plug didn't give, rolled along the floor
tumbling light, and then Dad was on his feet, in front of the chair, and he
had a gun in his hand he'd pulled from the cushions.

Bert fired his automatic.

There was a streak of light and stench of gun powder and a sound like
someone coughing out a wad of phlegm, and then Dad sat back down
in the chair. The gun he had dangled from his finger. He was breathing
heavily. He tried to lift his hand with the gun in it, but he couldn't do it.

He might as well have been trying to lift a steel girder.

Bert reached over and took Dad's gun from his hand and gave it to me to hold. He set the lamp up, then. The light from it lay on Dad's face like it had weight. Dad was white. I looked at him and tried to feel something, but I didn't. I didn't feel bad for him, and I didn't feel good about it. I didn't feel nothing. Not right then.

Dad was wheezing and there was a rattling in his chest. I guess the shot got him through one of his lungs.

"We can watch him die if it'll give you pleasure, or I can finish him, kid. Your call."

I lifted the pistol in my hand and pointed it at Dad.

Bert said, "Whoa."

I paused.

"No silencer," Bert said. He traded guns with me. "He can't do nothing, like you couldn't when you was a kid. Get up close and give it to him."

I moved close and put the barrel of the pistol to his head and pulled the trigger.

The gun coughed.

Now I had the box with the gun and silencer in it. Those many years ago, Bert had wiped my dad's gun clean with a dishrag, and dropped it and the gun on the floor. He had kept his own gun, though, and now I was to use it and get rid of it. I think it wasn't only about safety, about not getting caught. I think it was Bert's way to say he was done from then on.

Back then, when Dad was dead, we walked out of there silently and down the street quickly. I knew and Bert knew what we had done, and that was enough. We never talked about it again. Didn't even hint such a thing had happened.

I slept well for the first time in years. I finally got my own place, and eventually I took the projectionist job. Things had been all right until those guys came around.

Now things had come full circle. It wasn't just me I was protecting now, it was Sally and the Lowensteins. Under the gun and silencer there was the wedge Bert had used to jimmy the doors way back then. I saw there was a piece of paper under that.

There were three addresses listed on it. Two apartments were listed at the same general address.

The other had a place listed outside of town, almost out in the country. It was near the railroad tracks. For all the high-roller talk those guys blew out, they were just like my father had been. Living on the margins, the rest of it going for booze and women. Big time in the lies, small time in their lives, as Bert once said.

I put the gun in my front pants pocket. The grip stuck out. I covered it with my shirt and stuck the silencer in the other pocket. I put the wedge in my back pocket, where I usually carried my wallet.

I wouldn't need the wallet that night.

When I walked the gun, silencer and wedge were heavy in my pockets.

The first address was not far from where I was, not far from the theater.

Outside, I started to turn down the walk, and then I stopped. A car was parked at the curb. I knew that car. A man got out.

It was Bert.

"I decided maybe I ought to come," Bert said.

The apartments were easy and quick. Bert took the wedge from me and opened the doors. I went in and they were in bed together, naked, two guys. I had heard of such. I shot both of them in their sleep, Bert holding a flashlight on them so I could see it was them. They weren't the two who had come to see me, but they were part of the five, Bert said. The scammers, the thugs. It was over so quick they never knew they were dead.

At the other apartment we got in easy as before, but no one was there.

That bothered me, but there was nothing for it.

We drove out to the place on the edge of town and parked in a grove of pecan trees that grew beside the road, got out and walked up to the house. There was a light on inside. There were no houses nearby, though there were a couple within earshot, dark and silent.

We went to the windows and took a peek. There was a guy sitting on the couch watching TV. We could hear him laughing at something. The voices on the TV had canned laughter with them. He wasn't one of the two that had come to the theater, but Bert said he was one of the five.

Through an open doorway we saw the two who had threatened Mr.

320

Lowenstein step into sight. They came out of the kitchen, each carrying a beer.

We stepped back from the window.

"Alright," Bert said. "That's all five, counting these three. They're together. That's all right. You don't have to worry about rounding up the one that wasn't at the apartment. He's the one on the couch."

"You're sure?"

"I know who they are," he said. "They been around awhile. It's the ones I was told about, ones bothering the block. Until recent they just been guys walking around after other guys, now they're trying to carve some territory. This is all of them."

"What do we do?"

"Well, it's easier to kill them in their sleep when they can't fight back. But I got an old saying. You get what you get."

"Meaning?"

"Meaning there's one more than I expected, and I got to go back to the car, kid."

We went back to the car. Bert got a sawed off double-barrel shotgun out of the trunk. The stock was sawed down too. He opened it and slipped in two shells from a box in the trunk, and then he grabbed a handful of shells and stuck them in his pocket.

"Hoping I wouldn't need this. It goes boom real loud."

We walked back.

We waited out there in the bushes by the house for an hour or so, not talking, just waiting. I thought back on how it had been with Dad, me pushing that gun against his head, his eyes looking along that barrel at me. It was pretty nice. And those guys earlier that night. Didn't know them. Never talked to them, but considering they were all and of a same, I was alright with it. Maybe I was more like Dad than I wanted to be.

After a while, Bert said, "Look, kid. We can come back another time when they're sleeping, maybe the other guy is back in his apartment then, splitting their numbers, or we can be bold and get it over with."

"Let's be bold."

"There's a door on either side of the living room, and if we go through the back, one of us coming out on either side, we can get them before they got time to think. Another thing, anyone else shows up, more of them there than we think, we got to finish things. Hear what I'm saying?"

I nodded.

"Don't get us in our own crossfire," Bert said. "That would be bad form, one of us shooting the other."

Slipping around back, Bert took the wedge and stuck it in the door and pulled and the door made a little popping sound. Nothing too loud. Nothing you could hear over the blare of that TV set.

Inside he went right and I went left.

Only the guy on my side saw us before we cut loose. He was the tall guy that came to the theater. He had tried to pull the gun out from under his pants leg, strapped to his ankle. He should have found a better place to keep it. I fired the silenced .45. It made that big tuberculosis cough and part of his face flew off.

That's when Bert cut down with the shotgun. One barrel, then the other. Both of those guys were dead. A lot of them was on the wall. The sound of that shotgun in the house was like two atomic bombs going off.

Bert glanced at the TV. "I hate that show, that canned laughter."

I thought for a moment he was going to shoot the TV.

We got out of there quick. Going out the back way. The canned laughs roared on the TV.

The only thing that had touched the door was the wedge, so no finger-prints to worry about.

I expected to see lights on in the houses down the way, but nothing had changed. Two shotgun blasts in the night must not have been as loud as they seemed to me. Maybe no one cared.

Bert put the shotgun on the seat between us and we drove away. He wheeled farther out of town, on down to the river. He drove down there and we pulled under the bridge, got out, wiped down the guns just for good measure, then threw them in the river, along with the wedge and the silencer.

When Bert pulled up at the curb in front of my place, I started to get out. "Hold it, kid."

I took my hand off the door lever.

"Listen here. You and me, we got a bond. You know that."

"The closest," I said.

"That's right. But I'm going to tell you something tough, kid. Don't come around no more. It's not a good idea. I done for you what I could. More than I meant to. I got my past in that river now, and I want to leave it there. I love you, kid. I ain't mad at you or nothing, but I can't have you around. I can't think on those kind of things anymore."

"Sure, Bert."

"Don't take it hard, okay?"

"No," I said.

"It ain't personal, but it's got be like that. And throw away that gun box. Good luck, kid."

I nodded. I got out. Bert drove away.

Next night I walked Sally to her apartment, and every night after that because she was scared. Walked her home until the day before the thugs were supposed to come around.

Sally and the Lowensteins were worried, but Mr. Lowenstein had put aside the money for them. He couldn't see a percentage on his side. Sally said she hated it, but was glad he was paying.

Mr. Lowenstein had read the papers, read about the murders in the apartment house and in the house outside of town, but he didn't put it together with those guys we had talked to. No way he could have. He talked about it, though, said the world was getting scary. I agreed it was.

On the last night I walked Sally, she said, "I'm not going to come back to work tomorrow. After Mr. Lowenstein pays them, I'll come back, so I won't need you to walk me for awhile. I think after he pays them, I'm going to be all right on my own."

"Okay," I said.

"I don't want to be there when they come around, even if he is paying. You understand?"

"Understood."

I stood there for a long moment with my hands in my pockets. I was glad she was safe.

"Sally, putting that ugly business aside, what do you think about you and me getting some coffee next week? You know, before work. We can even go to the movie on our day off, and for nothing."

I tried to say that last part with a smile since we see the movies all the time. Me up in the booth, her over by the seats. She smiled back at me, but it wasn't much of smile. It was like she had borrowed it.

"That's sweet," she said. "But I got a boyfriend, and he might not like that."

"Never seen you with anyone," I said.

"We don't get out much. He comes around though."

"Does he?"

"Yeah. And you know, I got the college stuff in the mornings and work midday and nights, then I got to study. My time is tight. We get the one day off, and there's so much to do, and I got to spend some time with my boyfriend, you know?"

"Yeah. Okay. What's this boyfriend's name?"

She thought on that a little too long. "Randy."

"Randy, huh? That's his name?"

"Yes. Randy."

"Like Randolph Scott. Like that movie we showed last week. *The Tall T.* You said you liked it."

"Yeah. Like that. His name is Randolph, but everyone calls him Randy."

"All right," I said. "Well, good luck to you and Randy."

"Thanks," she said, like I had meant it. Like I thought there really was a Randy.

Sally never did come back to work after that. And of course the thugs didn't show up. Mr. Lowenstein got to keep his hundred dollars. All along the block, those businesses, they got to keep their money too. Guess someone else like those fellows could come along, but what happened to those five, it's pretty discouraging to that kind of business. They don't know what kind of gang there is that owns this block. There was just me and Bert, but they don't know that.

I like it pretty good up there in the projection booth. Sometimes I look out where Sally used to stand, but she isn't there, of course. Mr. Lowenstein never hired another girl to take her place. He decided people would come anyway.

I saw Sally around town a couple of times, both times she was with a guy, and it wasn't the same guy. I'm pretty sure neither of them were named Randy. If she saw me she didn't let on. I wonder what she'd think to know what I did for her, for all of us.

What I do now is I show the movies and I go home. I used to walk by Bert's place every now and then. I'm not sure why. I read in the papers that his wife Missy died. I wanted to send flowers, or something, but I didn't.

Just the other day, I read Bert died.

I like my job. I like being the projectionist. I'm okay with it, being up there in the booth by myself, feeling mostly good about things like they are, but I won't kid you, sometimes I get a little lonely.

About Joe R. Lansdale

As probably the only person in the International Martial Arts Hall of Fame who has received the Edgar, ten Stokers, the Grandmaster of Horror, the Raymond Chandler, the British Fantasy, the Spur, the Golden Lion, the Grinzane Prize, the Herodotus, and the Inkpot Awards, Joe R. Lansdale's extraordinary output has included more than 40 novels, 400 shorter works, numerous comic books, and a handful of screenplays as well as devising the Shen Chuan Martial Science. His acclaimed works landed him in the Texas Literary Hall of Fame and the Texas Institute of Letters.

His novels include *Dead in The West* (1986), *The Magic Wagon* (1986), *The Nightrunners* (1987), *The Drive-In* (1988), *Cold in July* (1989), the Edgar Award–winning *The Bottoms* (2000), *A Fine Dark Line* (2002), *Flaming Zeppelins* (2010), *The Thicket* (2013), the Spur Award–winning *Paradise Sky* (2015), *Jane Goes North* (2020), *More Better Deals* (2020), *Moon Lake* (2021), and *The Donut Legion* (2023). Beginning with *By Bizarre Hands* (1989), Lansdale's numerous short stories have been collected in several volumes, including *Writer of the Purple Rage* (1994), *High Cotton* (2000), *Sanctified and Chicken Fried* (2009), *The Best of Joe R. Lansdale* (2010), *Deadman's Road* (2010), *Bleeding Shadows* (2013), *Miracles Ain't What They Used to Be* (2016), *Terror Is Our Business* (2018, with Kasey Lansdale), and *Fishing for Dinosaurs and Other Stories* (2020). Lansdale has edited 15 anthologies, including *Razored Saddles* (1989, with Pat LoBrutto), *Dark at Heart* (1992, with Karen Lansdale), *Weird Business* (1995, with Richard Klaw), *Retro Pulp Tales* (2006), *Cross Plains Universe* (2006, with Scott Cupp), *Crucified Dreams* (2011), and *The Urban Fantasy Anthology* (2011, with Peter S. Beagle). He has also written comics for DC, Marvel, Dark Horse, IDW, and others.

Lansdale's most famous creation is the unlikely duo of Hap and Leonard. Hap Collins is white, liberal, and even-tempered. Leonard Pine, who is quick to anger, is Black, conservative, and gay. In a series of 13 novels, spanning *Savage Season* (1990) through *The Elephant of Surprise* (2019), and several novellas and short stories, the best friends encounter violence, racism, and adventure in their East Texas haunts. The often-humorous tales have garnered much praise and a legion of devoted fans. Many of the Hap and Leonard novellas and shorter tales are collected in *Veil's Visit* (1999), *Hap and Leonard* (2016), *The Big Book of Hap and Leonard* (2018), and *Born for Trouble* (2021). *Hap and Leonard: Blood and Lemonade* (2018) and *Of Mice and Minestrone* (2020) chronicle the young adventures of the duo, including the origins of their unique friendship. For three seasons, the pair were featured on the television series *Hap and Leonard* (2016–18), starring James Purefoy and Michael K. Williams.

Other works that have enjoyed the film treatment include the feature films *Bubba Ho-Tep* and *Cold in July*; "Incident On and Off a Mountain Road" for *Masters of Horror*; "The Dump," "Fish Night," and "The Tall Grass," all for *Love, Death & Robots*; "The Companion" for *Creepshow*; and *Christmas with the Dead*, which Lansdale produced with a screenplay by his son, Keith. He has written many screenplays and teleplays, most notably for *Batman: The Animated Series*. The documentary *All Hail the Popcorn King* (2019) explores the enduring legacy of Lansdale and his creations.

Joe R. Lansdale lives with his wife, Karen, in Nacogdoches, Texas.

About S. A. Cosby

S. A. Cosby is the *New York Times* bestselling, award-winning author of *Razorblade Tears* and *Blacktop Wasteland*. Cosby's books were *NYT* Notable Books and named Best Books of the Year by NPR, *BookPage*, Goodreads, *Library Journal*, and *Deadly Pleasures*, among many others. Cosby has won the *LA Times* Book Prize, the Anthony Award, the Black Caucus American Library Association Award, and the ITW Thriller Award; has been nominated for the Edgar, the Barry, the Lefty, and the Audie; and was a finalist for the Southern Book Prize and the Goodreads Choice Award.